BEAUTIFUL FIEND

NORTH SHORE STORIES

BOOK ONE

LOLA KING

Cover art by Wild Love Designs
Editing by Angie at Lunar Rose Editing
Alpha reading by Lauren Pixley

To all my girls who, on their way to their prince, lost themselves in the villain's arms.

CONTENT WARNING

This book is a dark romance for 18+ readers only.
It contains non con (*for real*) and dub con.
Seriously, there is non con from the hero who is not a hero at all and, in fact, a total villain.
Caden King is not morally gray, he is morally *pitch black* (and yet he is also redeemable – make it make sense)

Please, be aware this book also contains on page SA, mentions of SA, domestic abuse, and depression.

This book is a work of fiction that depicts sexual fantasies that might be triggering to some readers.
Please, understand that the fantasy starts on the next page and you are entering at your own risk—there will be no further warning and no safe word.
Consider this book a CNC scene and the only safe word/gesture at your disposal to end it is to close the book.

PLAYLIST

LET GO - LIL DUSTY G
Me & My Demons - Omido, Silent Child
Storm - Honors
MY HEAD - Layto
Bleed - Connor Kauffman
Fast Forward - You Me At Six
Take Me Away - New Medicine
Blood - Call Me Karizma
Kinda Scary - Call Me Karizma
A Girl Called Jazz - Omide, Tobi Swizz
The Kid I Used to Know - Arrested Youth
Lost It - Layto, Jaymmac
PLEASE - Omido, Ex Habit
Riot Girl - Good Charlotte
The Wall - PatrickReza
All In - Chri$tian Gate$

Crazy - Jake Daniels
Follow You - Bring Me The Horizon
Pain - Jake Daniels
Super Villain - Stileto, Silent Child, Kendyle Paige
Freakout - Gianni Caneti
ghost town - JVKE
Dangerous State of Mind - Chri$tian Gate$
November - PatrickReza
Bloody Valentine - Good Charlotte
Bodies - Bryce Fox
Body (slowed & Reverb) - Rosenfeld
Baby - Elvis Drew, Avivian
DiE4u - Bring Me The Horizon
Avril's Song - MOD SUN
Problems - Jake Daniels
Night People - You Me At Six
SWEAT - PatrickReza
Only - NF, Sasha Alez Sloan
Where Were You - girlfriends - Travis Barker
Can You Hold Me - NF, Britt Nicole
The Raging Sea - Broadside
Say Anything - Good Charlotte
Hurt Me - Suriel Hess
I miss you, I'm sorry - Gracie Abrams
Back in My Arms - Carlie Hanson
Somwhere Only We Know - Keane
Two Punks In Love - bülow

PROLOGUE
BILLIE

LET GO - LIL DUSTY G

Two Years Ago...

The screams of the crowd always resonate loudly, but it's the sound of the fallen that's deafening.

Tonight, we are the fallen.

Silver Falls is the epitome of the American dream. A beautiful U.S. city full of happy workers and growing families on the south bank of the Silver Snake River. Green parks, bright malls, and one of the best colleges in the tri-state area.

Just like every American dream, it hides its dark, dirty side not far from reach but far enough to turn a blind eye to it.

The North of the river is also simply known as North Shore. Overpopulated, with low to no-income inhabitants, the highest crime rate in our state, and enough criminals to fill up an average-size prison.

Our side of the river is split in two by the gangs who rule it. The Kings of the North Shore, led by the King family, and the North Shore Crew, captained by my dad and older sister.

Criminal organizations have a field day coming to our

town and offering deals to our petty gangs so they can grow their empires safely. This is precisely what the Bianco family did. The powerful Cosa Nostra family offered my dad a sweet agreement. They give us protection, money, and power over our rivals, and we work their riskiest crimes in exchange. The kind that would get us arrested and put in prison rather than them. The kind they can always say were never linked to them in the first place.

Thanks to them, in the last year, we took over most of the Kings' territories. Practically all their deals, and I'm pretty sure they're running out of options for themselves.

That's why they contacted the Bratva for help. They want the same kind of sweet pact we have, except with the Russians. The Wolves are a ruthless organization run by invisible men who rarely show their faces. Even their men on the ground are often hard to find. They're smart, cunning, and always make sure a wolf's face is the last thing you see.

Which brings me to the here and now. The Bianco family backs up our crew. The Wolves back theirs, and we have been battling over crumbs of business for months now.

It was about time to organize a fight in the Death Cage. The crime families decide who they want to send to settle the fates of us small gangs. The rules are simple, the Bianco family picks someone from NSC to fight, and the Wolves choose someone from the Kings. We settle this the good old-fashioned way; whoever is still standing in the end takes over our town.

It's archaic, violent, and deadly. But it works. It prevents all of us from killing each other. Only one person has to die to decide who of NSC or the Kings will rule the North Shore.

I wish I'd been picked. I'd have given anything to be in that ring and kill a fucker from the Kings. Not many in our crew can compare to my MMA skills. That's why I spent a few months fighting in Bianco's underground rings in California. But since I've been back, the head of the Bianco family has shown no interest in me or my fights.

No, tonight our side picked Jake White, a guy I met fighting in L.A. He's directly linked with Bianco. He's good, although I don't know how good the other guy is, and that could change everything.

I tighten my ponytail at the top of my head and hook two fingers in the silver chain around my neck. I run them along it, betraying my nervosity. Jake and I have kind of been dating for the last few weeks. He did it because he wanted to hurt his ex, and I did it because it was nice to have someone by my side for once. Someone warming my bed and giving me pleasure. I'm not the girlfriend type and never really wanted a boyfriend. I would not call what we had a relationship, more like a mutual arrangement. Nonetheless, I've started caring for him and don't want him to die tonight. The Death Cage, as its name points out, only spits one of its fighters back out alive.

My fingers tighten around my chain, and I bite my lower lip trying to focus on the fight. I'm not too close to the front, and I'm smaller than the average seventeen-year-old. Much smaller. I keep having to go on my toes and shift from side to side to try and make out what's happening past people's shoulders.

"I heard his girlfriend is here," a voice startles me. My stepbrother, Xi, is standing next to me, his sardonic smile plastered on his face.

He's pretending to act unbothered, but if we lose tonight, his side of the business will be the first to suffer. When his mom married my dad, he was given power over the drugs. He meets with our suppliers and spreads it all to our dealers. He gets the money back, takes his hefty cut, and gives the rest to the Bianco family.

If we lose tonight's fight, we'll lose Bianco. We'll lose our suppliers and Xi, his business.

"Yeah, she's here," I reply. Jake's girlfriend or ex, or whatever they have going on, tried to stop him from getting inside the cage. He did it anyway because he didn't have a choice. None of us do.

"She's at the front, you know."

I ignore him, going high on my toes to look at what's going on.

"She's gonna have a perfect view of him dying."

"Stop it," I snap. "You're being a dick just 'cause you didn't get to fuck her."

"Maybe I'm being a dick 'cause he got to fuck you." He shrugs as if he doesn't care, even though a second later, his face falls.

"What? What's going on?" Vast parts of the crowd erupt in cheers, and I watch some people start to make their way out. My people.

Pushing past the crowd, I see Jake on the floor, being strangled by the Wolf guy.

"Shit," Xi hisses as we both helplessly watch as Jake loses consciousness. "We need to get out of here."

A bell rings, and Jake's opponent stands up, his fists raised in the air and a bloody smile on his face.

My heart drops when I see Jake's unconscious body on the floor. "He's dead," I murmur to myself more than anyone else.

Xi grabs my upper arm and pulls me. "Come on, let's go." He drags me for a few feet, but a crowd shift separates us and as much as I look around, I can't find him anymore.

He knows not to wait for me. We have to split and run away before the Kings eat us alive.

I struggle to take in what's happening. Half an hour ago, I

was with him in the changing rooms, helping him prepare for his death.

Worse than that...*we lost.*

The tables are turning, and this town will belong to the Kings by tomorrow morning. I hear a gunshot and drop to the floor. Someone screams, and the crowd movement turns into a rush of panic. I stand back up right away to avoid what is about to turn into a stampede.

My phone beeps, and I grab it out of my pocket, going to a secluded space. More screams fill the huge warehouse. The Kings' crew is having a blast watching our downfall and they're taking advantage of the Wolves being here to get rid of some of us.

I look down at my screen and read the text from my sister, Emma.

> Emma: Where the hell are you? Caden King is looking for you. Go home right now.

My heart drops to my stomach. Caden is the youngest son in the *real* King family. The ones who started their crew. He is a ruthless bastard, completely unhinged, with a penchant for making people suffer.

During our high school years, the North Shore Crew has been ruling this town, and I've taken my fair share of pleasure being a bitch to him and his friends.

Now that they're witnessing our downfall, he will get his revenge. I know it.

My heart kicks into an unhealthy rhythm, and I hurry in the opposite direction the crowd is taking. They're all going to the main exit, and I'll go through the back, where I'm sure Caden won't be waiting for me.

Walking past the ring, I notice Jake's body is gone. There's a small girl still waiting in front of the ring. People are pushing past her, but she doesn't move or react. Her gaze is stuck to the exact spot Jake died.

It's Jake's girlfriend.

Just leave her here. Don't worry about her.

"Jamie," I call.

Fuck. I don't have time right now to be taking care of some girl who has no idea what is truly going on here. She didn't even hear me, lost in her own world.

"*Jamie*," I repeat in a hiss. "Wake the fuck up. We need to leave. This place is about to turn into Wolf Central, and if we stay one more minute, we're dead meat."

She looks at me, but her gaze is vacant. She's in shock and is going to get me killed.

"Come on," I insist. "Don't make me regret trying to save your ass." I grab her hand and make my way through the crowd to get to the back. I don't stop until we're outside. There aren't as many people here as inside, but some have found their way.

Someone calls my name, and I freeze at the sound of his voice. There's danger in it, and I know it's all for me.

"Fuck," I huff. I watch Caden King make his way to us, a carnal smile spreading on his stupidly handsome face. I take a step back, still holding Jamie. "Fuck. Fuck. Jamie...*RUN*."

Keeping her close, I break into a sprint, leading us to an alleyway I know belongs to us. Surely, they won't follow us there.

Things are changing.

What if they don't care about the limits we have set for our respective crews? This place is a perfect dealing spot and we had banned the Kings from coming here. That was before we lost a fight against them in the Death Cage, of course.

I lie against the brick wall surrounding the alley, holding

my ribs as I try to catch my breath. Turning to Jamie, my anger finds her as an outlet.

"We almost fucking died! You need to catch up, Jamie. I know...I know this is hard." My own voice breaks when it hits me that her boyfriend died. They loved each other. "But it happened."

"No," she whispers after a long silence.

"Yes," I insist as I put both my hands on her shoulders. "He's gone, Jamie. I'm sorry."

She explodes in sobs, talking about his family and friends and who will tell them. She falls to the floor and sympathy overcomes me. She just lost the love of her life.

"Shh," I crouch in front of her and rub her shoulders. "I'm sorry," I whisper to her.

"I can't...I can't, it hurts." She grabs at her chest, sobbing some more and calling out her boyfriend's name in vain.

"You're strong," I try my best to get her to calm down. "It's going to be okay."

She screams, and fear grips me. She's going to get us found.

"Shh, shh," I say as I take her into my arms, pulling her close. "I know this hurts, baby. I know. But please, you need to keep quiet. The Wolves have sent the Kings after us right now." I don't know why I keep talking and explaining everything to her. Maybe I need to lay down the facts for myself. To understand that this is indeed happening. "The Bianco Family lost an important fight, and the night is turning into a fucking hunt for North Shore Crew and anyone else affiliated with Bianco. If they find us..." I struggle to swallow down the fear. Nothing good will happen if they find us.

"Leave me here," she rasps. "Just leave me, please."

"I can't," I fight her. "Jake would have never let me. I can't do this to him."

"Jake is gone," she sobs loudly.

My heart stops beating when I hear hurried footsteps at one end of the alley.

"Right here!" a voice shouts. It's one of Caden's friends, Elliot. Both are just as fucking crazy.

"It's Scott," someone else adds, recognizing me. I recognize him, too. He's the other piece in their trio: Elliot's stepbrother, Ethan.

"Shit, shit, shit," I panic. I want to act strong and keep it down right now but, fuck, if they catch me, I'm worse than dead. I try to pull Jamie up, but she resists. "Jamie, get up. *Please*, get up," I beg her.

She finally follows, and I stop to look at the three shadows approaching us.

"Come out, come out, Billie," Caden sing-songs. A threatening melody that brings goosebumps to my skin. "We're hunting NSC bitches tonight."

My voice wobbles when I drag Jamie with me. "That's Caden King. We need to leave. We need to leave *now*."

We hurry toward the other end of the alley, but I stop and force her to stop too. Someone is coming from the other side. It's impossible to see who from here.

"Shit." My shoulders slump from the defeat. I let go of Jamie and run a hand over my face. This is not good.

I turn back to the three guys right by us and gather my courage. I cross my arms over my small chest and try to make myself look threatening. Or at least not like a little mouse about to be eaten. I'm not weak; I have years of MMA behind me. I won't go down without a fight. They can fucking count on that.

Caden gives me his most beautiful, carnal smile. "Billie Scott." He juts his chin toward Jamie. "Who's that?"

"I know who that is," Elliot says. He runs a hand through his blond hair. "That's Jake White's girl. Well...*was*."

"Looks like we got the best catch of the night," Caden mocks. His piercing green eyes dart to Ethan then back to Jamie. His friend gets the hint and grabs her by the arm, making her whimper.

"Leave her alone," I tell Caden. He's the one in charge, so there's no point asking his dogs anything. They only listen to him.

He takes a threatening step toward me, and his smile widens. It takes everything in me not to move back. "Now, why would I do that?"

Our height difference is ridiculous. I know the first impression I give. I'm small, with big doe-eyes, and on the skinnier side. But I know what I'm capable of. Caden King will not make me feel weak.

"The girl just lost her boyfriend. Don't be a dick, Caden."

"Talking about dicks." He smirks down at her. "How about I ram mine down her throat. She's single now."

The rumors regarding what Caden does to girls are sickening. What makes it even sicker, is that he prides himself on them agreeing to the shit he does to them. He's yet another guy on the North Shore with the biggest mommy issues who will never deal with it healthily. I've never had any real problem with him because our crew was in charge.

Until now.

Before I can help, Jamie is retching, holding herself against the wall and throwing up against it. She's been caught in the North Shore war, and she doesn't deserve it. Not after what she went through tonight.

I cut off the men's laughs with a stern voice. "How about you play your fucking games with someone who can take them."

"Yeah? You think you can take me, Billie?" Caden tilts his head and bites his full lower lip. Someone so sick shouldn't be so beautiful. His angled jaw tightens before he talks again. "With the state we found Kay in after she visited you guys, you're not gonna like what's to come."

His older sister, Kay, visited our crew a few weeks ago. She wanted a truce between our gangs. She wanted to stop the war. Of course, in true North Shore style, we beat the shit out of her and sent her back bloody and broken.

Karma really is a bitch tonight. And she's coming for me.

I almost choke on the fear for the second time tonight as I swallow it down my throat, but I don't move.

I feel a presence behind me, but I don't turn around. I can't turn my back to the Kings, they'll stab it.

"Take your catch and go away, King." His voice is unfamiliar. So when Caden and his friend execute his order, I know he must be a Wolf—someone more powerful than us, who doesn't care about what becomes of our fate.

Caden grabs me harshly, pulling me to him and making me grunt from his tight grip on my arm.

I keep my head high as his two friends come on either side of us, and they all escort me out of the alley.

I stay silent, using it as a protection, as we walk along the edge of the forest surrounding the North Shore. Despite my heart kicking and screaming, I say nothing when they taunt me. It's best not to encourage them.

"Should we take you to the forest?" Elliot sneers.

"Deep in there where no one can hear you scream while we torture you?" Ethan adds.

"We can make her dig her own grave," the first laughs.

I manage to keep calm until we stop in front of a matte green truck, and Ethan unlocks it. My body halts when I understand they're taking me somewhere, maybe where the rest of their crew is. Who knows what could happen there?

I don't think anymore, I just move. I throw back my free elbow and catch Caden in the jaw.

"Fuck," he spits as he lets go of me, taking a step back. Not waiting for them to realize what's happening, I make a run for it.

Despite running six miles every morning, my legs are just too short to outrun them, and Elliot is on me in a split second. He crashes against my back just as I reach the woods. I fall on my front, my hands and knees crashing against the dried pine needles and pebbles to protect my head from hitting the harsh ground.

He grabs me by the shoulders and flips me around before putting his heavy weight on my hips. "Where are you going?" he mocks. "Want to start the fun early?"

I grunt when he strikes me across the face. My head snaps to the side and my vision goes blurry for a few seconds. Blood tastes like copper in my mouth. My arms are trapped against my body, Elliot's thighs keeping them tight against me.

"Billie," Caden chuckles as he settles by my head, standing tall above me. Ethan is right next to him. "I thought you said you could take me, baby. I'm only taking your word for it."

"Fuck you," I hiss. "Fuck you and your entire crew, Caden. Enjoy this because I swear to God, you're going to suffer when we get back at you."

He doesn't say anything. His big, Cheshire smile is the creepiest thing I've ever seen. The moonlight is casting a shadow across his face, and he looks demonic. He lifts his foot and presses the sole of his boot against my cheek, pushing until the other side of my face is squashed so hard against the ground I can feel the pine needles digging into my skin and creating dots of blood on my cheek and temple.

I squeeze my eyes shut, doing my best not to scream from the pain of his foot crushing my jaw.

"Oh, believe me. I am going to enjoy every single second of this." He presses harder before letting go. I take a deep breath just as he tells his friends, "Put her in the car."

Not the backseat, of course. I'm roughly thrown into the bed of the truck and even hit my head as they roll back the shutter. I feel sick from the turns of the road, and I don't know how long I spend in there, but as soon as they open it again, I kick with both my feet. Instead of hitting any of them, they grab me before I can do any damage.

Elliot and Ethan are the ones holding me now, each grabbing an arm tightly enough to cut off circulation. I spit blood on the floor from when Elliot hit me. They walk forward, and I have no choice but to follow. Only when I look up, do I start to wish they had just taken me to the woods and made me dig my own grave.

They've taken me straight to Sawyer Price's house. He's their second in command, and his house has been turned into the Kings' HQ over time. I could not be deeper into enemy territory if I tried.

"If only you could see your face, little Scott," Caden cackles. I hate this nickname. My older sister Emma is the Scott girl, and I've always been little Scott so no one would get confused. I know he's using it to make me feel like a little girl who can't handle this.

"I think someone's just realized the situation they're in." Ethan's words freeze me to the bone.

They drag me inside the house no matter how much I wriggle around and try to kick them. There's a party going on in here, and everyone is drunk and high. The smell of sweaty bodies and the overwhelming bass of heavy music makes me dizzy. People cheer when they see me, congratulating Caden and his friends. They shout insults at me and the things they'll do once Caden is done with me.

Someone throws a drink at me, and I gasp as the cold liquid hits my skin. Ice slides down my white tank top, and I struggle against Elliot and Ethan.

"Bitch, wait until I get my hands on you," I hiss at the girl who's now snickering in my face. She slaps me and looks up at Caden.

"Nice," she smiles. She runs a hand against his chest and adds, "Don't be too long with her. I want to play too."

Who with, I'm not too sure.

Wherever they're taking me, it isn't easy to get there. We keep bumping into people who want to see me, hit me, insult me. I've had a few drinks thrown at my face by the time we reach the other side of the kitchen and go through another door. Once we're in, I realize it's a garage. There's shit everywhere, open cardboard boxes on the floor, and car parts spread throughout.

"You're popular among the Kings' crew. Aren't you, little Scott?" Caden asks.

"I bet many of the guys in this house wish they had caught you tonight," Elliott adds.

"They'd pay us a lot of money to do whatever they want with you," Ethan concludes.

I chuckle to myself and peer up at the three of them just as they release my arms. I take a step back for a proper view since they're about two heads taller than me.

"Let me tell you something," I say low. "If you kill me tonight, you'll have the entire North Shore Crew on your ass. You won't get away with it. And if you hurt me and let me go, I will come back with my stepbrothers and Emma. And you can be sure we'll get you when you least expect it. You might hurt me tonight, but you won't get out of it unscathed, either. So, if I were you, I'd just let me go before you get yourself in real trouble."

The three of them eye me for a minute before Elliot bursts into a loud laugh. Caden claps his hands slowly, and Ethan takes a bow.

"Wow, that was beautiful," Ethan cackles.

"Guys...she's going to come back with her *stepbrothers*. I'm so scared." Elliot pretends to shake and hold Ethan.

"Honestly, great speech," Caden says. He maintains his creepy smile when he adds, "Now get on your knees and open that pretty mouth."

I take another step back. This can't be happening. "Fuck all of you," I seethe at them.

It wouldn't be the first time I got on my knees to get myself out of a situation. Everyone on the North Shore learns survival techniques early in life. I've not slept with many people, yet no one can judge me for the number of dicks I had to suck to get myself out of trouble.

But never have I ever had to get on my knees for the Kings, and I don't plan on doing so anytime soon.

"I swear, Caden, I'll die before I agree to suck your dick," I snarl as I look around. Surely there's something here I can use to defend myself.

"If you want to tick dying off your list before sucking me, I'd suggest doing it right now," he says, approaching me slowly. I walk back, only stopping when I feel metal shelves hitting my back. "Because my cock is going to be down your throat in less than a minute."

The other two jump me, making my heart pump harder from the violence in their movements. They drag me to the middle of the room, and I fight with all I have. Which isn't much right now.

"Wait," Caden says, and hope grows within me. "She's right, guys. We're not going to do this right now." I relax my stance slightly, eager for this to be over. "Get her clothes off first."

"No!" I shout as Elliot grabs my jacket. Ethan grabs the front of my tank top, pulling so hard it rips from my body. I cry out when one starts holding my arms behind my back and the other rids me of my jeans. "Fuck," I gasp. "Caden, don't do this." Panic overtakes me, and I still when they violently rob me of my bra and panties.

I'm shaking, trying to convince myself that this isn't really happening. Not to me, not with them.

"I told you I'd get my revenge for what you did to my sister."

"She came to us," I fight back as my throat tightens. The cold air raises goosebumps all over my body, and I feel my nipples tightening as he approaches me. "You would have done the same to any of us if we showed up at your house. But this...we didn't do *this* to her..."

I cry out when he grabs one of my small tits. His huge hand covers it all, making it disappear within his grasp.

"No? You didn't do this," he tightens his hold on my breast, "to her?"

"No!" I whimper just before he lets go. "We might have beaten her up, but we didn't...we didn't..." I can't get myself to put an actual word on what they're doing. I struggle against Ethan, who's holding my arms behind my back. "Just beat me up," I whisper in defeat. "Please...just hit me and send me on my way. We'll be even."

I can take a beating. It wouldn't be the first time and I get hit all the time at MMA training. But I can't take what they're about to do.

I know his answer before he even says it. It's all in that sick smile of his. In those piercing green eyes as they light up with sadism.

"No."

"Fuck you!" I scream as Ethan forces me to my knees. "You're fucking dead, Caden, I swear."

"Am I? What a great way to die," he mocks me, undoing his pants. "While getting my dick sucked. Open, little Scott." I shake my head, tugging back until I feel one of the other guys grabbing my neck. At the same time, Caden fists my ponytail.

I hiss but do my best to keep my jaw shut as his hard dick comes to tap against my cheek. "Knock, knock." He pokes me playfully, having the time of his life. "See, that's just silly, Billie. Because now you're going to make me play unfair. We were having such a good time."

He nods to Elliot, and I feel him shift. While Ethan is kneeling behind me, holding my arms tightly, Elliot crouches next to me, with his hand still at the back of my neck. He winks at me, shakes his head to get his blond hair off his face, and casually brings his fingers to my nose, pinching tightly.

I fight back, wriggling and trying to gain back any sort of control, but I quickly lose my strength as the lack of oxygen gets to my head. In under a minute, my lungs are heaving with the need to breathe, and I gaze up at Caden, pleading with him silently to stop this.

"Fuck," he rasps as the tip of his dick traces my lips. "I love this look on you, little Scott. On your knees and at my mercy."

My body gives up, my mouth opening to drag air in, and just as I do, Caden shoves his cock past my lips so violently it hits the back of my throat. I retch around him, gagging as tears come to my eyes. Elliot finally lets go of me, but I'm still dying for air.

Caden must read my thoughts because his threats don't stop. "Bite, and there will be nothing left of you when your crew finds you. Ever had your jaw wired shut? Test me and find out."

That kills the fight in me.

He pumps into my mouth until said tears fall off my eyelashes and down my cheeks. "Very nice," he smirks down at me. I squeeze my eyes shut, the humiliation too much to process as reality.

My stomach twists as he goes further, and I'm scared I'm going to be sick all over him. I feel him shift before telling me, "Open your eyes, pretty girl." I do and recoil at what's in front of me.

His phone is pointing down at me. The flash comes on, blinding me and making me squint my eyes, but it doesn't come off.

The bastard is filming me.

I try to shake my head, except he goes harder. I plead with my eyes, twisting to pull at my restricted arms. There's nothing to do. My entire body is stuck, and a sob wracks my chest.

"Fuck, Billie," Caden whispers in a ragged breath. "It feels so fucking good to put you in your place."

Please, stop. Please, stop. Please, stop. I chant in my head. Surely, he'll hear it at some point.

I'm certain he does because he does the exact opposite. Just to spite me. He goes harder before pushing so far down my throat my nose hits his pubic bone. He's choking me. I can't breathe. He's going to kill me like this. I bend and turn, causing everyone's grip on me to tighten. Tears are flowing down my cheeks, and I've never felt so close to breaking in my entire life.

He pulls out, allowing me to take a deep breath. "Cad—" He doesn't let me finish, forcing his way back in. He increases his pace, his hand at the top of my head holding my ponytail so tightly I fear it's going to rip.

"Fuck, she's hot," Elliot breathes out.

"Come in her mouth, Cade," Ethan adds.

And he does. I feel him explode against my tongue and slow down. Even when he stops moving, I can't even spit it out or swallow with his hard dick still in my mouth.

"I'm going to take my dick out of your mouth, and you're going to show me my cum on your tongue," he says low, his phone still pointing at me.

I shake my head, so he puts on a fake sweet voice. "Do it, and I'll let you leave." Another sob threatens to come up my throat, but I keep it down.

"Don't spill," he grins as he pulls out of my mouth. I keep my lips tightly wrapped around him so nothing drips out. "Good girl. Now open for me. Show me the way I marked you."

I open my mouth wide, and he points the camera flash at my mouth. He pushes two fingers in, spreading it all over my tongue and making me whimper at the ferocity of his gesture. He pulls his fingers out, wipes them on my cheek, and says, "Now swallow like a good little bitch."

I swallow, holding my breath to try not to taste anything. Then I open my mouth to show him it's gone.

He cackles in my face and stops the video. "Have you ever considered a career in acting? You'd be an amazing porn star."

He takes a step away from me and zips up his pants, but behind me, Ethan hasn't loosened his grip.

"Let me go." My voice is hoarse from the face-fucking, and the attempted order doesn't mean much at this point. I sniffle and look up at Caden. "Let me go," I repeat, begging this time.

He shakes his head at me. "I'm not quite done yet. Put her on her back."

My heart drops in my stomach, making me feel like I've

swallowed lead. "No," I whimper. "Don't do this. Please, don't do this."

Ethan and Elliot force me onto my back, and I shriek knowing what's coming next. "You said you'd let me go!" I sob. "P-please, don't."

Caden spreads my legs as Ethan secures my wrists above my head. "Film her, Elliot."

"Don't, don't...Caden, please."

"I'm going to be watching this video if only to hear you beg over and over again," he taunts.

Then he does the last thing I expected. He drops his head between my legs and licks me from my entrance to my clit. I gasp, the shock so intense I don't even register that the light from the phone is back on me.

"Oh," he laughs. "You thought I was gonna hurt you. That's why you just lost your shit." He runs his knuckles against my clit, making me tremble. "No, pretty girl. I'm going to make you come."

He disappears between my legs, and I shake from the lurid feeling of him licking my clit over and over again. I have never had anyone do this to me before. None of the men I've ever been with went down on me, and the sensation is like nothing I've ever felt.

There's something that feels hard against my clit, that feels perfectly pleasurable, and I only realize after a minute or so that he's got a piercing on this tongue.

Pulling away slightly, I feel his breath on me when he talks. "Huh, sucking my dick got you a bit wet, little Scott. Did you know? Let's make it even better." He spits on me before his mouth is on me again, his tongue playing with my entrance before moving to my clit.

I try to keep my mouth shut, but he keeps going

relentlessly, licking me and sucking at my clit until a moan escapes me.

"Oh, fuck," Elliot laughs at me from behind the phone. "She's fucking loving this."

I shake my head. "I'm not!" I cry out, although it betrays my pleasure. I try to close my legs, but Caden's hands are tightly wrapped around my thighs, ensuring I can't move.

"Shit," I gasp as his teeth graze my clit. I feel my stomach tighten, my muscles starting to shake and my heart beating in my throat.

My orgasm is building slowly, and I begin to buck my hips against his mouth, chasing it desperately.

"She's gonna fucking come," Ethan taunts me. "You're going to come, aren't you?"

"No," I squeeze my eyes shut. But it builds higher and higher, curling inside me and making me feel hotter by the second. "No, no...No!" I scream as I come hard against Caden's tongue, my hips rolling, despite him slowing down.

Finally, he comes back up and smiles with glistening lips. "You taste fucking delicious."

Tears run down my cheeks as he lets go of my legs and stands up. "Why?" I rasp.

"Because," he says low, "with one video of you sucking my dick, you'll *probably* not get help after this. There's still a risk, though. Mean boys from the opposite gang made you do something you didn't want to. People could take your side if it got leaked. But with a video of you coming apart on my tongue? I know for sure you won't ever want anyone to see that."

Ethan releases me, and I curl into a ball on the floor. My entire body is in pain from everything that's happened, and I can't find the strength to get up anymore. I feel disgusting from what they forced on me: the humiliation and the pleasure.

"So," Caden squats next to me and caresses my hair as I try to stop the tears from falling. "This isn't going to get out of this room. Right, Billie? You're going to keep our little secret to yourself, or those two videos will be seen by every single fucking person who lives on the North Shore." He grabs me by the jaw and forces me to look at him. "Understood?"

I nod as another pathetic whimper escapes me.

"That's a good girl," he beams. "Now get the fuck out of here." He grabs my clothes and throws them at me.

It kicks me back into reality, and I dress in record time. They open a side door that leads outside, and I'm almost out when Caden calls me again.

"Hey, little Scott." His voice is soft, and I turn around, confused by the sudden change. He smiles tenderly. "Your cock-sucking skills are top-notch. Come back anytime." He explodes into a laugh with his friends, and they shut the door in my face.

I don't think, I run. It takes me almost half an hour to run back to my house, but I don't stop. Too scared of anything that could happen before crossing over to our territories. I wipe my face free of tears and zip up my jacket. I can't have anyone at my house seeing my ripped tank top. They'll ask questions I can't answer.

I push my front door open and walk right into the living room. My sister, Emma, and Xi are on the couch. Not far, my other stepbrother, Lik, is sitting on the armchair my dad usually sits on.

"Billie!" Emma shouts in relief. "Oh my god, where have you been? I texted and called." She hurries to me and looks down at me. She's much taller than I am and looks more and more like our dad as she gets older. "What happened to your cheek?"

Elliot hit me. I'd forgotten about that after the latest events.

"I fell running through the forest," I lie. "Some Kings chased me, but I managed to lose them."

"Fuck," Xi huffs. "This isn't good. It's not fucking good at all."

"I can't believe we're about to lose the North Shore," Lik adds.

"Everything is gonna become Kings' territory," Xi concludes.

Emma, the oldest out of the four of us, looks down at me again and frowns. She runs our crew with our dad, and I know she won't let us go down without a fight.

"We'll figure something out," she tells us. "We'll get together with the rest of the crew tomorrow. For now, I'm just glad you're all alright."

She digs her blue eyes into my muddy ones. "Are you sure you're okay?" Maybe she can feel me trembling; maybe it's her sisterly instinct.

Either way, I smile and nod. She takes me into a tight hug, and I breathe in her warmth and her strong perfume.

With the taste of Caden still on my tongue and the phantom touch of his soft lips between my legs, I lie to my sister. "Yeah, I'm okay."

1

CADEN

Me & My Demons - Omido, Silent Child

Today

I count the cash in my hand before looking around the room to ensure I've searched everywhere I could steal something. Jewelry? Done. Emergency cash they hide under their mattress? Done. Underwear drawers? Done and redone. I walk out and gaze at the family portrait hanging in their upstairs landing. I bet my ass there's a safe behind there.

I hesitate, tilt my head then turn around. Nah, I'm going to get caught for sure. I stretch my arms and walk down their double staircases. The houses in Stoneview are perfect for thieving. The parents are away most of the time and are too loaded to notice when things go missing.

The town is a half-hour drive from the North Shore, but our lives couldn't be more opposite. Only the rich and famous get to live in this city. The only problem with stealing here is getting in. It's hard to break into their houses to steal their treasures. They have top-notch security and it's practically impossible to sneak in without getting caught on camera or having guard dogs released on your ass.

Thankfully, I don't need to sneak in. I usually walk through the front door and smile brightly at their maid when they welcome me in. A technique I've perfected over time.

Strolling back into the living room, I observe the kid at the table, focusing on his homework.

"How is it going, buddy?" I ask, sitting down next to him. "I like the way your parents redid the bathroom, by the way."

"I'm not doing good at all," he mumbles, chewing on the cap of his pen and twisting the page of his notebook with his other hand.

I like Jordan, although his low confidence will get the best of him one day. I wish he could see how smart he is.

"Alright, let's have a look together." I grab his book and read the math problem several times before looking at what he started writing. "Okay, that's not a bad start."

For another half hour, I help him with the questions he didn't understand. Math comes easy to me. It's just another language to learn. It's simple and efficient. It makes sense. And, thank fuck, it never changes. Once you know something, you don't have to worry about it. It'll always stay the same.

A knock on the door takes us out of our hard work, and I peer up from the table to watch Jordan's mom walking into the room.

"Your two hours are over, Caden," she smiles sweetly. "Are you all done with your homework, pumpkin?"

Jordan nods and closes his textbook and notepads. "Yeah, Cade is the best."

I laugh softly and mess up his hair as I get up. Julianne grabs her purse and walks me to the front door. She fishes the cash she owes me for the lesson and hands it to me.

"You're amazing," she purrs before squeezing my bicep. Every single Stoneview stay-at-home mom drools over the North Shore poor boy who tutors their kids. They just love the rough look mixed with the kind heart. "Jordan loves you. Thank you for *everything*."

"My pleasure," I smile at her before pocketing the money.

"Same time next week?" she asks as she tightens her robe around her.

"Sure thing." I wave and walk to my shitty car. It looks pathetic compared to their luxurious ones.

Someone opens the gate for me, and I drive away. It's sad to see the way my surroundings deteriorate as I drive away from billionaire-town.

Silver Falls is average and the people here love life on the South bank, but it's definitely not Stoneview. I stop at the light just before turning onto the bridge and observe a family of four walking alongside the Silver Snake River. They've got a boy and a girl running ahead of the parents, giggling as they pick up leaves and throw them into the river. I rest my head against my seat and daydream about doing this with my kids one day. Getting out of the North Shore, finding a decent girl, and marrying her. Giving her about a million babies and watching them grow. If I don't end up in prison for killing someone, that's what I want.

Someone behind me honks, and I startle in my seat. The light is green, allowing me to turn right onto the bridge. I roll down my window and give the middle finger to the car behind me, my silver ring glinting in the sun, just as I accelerate and cross the bridge leading to the North Shore. It's a red, neglected truss bridge that barely fits a two-way system. On my side of the road, a sign says, *Entering Silver Falls North Shore*, as if to give a final warning. A chance to turn around in case someone went the wrong way. After this sign, no one can protect you.

On the other side of the Silver Snake River, the commercial street I was on before crossing is replaced by a rundown road surrounded by trees. No one really lives by the river here because it would kill the nice view people in the penthouses get from the South bank. We're all packed into the housing behind the woods. I drive straight through the woods and turn left onto the main road.

Two years ago, that wouldn't have been possible. Back then, most of the North Shore belonged to NSC, aka the North Shore Crew. The woods were theirs, and I would have had to take a longer route around it to get to my house and avoid their territories.

I smile to myself as I look at the town around me. We're the Kings. This town belongs to us. Every single abandoned building, every broken house, every cracked bit of the road and sidewalk. Ours. Even the abandoned cinema they had built when I was a kid, and the city was desperate to gentrify our area. They changed their mind quickly. After selling some parcels of land to property developers from Stoneview—who built condos and some shops no one here could ever afford—a few people moved here. Middle class who couldn't afford the South bank but still wanted something nice. Needless to say, they didn't stay long. Too many of them were robbed. They got scared and moved away. The buildings were abandoned, the cinema, the bowling alley, all of it was left for us to destroy.

And we did. Because that's what we do here. We can't afford shit, we're bored, and we turn against each other. And every single brick of those abandoned buildings belongs to the Kings now.

To me.

Since NSC lost the support from the Bianco family, they've

been reduced to nothing. They can't trade anything but drugs on the North Shore, and even that, they're struggling with their suppliers. They're fucking done, and they know we won our long war. Most of their crew has turned to us, joining the Kings so they could survive. If they want to eat and pay their bills, they work for us. If they want to feed themselves off our leftovers, they can stay with NSC.

I park in front of Sawyer's and close my door softly. I think if I slam it, it'll fall off. It's not like I'm completely broke. Between the North Shore jobs, the Stoneview thefts, and the math tutoring, I'm doing okay. But that money isn't for a new car. It's to get the hell out of this shithole. For that, I need much more, and I know exactly how. I just need Sawyer to approve my new idea.

I walk into his house and go straight to his kitchen. The guy only does business while cooking. My older sister, Kay, is already here and my dad said he was on his way. The Kings' crew was named after my family. My dad is at the head, and Kay should be his right-hand man. Unfortunately for her, she was born without a dick so my dad can't take it. So he put Sawyer in her place. He's not even family. No, my dad just valued his loyalty and violence. Apparently, I'm too unpredictable to be the second in command. I never told him I didn't give a shit and that I never wanted the role anyway.

Kay's not far behind Sawyer in our useless hierarchy, nonetheless, everything has to run past my dad and Sawyer before we put it in place.

"Hey," I say as I kiss the top of her head. "Look at you in a dress." She smiles at my compliment and dusts her dress. She hasn't worn one for more than a year.

"Yeah, well, getting out of the house and all."

"Thanks to me," I smile as I tap Sawyer on the back as a

hello. "Forcing you to get out of your house and back in business."

My dad walks into the kitchen and grunts a hi before sitting down.

"Nice to see you too," I tell him sarcastically. We're not exactly on the best terms right now. Thinking about it, we've never been. He thinks I'm a pussy for wanting to leave the North Shore, and I think he's a dick for abusing my mom to the point where she ran away from all of us. Great relationship.

"Alright," Sawyer says as he slides a chicken to roast in his oven. He throws potatoes on the table and gives us all a knife. "Get peeling, everyone."

We all start peeling our potatoes, and my dad gets us started on business. "I thought of your idea, Caden," he says low. "I'm not sure it's worth the risk. Sawyer can tell you more."

"Can't you?" I ask him with a little more vehemence than I wanted.

His answer is a grunt, and I share a look with Kay. "Great conversation," I mumble. "So," I say to Sawyer. "What do you think?"

"I think arms dealing gets people in jail." He's not much older than Kay, but he always talks like he's seen the world. The guy's never stepped outside the North Shore in his life. He's scared of growing our business because it could mean doing things he knows nothing about and losing face in front of us all.

"Please," I scoff. "Everyone deals arms. Fucking NSC still has that on us. How can you guys be so unambitious?"

"Will you be meeting them and doing the transports?" Sawyer snarls. "Cause I fuckin' won't, that's for sure. Get caught with that sort of shit, and you're not getting away.

Drugs and women are safer. Drugs are easily split into small dealers, and everyone from the richest fucker to the poorest enjoys women illegally. No one wants to save them."

I tighten my jaw to try not to insult him the first chance I get, running a hand through my dark hair and taking a deep breath. "*Obviously,* I'll find someone to do the risky task of moving the guns. We've got buyers all over town, even on the South Bank. This is a gold mine we've yet to explore."

"It's not just that," Kay says. My heart rate doubles when I realize she's on their side. We always have each other's backs.

She must see my disappointment because she continues with a soft voice. "Cade, you'll be getting guns from the Wolves. They're a dangerous organization."

"We already get our drugs and women from them," I argue back, trying to remain cool and collected.

"Yeah, but not directly. There's a process; we have middlemen. We don't have anything in place for that kind of trading." She tries to stay sweet, although the strong bitch who doesn't do business nicely is in the room. Not my older sister.

"I'm gonna suggest something," my dad intervenes. "Find someone willing to make the trips from the Wolves to our distributors. Then we can talk about it again."

Fucking asshole. He knows no one would do that kind of job for us. "Okay," I say anyway. "I will."

"Sure thing," Sawyer snorts. "You do that."

I stand up and throw a potato at his face. "Fuck off."

I leave without saying bye, hearing my dad tell Kay that I'll never find anyone. I text Elliot and Ethan to tell them I'm on my way to theirs and to roll me a joint. I need to fucking relax.

I park on their road and go straight to their shitty backyard. It's small, and the grass is always yellow no matter what, but at least it has some privacy due to the high bushes.

"Here's our genius," Ethan shouts as I make my way past

the two trash cans they use as a replacement for their broken gate.

"How were classes?" Elliot asks as he lights up the joint.

I sit on one of the plastic chairs next to them and shake my head. "I was at Sawyer's."

"Tell me you didn't miss classes, Cade. You're the only one of us who goes to college. Make your daddies proud." Elliot winks at me and pulls at the joint. He's older than Ethan and me by a year but always hangs out with us.

"I didn't have anything today." I'm the only one who goes, even though it's still the worst community college in the state.

North Shore Community College is overpacked with students who want a chance at life yet can't get out of here. It's a fucking joke because one of the best universities in the world is in Silver Falls. Unfortunately, it's unaffordable for any of us, even if we have the brains. No kids from the North Shore ever got a scholarship to attend there. They're too scared we'd bring trouble with us. We can barely afford our community college, to begin with.

The trash cans move and we all turn to watch Jade walk into the backyard. She zips up her coat as she walks our way. "Hey, fuckers," she grins. "I see you started without me."

"Do we have to call you whenever we light up a joint?" Ethan snarls. They're not exactly the best of friends. She fucked him first, and then Elliot after. She's been causing trouble between the stepbrothers for years. Jade is a beauty. Dark skin, pale blue eyes and thick, long brown hair. Her mom is Indian, her dad Portuguese, and she's a lovely mix of both.

She sits on my lap and wraps an arm around my neck. "Cade didn't start without me, 'cause he's a good friend." I grab her waist, lifting and putting her on the chair beside mine. Elliot passes the joint to Ethan as I dust off my jeans.

"Ouch, my feelings," she snorts.

Jade has been very clear over the years about wanting to have sex with me. I personally think she did well enough with the brothers and doesn't need to add me to the list. We're better as friends. She's fine with it unless she's drunk and texts me all the things she'd like to do to me.

"I bumped into Sophie." She smirks at me. "Such a pretty name for a huge slut like her."

Ethan chokes on the smoke as he explodes in a laugh.

"She's sporting a nice necklace," she continues before turning to me. "Yours." She drags her index finger from her ear to her chin, indicating what she means.

"What?" I shrug. "She's a good fuck."

Ethan passes me the joint, and I drag in the smoke as Jade keeps going. "Why do you always do this? Leave hickeys along their jaws. Like, everyone is so aware every time you fuck a girl."

We all chuckle, and I relax as the weed spreads through my system. "I like marking my territory."

"Women are not objects," she huffs. "You three are bad, but you're seriously the worst, Cade."

"Women are not objects," I agree. "But the women I fuck are whatever I want them to be. They have no issue with it, trust me." I wink at her and she takes the joint from me.

"Keep begging, and you'll get your turn at some point," Elliot adds. "You'll go through the three of us eventually."

She gives him a middle finger, and we laugh again. All of us but Ethan.

"Sensitive topic," Elliot adds just to make fun of his brother. "So, how was it at Sawyer's?"

"Shit," I say, putting my hands in my jeans. It's the end of October, so the winter cold is already starting to take over our

LOLA KING

town. Jade hands the joint back to Ethan and they all turn to me. "It's a big 'no' for arms."

Jade's mouth twists. "We kinda expected that."

"It's a risky move. Sawyer hates anything risky," Ethan adds.

"Yeah, but it would make us so much money."

Elliot smiles knowingly at me. "And fast."

"And fast," I confirm.

Jade huffs. "You just want to get out of here quicker. You still have another year of college after this one."

"Yeah, imagine the kind of money I'd have if I'm the one in charge of arms dealing for more than a year?"

The joint comes back to me, and I take a drag. I let my head fall back and exhale before saying, "They said if I find someone to be the middleman, they'll let me do it. Someone who'll take the fall if things go south."

"What will they do exactly?" Ethan asks. "Drive from your supplier to us?"

"Yeah, basically. And go to prison for us."

"I'm sure you'll find someone real quick," Elliot mocks.

"You have two solutions for that kind of driver," Jade says low. "Either you pay them a shit ton of money, or you blackmail them into doing it." She shrugs. "We all know you're tight as fuck when it comes to money, and you won't spend an extra cent than necessary."

I smile as I bring my head up and look at her. "So you're telling me to find someone to blackmail?"

"That's what I'd do. Or someone you can trust and who you can promise something to if they do the job right."

I nod slowly before tilting my head to the side. "Jade," I smile. "I'll fuck you if you move guns for me."

Elliot and Ethan laugh as my friend gives me the middle

32

finger. "I don't want your fucking dick. Just go stick it in Sophie for all I care."

Our laughs double, and she gets off her seat. "Whatever, I'm gonna get a beer."

"You've upset her," Elliot laughs.

"She prefers when she's the one fucking her friends over," Ethan adds bitterly.

I lick my lips as I stare up into the darkening sky. The sun is setting and the moon is rising. I'm a night owl, so I'm sure I'll figure something out during the late hours.

I've always felt more alive when the darkness surrounds us, and the stillness mutes the town.

2

BILLIE

Storm - Honors

"Thirty seconds left!" Dickie shouts to the three of us. He runs intensive training sessions at night, and not many of us can take his kind of intensity. "Come on! Hit that bag! Give it all you got!"

I feel him coming closer to me and I accelerate, trying to keep breathing as I hit the bag over and over again. My knuckles are hurting despite the gloves, but I don't care. I can fight without them if I want to, though Dickie has forbidden it. He said I needed to take care of my body if I wanted to take this seriously. I do.

I feel him at my side and the next thing I know, he's hitting me in the stomach. My abs tense, and I know he's not using much strength, even though I can feel it alright. "Come on, Billie. You can do better than that!" he shouts in my ear. He hits me repeatedly until the bell rings, indicating the end of the session.

He moves away from me as I take a step back and put a hand on the bag to stop it from swinging into my face. My other hand comes to my ribs, and I fold in half, panting and sweating. Fuck, I needed this to get my mind off things.

"Alright, everyone. Do some stretching and go home. We're done for today." He claps his hand and leaves the main room of the rundown gym.

It's really shit. The ring barely holds together, most of the bags are covered in duct tape from the tears over the years, and most of the neon tube lights are broken.

But it's free.

Dickie took over the gym after the previous owner died, and he's been doing his best to maintain it. We come on a 'pay-what-you-can' basis and since most of us can't pay shit, we train for free. He doesn't care as long as it keeps us off the streets.

I head to the shower after twenty minutes of stretching my sore body. The water is freezing, which makes me gasp as it sprays on my skin. There's no hot water in these changing rooms, but I don't care. I always shower here anyway because it delays me going out.

This gym is my safe space. I'm the strongest I'll ever be in here, and Dickie always keeps me safe, whether from the outside world or myself. He's aware of my potential and has been taking me to fight at other gyms in the area. I've won every single fight. He has so much hope that I'll make it far.

The only problem is that I'm forbidden to do illegal fighting anymore. I'm also banned from getting into petty fights outside of here and I miss smacking a bitch in the face. I do what I'm told, though, mainly because making it to professional MMA is more important to me than my pride when a Kings' bitch insults me. I need to keep my body safe, or I won't survive long enough to make it.

I turn the shower off and dry myself before putting on my tight jeans and tank top. I gather my brown hair in a high ponytail and zip my bag. Grabbing my phone on the bench, I check for messages.

> Xi: Call me back when you leave your mom's.

> Mom: Hi, angel, can you buy mama a pack of cigarettes on your way? Love you.

> Emma: Let me know when you're at mom's. Stay safe.

I huff and put my phone in my pocket before grabbing my gym bag. The cold smacks me as I leave the gym. Dammit, I should have brought a hairdryer. I walk to my car and throw my bag in the passenger seat before rounding to the driver's side. It takes a few tries and a lot of prayers to the gods above before it starts.

"Thank fuck," I whisper to myself. The sun has already set, and I turn my lights on knowing perfectly only one is working. I need to get it fixed, only I can't exactly afford it at the moment.

My stomach tenses as I approach the trailer park where my mom lives. I love her to pieces, and I will keep visiting her twice a week like I promised when we moved to Dad's but, fuck, it's always stressful to spend time with her. I'm never sure what state she'll be in.

I park right outside her mobile home and take a deep breath. Here goes nothing.

I climb the step she puts in front of her door and walk in. I'm instantly hit with the heat of the place. She must have turned all her radiators on. It smells of dampness, cigarettes, and all sorts of food, as usual. The TV is on, except she's not on her sofa. I look around and find her by the stove, stirring whatever is in the pot with a plastic fork.

"Hey, angel," she beams with a cigarette between her lips.

"Come on in, baby, and close the door. Give Mama a kiss." I shut the door and go to her. She's in a good mood, dressed and clean. Her hair isn't brushed, but I can't ask for too much.

I walk to her and give her a kiss on the cheek before taking the cigarette from her mouth. I stub it in her already full ashtray and leave it there. "I swear it sounds so weird when you call yourself mama," I say lightly.

"I know," she smiles. "That's why I do it. I'm making mac and cheese. The box kind."

"My favorite," I say softly. "How was your day?"

"Good, good. I had work at the store, and I went." She looks at me, expectant.

"That's amazing. Well done." It might seem like nothing to show up to work, but it's a big step for my mom. She often isn't well enough to even get out of bed. Knowing she went to work is a great thing.

Her eyes light up following my praise, and I feel guilty for all the times I've not been with her to tell her how good she's doing. That I'm proud of her for being alive.

"Some customers are so fucking shitty," she adds. "I swear I could slap them. This lady wanted a refund for a box I know she opened while she was shopping. We're a tiny convenience store. Did she honestly think I didn't see her?"

I chuckle and fill two glasses of water for both of us. "I wanted to slap a few people today, too. My Philosophy professor outed me in front of everyone for missing classes last week. There are hundreds of us in the class. It was embarrassing as fuck."

"That's your own fault. You should show up to class."

"I had a fight last week," I smile proudly. "Dickie took me to the South Bank for it. Their gym is insane. It has three rings and seats for people who want to watch. *Seats*, Mom. How cool is that? You could come if you want next time. I won, you know?"

"I don't want to see you fight," she snaps back. "Why would I want to see my daughter getting beaten up?"

"That's my point," I insist. "I don't! I kick the shit out of them."

"Whatever, there's always someone bigger and stronger than you." I shrug, and she changes the topic. "Did you get me my cigarettes?"

"No," I snort. "When do I ever? That shit is bad for you."

She rolls her eyes. "So is fighting, and you don't see me stopping you."

Once she's done cooking, we settle on the sofa with our bowls of mac and cheese. We change the channel to put a soap on and eat silently.

By the time we're finished, I clean up as she snuggles on the sofa. I use the occasion to clean her entire kitchen area and wipe the counter. I wash the dishes she's been leaving in her sink for god knows how long, dry them, and put them away. I sweep her floor, mop, and then move to the TV area. I dust her shelves and clean the table. Then I grab all the dirty clothes and wash them for her before putting them all to dry. By the time I'm done, the trailer is squeaky clean, and she's falling asleep. My shoulders hurt; I'm exhausted, but at least she's got a comfortable place to spend the rest of the week.

I sit down next to her and put a hand on her cheek. Her eyes open right away. "I'm leaving you the bedroom," she says in a groggy voice. "I'll take the sofa."

She always does that when I sleep over. Unfortunately, tonight I'm not. "Sorry, Mom. I'm not sleeping here."

"Why?" The sadness in her voice breaks my heart, but I can't let it get to me.

"I have classes early tomorrow, and I can walk to college from Dad's."

She nods. "How is he? How's Aisha?"

"Good. They keep inviting you over. You should really come sometime."

"I'm okay here," she nods to herself.

My mom and dad didn't divorce on bad terms. Their love faded over the years because of her illness. It was too hard for Dad, and she loved him, so she let him go. She's not angry and has even met his new wife, Aisha. She's Lik and Xi's mom. She's happy for them. As happy as Mom can get.

I give her a kiss on her forehead and point to the tea I just finished making for her. "Drink that. It's chamomile and will help you sleep."

"Goodnight, angel," she says as I get up. "Say hi to Emma for me."

"Of course, Mom. Will do."

I leave and get back to my car. As soon as I'm in, I call Xi.

"Hey," I say as I drive away. "What's up?"

"*I know you're going to be super mad at me, but I have a huge favor to ask you.*"

"Go on," I say warily.

"*One of my guys got jumped by some Kings. They took all his cash. He wants to get rid of the food he has left so he can take a break. He's on edge right now and doesn't want anything on him. Can you pick it up from him?*"

And by *food*, he means *drugs*.

"Why don't you go?" I huff.

"*I'm with Emma dealing with some other shit. Come on, Bil's. It'll be quick.*"

"Is there a lot?"

"*He's a distributor, so, yeah. Enough to distribute.*"

"Xi, you know I can't do that shit anymore. If I get caught, I can kiss goodbye to professional MMA—"

The phone scratches, and Emma's voice is next on the line. "*I know this is shit, Bil's, but he lives really close to Mom's. The guy is traumatized right now, he wants out for a bit and we need to keep selling.*"

"What kind of gang dealer gets traumatized for getting jumped? Happens to literally everyone."

"*Please,*" she insists.

"Whatever," I huff again. My sister wouldn't put me in danger. "Just give me his address."

"*You're a lifesaver,*" Emma adds. "*I'll text it to you. How's Mom?*"

"You'd know if you visited her," I snap.

"*Don't be like that, please.*" The guilt in her voice annoys me. "*You know I can't take it. It's too hard for me to see her.*"

But somehow, she assumes it's fine for me.

"Just text me," I say before hanging up.

It comes a few seconds later. The guy lives two minutes from where I am, so I guess it makes sense for me to head out.

Once I knock on his door, he opens it like he's been waiting. He shoves the bag at me and shuts the door in my face.

"You're welcome, fucker!" I shout at his door. Dick.

I had to park my car down the road and I've got a few minutes to walk, so I put the backpack on my shoulder as I stroll back. I haven't walked for thirty seconds when I see blue lights in front of me. I turn around, my heart already beating out of my chest. There's a warning siren. A short *woo* that tells me they're here for me.

"Fuck." I break into a sprint as I realize this is a setup. Not by my sister, of course. No, their dealer has switched sides and is attempting to take us down in the process—typical Kings' style.

I hear behind me, "Stop right there!" But I keep running. My lungs burn as I get in an alley they can't reach with the car and sprint through. On the other side, I take a sharp left and enter a residential area. I keep looking for the street sign but don't have time to slow down. I have no idea if I'm entering Kings territory or not.

I run some more as I see blue lights not far away. I jump over a cemented wall and hide the bag under a bush. I fucking hope this is an NSC street still. Now lighter, I jump another fence and end up in someone's backyard. I exit through the front and run until I can't anymore. I hear another shout, and I know this isn't over.

Barely catching my breath, I cross into the woods and come out the other side. I run into a new street and my heart stops.

Shit.

I'm in Kings territory. I don't know the name of the street; I just recognize the crown spray-painted on the sign. A cop car comes my way as I'm about to turn around. I have no choice but to keep running. I take another turn, but I know if I don't hide, they'll keep coming after me. If a King finds me, my life is at risk. I try to ignore the memory crashing back of the last time I got caught by people from the Kings crew.

I jump into someone's bush and fall onto the other side. The branches scratch my face, arms, and neck, but I roll onto my stomach and plaster myself against the yellow grass. I wait until the car drives past and then until the blue lights disappear before releasing my breath.

"Well, well, well. Would you look at what the pigs dragged in?"

I recognize all too well the sound of the smug voice. Out of all the Kings that could have found me in their backyard tonight, it just had to be Caden.

3

BILLIE

MY HEAD - Layto

My heart stops and I roll onto my back, hurrying to my feet so I don't get caught in a weak position.

"I swear," Caden smiles. "We've spent the evening wondering who we could blackmail into doing a shit job for us. And here you are, falling into our laps like a godsent gift."

I gulp, noticing the people with him. Elliot and Ethan are sitting on plastic chairs on Caden's left. On his right is some girl I don't know. I've seen her before, although have never dealt with her directly.

I eye the backyard, looking for the exit, while Caden gets off his chair and approaches me slowly. He's got that predatory way about him that I hate. I've managed to avoid being in his vicinity for two years. Since that night, I have done everything in my power to forget and move on. Now here I am, choosing his *fucking* backyard to escape the cops.

Noticing the trash cans on the other side of the yard, I take a slight step to the left. His smile widens, and he shakes his head. "No, no. You ain't going anywhere, little Scott."

Deciding to ignore him, I make a beeline for the exit. I kick a trash can out of the way as I sprint onto the street. I don't make it a few yards before one of them whistles down the road. A few seconds later, members of their crew are coming out of two different houses on the street. A group of them blocks my way, and I spin around, but I'm forced to stop dead in my tracks.

Caden and his friends are waiting patiently, not far from me.

"Is that Billie Scott?" someone asks.

"NSC bitch in our territory. Someone's begging for trouble," another person adds behind me.

I do my best not to panic, even though fate is not exactly in my favor right now. All this for a bit of powder Xi should have picked up himself.

"It's okay." Caden smiles carnally before taking a step toward me. "She's with me." He takes his time walking to me, knowing perfectly well I've nowhere to run anymore. "And she's coming with me," he says as he grabs my wrist. "Aren't you, pretty girl?"

Fury is a small word to describe how I feel right now, but it's him or my body in a bag. I give him a slight nod and follow as soon as he takes a step. Slowly, his crew spreads out and people go back into their respective rundown houses.

Me? I'm stuck following him, Elliot, Ethan, and that random girl back to their house.

"Welcome to our humble abode," Elliot cheers as he opens the door for us. I'm assuming it's the stepbrothers' house, then.

Caden doesn't release my wrist until I'm sitting in the middle of the sofa in their living room. Elliot and Ethan are on either side of me to ensure I don't go anywhere, and Caden sits on the coffee table right in front of me. He puts a hand on my knee, and I push it away instinctively.

"Don't touch me," I snap.

"Someone is feeling feisty today," he says, amused.

"What do you want?"

The girl with them sits next to Caden and cocks an eyebrow at me. "Do you often talk like this to people who hold your pathetic life in their hands?"

I lean back against the sofa and cross my legs. "Go ahead. Kill me."

They would have never taken me back here if they wanted me dead. I know that for sure. No, Caden's got a sick game in mind, and he wants to use me for it. I'll say whatever he wants to hear as long as I can get the fuck out of here quickly.

The girl narrows her eyes at me, shooting daggers and making me want to taunt her some more.

"I must warn you, though. If you don't have a gun to end me, I'd suggest you just let me leave. You don't want to have a fistfight with me. Trust me on that."

Apparently, she's ready to risk her life because she goes to get up, spitting a 'bitch' at me in the process, but Caden puts an arm in front of her.

"Jade," he says coolly. "Behave."

"Fuck this girl," she snorts before going to sit in an armchair, away from me. "Just kill her already. She's no use for us."

"I saw you fight, you know," Ethan says. "You fucked that Silver Fall girl up."

"I did," I confirm as my pride grows bigger. I don't hide from compliments when it comes to what I'm good at.

"Dude, you should have seen her," Elliot adds as Caden cocks his head, starting to show interest. "She's got skills."

"I don't need someone with fighting skills, though." Caden

runs a hand through his black hair before leaning forward. "Can you drive, Billie?"

"Come on," Jade cuts through our conversation. "You can't possibly want to use this bitch for such an important job."

"What job?" I ask. They all turn to me silently.

"No one's talking to you," Jade snarls.

"Do you bite, Jade?" I tease her. "Or do you just bark like a cute little puppy?"

Ethan chortles, attempting to hide it by running his hand over his mouth.

"I'm going to kill the bitch," she seethes as I smile at her. My hands are damp from holding them into fists, and my voice isn't as assertive as I wish, but I got to her, which means one point for me.

"Answer my question." Caden's ridiculously emotionless voice brings me back to the situation in front of me. "Can you drive?"

"No," I lie.

"Sweet," he beams. "That means you and I can spend time together while I teach you. It's super simple, you'll see. Just you and me cramped in my car while I show you how to use my stick." His deep green eyes cut through me. Monsters hide in them, telling me everything he'd do to me if I ended up in his car.

I bite my tongue, not knowing how to get myself out of the situation I just created for myself.

"Unless you were being a smartass and you *can* drive. Should I ask my question again?"

My silence nudges him on.

"Can you drive, little Scott?"

"Yes," I push past gritted teeth.

"How amazing." He leans back, supporting himself with

his hands behind him on the table. "I've got a great job for you."

I reach into my pocket, pull out my pack of gum, and pop one into my mouth. I need something to distract myself. "If it's illegal shit, count me out."

Ethan and Elliot laugh on either side of me. "Isn't it just so cute that she thinks she has a choice?" Elliot says.

"Just. So. *Fucking. Cute*," Ethan adds.

"I won't say it's legal, but I can promise it's simple. You take a car to a place, let some not-so-nice people fill the trunk, and drive it back to me. No peeking at what's in there, no detour, no complaining. You drive there and drive back. Period."

A panicked snort escapes me. "You've got to be joking."

He gets up slowly and leans over me until he can hold himself on the back of the couch. His face is inches above mine, and I feel his breath on my face when he talks. He smells of weed and mint. "You've had to deal with me before. Did it seem to you like I joke a lot?"

A shiver runs down my body from remembering what happened the last time he had me within his hold. Not only how humiliated and destroyed I felt afterward, but the shame of knowing I touched myself to the memories of him. My brain must have idealized the situation. Over two years, my mind must have forgotten how utterly broken I was after what he did.

It's the only explanation for why I feel so pleasurably tense as he remains close to me. The only reason I feel my stomach twisting in the best way as he smiles grimly at me.

He cocks his head to the side, undoubtedly waiting for my answer.

"No," I push past my tight throat. "You don't joke a lot."

"No, I don't joke around with NSC bitches I can use for my own gain," he confirms.

Swallowing my pride is bitter, though now is not the time to play smart. With his knee, he kicks my leg off the other and settles in between them. The same feeling of dread I had two years ago comes back, replacing the warmth in my stomach. The simple gesture of him settling between my legs reminds me of the moment he had forced them apart to humiliate me. I shift, fear taking a tight hold on me.

"Now, I think you're dying to help me out. Aren't you?" he says calmly.

I shake my head slowly, trying to figure out if I can still avoid doing a dangerous job for him or if I'm genuinely, royally fucked.

He doesn't like my answer because he steps back and reaches for his phone on the table. "Do you know what I'd hate to have to do with those videos I have of you, Billie?"

Yes. I do know.

My nails bite into my palms. "You wouldn't..."

He explodes into a cold laugh. "Didn't you also think I wouldn't make you suck my cock? And that I wouldn't force you to come from my tongue only? Shit, baby, you truly don't know me."

"What? You went down on her?" Jade chokes.

"Don't believe me, Jade. Just check for yourself."

He taps on his screen and throws his phone at his friend.

"Don't!" I try to get up, but Elliot and Ethan are too quick. I'm smacked back onto the sofa in a split second, their hands on my shoulders. The moment my loud moans resonate from the phone speakers, I squeeze my eyes shut.

"Turn it off," I grit.

"What a fucking slut," Jade snorts. "Desperate enough?" she says as she looks up at me.

"Just turn it off!" I shout at all of them. "I'll do your fucking job, Caden."

48

He grabs his phone from Jade. "Hey!" she complains. "She was just about to come."

"No need for more," he smiles. "Billie is going to behave from now on, aren't you, Billie?"

I grunt a vague yes, barely able to breathe through the humiliation.

"That's what I thought." He pats the top of my head condescendingly. "Come on, let's get you back to NSC territory. I'll escort you so you don't get killed or anything."

Ethan and Elliot release me and I'm up in an instant. Caden walks out with me, and we start the long road back to where I parked my car. I'm silent the whole time. He makes a couple of phone calls and meets some guys he knows on the way, giving them random tasks to do over town. I simply keep walking and he always catches up.

When we reach my car, he opens it for me. "You came all the way to our territory. You're risking a lot here," I say, secretly wishing someone would jump him and kill him on the way back.

"Gotta make sure nothing happens to you. A pretty girl like you walking alone at night. Who knows what kind of monsters could get you?"

He knows just as much as I that he's the worst monster I could bump into. Ruthless, unhinged. I can't think of one sweet quality to describe Caden King.

"Careful," I say sarcastically. "One may think you care."

He wraps an arm around my waist and brings me close. So close my nose is practically touching his chest. He smells clean, like the sea. It feels aquatic and fresh. It's reassuring and comforting for such a callous man. Wrapping a hand around my throat, he forces me to tilt my head up.

"You're my investment now, little Scott. You can bet your

ass nothing is going to happen to you. Not until I'm done with you."

I push at his chest, and he lets me go easily.

"Give me your phone."

"Great," I huff as I take it out of my pocket. "Now you want us to text and shit. Real cute."

He smirks as he grabs it from me and calls himself.

"It's to make sure you get your goodnight texts from me, you know."

I shake my head, grab my phone back and get into my car as quickly as possible. I need to be away from him, then I'll figure out what to do.

He holds onto my door, stopping me from closing it. "I want you at Sawyer's house tomorrow at nine p.m."

"Sawyer's?" I choke. "The Kings will have my head before I can even reach his road."

"Nah," he smiles. "You're mine now. No one hurts you. No one stops you from working for me."

My heart somersaults at his words. It's the wrong kind of attention, but it's attention, and I haven't had that in too long to be able to ignore it and pretend it doesn't affect me.

"Nine p.m., got it? One minute late, and I'll start to leak that video."

I clench my jaw, then I nod. He finally releases my door and I slam it shut before leaving.

All I had to do was stay away from illegal business, and here I am, right in the middle of it.

4

BILLIE

Bleed - Connor Kauffman

"Billie! What the fuck is that?" My heart jumps as my dad's angry voice pierces through my headphones.

It's not his shouting that scares me; it's that I feel like I've been caught doing something wrong even though no one's seen me. I leave Caden's Instagram and get over the fact that no one caught me stalking, it's just my dad wanting to talk to me.

I jump off my twin-size bed and walk to the living room. He's in his usual armchair while Emma is watching TV on the sofa. His bushy eyebrows are furrowed as he looks down at his phone. My heart drops instantly. Did Caden release the video? It's five p.m. I don't have to meet him until nine. Why would he do this? Maybe he was just fucking with me yesterday and was planning to release the video no matter what.

My dad looks up, hot anger emanating from him. "Why is Lik telling me you haven't been attending any of your college classes?"

The fucking snitch. I roll my eyes as my shoulders relax and let out a sigh of relief. "I've been busy," I tell him.

"Busy?" he snorts. "What could you possibly be busy with since you've stopped working for me so you could pursue your 'dream' career."

Fuck I hate when he's like this. "I wasn't 'working for you', Dad. I was dealing drugs for NSC."

"I am NSC," he snaps back. He just can't get over the fact that he's old and can't be our leader anymore.

"Sure," I nod. "And I'm sure it must be horrible that your daughter decided to give a real career a chance rather than work for your gang. I can't risk being arrested and missing a fight. This is important to me."

"Fighting is not an actual career. You will never make money out of it. Your real career will come once you go to college and graduate and find a goddamn job. In the meantime, you're bleeding me dry for no reason."

"I don't have any use going to college," I argue back. "My time is better spent at the boxing gym."

"Look, pumpkin," he huffs, running a hand through his beard. "I don't care that you don't work for me anymore. Of course, I prefer you not to be involved. Of course, I don't want you arrested. But your sister didn't go to college so that you could."

"I never asked for that!" I defend myself. "That was your decision, not mine."

"Billie." His stern voice stops me from fighting any harder. "We lose money daily to try and give you a chance at life. That shit costs me three grand a year. Do you have any idea how hard it is for us to try and make that work? Don't be ungrateful. Just show up to classes and try your best."

Three grand. We're one of the cheapest community colleges in the U.S., I get the most affordable fee since it's my district. And yet we can barely afford it. I never even asked to go; they all forced me to.

Keeping quiet, I simply nod. Emma gives me an apologetic, tight-lipped smile before her eyes go back to her phone. Her face falls.

"Fuck!" she snaps.

"What?" I ask automatically as I head over to her. Something bad happened, and I can only hope that no one I care about is hurt.

Emma puts her thumb between her teeth, biting the acrylic nail extension. "Crook's dead."

"What?" I gasp as I look at her screen.

"Don't look," she grunts, pulling her phone away and giving it to my dad instead. But I saw the picture that was sent to her.

Crook is one of Emma's close guys. He usually takes illegal bets on anything across town, but a couple of weeks ago, she sent him to spy on the Kings. They've been stealing people from our crew anyway, so it wasn't weird to them that Crook switched sides.

It seems they caught him reporting to us.

In the picture, his tongue was cut out and stapled to his naked chest. They bashed his head in so much that his nose was flat and caved inside his skull. He was in a pool of his own blood, and I'm sure the bullet to his forehead came after they tortured him. I know who did it because, right under his tongue, someone carved a massive crown on his chest.

Caden's signature.

My dad's eyes narrow on the phone as he reads out loud. "This is what happens to snitches. I shot him in case, but he opted for the coward's way to go."

"Fuck," I huff.

The Kings are vicious. They pride themselves on killing

people from fear. They torture them so much that their heart gives out. And they call that *the coward's way to go.*

"Caden King gets more dangerous and unpredictable by the minute," Emma says low. "He's out of control."

My dad runs his big hand across his face. "I told you it was a mistake to send Crook."

Instead of acknowledging the criticism, Emma answers without an ounce of emotion in her voice. "We'll lay low for a bit. Let Caden calm down. Then we'll strike again."

"That's not a good idea," I jump in.

"You said you didn't want any part in this," she hisses at me. "Go to your fucking room and let the adults handle it."

Narrowing my eyes at her, I swallow the fact that she just threw my own words in my face and stride back to my room.

At nine p.m. on the dot, I am parked on the street, just opposite Sawyer's house. Caden was right; no one bothered me. Some guys looked a little too closely for my taste when I was stopped at a traffic light, but they backed away as soon as they saw it was me. I guess I'm more or less safe from the Kings. As long as Caden decides so. Still, it's fucking terrifying to be here when I know what he did to Crook not even twenty-four hours ago.

My phone beeps at 9:01.

> Caden: I guess you didn't take my threat seriously. I said not one minute late.

I speed-type to reply as quickly as I can.

> Billie: I'm right outside!

> Caden: Come in. We're in the kitchen.

Great. He doesn't even bother coming to me. Walking to Sawyer's house feels the same as heading to a death sentence. My hand trembles when I knock on the door, and I force myself to calm down. This is going to be okay. I just need to do a drive for him. I don't even have to look at what's in the trunk.

I slip two fingers beneath the chain around my neck and rub it to bring me peace.

You're going to be okay.

No one answers, so I push the door open and walk right into their living room. My stomach tightens with fear when I remember the last time I was here. I hurry, walking straight into the kitchen, and face the people in front of me.

Sawyer, whom I know from the many times he had fights with my stepbrothers, is leaning against the kitchen counter, sharpening a knife, and staring at me as I placate myself against the door I just closed. He watches me as my eyes stay stuck on the knife.

"I'm about to cut some meat," he says with a voice that makes me wonder if I'm the meat.

Caden is sitting at one end of the table, and his older sister Kay is across from him.

Fucking. Kay.

She cocks an eyebrow at me as she gets up from her chair and walks to me. To say we have a complicated history would be the understatement of the year.

When I was thirteen, and she was seventeen, Kay and her girls found me after school and forced me to go to their side of the town. Once we were away from everyone, they beat the shit out of me, leaving me for dead. I was in the hospital for weeks, bleeding my dad's money dry. I still have a long scar on my left forearm from the surgery after she broke my arm and one just below my right ear from when she beat me repeatedly with a knuckle duster.

That wasn't even the worst part. They did it because of some guy my sister, Emma, and her were fighting over. It wasn't even something I was involved in or that I could have controlled. I was barely a teen, small and defenseless, and there were three of them. I loathe this woman more than any other.

The only good thing that came out of it was that I started boxing after that, promising myself I would never be weak again. Now I *wish* she'd try and find me when I'm alone. Just to beat the shit out of her and leave *her* for dead. Just to give her a taste of what it's like to be the girl who can't defend herself.

I'm terrified of every single person in this room, but I'll die before letting Kayla King think she can intimidate me ever again in my life.

I push away from the door and meet her before she gets to me. She's pretty tall compared to me, yet I glare up at her with all the hate I have for her. I cross my arms at my chest, attempting to make myself more threatening, and wait for her to say something.

She puts a hand on her hip and tilts her head, her hair flowing to the side. It's black like Caden's.

"Isn't it so comical that you will be working for the Kings? I bet I'm the person you hate the most in this town." She bends down slightly, her hands on her knees, pretending she's talking to a child. "I bet you can still taste blood from that time we kicked your skinny ass. Now look at you, doing jobs for me."

I can't control myself. Despite knowing I shouldn't fight outside of the gym, that I shouldn't risk hurting myself and especially my hands, I shove her hard. She's forced to take a few steps back and before she can react, I swing. My fist

56

connects with her cheek in a loud smack of flesh upon flesh, and she falls to the floor with a loud grunt.

Sawyer and Caden are on us the next second. The former helps Kay get back up as she screams something about me being a cunt, and Caden grabs me by the waist in a bear-like hold, lifting me until my feet can't touch the floor.

I fight in his hold, scratching his forearms. "Bitch, talk to me again!" I scream at her. "I dare you. Open your fucking mouth so I can end you." I wriggle in Caden's arms. He's laughing behind me, making fun of my outburst. "Let me go!" I rage. "I ain't doing shit for you!"

"You're a real tiger, little Scott, aren't you?" he keeps teasing.

"You're fucking dead," Kay shouts at me. She spits blood on the floor then comes for me. Sawyer lets her, an amused smile plastered to his face.

Before she can reach me, Caden puts me down and pushes me to one side before extending an arm to Kay, putting himself between us.

"No one's dying tonight," he says more seriously.

She slaps his hand away and tries to go for me again. Good, I try to push past him, but he grabs my upper arm tightly then pushes Kay back softly.

"Back off. This is my first and only warning. The girl works for me. You're not fighting with her."

"She works for *us,* and only if I decide so," she seethes.

"Fucking drop it, Kay." His voice turns a degree of cold that makes me shiver. His sister seems to notice too, because she takes a step back.

"Alright," Sawyer cackles to ease the tension. "No need to let out your nasty side, Cade."

Caden runs a hand through his messy hair and tightens his grip on me. Sawyer and Kay's reactions make me wonder why I'm not the only one afraid of his 'nasty' side. Do they know it too? Are they scared of him?

"So," Sawyer announces as he grabs his kitchen knife again. He removes a big rack of ribs from the fridge and smacks it on a wooden chopping board. He starts cutting in between the bloody ribs, making my stomach twist with disgust. "Take a seat, Billie."

His hand still wrapped around my arm, Caden guides me to the table and pulls a chair out for me. It's not until I'm sat that he lets me go to take back his seat at the head of the table.

Kay sits back down in her initial place, across from Caden at the other end. I have Caden on my right, Kay on my left, and I'm facing Sawyer's back as he chops ribs on the kitchen counter.

"Are you ready to work for us?" Sawyer asks without turning around.

"Doesn't work include some kind of money or reward?" I say calmly.

He chuckles to himself and shakes his head. Turning around, he points the knife at me. "I guess your reward will be the entire town not knowing how sweet your moans sound when Cade has his head between your legs."

I feel the blood draining from my face as my heart accelerates. I turn to Caden, my lip curling as I wonder if he truly showed the video to Sawyer. And if so, how many other members of the Kings crew have seen it?

As if he can read my mind, Sawyer adds, "Yeah, he showed it to me. I had to make sure we really had something to blackmail you with." He settles down in front of me and places his hand holding the knife on the table. "Don't worry. It's only because he has to run everything past me. Your secret is safe as long as you don't fuck us over."

I stay completely silent, starting to suffocate from all of them being so close to me.

"You ain't gonna fuck us over. Are you, Billie?" he insists.

Under the table, Caden kicks my leg, spurting me into replying.

"No," I seethe.

In an unrealistically quick movement, Sawyer grabs my forearm and slams it on the table. He holds it firmly enough to stop the blood from flowing, and I gasp in fear as he raises his knife above his head. "Because I swear to God, if you fuck us over..."

He swiftly brings the knife down and a piercing scream escapes me, incapable of stopping myself. He stops right above my wrist, the razor-sharp edge barely touching my skin. "I will put you on that kitchen counter and chop your entire body myself. Understood?"

The blood from the ribs drips onto me as my entire body trembles, struggling to believe that he didn't just cut my hand off my body.

I nod repeatedly, the movement jerky and making me dizzy. Sawyer smiles and finally releases me. I snap my hand back, wiping the meat's blood against my jeans and hiding my hands below the table.

They all burst into laughter. Sawyer slams his hand on the table and throws his head back as he laughs at me. Kay wipes tears as she says to Caden, "Oh my god, the face she's making."

Caden gets up from his chair as they begin to calm down. He settles behind me and lowers himself to talk in my ear. "Come on, little Scott. Let's get you on the road because I'll do so much worse to you if I'm not satisfied with your work. I'm a very demanding CEO."

I barely have time to register his words when Sawyer starts

talking again. "Cade will go with you tonight, and tonight only. After that, you're on your own."

"After that?" I ask, utterly lost.

"For the other weeks," Sawyer insists like I'm dumb.

"What other weeks?" I retort. "This is a one-time thing."

"You honestly think we would go through all this trouble for a one-time thing?" Kay sniggers. "Don't be stupid."

I turn in my chair to peer up at Caden. "That's not what we agreed."

"Come on, get up. Let's go." He doesn't even deign me with a response.

I want nothing more than to leave this house, so I follow Caden outside quietly. As soon as we're by my car, I circle back to the problem.

"That's not what we agreed, Caden," I rage, finding some of my strength back now that I'm not surrounded by three Kings. "I'm going to do this job for you, and that's it. You can find another person to blackmail after tonight, because I'm not doing it weekly."

In a split second, he flips me around and wraps his hand around my throat. My back hits the side of the car as he pushes me. My defenses kick in, and I attempt to knee him in the stomach, but he grabs my leg easily and pushes it back down. When I try to throw a punch, he swats it away like it's nothing to him. His hand tightens around my throat and the lack of oxygen stops me from trying anything.

"We didn't agree on anything," he rumbles low. "You do what I say, and that's it."

Both my hands are holding his forearm. It's strong, veiny, and I can feel he's holding back his strength even though he's already hurting me. His fingers on my skin are burning a fire of conflicting emotions I can't control.

"You need to learn how it works with me, Billie. I order, you obey. Period."

I can see that he won't let go until I stop fighting back, that he wants me to agree to his words, to submit. Despite that, I thrash around and fight until I understand there's no point.

He smirks when I start to lose my strength; when he sees I'm about to give up. I turn manic when my chest heaves and I tap at his forearm rather than attempting to get him off me.

"Put both your hands at your side," he tells me calmly. "Show me you're going to listen."

The lack of oxygen is getting to my head as I feel my vision narrowing. Left with no choice, I let go entirely and allow my arms to fall by my side.

He squeezes a little longer for effect and finally releases me. I gulp in the frigid night air and bring a hand to my chest as it burns my lungs with every intake of breath. He steps back as I hunch over, feeling like I'm going to be sick. When I finally feel like I'm not going to pass out, I straighten up again.

"Anything you'd like to add?" he asks with his mocking grin twisting his mouth.

I shake my head, still too shaken to even talk.

"That's what I thought. Get in the car."

I quiver as I turn to the car and get in the driver's seat. He gets in next to me, and I start the engine.

"Where—"

"I'll guide you."

It takes all of me not to retort something.

"What the hell is wrong with your car?" he asks seriously. I shrug, not knowing what he means, and pull out of the parking spot.

"Your light, Billie. Do you not have two working headlights?"

"Oh, that." I've gotten so used to driving with only one

working light that it doesn't strike me as something wrong anymore. "Yeah, it's broken."

"You need to get it fixed."

"I don't have the money," I say quietly. Everyone is poor on the North Shore, but it's always embarrassing to be doing worse than the others.

"Take a right here. Get on the highway toward D.C.," he indicates. "I know someone who'll fix it for you. She owes me one. I'll take you during the week."

"Right," I snort. "As if I'd ever leave my car with someone from the Kings' crew. She's going to cut off my brakes."

"I can't have you giving the cops any excuse to arrest you while driving for me. You're getting your car fixed."

"Fucking hell," I huff. "Your voice makes me want to punch walls, Caden."

He chuckles, and I can sense his green eyes piercing through the side of my face. I maintain my focus on the road as I pull onto the highway. My hands tighten on the steering wheel, and I check my side mirror before pressing hard on the gas pedal.

"You're kinda hot when you're angry and focused."

"Don't," I snap. "Don't tell me how you find me."

In my peripheral vision, I feel him relax against the seat and spread his legs comfortably. "Why not?"

My heart beats hard against my ribcage, anxiety enveloping my body like a coat of dread.

"You know why." I force myself to push the words past the heavy lead in my chest and the dryness of my throat.

"Oh." He titters to himself before his sick voice perforates any sort of bravery I keep trying to put on. "Because I made you suck my cock."

A wave of nausea makes me tremble, and I can feel my back spasm.

"I wouldn't have done it if I didn't find you hot as fuck, little Scott. We're from rival crews. There was only one thing to do once I got you all alone."

"What?" I snort sarcastically. "Break me?"

His hand comes to the back of my neck, cold fingers that belong to death itself. "I could do it again, you know? We're alone in your car. I'm stronger than you. I think you're quite irresistible in your tight little tank top. I could wrap your ponytail around my fist. I also would really, *really*, like to see tears in those big doe eyes of yours again."

"Stop," I hiss. I try to shrug him off, but I'm driving eighty miles per hour and can't do any sudden movements.

"I've watched those videos so many times. Especially the one where you suck my cock and swallow. Gets me hard every fucking time."

My throat is so taut I can't breathe. My chest struggles to expand no matter how hard I try to force oxygen into my lungs.

"Get your hand off me," I heave. "Stop touching me."

I've spent the last two years battling with myself over what he did to me. The days after it happened, I couldn't speak or leave my house. I showered enough times a day that my skin was raw and red; it stung. Every time I tried to leave the house, I was too scared to bump into him. Every time my phone chimed, I was petrified the videos were viral.

It took me weeks to find a semblance of normalcy in my own house, but I still couldn't be out on my own. I'd always tag along with Emma, Xi, or Lik.

The worst thing is, I got so good at hiding it everyone thought I was still strong Billie. The one who kicks ass and doesn't take shit from anyone. They all thought my passion for MMA made me the toughest they'd ever seen. No one realized that the boxing gym was the only place I could forget about

Caden. About the musky scent of his crotch against me. About the choking feeling of his cock down my throat and the sickly taste of his cum on my tongue.

No one knew the boxing ring was the only place I didn't think of the pleasure he'd forced on me. I didn't want to come that night. I didn't want it to feel good. I never hated myself more than when I started associating sucking his dick and having his tongue on me as being things that got me wet.

The two events of that night mixed into the memory of the most earth-shattering orgasm of my life. The fear, the humiliation, the idea of two people watching us and being recorded. The fact that I was forced...it all melted into associating pleasure with a situation that I know traumatized me.

And yet, when Caden is near, when I smell that same marine cologne and the scent of weed and mint, when I hear his mocking laugh and his deadly voice, or when I see his wicked smile...my heart beats strangely. Fear and confusion blend, sickening me.

Instead of lifting his hand off me, he tightens his grip because he's a sick fuck who gets hard from torturing people.

"Don't be scared, little Scott." He massages the back of my neck, and that sick feeling melts into warmth, trailing down my back. "If I wanted to have you again, I wouldn't have waited two years for it."

A sense of safety comes over me. That's true. Caden's reputation has always preceded him. The sick King. The brutal son who takes pleasure in torturing his enemies. The villain that even criminals like us fear. No one wants to end up face-to-face with Caden. He's too unpredictable. Too *deranged*.

I thought he was done, but he keeps going. "See, if I wanted to have your pretty lips wrapped around my dick, I would have followed you after school and cornered you in that narrow alleyway you take to go back to your house. I'd have put you on your knees in the dirt, stuck between the wall and me, and fucked your mouth until you passed out. Then I'd have left you there, only for you to wake up alone with my cum dripping down your lips."

My stomach tightens at the thought, but I keep my eyes on the road and do my best to breathe properly.

"If I wanted to have your pussy, I'd have just broken into your house during the night and covered your mouth with my hand while I ripped your pajamas off your little body and bent you in half to fuck that tight cunt."

He finally lets go of my neck and points to the exit I should take. "But see, I didn't. So you're safe, baby. As long as you don't tempt me to hurt you."

I switch on the indicator and exit the highway, feeling so hot I am genuinely considering rolling the window down.

He's right, after all. If Caden wanted to hurt me some more, he would have done it long before tonight. If he'd wanted to harm or humiliate me after that night, my avoiding him wouldn't have changed anything. He would have done it anyway.

He simply didn't want to.

And for some mysterious reason, it feels oddly disappointing to realize that.

5

BILLIE

Fast Forward - You Me At Six

The rest of the way takes us through muddy roads surrounded by trees. It's only once we're deep into the forest that Caden tells me to stop. There is nowhere to park, so I just stop along the trees.

"Turn your lights off. Or *light,* I guess." Just as I do, another car comes our way, its headlights blinding us and stopping us from seeing who's driving. I know it's a bigger car than mine, higher too, but that's about it.

Caden opens his door, letting the cold air and smell of the pine trees into the car. "Stay here. Don't move."

I watch him walk over to the other car. The window must open because someone hands him what looks like a black cloth. Caden comes back to sit in the car with him.

"Damn, it's cold," he says as he closes the door again. "Alright, here's how it's going to work. Every week, I will give you a time you have to be here. You show up on time. Then you turn the car off and wait for them. Once you see their cars, you put this on."

He gives me the cloth they handed him, and I eye it suspiciously.

"What the fuck is that?" But I get my answer as soon as I grab it. "Are you kidding me?" I hiss. "I'm not putting a hood over my head—"

"Put it on. Now."

Something clicks, and I finally understand who's giving him the goods. "Brave of you to get supplies from the Wolves," I say. I don't know what they're supplying him with, but it looks like he's deep into it.

"Smart little thing you are. Now, if you know what's good for you, you know you don't want to see a Wolf's face because—"

"It's the last thing you see," I cut him off. The Volkov organization is notorious enough for everyone on the North Shore to know their motto. "But you just saw them."

"Yeah, well, they make exceptions for fuckers who bring them a lot of money. You don't make them any money. So you put it on, then you put your hands on the wheel and wait. They'll come and load your trunk. When they're done, they'll tap your window. You wait until you hear their car has left, then you can take the hood off and leave too. That's the first part. Simple enough?"

I nod despite feeling the fear heavy in my stomach.

"Now be a good girl and put that hood on for me."

"For fuck's sake," I mumble as I put it on with trembling hands. Everything that is Caden-related makes me want to drop everything and run away.

Searching blindly in front of me, I grab the wheel tightly. It's stuffy in here and it smells of dust.

"I swear to god, Caden," I say between gritted teeth. "If this is a setup..."

"Then you die," he says lightly. "Better than your videos being leaked, believe me."

I startle when someone opens my trunk.

"They're just going back and forth with the products. Relax."

"Easy to say when you're not the one with a fucking black bag on your head."

I feel him shift before his smug voice reaches my ears. "I can help you relax if you want."

"Not even in your wildest fucking dreams will you ever touch me again," I hiss.

Not caring one bit about my opinion, his hand comes to rest on my thigh, and I tense even more.

"Don't touch me," I rage. I go to take the black bag off, but he stops me with his other hand.

"They'll kill you." The sentence is so simple yet so effective.

"Then let go of me," I say as calmly as possible. He lets go of my wrist but tightens his hold on my thigh.

"Caden..." All my muscles stiffen, and my hold on the steering wheel threatens to break my bones.

"Just don't move, little Scott." His hand slides higher and I'm too late to close my legs. When I do, it only reinforces the presence of his hand against my pussy. My jeans feel rough as he starts rubbing me.

I shift, but it doesn't change anything. I would need to remove the hood and jump out of the car to avoid him.

"If you do anything else but stay still, these guys will put a bullet through you so fast you won't even realize how you died."

His fingers push against me, and my clit starts to tingle. The fear in my stomach doesn't disappear, but it welcomes the tension that wants to snap like an elastic band.

"Don't," I whisper groggily. Electricity leaves his hand to travel up my body and make my heart beat faster.

"I don't know if you remember, Billie, but telling me not to do something rarely gets me to stop."

He presses hard and uses my jeans to rub against my clit. My thighs tighten and uncontrollably squeeze his hand to keep it in place.

"Shit," I pant.

"It's okay if it feels good." I can hear his sick smile spreading and feel his deviant side relishing in the situation.

"It d-doesn't. Stop it." He presses harder, and a moan slips past my lips before I pinch them together.

"Are you sure?" His rubbing intensifies. "Are you sure it doesn't feel a little bit good?"

His other hand slides under the hood and I feel something against my lips. He's trying to get me to open my mouth with his thumb. "Just let it out. Give it to me."

I shake my head, biting my lips so he can't make me open them, but my hips are starting to roll, following the movement of his hand and chasing for release. I can sense a moan forming at the back of my mouth.

"Just let it go, baby. Show me how good I'm making you feel." He firmly wraps his hand around my jaw, forcing my lips to spread and my mouth to open. At the same time, he presses harder against my jeans and, ultimately, my clit.

I cry out in a groan. "No..." I pant as I feel myself getting closer and closer. "Caden...I don't want to come. P-please."

"Shh." His breath is against my chest, and I hadn't even realized how close he was. I'm practically heaving with a need to come. When his lips meet the swell of my right boob, and he starts sucking violently, I wholly let go.

With my hands tight on the wheel, I rub myself against him, buck my hips and chase the orgasm I can't resist anymore. He bites my breast harshly and I come apart on his hand.

He keeps rubbing me until my cries become whimpers and finally lets go of me completely.

In a forceful movement, he rips the hood off my head. Automatically, I squeeze my eyes shut, as scared to see a Wolf as anyone would have been to see the boogeyman.

Caden cracks a laugh. "They're gone, little Scott."

I slowly blink my eyes open, unsure if I can trust him. "I..." I gulp, suddenly realizing how hot I am. It was stuffy under that bag. "I didn't hear the tap on the window."

"No," he smiles and tilts his head to the side, observing me. "You were preoccupied with something else."

He reaches out to me with his hand and wipes my forehead. I only notice now that I've been sweating. "Had a good workout?" he mocks me.

I push his hand away with as much violence as I can muster in his presence. "Stop it," I rage. "Why? Why did you do this?"

"You liked it," he shrugs.

"I didn't *want* it," I shout while he is perfectly calm.

"Your body disagreed."

"I don't care! I don't want you. Do you understand that, or is your self-contented, pathetic brain incapable of processing rejection?"

He opens the window, relaxing in a way that shows he doesn't give a damn about anything. "Rejection doesn't exist when I can take what I want, whenever I want."

The shock is too great to handle. Is he serious?

"When you're done gaping, will you start the car and finish the job? I won't be with you next week, so I need you to know what to do." His casual tone pisses me off even more.

I feel the line between my brows trembling and contorting

from the frustration. I pinch my lip together, stopping myself from saying anything I would regret. I want out of this. I need to find a solution before he eats me entirely. Before I disappear within his resolve.

I start the car and follow his instructions. I silently drive to someplace on the North Shore while he makes a few calls.

My body is still tingling, electrified from the orgasm, and I can't help but think about the pleasure he brought me. About how my body *disagreed,* as he says.

Once I'm parked in a vacant parking lot where weeds have grown between every crack, he asks me to get out of the car.

"You'll come here after getting everything from the Wolves. Someone will come to get the car and bring it to the warehouse you see over there."

I look at where he's pointing, barely able to make out the shape of the warehouse from the lack of light. A car is approaching us, and then two men exit it. One is a gigantic beast I would never want to fight, and the other is a short man with a scar going from his ear to behind his head. The short man talks with Caden briefly, but I can feel their reluctance to say much in front of me. Caden introduces me as his 'driver', and tells them not to accept anything from anyone else. The guy takes my car away and follows the other vehicle back to the warehouse.

The cold night turns freezing now that I've fully come down from the orgasm and I'm not in my car anymore. I look away from Caden to avoid having to talk to him. Every time he opens his mouth, I loathe him a little more.

I feel his presence behind me before he speaks, his heat warming my back.

"You know," he says low. "For someone who doesn't want me, you've come twice for me."

"Shut up," I push past gritted teeth, not even turning around.

From behind, his hand comes around to rest on my right tit, where he bit me earlier. "I think it's strange that you can come from being forced. I also think it's hot as fuck." How can someone say such horrible words with a voice projecting absolutely zero emotion?

I snap around and push him hard enough to make him stumble back.

"Someone's not loving the truth," he scoffs.

"What do I need to do for you to just stop. *Fucking. Touching me.* I thought you said you weren't interested. I thought you—"

"I didn't say that." His voice turns a shade of dark that makes me tread backward, increasing the distance between us.

"You said it earlier in the car," I attempt.

"See, I think you only heard what you wanted to hear. I said if I wanted to have you again in the past two years, I would have."

"Exactly, then stop! Just fucking leave me alone."

"I didn't want you in the past two years. But maybe I want you now. Seeing you again, all weak and miserable, back to being at my mercy...maybe I want to take advantage of that."

I shake my head. "You're so fucking sick," I hiss.

"You have no idea how much. I've been so tame with you. You can't even imagine what I could do to that tight little body of yours."

My throat dries up and I feel a pulse in my clit again.

What is wrong with me?

How can his words make me feel so hot?

"Just find someone else," I whisper, turning away from him

73

again. "If you've got dangerous needs, find someone who's willing to experience them with you. I'm not."

He's about to respond, but the two cars appear again. The short man gets out of mine and walks to Caden.

"All done." He gives him a black bag overflowing with wads of cash and nods. "Pleasure doing business with you, King." Caden doesn't reply; he just nods back.

The short man turns to me. "We'll see you next week." He climbs back into the other car, and they disappear into the distance again.

"And then you come for me."

"I am not coming for you again!" I shout in exasperation.

He bites his lower lip before a huge smile spreads on his face. He shakes the bag at me. "I said you come *to* me, little Scott. To give me the cash."

I feel my cheeks heating to the point that steam could evaporate into the cold air. I honestly thought he said come *for* me, but I must have misheard.

"Whatever," I spit before rounding my car.

Instead of getting in, he follows me, forcing the hair on my neck to stand.

"If you're that desperate to come again, you just have to beg nicely," he sniggers from behind me.

"You know what?" I turn around swiftly, and before he can take a step back, my fist flies to his cheek.

He stumbles back, dropping the bag and touching his cheek. "Fuck!"

"Does this look like I'm desperate for you to touch me again?"

I'm annoyed at myself for taking the risk of hurting my hand, but I feel fine, and my next fight is in a week. Plus, there's nothing like seeing Caden King's cheek swelling slightly as it bruises.

"Billie," he teases as he straightens back up. His jaw moves from side to side as if checking it's not broken. "You just propelled the sexual tension through the roof, baby." He winks at me before grabbing the bag and putting it in the back seat. He walks back to his side of the car and climbs in, so I do the same.

"Fuck right off to hell, Caden," I mumble as I start the car. "Seriously."

He laughs heartily. "Can I take you with me?"

6

BILLIE

Take Me Away - New Medicine

Jab. Jab. Right hook. I take a step back, sliding to the side to avoid her attempt to hit me back. The bitch is almost done. I can see her jumping and shaking her arms, exhausted and trying to keep up.

She has no chance against me.

I give her a kick to the ribs, and she falls on her side. I can barely hear the crowd cheer, too focused on my chance to win.

Jumping on her, I sit on her hips and throw my fists at her face. Her arms come up to try and protect herself, but she's done for. I put all I have into my punches. When she protects herself too well, I go for the ribs and the stomach.

Caden's face comes to my mind, and I hit harder. I'm dying to take back control for what he did last week and two years ago. I just want to hurt someone else's body as he hurt mine. I just want to force her to take what I have to give. I'm struggling to breathe. Raining punches on her is taking all the energy I have left, and if she doesn't tap out soon, I'll have used all my strength for no reason.

I hear Dickie shout something in the background. I think he's telling me she's not tapping out. But it's too late now. I've come this far and need to dig up more energy and finish this. I hit her with a hook, somehow avoiding the arms in front of her face and getting her in the jaw. Blood spurts out of her mouth, and her eyes roll to the back of her head.

"End it!" Dickie roars. The girl's coach follows with the same order to the ref. If he doesn't end it now, she will get seriously injured. She's unable to defend herself anymore, and he needs to call T.K.O.

Is it my problem, though? Absolutely fucking not. This bitch will take until I'm forced to stop.

It's not until her arms fall to her side that the ref is on me. He pushes me off her and signals that the fight is over. Next thing, he kneels next to her, checking whether she is still conscious or not, but I don't care anymore. The crowd's cheers are bringing life back to my exhausted body and I get up, running around the cage and lifting my arms up to encourage them. I spit my mouthguard out and go to the side of the cage where Dickie is waiting for me. I climb up and bend over the edge as he takes me into a hug.

This is a shit cage. The crowd must be thirty people at best. The judges are sitting on broken plastic chairs, and the mic the announcer uses to inform us of the winner screeches into the air, rendering us all deaf for a few seconds. We're in a worn-down gym with not much at all, and I know that even the changing rooms barely have any water pressure.

Yeah, it's all shit, but it's a win. And as I come down from the grill of the cage and go by the ref so he can announce the winner—perfectly knowing it's me—I imagine the crowds of people who will cheer for me when I become a UFC fighter. I imagine the cameras flashing when I lift the belt high up in the air. I allow myself to escape the North Shore, to escape Silver Falls.

I see myself in a place where I don't know anyone, but everyone knows me for being the most ruthless fighter they're ever seen. They'll look at this 115-pound tiny girl who barely makes it into Flyweight, and they'll drop their jaws to the floor when they see me win.

There will be no drugs, no pressure, no lack of money. There will be no Kings crew trying to hurt me. Caden will never make it out of here, and I will be far away from him and his gang before he can harm me beyond repair. I know it. I feel it with the way the music and uproar make the floor of the cage vibrate.

The ref takes both my hand and my opponent's as the presenter speaks. He's not actually a presenter, more a guy who loves putting on a show for a few bucks.

"Tonight's win goes to the tiny fighter we've started calling *unbeatable*," he shouts into the mic. He's done many of my other fights, and everyone is starting to know my reputation in Silver Falls, South Bank and North Shore alike. "This is her fourth win this year and her *third* T.K.O., ladies and gentlemen."

My heart is beating so hard that I struggle not to tremble with excitement. My whole body is burning, emotions flooding my chest, and I almost want to cry. There is no better feeling than what comes next.

"The winner of this fight by T.K.O. is...Billie *the unbeatable* Scott!"

The cheers and screams make my knees weak. Apart from my family, I know none of these people. Dickie wraps me in his arms before lifting me on his shoulders. I raise my fists to the sky as he does another round of the cage. My huge bear-like coach has the personality of a marshmallow when we're outside the gym, and as I look down, I see him wipe a tear of happiness.

Dickie is a war veteran. When he returned from Iraq, his wife left him and took his two daughters with her. He had nothing left except fighting. She would only let him see his daughters when she needed money from him.

He was not a good man back then, though no one on the North Shore judges anyone on their past, especially me. He took his anger out on poor guys who looked at him the wrong way in bars. He lost his money and visited jail more than a few times. One day he got a call saying his ex-wife and kids had been in a car accident and were all dead. Two little girls, four and seven years old, gone, because his ex-wife had started dating a maniac who couldn't control his anger. He never got to say goodbye. All he could do for closure was kill the fucker. No one ever found out. He didn't get convicted or do time, and I think that was fate telling him it was his chance at a new life. He had nothing and no one. So, he became a boxing coach.

I met him in L.A. The year the Bianco family was backing up our crew, I was sent to fight illegal fights for three months. A way for us to show our loyalty. That, among many other things. If big organizations keep us as low-class criminals, they always have something to hold over our heads.

Dickie saw the potential in me right away. He was working for Bianco too back then. When I went back to North Shore, he followed me. And when Bianco got put away, he took the rundown gym that's on North Shore Crew turf and told me to drop all illegal shit I was involved in.

I have no doubt he sees his little girls in me. With every win, I see the pride in his eyes and the tears shining. Every time I get into fights outside the gym and kick some Kings Crew bitch's ass, he looks at me with that disappointed expression that silently tells me to do better.

He knows I want to get out of this shithole. He knows I want not only my UFC fame but a nice life far away from here. Make good money from fighting as long as possible, and when I'm done, move to some nice small town where people gossip about who took two parking spots at the grocery store. About whose kids are bad because they once saw them smoke weed. A humble marriage, possibly some kids. Some white picket fence and a small house. Waving at my neighbors when I leave for the boxing gym. I'd discuss how I used to be part of UFC over a glass of wine with them and shock them with YouTube videos of my best fights.

I simply want to be somewhere else. Anywhere that isn't here.

Dickie knows that, and he's trying so hard to get me out of this life. I dread disappointing him. But on nights like this? When I see him wipe a tear at how proud he is of me, I feel light as a feather. I feel like I can fly so far away from here North Shore of The Falls would just be a small dot on a map and bad memories.

Grabbing me by the waist, Dickie lifts me off his shoulders and sets me down. He hugs me so firmly that I feel a ball of emotion gather in my throat as my face hides against his belly. He truly is a gigantic man.

Some random local journalist takes a picture of both of us. I'm going to make the local news. Probably on that last half page, the one they dedicate to sports. I don't care. My stomach flips with excitement, and I raise one winning fist to the sky. My face is probably bruised from the few punches the other girl got in. They call her Feisty Cathy. She didn't stand a chance against me, although I do feel blood trickling down my eyebrow from when she punched me hard in the first round. That was before I annihilated her. She lasted three rounds. The third was obviously cut short by the T.K.O.

"Come on. Let's get you showered and changed. I need to check that eyebrow again," Dickie says as he nudges me.

Before I make it off the ring, the presenter, who loves to put on a show, comes to me with the mic and asks the same questions UFC fighters are usually asked. Instead of having a cameraman with him as most professionals would, he's just got his phone, filming himself. "Billie, Billie! This is for my YouTube channel *FollowTheFight*. My subscribers saw you live tonight, and they love you! You only have one more fight to win before facing the current local Flyweight champion. We have no doubt you'll get there, but she's never lost a fight. They call you 'Unbeatable Billie', but they call her 'Killer Clover'. How do you feel about that?"

I laugh at how serious he is about this. He points his phone camera at me, and I love it, so I play the game. "I'm coming for you, Clover." I stop at that, not wanting to say something I'll regret.

I follow Dickie to the changing rooms, and he gets his first aid kit out as I go to the showers. I untie the tight French braids I have on when I fight and relish in the warm water trickling down from my skull to my toes. Once I'm out and dressed back in tight jeans and a tank top, I find a bottle of water and some Advil next to my gym bag. I keep the towel on my shoulders as my long, light brown hair dries.

"It's stopped bleeding," I tell Dickie as I pop an Advil in my mouth and down half the bottle.

He still comes to observe me, leaning down with a penlight as he checks for severe injuries.

"That's what I like to hear," he says in his low grumbly voice. "Your cheek is a bit swollen. Let's put some ice on it." He cracks an icepack taken from his kit and gives it to me so I can apply it against my cheek.

"Alright," he says. "There's someone who's been waiting

outside to meet you."

He walks to the door and opens it to a man in a suit. He looks rich. The kind of rich that either means he's up to no good or he has opportunities for small people like me. Maybe both.

He walks into the room with a confidence I could never have and extends his hand to me. I look at it for far too long, wondering who he is, noticing the stark difference between him and us. I'm wearing the same clothes I always do and Dickie the joggers and hoodie he can't live without. The man's wearing the kind of suit that costs the amount of money I could only ever dream of.

Shit, I bet it's tailored.

"Hi, Billie. I'm Taylor Davis."

Taylor in the tailored suit.

Shaking my head, I try to bring myself back to reality. "Um, hi," I finally blurt out. I awkwardly put the ice pack down and shake his hand, realizing too late that my hand is wet from the ice. Feeling self-conscious, I take the small towel from my shoulders and tie my hair in my usual ponytail.

"Taylor is an old friend of mine. He's a professional MMA agent, and he came to see you fight tonight." Dickie can barely hold back the smile spreading on his face.

I blink up at Taylor, not believing what I'm hearing.

"Sorry, what?" I finally say.

"You've got some real talent there, Billie. You're a fighter if I've ever seen one, that's for sure. Dickie's been begging for me to come to one of your fights for months. I regret not coming sooner."

It takes me a minute to pick my jaw up off the floor.

"Bil's," Dickie smiles. "What T. is trying to say is that he wants to represent you and put you forward for professional fights."

"What?" I whisper. I grab the bottle of water I'd put away and down the rest before squeezing it past its limit. "W-what do you mean by professional fights?"

"Well," Taylor finally says. "We'll start with some small local pro fights. Earn you a reputation within the East Coast and—"

"Wait," I choke. "By local, you mean East Coast?"

"Yeah, we won't be able to get you to the West Coast this year. But who knows, maybe we can get you a fight for King of The Cage or Elite Xtreme Combat next year. Who knows, we might even get you to Road FC by the end of next year."

"Road FC." I inhale in shock. The South Korean lower league has seen some of the best women fighters, including the current UFC champion.

"Of course." He nods like it's no big deal. "You're small and skinny, though. So we have a lot of work ahead of us. We might need you to change weight class, so be prepared to put on weight." He smiles softly at me. "I'll take good care of you, Billie. I'm one of the best in the game, and if you let me, who knows where you'll be in two or three years. UFC is on the table for you, girl. You just have to put in the work."

Put in the work. So I can go to the UFC.

This is what I've dreamed about for as long as I can remember. Making money out of my passion. *Getting away from the North Shore.*

"Well," I huff as I fall back on the bench. "Shit."

Dickie cackles a laugh. "She's not used to good news, T. Give her a minute."

"Alright," Taylor smiles. "I will, but time is money. So, I'm going to give you my card and you can call me if you're interested."

I snatch the card off him and practically shout, "I'm interested!"

He joins Dickie in the amused side of the room and taps his shoulder. "I like her already. Email me, Billie, and I'll send you a draft of my contract. If you sign, I'm yours. In the meantime," he gives Dickie a serious look before looking at me again, "no drugs, no alcohol, no fights outside the gym. And absolutely *no* involvement in illegal activities. Keep training hard, and don't injure yourself."

I gulp at the mention of illegal activities, even though I nod.

"Our contract will have a clause that states I will only take you on if you win this local amateur championship," he continues. "I need someone with no losses, or you'll have no credibility out there. I'm not worried, in any case. You're going to give Killer Clover her first loss, aren't you?"

I nod, but I know he can see the hesitation in my eyes.

"This is the real deal now, Billie. You go for it, or you're left behind. There are thousands of great fighters out there. Show me you're more than great. Show me you're exceptional."

He nods at Dickie and finally heads out of the room.

"Oh my god!" I shriek as I jump up and into Dickie's arms. "How long have you been planning this? Why didn't you say anything? Oh my god...oh my god!!"

I release him and stare at him with tears in my eyes. "Thank you," I finally drop quietly. "Fuck, Dickie. Thank you."

He messes my ponytail and cracks a smile. "It's all you, kiddo. But you heard him. Time to take this shit seriously."

"I know." I nod enthusiastically, even though I realize it's impossible for me to stay out of trouble for now. But I won't get caught. I know I won't get caught. I need this like I need air. I'm going to win, and I'm going to become a professional MMA fighter.

I fucking deserve this.

7

BILLIE

Blood - Call Me Karizma

"Bil's!" Emma shouts as I walk out of the gym. Some people have gathered, having drinks out of their trunks and using the parking lot's lights to have their post-fight party. "You were unbelievable in there!" My sister takes me in her arms and gives a quick hi to Dickie.

He nods to everyone hello but doesn't actually stop. "Get some rest, Billie," he says before getting in his car and driving away.

"Yeah, fuck that. We're celebrating your win." Xi turns to me with a bright smile. He and Lik take me in their arms and hug me until I can't breathe.

"That's my little sister, y'all!" Lik shouts at whoever wants to hear.

"She'll kick your asses if you fuck with us," Xi adds before we all burst out into a laughing fit.

Feisty Cathy makes her way to us. Her face is bruised, and her left eye is swollen shut, but she beams at me. "You're one hell of an opponent, Scott," she says.

I nod and smile. Now that I'm not competing with her anymore, I welcome my fellow North Shore Crew girl into a hug. "You're not too bad yourself."

"Yeah," she smiles awkwardly as we separate. "Not unbeatable, though."

I shrug, not really knowing how to answer.

"Anyway," she cuts it short. "We're all going to the Death Cage warehouse. Someone is fighting in the smaller ring. Just a small NSC vs. Kings fight, nothing too serious. We're gonna take bets on us if you wanna join."

I glance at my sister and stepbrothers, about to say no, except Xi beats me to it. "Fuck yeah. I want to see more blood tonight."

"I don't know," I hesitate. "I can't get involved in shit like that too much anymore."

"You're not the one fighting," Emma insists. "And if things go south, we'll be out in no time."

"We got you, Bil's," Lik smiles. He's got the most contagious smile I've ever seen in my life.

He plays with his nose ring as he waits for my answer. He's got a fashion sense that demands constant attention. It calls to everyone. Earrings, nose piercings, pearls around his neck, and a lock necklace he never takes off. I love how much effort he puts into it.

"Alright," I give in. "But I'm leaving as soon as I feel too tired."

"'Course you are." Xi winks at me. He's a few years older than Lik and usually a little more serious than him.

Xi takes care of drugs and hiding bodies for NSC. Lik has long stopped actively participating. He has found himself a nice hitman boyfriend who takes care of him and earns money for the both of them. They've moved in together, and he now goes to college with me while living his best life, trying to stay away from North Shore troubles as much as he can. Only tonight, it seems he wants to have a bit of fun.

It's only a small fight and a bit of betting. And as Emma said, if things start to heat up, I'll just leave.

We arrive at the warehouses piled up in Xi's car. *Rockstar* by Post Malone is playing so loudly inside we can hear it as soon as we open the car doors.

"I love a good Friday night fight." Xi grabs some beers from his trunk and hands one to everyone but me and Lik. He knows I don't drink. Taking care of my body is essential.

"Here's a water for our future UFC champion," Lik says as he gives me a small bottle.

I've had time to update them on the ride here, and now they just won't leave me with it.

"Oh yeah," Emma adds, doing a little dance. "My sister is going to be rich."

"Guys, I have to start with beating Clover. And before Clover, I need to win my next fight leading up to her. So let's not get ahead of ourselves here." I emailed Taylor from my phone as soon as I sat down in Xi's car. I'm not waiting for another opportunity. This is my chance. But I don't want to hope for anything and their optimism is scaring me.

The heat of the crowd hits me as soon as we enter the warehouse. It contrasts with the cold night outside, and I'm glad I left my jacket in the car. The music is loud, *Smells Like Teen Spirit* now blurting out of some speakers. Everyone has started to gather around the small ring, and my siblings and I make our way through the mob to end at the front. We quickly recognize what side of the room our crew is on and don't mix with the other guys. Even the ones I don't know, it's still easy to tell them apart. Everyone who is part of the North Shore Crew has a dagger tattooed on them, with the letters N.S.C. on the handle. Mine is between my breasts, dipping onto my sternum, just like my sister's. Xi's is on his shoulder, and Lik's is on his forearm, below his elbow.

In contrast, all people who are part of the Kings crew have a crown tattooed somewhere on their body. People choose wherever they want to tattoo based on which crew they side with, although Caden's is famously on his neck for everyone to see he's part of the *original* Kings.

Because we don't want stupid-ass fights to stop us from enjoying our evening, NSC comes in through one entrance and the Kings through the opposite one. We occupy one side of the ring and their crew the other side. No mixing. We all know the lightest spark starts a wildfire between us, but we also want to see our fighter beat the other one.

I can't see Caden tonight and it keeps my spirit light. I want to have fun, to celebrate my win. What's better than watching NSC win an underground fight after the good news I got?

We don't do much else in this town. When people are not stealing or dealing, they hang around in parking lots, in front of the high school or local grocery store. We make bets on illegal fights and keep the war going with the Kings. Just like any other wrong side of the tracks, we're bored and abandoned by the government. We do what we can to keep ourselves sane and occupied.

Xi opens another beer by the time we settle right in front of the ring. The warehouse is packed, but everyone lets Emma through since she's essentially everyone's boss.

In our corner, a guy I don't even know is jumping on the spot and rolling his shoulders, waiting for the fight to commence. Unlike the MMA gloves I wear, this guy isn't wearing anything.

I used to do that, but I would never risk fighting with bare hands again.

"Who's that guy?" I ask Emma.

"That's Titan," she smiles.

I raise an eyebrow at her. "Titan. Who uses ridiculous names like *Titan*?"

"You can only wear a shit name if you earn it," Lik agrees with me.

"Oh, he's earned it," Emma nods. She grabs the kid who takes the bet money by the back of his neck and gives him fifty bucks. "Place that on Titan."

"What the fuck," I choke. "Stop flaunting your money. You could have given that to me. I can't even take my car to college 'cause gas is so expensive."

"When Titan wins, you can have those fifty dollars. I'll take the rest."

I shake my head and turn toward the ring again. My heart drops when I see Caden in it. He's topless, and I have a perfect view of his defined arms. I've never seen him without a shirt on.

Usually, he parades around town with ripped jeans and a black t-shirt. He's got an edgy, punk look with chains hanging from his jeans and a leather jacket. Usually, he's wearing layers of silver necklaces around his neck and a silver moon earring with multiple thick rings on his fingers that people on the receiving end of his fists will never forget.

But not tonight.

No, tonight he has on black gym shorts that hang low on his hips and show his white boxers and perfectly carved Adonis belt. His rings are gone, as they're not allowed even in underground fights, but mainly...mainly he's topless, and my heart just won't get over it.

Caden is not a big guy. No, he's the kind of tall and perfectly defined type of man. Muscles only and nothing else. They are so prominent right now as his tattoos move over his chest and stomach as he laughs. His bestie Ethan must have said something to mock Titan because Caden throws him another look before practically bending in half from laughter.

A band tightens around my lower belly as his deep voice reaches me and he runs a hand through his hair. He's not warming up. He's not jumping around getting ready by throwing punches into thin air like Titan is. He is just... laughing. He's carefree and so unaware of the danger from the beast that seems to be twice his size.

A bell rings from somewhere. There are no refs in our fights, just a random bell that starts the round and a guy falling unconscious to end it.

Caden turns to Titan and gives him his most demonic smile. The easy laugh now gone as the man I know he truly is, takes over.

They gather around each other, jogging in a circle for a few moments. Titan wastes no more time. He charges Caden, but the latter is too quick. He avoids the double punches and circles the ring.

"Might wanna try that again, big boy," Caden taunts him.

They exchange a few punches, yet both seem entirely unreceptive to pain. I get it. Adrenaline is numbing the pain right now, but one will fall before the other, and Caden is practically avoiding everything.

Caden manages to corner Titan close to where we are standing and punches him so hard three times blood spurts all the way to my feet. He looks up as Titan wobbles, and his gaze locks with mine.

I feel the world disappear as his piercing eyes cut through mine. My soul gets agitated, and my stomach flips. There is no one else in this room except the man who has taken pleasure in hurting me. My body and brain refuse to acknowledge that they shouldn't let him make us feel this way. He is as beautiful as a god and as dangerous as the devil himself.

Caden must be as shocked as I am because Titan manages to land a powerful punch to the side of his face and he is forced to take multiple steps back as he comes back to reality.

"What the fuck just happened?" Emma snorts. "King was winning, and he just stopped fighting."

"He did?" I ask, completely lost.

"What were you looking at if not the fight?" Xi mocks me.

I was looking at Caden King, only not the way everyone else was.

I was looking at the way his sweaty chest was moving up and down so quickly the massive tattoo of a snake eating its own tail was trembling. I was looking at the way his abs tensed, and the skull wearing a crown was dancing with the clock set to midnight, both inked into his skin.

And now I'm letting him hypnotize me again. His fists are moving fast, his muscles flexing, and his countless tattoos rippling on his arms and shoulders.

With one last punch, he knocks out Titan. The ring shakes when our beast falls to the ground.

The Kings crowd explodes in cheers and Caden smiles proudly at them. His eyes have a dangerous glint of excitement as he turns to me, and I stumble back into Lik.

My stepbrother looks down at me, putting a hand on my shoulder. "You okay?"

I can only nod as my eyes return to Caden. He's showing his closed right fist to the crowd. It's bloody, but the letters on his knuckles are as clear as ever. K. I. N. G. I'm hot and bothered remembering what he did with those fingers—the way he rubbed against my jeans and made me come.

He sticks his tongue out, winking, as some of his friends take pictures of him and it shows the piercing he's got on it.

My knees almost buckle as the phantom touch of that piercing on my clit awakes a need in me. The things he did to me...

You didn't want him to! My brain tries to fight my body. Right. I didn't want to. Then why do I wish he'd jump out of the ring right now and kiss me in front of the entire crowd? Why do I want him to grab my ponytail and, as he does so, claim me like the violent man I know he is?

Caden must catch me fixating on him because his eyes dart to mine, and he winks at me before turning to join Ethan and Elliot.

"Let's get out of here," Emma huffs. "Fucking lost fifty dollars. Titan is useless."

"Big doesn't mean strong," Xi says as I feel them walking away. "Look at Bil's. Tiny fucking thing beating the shit out of everyone."

Their voices fade, but I can't seem to move. My gaze keeps following Caden as he jumps out of the ring and hugs his friends. Jade, that same girl who was at Elliot and Ethan's house, jumps on him, forcing him to give her a piggyback ride.

"...llie."

She drops a kiss on his sweaty temple as he grabs her legs, and they all head outside through their door, following the Kings crowd. My stomach twists and I want to punch myself for how I feel.

"Billie!"

"What?" I startle. Lik is right next to me, shaking his head at me. "Wake up, girl. We're leaving."

"Yeah. I know that," I smile dumbly.

"You sure you're okay?" His gaze darts to Caden and his friends as they cross the huge doors to leave, then back at me.

"I'm totally fine. Let's go."

As we head out, someone bumps into me. He doesn't even

apologize, and I notice the crown tattooed on his shoulder. What's that guy doing on our side?

"Dick," I throw back without stopping.

The moment I'm by Xi's car, I understand what happened. "Fuck," I mumble to myself. "The bastard took my phone." I tap my front and back pockets then check my jacket. "I'll be back," I huff at them as they wait in the car.

There's no need to start anything; I'll just get my phone back and leave. Now is not the time to get into unnecessary drama.

I scan the parking lot but can't find him, so I head back into the warehouse. He's not part of the few people left in there, either. Huffing, I walk to the other exit, knowing that's the only way for him to join the Kings' side of the parking lot. As if I want to go through a crowd of their crew right now.

I'm not the kind of NSC girl who has the luxury of disappearing into a crowd of Kings if they don't manage to see my tattoo. Emma is our leader, and I'm her sister. Everyone knows my face. I fought in that same ring Caden did too many times for them to forget it. I get into fights with Kings' girls regularly.

I've got no choice except to pull the hood of my jacket up and zip it all the way to try and go incognito. I make my way to the parking lot they use and look for that random guy. I end up finding him on the other end, smoking with a few other men I don't know. And what a surprise, my phone is in his hand.

Shoving past a few people and keeping my head down, I finally reach him. "Hey, asshole," I call him out. "You know you're the reason Kings and NSC have useless feuds? Give me my phone."

He and his friends look down at my small frame and chuckle at each other. "Can't hear you from up here, babe."

"That's fucking hilarious," I grumble. "Just give me my phone and save yourself the humiliation of getting your ass kicked by a girl half your size."

He lifts his hand high above his head and exhales the smoke of his cigarette in my face, causing me to cough. "Why don't you try and grab it?"

"What the fuck. Seriously, how old are you?"

He shrugs. "Old enough to love playing games with hot babes."

I run my tongue against my teeth, trying to rein in the anger starting to boil in my veins. "Just remember you asked for this," I mutter as I pull down my hood. Before he can move, I knee him in the balls.

Hunching over, he drops my phone and I pick it up. "You fucking broke the screen," I rage.

Now that his face is low enough, I'm dying to knee him in the nose, but I know this will get me nowhere. Instead, I turn around and take a step to leave.

Before I can take a second one, someone grabs me by the ponytail and pulls me back. I grunt as he drags and throws me into his friend's arms. Said friend turns me around, forcing me to face the guy I just hit, and his arms wrap around me, constricting my arms to my body.

Not waiting for them to act further, I stomp hard on his foot. As soon as he releases me, I elbow him in the nose. "Fuckers think you can manhandle me?" I spit at them. "Stay the fuck away."

Of course, they don't. The one who initially had my phone charges me and then picks me up. When he sets me back down, it's only to shove me at another guy. I lose my footing and fall into his friend's arms. The first one uses the opportunity to slap me so hard in the face I see stars.

"Shit," I grit.

"Fucking NSC bitches thinking they're strong. Notice how all of them are just way too confident?" he says.

The last one of the trio grabs me by the hair before pushing me onto the first one and then back to his friend. I lose my bearings and keep tripping over as they toss me around in a circle.

"This is my new favorite game," one snickers. I'm dizzy and not sure which one it is anymore.

Just as I'm about to land in the hold of another, someone grabs me by the upper arm and pulls me away. I glance around, taking a few deep breaths until I feel like the ground isn't tilting anymore.

My eyes practically pop out of my head when I realize the hand on mine belongs to Caden. He's back to wearing his ripped jeans with a chain attached from the back pocket to the front. He's topless under his leather jacket and my heart squeezes at the sight.

"Boys," he says with half a smile. "Three against one, that's not exactly playing fair, is it?"

As if he knows anything about playing fair.

"The bitch kicked me in the balls," the one who had my phone grunts.

I struggle in Caden's hold, trying to go for the guy again. "You stole my phone, assh—"

"Tsk, tsk," he tuts at me, reeling me back. "You let a five-foot girl kick you in the balls, man? Sounds like a *you* problem. Not really her fault, is it?"

The other guy comes to his rescue when the first stutters his words. "Who fucking cares, bro. She's NSC. Let's give her a good lesson and send her back."

His two friends nod in approval and my stomach becomes heavy.

Not again.

Caden exchanges a knowing look with him and steps forward, still holding me. "I get the idea." Madness is pouring out of him, making him tighten his grip as we get closer to the other men.

My heart is beating in my ears while fear wraps around me. I shake my head, trying to stop memories from two years ago from flashing into my mind.

Caden unzips my jacket, displaying my skin-tight, white tank top. "You want to play with her, don't you?"

They all nod. One even licks his lower lip like the disgusting dog he is.

My body feels foreign as their eyes run over me. I attempt to backpedal, but Caden settles behind me.

"See, the problem is," he pulls my top low enough that the top of my boobs is showing. Then he pushes his index fingers hard against the bruise he left on me last week, making sure to hurt me in the process. "This, boys, has Caden King written all over it. And I'm afraid if I see you touch what's mine again, I will have to kill every single one of you in the most sadistic way you've ever seen. And," he inhales through clenched teeth, "it will be fucking bloody. Believe me."

In unison, the three men take a step back.

"Sorry, man. We didn't know."

"I fucking hope so." His hand grabs one of my boobs. My eyes peek down, watching his knuckles crusted with blood squeezing hard and making me wince. "Cause I really, *really* hate people touching my stuff."

"She didn't have the...the usual, you know?"

And by the *usual,* he means the necklace Caden leaves on every woman he fucks. Every time I see a girl walking around with hickeys going from just below her ear to her chin, I know Caden had sex with her. Most of the women in Kings Crew wear them like a badge of pride. When we were in high school, they'd act so cool because they were another girl he marked with possessiveness before ignoring them.

"Well, that's because I haven't fucked her yet, Matthew," he says with a silent 'duh' at the end. "Maybe I'm trying to be a gentleman here," he concludes, his hand still on my tit and his grip bruising my arm.

The perfect gentleman.

"Okay, now run along before I fuck you up," he tells the three. They're gone in mere seconds.

I struggle out of his grasp, and he finally lets me go. I rapidly twist around to face him and point my index finger at him. "I didn't need your help," I rage at him. "Even less your hands on my body. And let me make one thing clear: You and I will never—and I mean *never*—have sex together. Do you underst—"

"What the fuck?" he grounds out as he wraps a hand around my jaw and tilts my head to the side.

"Cad—"

"Did they hit you?"

"What?"

"Your cheek," he insists, his grip tightening. "It's swollen. So, it's a simple question." He brings his face down and closer to mine. "Did. They. Hit. You?"

My thoughts become liquid and escape me as his warm breath caresses my face.

"I—y-yeah, but the swelling is from my fight. They didn't hurt me." He doesn't react, so I add with determination, "I can take it."

He straightens up and smiles. Why do his grins always feel so ominous? "Your fight, huh?"

"Yeah, let me go now."

Surprisingly, he does. As he retreats, a shiver courses through my body. I zip up my jacket, but it's no use. I don't need more layers of clothes. I need Caden King's skin against mine.

"You're the toughest little cookie, aren't you?" he mocks me.

"Fuck off, Caden," I throw, starting to leave. He grabs me by the wrist and stops me.

"Next Friday. You've got a transfer to make for me. Be at the location at one a.m. Don't forget to put the hood on when you see their car coming."

I wrench my wrist away from him. "Sure, boss," I smile sarcastically as I walk away.

"I could get used to you calling me boss," he shouts at my retreating back, so I make sure to flip him off.

8

CADEN

Kinda Scary - Call Me Karizma

"That's it for today, everyone. Make sure to hand in your essay before you leave."

I fish the sheet out of my bag and hurry to our professor's desk, dropping it there before I head out.

Writing essays about the history of mathematics isn't exactly my passion, but it's something I chose. I want all chances on my side when I eventually apply to be a math teacher.

It'll happen one day. Once I'm out of this shithole of a town.

In the meantime, I need to make money. I hop in my car and put on *Gucci Coffin* by Josh A and iamjakehill so loud it practically shatters my windows. Then I floor it all the way to Stoneview. I can't afford to be late for any tutoring lessons.

The rich kids eye my shitty car as I drive past their prep school so I lower my window and offer them my ringed middle finger. I hear one of the girls in a group talk to her friend as I'm forced to stop at a red light.

"That's Caden King," a tall blonde one says.

"He's part of a gang. Did you know?" the other adds.

"So hot," the third concludes.

"I would literally give my left kidney to attend a North Shore party," the first one starts again.

Ah fuck. They're gonna talk to me, aren't they? I tap my finger on the wheel as I pray for that light to turn green before they reach my car.

No such luck, sadly.

"Hey, you're Caden, right?" the blonde one asks as she leans a hip on my car and rests a hand on my door so I can't put up the window.

I lick my lips and give her a smile. "At your service, Stoneview princess."

She rolls her eyes, pretending not to be affected. "Don't you tutor Harry Malone?"

"That's right. Gotta make honest money somewhere."

"I'm really struggling with math too." She pouts, pushing out her lower lip before giving me a bright smile. "Maybe you could help me."

The two girls behind her giggle.

"My schedule is full." I'm a bit done with her shitty flirting. When is this fucking light turning green?

"Okay, well, just invite me to one of your parties, then." She flips her blonde hair over her shoulder.

"You wanna come to a North Shore party, princess?" She nods and bites her lower lip. I reach into my pocket, pull out my switchblade, and press to get the blade out. "How healthy is that kidney of yours?"

Her eyes practically pop out of her head as she takes a step back. "What the hell!"

I cackle, throwing my head back. "Go back to your prep school."

The light finally turns green, and I speed away.

"Hey," I smile sweetly as Harry opens the door.

"Hey, man. Come in."

"Caden, hi!" his mother exclaims from the living room as we're walking up the stairs to his room.

"Hello, Mrs. Malone." I wave.

"Oh please, Mrs. Malone is my mother. You know to call me Chantale."

"Of course, Chantale," I force before following Harry.

We settle at his desk in his bedroom and go over his homework. The kid isn't even bad at math, his parents just love spending money. After reviewing his work, I give him a few more complex problems to solve. I check my phone and find the text I've been dreading while perfectly knowing it was inevitable.

"Alright, I'll give you fifteen. Just gonna make a call outside."

He nods, already immersed in the exercise, with his nose practically touching the notebook in front of him.

I come out of his bedroom and climb another set of stairs. The long hallway leads me to the master bedroom. I don't knock, simply push the door open and lock it behind me.

"Took you long enough," Chantale says. She's sitting at her vanity in nothing but a see-through pink nightgown.

I can see *everything*. From her erect pink nipples to the black hair covering her pussy.

"Come here," she says in a sultry voice. "Take your top off."

I take my *The Offspring* black hoodie and my t-shirt off at the same time, throwing them to the floor. Her eyes take in the tattoo on my chest, following the unending ouroboros. Then she takes in my cut abs and bites her lower lip. "Hurry," she breathes out.

I walk to her and let her run her hands all over my stomach. I merely stand still, my arms hanging by my sides, and try my best not to react.

"Get on your knees." She smiles, spreading her legs and bringing her nightie up to her waist.

I clench my jaw and force my mind to blank before sinking to my knees in front of her.

"Lick me, Caden," she says with enough anticipation she's already trembling. "Tell me you want it first."

"I want it," I force the lie past my throat.

"No, no. You know how to call me."

My stomach recoils before I can say it. "I want to lick you, Mommy."

"That's right, baby boy. Go ahead."

Bringing my head between her legs, I don't think about it. I make out with her pussy before pushing my tongue inside. Then I lick her clit in long strokes before nibbling it and accelerating.

"Yes...yes...that's right...oh my—fuck. Caden!" Her hands are in my hair as she grinds against my mouth. She messes the strands and pulls to keep me close against her.

I keep being relentless on her clit until she comes all over my tongue. She keeps bucking until she's done riding her orgasm, then finally lets me go. I fall back on my ass, wiping my mouth and feeling the disgust poisoning my entire body.

She gets up quickly, hurrying to her bed before bending over the end of it. "Come fuck, Mommy."

For fuck's sake. This woman has more issues than the *Good Housekeeping* she keeps in her living room.

Before lowering my black jeans, I settle behind her and grab one of the rubbers I always have when I go to her house.

I've got a semi, but I'm not even hard enough to roll the condom on. She's shifting her hips eagerly, her pussy wet from my spit and her own lubricant.

"Be a good boy for Mommy. Fuck her good," she pants into the bed.

I try to get myself hard, except her waving her pussy at me is doing nothing. Fuck, I'm usually fine fucking this woman.

I bite my lip and think of the latest thing that got me rock-hard. Big, brown doe-eyes flash in my mind. Her small face and plump lips. Her feistiness and the way she always yells at me. I imagine her small tits in those tight tank tops she always wears. The bruise I left on her. I see her on her knees in front of me, with her mouth full of my cum, and I hear the noises she makes when she pretends she doesn't like the way I touch her.

Before I know it, I'm burying my cock into Chantale. I fuck her hard, imagining Billie Scott on the bed before me. My hand comes to the back of her head, and I press her into the mattress as I go at her relentlessly.

"*Shit*," I hiss as I come the quickest I've ever had.

When I come back to reality, Chantale is squirming under my grip.

"For heaven's sake, let go!"

I release her and take a step back.

"Good Lord, Caden," she gasps as she turns around and sits up. "I don't think you've ever fucked me so hard." Her eyes are glassy, and she has a dumb smile on her face. "I'm not sure I'm a big fan of the pretend choking, though. Does Julianne like it? I'll have to ask her."

Of course, all the Stoneview moms I fuck behind their husbands and children's backs discuss me behind mine.

Fucking sickening vultures. It must feel powerful to gossip about how good the kid from the wrong side of the tracks fucks you while they sip champagne at the country club.

I'm not even listening to her babbling anymore. I walk to the en-suite, holding my jeans mid-thigh, and remove the condom before cleaning my cock with some tissues. I rinse my mouth, feeling sick from the musky taste of her pussy, and I use some mouthwash to get rid of it. I zip up my jeans and desperately try to rearrange my black hair, to no avail. It's to my ears and always messy no matter what I do. Strands constantly fall into my eyes, and I run a hand through them to try and see clearly.

When I walk back into the bedroom, she's rummaging through her purse. I put my t-shirt and hoodie back on. She hugs me tightly from the back as a hand full of cash appears in front of me.

"There's a tip there for the commitment you put into fucking me."

It's always the same feeling I get when I take the money. Revulsion rolls over my entire body. My mind goes into overdrive, and I feel like tears will explode from my eyes. My throat is always so tight, my 'thank you' comes out mumbled as I try to push down the nausea.

Then, when I put it in my pocket and walk back to the kid's room whose mom pays younger men for sex, I think of how beautiful my life will be when I leave the North Shore for good.

After Harry Malone, I tutor Jordan, aka Julianne's son. It's the same thing, just a different woman with different needs.

At least Julianne doesn't make me call her mommy. She's more into the bad boy look. She wants to be spanked and fucked in the ass because her husband is a devoted member of their church and would never do the kind of things I do to her. Whereas Chantale likes to give me the cash directly,

Julianne leaves it on the table, too ashamed of what she's just done.

Either way, I keep my mouth shut and take it. And when I feel particularly disgusting, I help myself to a tip behind their backs.

By six p.m., I'm back home with almost two grand in my pocket. Three tutoring lessons and three fucks, plus what I stole from them. Stoneview moms pay a lot of money to fulfill their dirty desires.

I push the door open to our rundown house and go straight for the bathroom. Kay tries to talk to me, but I feel too dirty to even stop. It's only when I've showered for half an hour under burning water and put some clean clothes on that I walk back into the living room.

"How was your day?" my sister asks, folding some laundry.

"I really wish all the girls who have ever tried to out-throne you could see you folding laundry in such a housewife attire."

She cocks an eyebrow at me. "Do *you* fold laundry? Does dad? No. Someone has to fucking do it."

I grab my phone and keys, putting them in my pockets before heading to the door. "Have fun."

"Where are you going?" she shouts at my retreating back.

"To kill a few fuckers."

The best thing is, I'm not even joking.

"Remind me why we've been sitting in front of Matthew's since seven?" Elliot asks as he grabs chips from the bag on his lap.

"Waiting for the devil's hour." I smile at him in the mirror from the driver's seat.

"I could swear that's at three a.m.," Ethan adds next to me. "I'm not waiting here till *three*, man. I've got shit to do."

"People to fuck," Elliot says, wiggling his eyebrows.

"Like Jade?" I wink.

"Fuck off with Jade. Both of you."

"Come on, brother," Elliot insists. "She's an amazing fuck, and I never had any intention to keep her after I had her. You can have her back now."

"I don't want your sloppy seconds, Elliot," Ethan snarls. "Plus, she's into Cade now. Right?"

"No thanks," I snort. "She's always been into me. I just never wanted her back."

"Poor Jade," Elliot sighs mockingly. "She just wants to fuck us in peace. We're the ones causing trouble."

"I'm gonna choke you with your chip bag," Ethan threatens coolly.

"Talking about choking. Did you try on Jade? Cause I did and—"

"His girl's gone," I cut him off. "Elliot, grab the zip ties in the back. I'll find a window to sneak in. Ethan, you go through the front door."

"His two goons are with him," Elliot warns me as we get out of the car.

"That's the whole point."

I disappear to the back of Matthew's house and climb through his kitchen window. Once I'm in, I almost cough from the disgusting state they keep the place in. What the fuck. There's food floating in a sink blocked with filthy water. The sides are covered in grease and dust and the table isn't visible below the cans, dirty dishes, and old newspapers.

"Gross," I mumble to myself. I hear Ethan knocking on the door and convincing Matthew to let him in. He's using a random excuse about Sawyer sending him to talk about the new drug they're going to sell to the Stoneview kids. In truth, NSC still mainly sells to Stoneview. Especially the coke they're such big fans of. We're starting to take over the pills, but somehow the rich kids still prefer to deal with Xi and his crew. Probably because he fucks most of the girls there.

I wait until I hear them talk in the living room and until Matthew's two friends, Joe and Rico, join the conversation. I quietly make my way out of the kitchen and open the front door to Elliot. He's holding a plastic bag full of zip ties and grinning brightly at me. I turn around and notice a bowling bag on the floor. Leaning down, I pick up the heavy bowling ball and slide my fingers through the three holes before looking back at Elliot.

"Love the new style," he whispers before we walk into the living room.

"Caden," Matthew startles as soon as he sees me. "Fuck man, how did you get in?"

"Through the window," I shrug. "Your kitchen is disgusting, by the way." I don't even give him time to answer. "I didn't know you bowled. That's kinda cool."

"Oh, it's my lady's." He waves a hand in the air, dismissing it.

"Huh. You're a lot less cool, suddenly."

Walking deeper into the living room, I put my back to the TV as I face them. "Why don't you take a seat, boys."

The three of them go to sit down on the sofa, but I tut them. "Chairs."

There are precisely three chairs around the circular wooden table behind them. Matthew and Rico grab one each, but Joe takes a step around the coffee table and toward me.

"You know what, bro. I just remembered, my girl is waiting for me to have dinner. So Imma head out. I'll catch you—"

Blood spurts as soon as the bowling ball hits his face, and he falls to the floor unconscious.

His head cracked with the force of my hit.

"Shit," Rico whimpers. "Caden—"

"Sit down. Now," I say calmly to both of them.

Matthew is a big man. Much bigger than me. But he is practically pissing himself as he sits down on the wooden chair he pulled out. Rico follows, his entire body shaking like a leaf.

"Arms behind the chairs, boys. We don't have all night."

They're too frightened to do anything else but obey. Elliot gives his stepbrother a few zip ties, and they quickly tie their wrists behind the back of the chairs and their feet to the wooden legs.

"I just want to be very clear," I explain as I walk to them, warming up my wrist with the heavy black ball in my hand. "You're both being killed tonight because you touched what belongs to me. And the unfairness in all of this is that you couldn't have known. Fuck, I didn't even know myself until I saw you three fuckers messing with her."

Elliot and Ethan give each other a puzzled look but they stay quiet.

I don't give a shit about Billie Scott.

That's what I have always told myself. I didn't even need to tell myself because I didn't think of her except when I sometimes needed a quick rub and watched her orgasm on my phone.

But then she showed up like a fucking runaway and decided that fighting me, instead of listening to me, was the best choice. That stirred something in me. Challenge. The feisty little thing keeps wanting to talk back and push me away when her body is so responsive to mine that it's like it was made for me.

I shouldn't care that a few people from my crew bothered her.

But her cheek was swollen, and she looked like she'd been backhanded or something. She said it was her fight, but she did confirm they hit her.

I don't like that. I really don't fucking like that at all.

I decided I want Billie. At least for now, she's *my* toy. Mine to torture and drive crazy. Until I'm bored with her, none of these fuckers get to approach her.

I smile at said fuckers, knowing it scares them even more. My smile *always* brings fear to the people facing me. "Thank you so much for making me realize even a wicked soul like mine still has a chance at chasing love." Of course, it's not love, but I do like a bit of dramatic effect. "Unfortunately for you, I can't stand knowing you three have put your hands on what's mine."

"P-please, Caden," Matthews starts crying. "We didn't know...we didn't know, man. It'll never happen again."

"Oh, it won't," I nod. "That I'm sure of. Which one of you hit her?"

They look at each other before Rico spurts, "It was Matthew. It wasn't me. It was him!"

I look at Elliot and Ethan. "You two better have my back better than this pussy here if we ever get in this kind of situation."

"Man, I'll die before I give you away," Elliot sniggers.

"We'll never be in this position," Ethan adds with certainty.

I tilt my head to the side, thinking for a minute. "Cocky, yet true."

Now that I'm standing before Rico, I pull my arm back and smash the ball into his temple. He cries out, and I do it again and again and again. Until his whimpers and tears quiet down and his chest stops moving.

"Snitches get stitches. Am I right, Matthew?"

"Fuck...fuck...fuck," he panics. "Caden, please. Sawyer likes me. Fuck...your dad works with me all the time. Please, man...p-please don't kill me."

"Hey, hey, calm down. You're hyperventilating."

He nods, trying to calm down, but a sob explodes from his mouth less than ten seconds later. "Please..."

"Are you a snitch, Matthew?" I ask.

"No!"

I put the bowling ball on the wooden table and crouch in front of him, grabbing the plastic bag of zip ties. "Then you're good. Chill, will you?"

He seems to calm down. Tears are still running down his face, but his body has stopped shaking. I slowly walk behind him, throwing the remaining zip ties in the bag on the floor.

"Ah shit, man," I add. "No, sorry, you're not good at all." I place the plastic bag on his head and pull until I'm sure it's taut against his face. He thrashes around, and I can't help a huge smile from spreading on my face. "Snitches get stitches. And men who touch my girl get a bag on their fucking head," I growl, pulling harder.

I keep hold of him until his body slacks. When I let go, I look back at Elliot and Ethan, proud of myself. "Alright. All done."

"Your girl?" Ethan finally asks.

"Yeah," I huff as I run my hand through my hair, trying to get strands out of the way. "Billie and I are gonna be a thing. Didn't you know?"

"Does *she* know?" Elliot shakes his head at me.

"Billie Scott is not your girl, Caden," Ethan says as if I'm the craziest fucker on the planet.

"Yeah, well, not right *now*," I fight back. "These things take time."

"What things? Kidnapping?" Elliot scoffs. "Dude, you two are never gonna be a thing. She's NSC. Oh, and let me think..." He puts his index finger on his chin, pretending to be deep in thought. "Right, she fucking hated our guts after what we did to her two years ago. Now that you're blackmailing her into moving shit for you, I'm pretty sure she daydreams of putting a bullet through your skull."

"Yeah, but—"

"Caden," Ethan says seriously. "If your dad knew you were killing Kings to defend the honor of an NSC girl, he would choke you, brother. Fucking *think* before you act."

I'm an impulsive fucker; that's not new. But my friends never had an issue with it before. The problem is, once I have an idea in my head, I have to execute it. I had this sudden urge to make Billie mine since I made her come in her car, so that's what I'm going to do. Make her mine. Matthew and his guys pissed me off, and I had to end them. That's just how I function.

I want Billie. I must have her, or I will fucking lose my mind. I don't accept defeat. Ever.

I tilt my head to the side, staring at Ethan. "Alright, well, my dad doesn't have to know shit," I say simply.

"Believe me, he won't," Elliot chuckles. "I'd like to keep my head attached to my body if you don't mind. You might have the King last name, but we don't."

"Anyone else we have to kill tonight because they did something bad in your fantasy world where you have a chance with Billie Scott?" Ethan asks.

I shrug. "Nah, we're good."

"Sweet, let's get some food," Elliot claps.

"I'm fucking starving," I agree.

On the way out, I call one of our guys. "Oran, my man," I say sweetly into the phone. "Listen, I just saw a few NSC guys leave Matthew's house. I'm on my way to something now, though. Can you check on him? Hopefully, he wasn't there and they just stole some shit, but I want to make sure our guy is okay."

My lie falls so effortlessly off my lips that I feel like a supervillain in a hero movie. Oran is going to find three dead bodies and put them on NSC—a perfect end to a really shit Monday.

9

BILLIE

A Girl Called Jazz - Omido, Tobi Swizz

My keys drop just as I try to stick them into the lock of my front door, and I have to hold back a shriek of frustration as I bend down to pick them up. Today is not my day. I went to classes and got reprimanded by three of my professors for not showing up last week. I thought the teaching staff wasn't meant to care at college.

Then, I was less than average at training, and Dickie was on me telling me he knew I was at the warehouse last Friday for an illegal fight. It didn't matter that I was just watching; he was still mad at me. If he loses his shit for that, I can't imagine him knowing I'll be moving supplies for Caden tomorrow.

A bark resonates behind my front door and I take a step back, keys now in my hand. Is there a dog in my house?

I hear my dad shouting something and Emma screaming.

What if some Kings have shown up with a dangerous dog and are threatening my family?

I'm pushing the door open before I can even finish my

thought. My Kershaw knife is out and I'm pointing at whatever I will find behind it.

"Put that shit away!" Dad shouts before I can register what is going on.

Emma is standing on the sofa with a gun in her hand, pointing at a huge Doberman running in circles around the living room. My dad is chasing after it, a collar in his hand, clearly trying to put it on the dog.

None of them have even noticed me yet. My dad just shouted his words at my sister for her to put the gun away, I suppose.

Her response is another scream as the dog comes to bark at her, and she points the gun down. "Dad, you know dogs terrify me! Why would you do this, for fuck's sake?!"

"What the hell is going on," I huff as I throw my bag down by the door and advance into the living room.

"Billie!" my dad shouts in surprise. "I thought you were at your mom's tonight."

"She didn't want to see me," I shrug, pretending I'm not affected when my heart is actually broken by it. The problem with my mom's illness is that when she needs to isolate, she will hate the entire world. Her children included. When I showed up tonight, she wasn't the cheery woman she was last week. She slammed the door in my face without a word, and when I tried calling her, she simply said to leave her alone before hanging up on me.

"Aw, no. I'm sorry, kiddo. You know it's not your fault, right?"

I nod silently, and another bark, followed by a shriek from Emma, ends the conversation about my mom. I put my knife away and snicker at Emma. "That screaming woman on your sofa runs your crew, you know?"

"Shut up," Emma fights back. "That dog is dangerous. Leash it already!"

I observe the beast wagging its tail and attempting to lick Emma's shoes. The dog does a circle trying to bite its tail and then barks at Emma again. It turns to my dad, though as soon as he steps forward toward the dog, it runs around the room again.

"It thinks it's a game." I roll my eyes. "You two are so bad with animals." I take the collar from Dad and whistle at the dog. I tap my thigh, and it barks happily as it trots to me. "Hi, beauty," I smile. "What have these two been up to, huh? Com'ere." As soon as it settles by me and does a circle, I notice the lack of male apparatus. "Oh, you're a pretty girl!" I say happily. She rubs against me as I kneel in front of her. As she tries to nestle in the crook of my neck, I slip the collar around hers.

"There you go! What a good girl," I cheer. I stand back up and keep petting her as I turn to my dad. "So, you've got a dog now?"

"No," he smiles. "*You've* got a dog now."

"Me? Why?"

He approaches me as Emma gets down from the sofa and sits down with a hand on her chest, trying to calm her heart.

"I know you're having a hard time at the moment, kiddo. I don't know what it is exactly, but a dad knows when his little girl isn't feeling safe."

"Dad—"

He puts a hand up. "If you don't want to tell me, I won't force it out of you. You can take your dog with you wherever you go. It will be an extra layer of protection. Until you feel ready to let me know what's going on, just know I've got your back."

Tears spring to my eyes, threatening to fall. My throat is

too tight to talk, so I say nothing. I simply nod a few times. It's almost imperceptible, but I know he sees it because something breaks in his eyes. Almost like he was hoping he was making it all up. Acting like an overprotective dad. Now he knows for sure that something's wrong, and he feels powerless. Just like I do.

Out of pure need, I take my dad in my arms and bury myself against him. He holds me tightly and I feel my new dog attempting to come between our bodies. It makes us both laugh as we pull away.

"What are you gonna name her?" he asks me as he runs a hand through his beard.

"Mmm," I start to think.

"Murderer," Emma mumbles behind my dad.

The dog barks at her, and I bend down to pet her. "You're the cutest thing I've ever seen," I tell her like I would a baby. "Murderer is too much, Em. How about Murder," I smile as I straighten back up.

"Oh yeah, so different." My sister rolls her eyes.

"Should keep a few ill-intended people at bay," my dad smiles.

"Yup."

"You're keeping her in your room, you hear me?" Emma complains. "I am not having this thing running around the house. And keep her far away from my hair extensions!"

"Yeah, yeah," I wave her off as I grab Murder by the collar. "Come, girl."

We go to my room, and she settles on the floor in front of my bed immediately. I go back to the living room and get her a bowl of water. My dad gives me a toy and some food he bought her. So I put that in my room too.

I only fall asleep around one a.m. I'm having too much fun with Murder and can't come down from the giddiness.

For the first time in a long while, I fall asleep without fear in my stomach because I can hear the soft snores of Murder on the floor by the end of my bed.

I feel something is wrong when a noise wakes me up. It's soft, quiet, but I hear it anyway. It slips into my dream and makes me feel uneasy. I don't fully wake up until a hand lands on my mouth, pressing harshly. It mutes the screech that would have come out otherwise, and I fight against it right away. My defense mechanism kicks in, and I punch the shadow in front of me. A grunt escapes them, and I grab their forearm, twisting myself until I can push them off.

I'm free for a split second but am now too shell-shocked to scream past my panting breaths. I go for my bedside table, attempting to grab the knife I keep there. Only he's quicker than me and takes it before I can.

I already recognize the smell of Caden. It's fresh. Something aquatic with a tinge of weed and mint from his breath. I can make out his wicked smile even in the night and the way his hair falls on either side of his forehead.

He pushes me against the mattress and settles on my thighs, stopping me from getting up. He uses my own knife against my throat, leaving it to gently touch my skin, forcing me to be still.

"Shh." He smirks. "I'll only hurt you if you resist."

"What are you doing?" I pant. My heart is racing so fast it makes me feel sick. My eyes drop to catch the knife, but I can only see as far as his wrist.

"It's six a.m.," he says casually. "The sun is about to rise, and I thought I'd come and be your alarm clock."

I feel the blade against my throat as I gulp down my fear.

"I-I don't need you to be my alarm." I bring a hand to his

forearm, gently trying to pry it away from my artery.

"Don't try to move me away, little Scott. I want you to feel that I hold your life in my hands."

"I can't breathe," I lie.

"Nah, you're fine."

He lowers himself and buries his nose into my long hair. He inhales deeply, and I feel him tremble. "You smell good," he finally says against my ear. I can feel him growing hard against my thigh, and that same conflicting feeling I get around him comes back, making me hate myself in the process.

"Get off me, Caden," I grunt. "My dad is going to get up soon. You don't want him to find you here."

"That old man? Don't make me laugh."

"Just...what do you want?" I whisper. I sound desperate, but that's the way he always makes me feel. How am I meant to be the tough girl everyone knows me to be when I'm facing the man who took chunks of my soul two years ago just to burn them into ashes and keep the hot remnants for himself?

"What do I want? Oh, I like that question." He straightens up, and his demonic features petrify me. "What I want is for you to stay still and quiet while I run your knife all over your tight body." He starts moving the blade from my throat and hooks it to the neck of my oversized t-shirt. In a swift movement, he cuts into it and keeps going down until it's split in the middle all the way to the hem.

My chest is moving up and down quickly, fear making me pant. He pushes the two sides of the shirt off me, exposing my boobs and stomach.

"Shit," he hisses.

I struggle to stay still, my hands turning into clenched fists as he runs the point of the blade down between my breasts and down to the cotton panties I'm wearing. Goosebumps follow the cold trail of the knife.

"What I want," he continues, "is for you to let me fuck you. Let me sink my cock into you and make you scream, baby."

Do it, is at the tip of my tongue. Because I just want to know what it feels like. I want to feel him inside me and attempt to satiate the strange feeling I get when he's around. I want to give it a chance and finally feel good and aligned with my desires when he touches me.

But I can't.

Because our gangs are at war.

We're enemies.

Because he blackmails me into doing illegal jobs for him.

Mainly...because he forced me when I wasn't feeling that way about him, and I can't get over that.

I shake my head, fear tightening my chest because I know that this word means nothing to him. I say it anyway. "No..."

"Why, Billie?" he grounds out between gritted teeth as the knife slides under my panties. "Why don't you ever want to cooperate with me, huh?"

"Caden," I panic, struggling to keep my voice to a whisper. Even if I didn't know what would happen when he loses it, the rumors are terrifying enough that I can't control the plea that falls off my lips. "Don't hurt me."

"Shh. Don't be scared, baby. I won't hurt you." He runs his thumb against my trembling lips before traveling all the way down my body and resting it on my panties. Right where my clit is.

"Let me play just a little, and then you can reconsider if you want me to fuck you or not, okay?"

I shake my head again, but I'm forced to freeze when he starts rubbing his thumb against my clit. The knife comes to rest against my throat again and I don't dare move. The problem as he starts forcing pleasure on me, is that I don't even want to move away. I just want to let him take control and relax into bliss.

My hips shift and my legs spread apart when he quickens slightly. His rhythm is perfect, the pressure not too much and keeping me chasing for more. A gasp of pleasure escapes my mouth, and his focused eyes brighten. He smirks from his position above me and keeps going exactly the same. I struggle to breathe, wanting to beg him to hurry and slow down simultaneously.

I can feel the tension in me, ready to snap. A moan bubbles at the back of my throat, and he puts the knife to the side before slamming his hand over my mouth.

My eyes widen, and he lowers himself to talk into my ear. "We wouldn't want your daddy to hear you come under the enemy's touch, would we?"

My chest rises quickly and deflates just as he pulls his hand away from my clit. He pushes my panties to the side, and I feel one finger at my entrance. I can't say no, not with his hand covering my mouth, but it's not *no* that I want to scream.

I want to beg him to push in. I want to feel him stretch me. I want his warmth deep inside me. I buck my hips, inviting him to do it.

And at a torturously slow pace, he pushes a single finger inside my dripping pussy. My long moan is blocked by his hand.

He pulls out and brings his hand to his face. Dawn is shining a low gray light past the clouds outside, and I can see him much clearer than I could when he arrived. His green eyes hold mine as he opens his mouth and slides his middle finger inside it. He wraps his lips around it and pulls it out, grunting low in his chest.

His smile is proud and destabilizing. "You taste as good as the last time, baby."

I should freak out at remembering when he forced his head between my legs. The way one of his best friends was holding me down, and the other was filming me.

Yet, all I can think about right now is having him back inside me. And thankfully, that's all he wants too. He pushes his finger back in and hisses. "Why are you so fucking tight? You're no virgin, Billie. I know that much."

I might as well fucking be now. I've not let a man near me since that fateful night two years ago. Although I would never tell him that. He'd be way too happy about it.

My body burns as he starts moving in and out of me.

It's one finger.

From a man I hate.

And yet, I can feel sweat running down my neck. I can feel myself under so much pleasure I want to weep. He inserts another one and bends down again to kiss my neck.

As he thrusts his two fingers into me, he trails kisses down my throat and collarbone until he's just above my tits. He kisses the top of the left, then the right, and before I know what's going on, he's biting and sucking. I twist out of pleasure, writhing under the tension.

Why do his teeth on my skin feel so good? I know he's bruising me. I should feel exposed and used, but I just want to let him in. I just want to let myself fall.

I explode as soon as he curls his fingers and rubs against the magic spot inside me. I tremble as I come undone, riding the wave of my orgasm until I can't anymore.

I finally come down when he pulls his hand away and straightens up.

The problem with falling is that, eventually, you hit the ground.

As his warmth dissipates and I'm left cold, half-naked, and with a ripped shirt, a loathing comes over me. I push him off me.

"Oh my god," I gasp. "Get off me!"

My shout wakes up Murder and in a split second, she's barking at Caden, who's just fallen onto the floor. Baring her teeth, her mouth drips with saliva. She barks again and Caden stands up.

"Holy fucking shit," he laughs. "Has this thing been here all along?"

I hear a door in the house and heavy steps in the hallway.

"Bil's!" my dad shouts.

My eyes practically pop out of my head, and I look at Caden. Murder barks at him again, and he puts a hand in front of himself. "Nice doggie..."

RUFF!

A knock on my door makes us both jump. "Bil's, are you okay?"

No, I'm not fucking okay.

In fact, I'm speechless.

I eye my knife, which Caden left on the bed and his eyes follow where I'm looking.

"Don't you dare," he mouths. I slowly move my hand toward the knife, and he pounces on me, grabbing it and pushing my head against the bed. Murder barks and rages, jumping on the bed too. He retreats just as my dad pushes my door open.

"I'm coming in," Dad announces loudly.

I become suddenly aware of my nakedness and grab the covers to pull them up to my chin. I look to my right and Caden has disappeared, though Murder is still barking like a mad dog.

"Calm down, girl," I say softly, tapping the tiny space between me and the wall. "Come."

"Are you okay?" my dad finally says, and I stare at the gun pointed at the rest of the room.

"Dad! I'm fine," I exclaim. "Put your gun down, for fuck's sake."

"Yeah, yeah," he grunts. He scratches his beard and looks around. "Are you okay?" he repeats for the millionth time. "That dog scared me."

"I'm okay," I say weakly, the events just crashing into my head. "I-I must have had a nightmare, and she started barking. Maybe I made a noise or something."

He grunts again and coughs up half his lungs because he won't stop smoking.

"Alright, I'm gonna make some breakfast. It's seven. She better not wake us up like this every day, the damn thing. Aisha had a near heart attack."

Murder yelps at my dad like he betrayed her, and I force a small laugh. "She'll be good."

"And don't forget to lock your window at night, pumpkin," he throws casually.

"I did—" I cut myself off when I notice I didn't. I *always* lock my window. North Shore is not a place you can trust. Psychos will sneak into your house during the night and slit your throat. Or give you a mind-blowing orgasm.

I must have felt safe with Murder and let my guard down —rookie mistake.

My dad finally leaves my room and I jump out of bed, startling my dog. "Where the hell are you hiding?" I hiss at my empty room.

He comes out from underneath my bed and stands up, forcing me to look up at him as he plasters his smug smile on his face. "You didn't lock your window last night, pumpkin," he mocks me.

Murder growls violently as he takes a step away from the bed. I wrap my torn t-shirt around me when his eyes start burning a hole through my tits.

"You should leave before I get my dog to eat your face."

"My pretty face?" He plasters a hand against his chest in betrayal. "You wouldn't dare."

"Leave, Caden," I seethe.

"I bet I can get that dog to like me. Right, doggie?" She barks at him, and he jumps back. "Just give her time. She'll warm up to me." He pierces his stare into mine. "Like you."

"Fuck you," I whisper harshly. "Get the fuck out of my house."

I push at his chest, but he grabs my wrists easily. "I should tell you why I came, I guess."

"What?"

"Well, I didn't come just to watch you orgasm."

My mouth falls open and I snap it shut.

"I'm taking you to my friend's garage before she starts her day. She said she'll look at your car today if we show up before eight. We should hurry. We need to get your headlight fixed before you do the drive tonight."

He releases my wrists and tilts his head to the side. "I guess you should get changed. I'll wait for you outside. Don't be long."

I watch, speechless, as he climbs out of my window and onto the streets. Our house is only a single story, and it's so easy to get in. Hence why we make sure all the windows are always locked.

How could I have been so careless?

I'm forced to skip breakfast and promise my dad I'll be back by noon. I have no classes on Fridays and typically like spending the day with him. Aisha is already cooking for the family dinner she holds every week and I make sure to tell her how good it smells before leaving.

Since we lack a driveway, my car is parked down the street. Caden is waiting by it, leaning on his own car. I've brought Murder with me, and she's so big she's the one leading me by the time we arrive. The fact that I'm trotting after her makes Caden chuckle and raises my hackles.

"A tiny thing like you won't ever be able to take a Doberman on a walk."

"Don't judge a book by its cover," I say, jutting my chin high, pretending I'm not out of breath from the fact that I had to jog after her and put all my strength into not dropping the leash. "I'm strong enough to handle my dog."

He nods, pinching his lips as if stopping himself from laughing at me. "You sure can, tough cookie."

His eyes drop to my hoodie, and he cackles. "Good Charlotte? Trying to make yourself look old or something?"

I tug at my Good Charlotte hoodie. It's the cover of an old album of theirs and says *The Young and The Hopeless* on it. "They're a great band."

"Were you even born when that album came out?"

"We're the same age," I say annoyingly, narrowing my eyes at him.

He shrugs. "I don't know. Apparently, you're forty and used to listen to Good Charlotte in your young days."

"Oh, shut up, will you?"

"Let's go," he snickers as he heads into his car.

I let Murder into the back of mine and climb into the driver's seat before following Caden all the way to the garage.

He parks in the lot right outside, and I stop my car right beside his. I let my dog out and grab her leash before he joins me.

"You're gonna take her everywhere you go, now?"

"Yup," I pop the 'p' and smile at him as she growls his way. "She can sense when people only want to hurt me."

He cocks an eyebrow at me, and our conversation is cut short by a girl in an oversized denim jumpsuit coming our way. She's wiping her hands with a cloth, removing black grease off them.

"Hey, Cade," she beams brightly. And just like that, I know he fucked her.

"Ashley, Billie, Billie, Ashley." I nod at her, and she does the same. Everyone knows I'm NSC, there's no need to pretend otherwise.

"It's just a light," Caden says, as if justifying bringing a car from the opposing gang to her garage. "She's doing a job for me. Can't risk her getting arrested."

"No judgment from me," she replies, approaching my car. "It won't take me long."

"We'll be at the Basement," he tells her. "Just call me."

"Got it," she throws back without looking at us.

I know the Basement. It's a shitty diner not far from here. I've never been because it's always been in Kings' territory.

I follow Caden across the road and down two blocks. "I'm not hungry," I repeat for the third time once we get there.

"No?" He turns to Murder. "What about you, girl? You hungry? Huh?"

She starts wiggling her tail and gives him a sweet *woof!*

"That's what I thought. Come on." He snaps his fingers, and she follows him inside. I've got no choice except to follow or drop the leash.

"Fucking traitor," I mumble at her.

We walk down a flight of stairs and into the basement that gave its name to the diner.

"What sort of food do you like, Billie?" Caden asks casually as we slide into a booth.

I attach Murder's leash to the metal leg of the table and sit back. The old vinyl of the bench creaks under me. Most of it is taped back with gray duct tape and the plastic of the table is falling apart. Not too bad for a North Shore diner. It smells good, of frying oil and pancake batter.

I finally look up at Caden. "I'm not making small talk with you. We're waiting for my car that you're fixing because you're blackmailing me into doing a dangerous job for you with a video of me that you have from sexually assaulting me. If you think I want to make small talk, you're strongly mistaken."

He runs a hand through his hair and grabs a laminated menu. "I personally love pancakes with just the sweet stuff on it. None of those savory bits like bacon and eggs. I just want blueberries and maple syrup. Maybe some chocolate sauce."

I ignore him, grabbing my own menu so I don't have to gaze at him. When he realizes I truly don't want to talk, he adds, "I hope it'll taste as sweet as your pussy."

I snap my head up from my menu and beg for my look to kill him. "What did you just say?"

"I'm saying I want to make you come again. Hopefully, now that you've given in once, there won't be so much resistance next time."

"You're sick. You're actually. Fucking. Sick. I did not give in."

"Oh..." He leans back, hitting the softness behind him, and shakes his head. "What were those noises you were making, then? Cries for help? They sounded a lot like moans to me."

"Stop it," I rage. "You had a knife to my th—"

"Hiya, my name is Cleo. I'll be your server today. Can I get you any hot drinks?" The lazy voice of the waitress, who clearly wishes she was anywhere else but here, brightens when she looks up from her notepad and sees Caden. "Oh my god, Caden. Hi!"

It takes me a moment to understand why they know each other. When I notice the hickeys on her jaw and how she's turned a dark shade of red, I want to jump and strangle her.

Ignoring the way she is currently melting for him, Caden keeps his eyes on me. "Can I have a black coffee, and Billie here will have..." They both look at me expectantly.

"Just a water. No ice," I push past my rage.

"I'll also have the blueberry pancakes with maple syrup and some strawberries, please."

"Alright." She writes it down. "Anything else?"

"A baptism to clean my entire soul," I mumble as I put my menu in front of my face so I don't have to see her anymore.

Caden snorts and dismisses his great friend Cleo. As soon as she's out of earshot, I slam my menu on the table.

"I cannot believe you. Did you break into my house right after you left hers, or did you have a little sleep before coming over?"

He licks his lips and smiles, clearly loving this. "I will shout to this entire diner that you are my girlfriend and I will never touch any other girl if you admit that you wanted me earlier. That you wanted me to sink my cock into your tight pussy and fuck the living soul out of you until you meet God and realize it was me all along."

A rush of heat courses through my body at his words. I undo my ponytail and redo it to buy myself some time while I try to get my brain to come up with a response.

I fail.

"Well," he shrugs. "In that case, I don't think you get to be jealous. Although just to reassure you, I fucked Cleo last week. The hickeys just last a while." He smiles as if this isn't totally fucked.

"As long as you stop touching me, I don't care what you do."

"Ah, no. See, that's just not possible."

"Why?" It comes out as a genuine, soft question before I can try and make it sound violent.

"Because I want to make you mine," he says in simple honesty. "I don't know why. It took me by surprise, because I had completely forgotten about you these last two years. Then you just showed up in our backyard like a gift from the divinities, and I haven't been able to get you out of my head since."

"It's been two weeks," I whisper. "You don't even know me. You can't just stake your claim—"

"But I am. I'm fucking telling you you're mine, and you'll come around to understanding it too."

I can see him getting heated. His hand is now on the table, and he's leaning over so closely I can feel his warmth.

"You just keep fighting back, Billie. I'll make you cave, eventually."

"Is that how you convince girls to be your girlfriends?"

"No," he snorts. "I don't do girlfriends. But I'll make an exception for you."

"You're Kings crew, Caden. And I'm NSC. I'm doing this job because I have to. Don't mistake my compliance for genuine interest because I have none toward you. I think you're violent and cruel. You take what you're not given because you're entitled. And to be totally honest, I don't think you're capable of affection. Let alone love."

A shadow of danger crosses his green eyes as the air around us seems to drop a few degrees. He runs his tongue against his teeth and clenches his jaw.

"You're gonna regret this," he simply says. The waitress brings our drinks and his food and I use this occasion to excuse myself. I undo Murder's leash from the table and don't even look at Caden when I say, "I'll wait for you outside."

We don't talk when we pick up my car. There's nothing to pay because Ashley owed Caden a favor and I climb in my car without saying a word to him.

He grabs my door before I can shut it. "Don't be late tonight. One a.m. at the meeting point. I won't be there to convince them not to kill you if you fuck up, so you do everything as I told you. Bring me my money when it's all done."

"Sure," I mumble as he lets go. I slam my door shut and drive back to NSC territory, feeling a hundred times lighter when I'm back on the streets I recognize.

10

BILLIE

Two Face - Jake Daniels, Omido

The hood makes my skin damp and sticky. I can feel my own breath in there and the way it staggers every time I hear a movement. There must be two or three of them going back and forth between my car and theirs. I can't believe I'm in this situation. How many times is Caden going to make me do this? It's the first without him, but I must admit I felt safer when he was in the passenger seat. It was easier to pretend nothing else was happening when I was busy focusing on his hand between my legs.

I couldn't take Murder with me. What if they shoot her for barking at them? The Wolves spare no one. I hear the tap on my window and focus. As soon as I hear their car leaving, I take the hood off and exhale. This whole ordeal is fucking terrifying.

I start the car and drive to the other spot where I know I'm meant to meet the men who take whatever is in my trunk and turn it into money. I'm guessing they're the buyers of whatever

Caden is selling. Or another type of middleman who hides it while they wait to distribute the product.

Like last time, the guy disappears with my car and brings it back before leaving in another vehicle. The bag of cash is in my back seat and it's time to bring it to Caden.

I get into my car and drive to Sawyer's house. A cop car overtakes me on the way and my heart almost explodes. I might not have the product on me anymore, but I could never justify the amount of money I've got in my car.

I stop behind whoever is parked in Sawyer's driveway and text Caden. I have to wait fifteen minutes for him to finally text back.

Caden: Bring it to my house.

Is he for fucking real?

Billie: Dick.

I start my car again, but someone is right there as I look in my mirror.

"Oh my god," I startle with a loud gasp. Sawyer walks around and taps at my window.

"How we doin' over here?" he asks lazily as I roll it down the slightest.

"Um, fine."

"That my money in the back?"

His?

"I thought it was Caden's," I reply with as much calm as possible.

"Potato, pot-ah-to. It's Kings' money. Give it to me." His voice is a little more violent. He hooks his fingers in the small gap in my window.

"Caden just told me to bring it over to his house."

He smiles and lets go before stepping back and putting his hand up in a sign of innocence. "Must be a misunderstanding. Give it to him, then. I'll make sure he and I are on the same page next time."

I frown at him, my finger tapping against the wheel. It's obvious he can't be trusted. Apart from being a King, he also seems to want to fuck his own crew over. I start my car and pull out of his driveway.

I'm not sure if I should tell Caden that Sawyer tried to take the money. Maybe it's all truly a misunderstanding, except the guy gives me all kinds of bad vibes.

By the time I get to his house, I conclude that this is a Kings problem. They can destroy themselves from the inside for all I care.

Caden's house is noticeably busy when I park in front of it. He comes out quickly and barely acknowledges me when he grabs the bag.

"That's a real good girl," he mumbles to himself, peeking at the amount of cash. Somehow, even when he's not addressing me directly, he manages to mock me. Once he's done, he finally gives me the time of day. "Get out of the car."

I eye his steamed windows. There must be a lot of people in there but there is no party going on or anything. I step out of my car, but I stay close. "I don't want to go inside your house."

"You're not invited to go inside my house, little Scott. Maybe when I fuck you, I'll give you the honor."

I clench my jaw, trying to hold my insults back.

Just give him the money and go home, Billie.

Dropping the bag next to him, he brings a hand to my face and caresses my cheek. I slap it away and look at anything but him.

"Billie," he says softly, still portraying the danger he hides within himself. It's *too* soft. The calm before the storm. "You know I can make you do whatever I want, right?"

My heart drops, my stomach catching and throwing it back to my throat. I don't answer, so his thumb comes to caress my lips. "Imagine your sister and your dad getting that video on their phone. Your entire crew losing respect for you and your family. You guys would be fucking killed in public for the simple fact that you let a King shatter you to pieces with his tongue."

"Stop it," I grit. He pulls his thumb away from my lips and caresses my throat, where my heart is beating so harshly my skin is trembling.

"I like that I scare you." The confession sounds desperately honest, and it terrifies me. "I like that you have no choice but to do exactly what I say because I'm not someone who ever takes no for an answer."

"The fact that you have to blackmail me for that makes you a coward. And weak." My throat is tight from the fear, yet my small voice still resonates with truth.

"You're making me sound like a bully," he laughs. Then his eyes light up with excitement. "Am I a bully?"

"Are you proud of that?" I scowl at him, not understanding what goes on in his head.

"Oh, come on." He smiles. "It's fun. Remember how you were the bully in our sophomore year? NSC had the Cosa Nostra's protection, and you were such a fucking bitch." He looks around. "Lik used to make me fucking eat dust, and I couldn't get back at him because I knew Sawyer and my dad would kill me if I started something they couldn't finish."

"Lik isn't me. I minded my own business."

"You beat up my sister," he snaps before his hand slams against my car window, making me shrink into myself. "You started minding your own business *after* Bianco was put away. *After* I made you suck my cock. You started minding your own business because you were *scared*. Before that, you were a proud bitch who loved beating up Kings girls for no reason and laughed when her stepbrother knocked my head against lockers."

"Okay," I nod. "Thinking your crew owns the North Shore makes you feel invincible," I admit. "I was a bitch. Happy?"

"You don't even remember that you once stole Jade's lunch money and made her crawl around the cafeteria if she wanted it back. Like a real *bully*."

"I had never met Jade before seeing her at your house. That wasn't her."

"It was her." He runs a hand across his face, getting pissed off at me. "It was her, Billie. Her teenage years weren't exactly kind to her, and she had the biggest fucking glow-up of all times since, but it was her."

Well.

Fuck.

He chuckles to himself and steps away from me. "Oh, the things I could do to you."

"Stop it, Caden. We're not in fucking high school anymore. Plus, you got more than your share of revenge." I wish my voice didn't come out as the most pathetic squeak, but here I fucking am. A tiny mouse fighting the giant predator Caden has become over the years.

"Get on all fours," he says calmly.

"You can't be serious," I scoff. "That was more than two years ago."

Grabbing his phone from his jeans, he unlocks it and starts scrolling. "I can't wait for everyone to see the videos. Which one should I start with? I really think your orgasm is the worst one for you."

"Stop!" I try to grab his phone as he pedals back.

"Get on all fours, Billie. Show me how you crawl."

"You're...I...fuck, I hate you," I snarl.

"There are a lot of Kings inside my house right now. Should I invite them to watch?"

I'm hyperventilating, anger and humiliation making me shake. "Caden, stop," I plead.

"You don't want to do what I tell you, little Scott?" I don't know what it is tonight, but he's *angry*. This morning he fixed my car and told me he'd make an exception if I wanted to be his girlfriend. Insane, yes, but at least he wasn't hurting or humiliating me.

Tonight, his wicked side is out to play, and I don't know what to do to escape him alive.

"I'm just..." I take a deep breath. "I'm just trying to make you see sense right now."

"I don't want to see sense. I want to see you on all fours. Do you prefer here or inside the house?"

"Caden!" I rage. "Just drop it. It was a long time ago. Get over it."

"You want me to get over it?" he scoffs. He grabs the bag of money and straightens up before his hand shoots to my ponytail. "I tried to keep this between us, Billie." He's close enough this time that I can feel his breath, and there's no mistaking what's happening.

He's drunk.

"Let go," I shriek as he starts walking and dragging me along.

"I do love that hairstyle for you. It's a nice little leash."

He pushes his front door open and brings me inside with him.

As I assumed, it's not a party. It's worse. They're having some sort of small get-together with their closest friends, and all their heads turn to me as we cross the threshold of his house.

"Everyone," he exclaims. "You know Billie Scott."

"What the damn hell are you doing, Caden," his dad scolds as the son drags me into their living area.

"Getting over some stuff." He drops the money in the corner of the room and drags me with him to the middle. "Billie said I should get over what she did in the past. I thought, hey, why not all do it together, right?"

Caden's sister, Kayla, looks right at me, her hatred for me buzzing in the air. I can't talk anymore at this point. Any begging or pleading is a weakness not only for me but for my entire crew. Fighting is stupid and will make my situation worse.

I'm stuck.

I'm stuck with ten or so people looking at me, sharing a need to make me hurt.

Still holding my ponytail, Caden grabs a beer on the table and downs it. "Kay," he slurs. "Wanna remind us of what happened that time you went to the Scott's house to ask for a truce."

"No, Cade," his sister huffs. "I don't want to get into the details, thank you." I notice she's the only one not drinking. Could she help me?

She smiles at me, obviously seeing the hope in my eyes. "But I will very much enjoy you teaching the bitch a lesson or two."

"Okay, well, whatever." He waves a hand in the air. "I know how we found you. No one is allowed to beat up Billie, though, 'cause she moves shit for me. Need the girl alive and all. But we can find other stuff, don't worry."

I shift on my feet when he turns to Jade, and I have to turn with him. "Jade. We're gonna get you settled, too, okay?

I remember how she treated you in high school. Don't worry."

Jade smirks and relaxes in her seat. "I knew this evening was going to be good."

He smiles at everyone, like a ringmaster about to present his circus. Ethan and Elliot are sitting on either side of Jade, taking in the situation with surprised yet happy expressions. There are a few other people, but I don't know them.

"Well," Caden nods to himself. "Billie, here, said we have to get over it. And I thought, why don't we show her what she did and then see how *she* gets over it, huh?" In one sudden movement, he pushes me to the floor and I'm forced to catch myself on my hands and knees.

I attempt a deep breath that falls short and stare at my hands on their rundown carpet. If I do this in front of them, they will never let me forget it.

If I don't...I don't want to know.

My heart is beating loudly in my ears, pounding in my head, and shortening my thoughts. So much so that Caden's voice is barely a ringing sound in my ears when he talks again.

"Come on, little Scott. *Crawl*." Trying not to explode into tears or pass out, I take a tentative tread, glaring at the floor. "That's it," he says, satisfied. "All the way to Jade."

I do it. It destroys the entirety of my pride, but I know I have no choice. Some people walk into this house and never come out alive. Caden broke me before, and I survived. I can do it again. He has the audacity to complain about me bullying Jade or beating up Kay when he assaulted me. Nevertheless, there's no reasoning with him, and I want out of here. So I do it. I crawl to Jade and wait by her feet for Caden's next order.

"Holy shit," Jade laughs. "I'm filming this."

"No." Caden's refusal is an order no one would dare to

disrespect. "Go around the room, Billie. Show us how pretty you are."

I don't think he meant the last bit, because he chuckles to himself when there's a short silence. Everyone must be looking at him with wide eyes, but I don't want to lift my head and see them.

"What?" he insists. "She is fucking pretty. Go on, Billie. Crawl."

I do it fast, my knees hurting and my wrists straining, but I don't care. I go around as quickly as possible while they make fun of me and throw insults at me. When I'm by Caden again, he puts a foot on my back and my arms buckle. I manage to hold myself in position and I don't say anything.

"The Kings have a new pet," a random guy says happily. I hear two beer bottles clinking and want to die on the spot.

The nightmare is almost over. He can't keep you here all night. You're going to be home soon.

"For fuck's sake, Caden." His dad's frustrated voice breaks through the sniggering and mockery of me. "Get her out of here. I want to enjoy my night."

"Dad, don't worry about it." His drunken voice is full of feelings, so different from the emotionless monotone he usually has. "We're just doing a little experiment to see if we should get a real pet or just keep Billie."

"You want to use the girl for your jobs, be my guest. But don't bring her to my house and abuse her like a stray dog when we've got better things to do."

I peer up at Caden's dad, trying to see if, against all odds, the leader of the Kings will let me out of here. But he's up and putting his empty beer on the table. He turns around and heads toward the hallway.

"What," Caden laughs, shouting at his dad's retreating back. "Isn't that what you did with Mom, though? 'Cause I remember why she fucking left. I know why she doesn't want to talk to any of us."

"Stop it, Cade," Kay intervenes in an angry hiss.

"Come on," he keeps going. "I abuse my women because that's what you've always shown me, Dad!" He keeps laughing maniacally before looking down at me. His voice drops, then. "Get the fuck out of here," he spits at me, taking his foot off my back.

I'm up in a split second, escaping his house. But of course, he's after me, following me outside.

"Little Scott," he calls as I'm about to enter my car. "Didn't I tell you you'd regret your words this morning?"

His smile is so devilish, it's almost surreal. My jaw drops to the floor before I can get a hold of myself.

"This wasn't about Jade or your sister," I finally whisper as everything becomes clear.

"Aren't you the smartest girl?"

"You just wanted to make me regret turning you down."

He nods as he approaches me, cornering me against my car. "I just wanted you to understand something. Be nice to me, and I'll be nice back. Refuse me anything, and you'll pay the consequences."

He leans down and leaves a surprisingly soft kiss against my forehead before straightening back up. "I'll see you soon, Billie."

God hates me, and only the devil welcomes me. His name is Caden King.

11

BILLIE

The Kid I Used To Know - Arrested Youth

On Tuesday morning, Caden texts me that he'll need me on Wednesday and Thursday night. I'm going to have to cancel my Thursday night with Xi, so I call him right away.

"If it's not my favorite stepsister."

It always feels a little strange and forbidden when Xi calls me his stepsister. Lik truly sees me as family, and he dropped the *step* before the sister a long time ago. Xi doesn't do it because our history is different.

"I'll tell Emma," I tease. "Look, I can't come over on Thursday. I've got early training on Friday, and I want to get a good night of sleep." The lie slips so effortlessly past my lips that I surprise myself.

"Why are you doing me dirty, Bil's? I thought you loved me."

"I do!" I laugh. "But I'll see you on Friday for family dinner and we can have game night next Thursday."

Xi lives in the house they lived in before his dad died and his mom married my dad. He's the oldest out of Lik and him. He pays for the rent, so he considers it his house. Every

Thursday, I go over so we can play PS4 and shout at each other over who's the best UFC3 player.

"Yeah, yeah. Miss you already."

"Miss you, too. I'll see you on Friday."

We hang up and I get off my bed, snapping my fingers and whistling for Murder to follow. I grab her leash in the living room and look around the house. Everyone is gone, and no one will be on my back for not attending classes today.

"Come on, baby girl," I exclaim. "Who's excited for a walk?"

She runs to the door, wagging her tail with excitement. I grab my phone and headphones, and I open the door.

I put my music on shuffle and *Head* by Layto comes on. I bob my head as I walk down the street, or rather Murder leads me down the street.

After ten minutes of walking around and letting her do her thing, I bend down to tighten my laces and straighten back up.

"Time to exercise, baby." I redo my ponytail and start jogging.

For an hour, I push my body past its limit, sprinting when I think I can't do it anymore. I'm careful to track my calories to make sure I eat accordingly and not lose weight. Running is to work on my fitness and endurance, and I must always be careful not to lose mass. I'm stretching my leg against a wall, Murder playing on a patch of grass further down the road, when I hear some snickering past the music in my ear. I pull my headphones out, rolling the string around my phone and tucking it in my leggings pocket against my leg.

"If it isn't *unbeatable* Billie," I hear as I turn around.

Caden's friend, Jade, and three other girls come to crowd me against the wall.

"Great," I say bitterly. "Is Kings' turf getting a bit too

crowded now that you've stolen half of our crew? Is that why you're venturing onto our territory?"

"Someone should keep up with the shit going on around her," Jade mocks me. "This isn't yours anymore."

My chest tightens at the revelation. When did this happen? I want to look around and check for the street sign, but she'll just use the occasion to attack me.

"So," Jade smirks. "How is it being Caden's little bitch?" The reminder of what happened Friday at Caden's house makes me want to disappear on the spot. "He can't stop talking about you and how you're *so* compliant."

I don't miss the undertone of jealousy. "Don't worry. I'm sure he'll be over his obsession very soon. Then you can go back to begging for his cock."

She explodes in a laugh and claps her hands. "Aw, girls. She thinks he actually gives a shit about her." Her voice drops. "You're just a life he doesn't care about sparing, Billie. Why do you think he's not asked anyone from his crew? He can make money off your back, doesn't have to pay you, and if you go down, no one will care. You truly are the Kings' new pet."

Clenching my jaw, I have an internal fight with myself. Thinking of what's important—and ignoring how I want to smash Jade's face against the wall—I swallow my pride and nod. "Whatever. I was leaving anyway."

"And now you're not anymore," she spits at me.

The brunette to her right looks me up and down. "I'm dying to check if you're truly unbeatable."

I recognize her from amateur MMA. I think her name is Reilly. She's two weight classes above me and looks like a wall of muscles compared to me. But she also lost her last two fights.

"In the ring? With rules?" I say. "I'm not entirely sure." I narrow my eyes at her before adding, "But on the streets? Bitch, I'm giving you an out now before you truly piss me off."

The two blondes on Jade's left snort. My gaze goes to them, and I don't even have time to look at Reilly again. All I feel is her fist against my cheek.

I stagger back, caught by the wall, before exploding into a laugh. "You're gonna have to try a bit harder than that."

I'm on her the next second, raining punches on her as she falls backward and onto the ground. Someone grabs me by the ponytail, pulling me off her and then I get a kick on my back, forcing me to retreat slightly. Without knowing who it is, I twist and grab the back of their head before pulling down as I bring my knee up and hit them in the nose.

I recognize Jade's voice when she shrieks, and blood spurts all over her face as she recoils. Turning around, I use the minor reprieve to whistle as the two blondes hesitate. A loud bark is heard as Murder sprints her way back to me. I grab one of the blondes and throw her toward my dog. She cries out as Murder unleashes on her leg.

Reilly and Jade are back on me despite having bloody faces. The former grabs me from behind, holding my arms behind my back as Jade punches me in the face.

I lose my focus for ten seconds, unable to defend myself and take a few hits. But if MMA teaches you anything, it's to keep going under the pain.

I grunt while pushing myself against Reilly for balance and kick Jade in the stomach.

"Lea!" Reilly shouts from behind me. The blonde my dog is not attacking, and who simply standing there uselessly, starts shaking her head, wondering what to do. "Call the guys," Reilly orders her in panic.

"You're such a fucking coward," I grunt as I do my best to make us both fall backward. The problem is that she's so much bigger and heavier than me that she feels like a wall behind me.

I whistle again, and Murder comes to bark at Reilly. She lets me go in fear of getting bitten and I turn around, striking her tactically in the chin. I see her lights blacking out in a split second and she falls unconscious to the ground. Next, I'm on Jade. I grab her by the hair as she tries to run away and shove her to the ground. My kicks to her ribs and stomach make her screech, and I only stop when I see she's lost the strength to defend herself anymore.

I grab Murder and the pouch that I've attached to her. I take my switchblade out and open it.

"Fucking come at me and see what happens," I say to Lea, who is stepping back anyway. I sit on Jade's chest and hold her face between my knees.

She gargles something, spitting out some blood, but she's barely conscious. I bring my knife to her face and carve her with the tip of it. One line from the corner of her eye, across her temple and until her hairline.

"Gave you a nice NSC pathway of tears. Look at it next time you think yourself bigger than you actually are," I seethe in her face with all the rage I hold.

When someone messes with our gang, we don't always kill them. Sometimes, we give them what we call the pathway of tears. Because once they're on the floor crying, this is the way their tears will fall. That way, they never forget they once lost a fight against us.

The Kings have their own mark. I know people in our crew who walk around with a messy crown carved into the side of their neck.

A loud exhaust startles me, and I hear one of the blondes muttering I'm dead.

I spit blood on Jade's face and hear her whimper

underneath me. I jump to my feet and whistle for Murder, who's been barking at the blondes all this time.

I turn around to face a matte green truck and recognize Ethan's car.

"Fucking bitches," I tell them.

"Scott!" Elliot shouts as he hops out from the passenger seat and Ethan from the driver's side.

"Fuck my life," I mumble as I look around. I'm going to have to sprint to the woods if I don't want to end up in a body bag.

"What the fuck," I hear Elliot's shocked voice. "Yo, Reilly."

"She's out, brother."

"You fucking K.O-ed Reilly? You psychopath," Elliot says with a little too much pride in his voice to sound angry.

My eyes dart to the forest again. Will they catch me if I run?

Ethan sees where I'm looking and shakes his head. "Don't even think about it."

Both their gazes land on Jade, and I bite my inner cheek. When they look at me again, Elliot has lost his usual spark of humor, and Ethan's normally unbothered stance has turned into tension in his body.

"I'm gonna fucking kill you," Elliot says.

"She attacked me," I defend. "I—"

"You're on Kings' territory, little bitch," Ethan snarls. "Rules are rules. Only NSC seems to be unable to respect them."

"I didn't know!" I shout. "I was defending myself," I add, dejected. The bitches I beat up don't scare me. But when it comes to Caden, Elliot, or Ethan, I'm always brought back to that night two years ago, and my bravery slips through my fingers every fucking time.

As soon as they take a step toward me, Murder barks at them.

"She'll bite you," I say in a weak warning as they keep approaching.

Ethan reaches for the back of his jeans and comes up with a gun. "I don't give a shit about animals. I think you should know that. Call your bitch back."

What kind of psycho doesn't care about animals?

"Don't," I put my hands in front of me and whistle at my dog. "Easy. Come here, girl."

"Drop your fucking knife," Ethan says. The two men clearly care about Jade. I'd never realized it before and I'm starting to regret having unleashed on her.

I drop my knife as Murder nestles against my leg with one last growl at Ethan. Elliot is saying soft words to Jade, helping her sit up against the wall, but her head keeps falling against her chest. There's too much blood on her face. Thank fuck, neither of them can see the pathway of tears on her yet.

Ethan is pointing his gun at me, but his eyes are on Jade and I use the occasion to slip my hand inside my leggings pocket and press the home button five times in a row. This automatically sends Xi my location along with a text that says S.O.S. It's always been his number because he's my closest friend. I put that system in place after that fateful night with Caden, Elliot, and Ethan. Xi never asked what happened. He just agreed and said he'd be there if I needed him. I know he will always keep his word.

Ethan keeps his gun on me for a solid five minutes as Elliot helps Jade. The two blondes are on the phone with other crew members, and the more I wait here, the more I risk my life.

My hope is running low, and I thank God when I see my stepbrother's car slowly drive past us. None of them notice him, too busy threatening me or taking care of themselves. He pulls down his tinted window, and I see him with a finger on his mouth, telling me to keep quiet.

He keeps driving, and I'm assuming he's going to park his car somewhere they can't see it. I only have to wait another minute before he shows up. I let him walk quietly behind Ethan and point his own gun to the back of his head.

"Get the fuck away from her right now."

Before the Kings crew people can react, another car arrives at full speed and stops right by Ethan's truck. Four windows roll down, and they shoot at it. The sound of guns and bullets against metal renders us all deaf. Ethan's windows explode, and the front of his car starts blowing smoke. Chaos ensues.

Xi hits the back of Ethan's head with the handle of his gun so hard he practically passes out from the hit. Falling to the floor, he's not a threat anymore. I grab his gun and step over just as more Kings appear.

"Fuck," I huff.

It's not often that our crews come to full fighting. We have 'rules' in place and as long as everyone stays in their lane, it doesn't end up being too bad. I fucking hate being the source of the current mess we're in.

Some of our guys are fist-fighting Kings and some are threatening the others with guns. Murder is whining away, losing her mind from the gunshots she heard.

Xi is on Elliot as he helps Jade up to try and get her out of the way. He grabs him by the back of the neck and throws him to the floor before pointing his gun down at him.

"If I see you near her again, I'm going to burn your fucking house down with your entire family in it." He shoots, making me shriek in surprise. The shot was far from his head, into the ground. But Elliot has curled into a ball, with his hands on his ears as he grunts in pain.

"Cops!" someone shouts, and everyone starts running away.

"Come on, Bil's. Get in the car."

I follow Xi to his car, helping my dog into the back, and we drive away in a screech of tires. In the mirror, I can see the Kings' crew spreading out and ours getting back into their cars.

Xi's eyes dart to me and his hands tighten on the wheel. "Are you okay?" he asks softly.

I pull down the passenger mirror and look at my swollen lip and bleeding brow.

"Fuck," I push through clenched teeth, hitting my head against the seat. "My face."

"Are you hurting?" Xi asks worriedly.

"No," I say. "But Dickie is going to fucking kill me." I look down at my bleeding knuckles and notice my right index finger is swollen. "Fucking...*fuck*," I breathe out. "Fucking bitches."

"It's gonna be okay." Xi's hand comes to rest on my thigh, and his touch brings me calm.

"They cornered me," I pant. "They fucking attacked me. What was I meant to do?"

"Bil's calm down. I can come with you to training tonight. We'll tell Dickie the truth and he'll understand."

I run my hand against my face, feeling tears threatening to spill out now that the adrenaline is running low. "I'm sick of this place."

"I know," he says with an understanding only people on the North Shore have. "I know, babe."

His hand tightens around my thigh reassuringly, and I can finally take a full breath.

12

CADEN

Lost It - Layto, Jaymmac

"Holy shit," I explode in a laugh as I walk into Elliot and Ethan's living room.

I always go to theirs after I've been to Stoneview. I usually shower at my place and then seek their company to keep my mind away from hating myself.

Chantale 'recommended' me to a friend of hers last week. Told her she should absolutely get that great math tutor from the North Shore. So today, I've had to suck off a bitch's husband just because what turns her on is watching her man dominate another. I kept fucking eyeing the money on the table the whole time, promising myself it would be worth it. At least he was hot, and I've been with men before. The only issue is that I'm a top, and he's a top. Obviously, I don't get to decide in a situation where I'm being paid.

Looking around the room, I can't help but laugh again. Ethan is holding a bag of frozen peas to the back of his head and Elliot's tending to Jade on the sofa. His left ear has dried blood that's trickled from it.

Jade's got a gauze taped to the corner of her left eye and two cottons neatly tucked in her nostrils. She's holding ice to her cheek, and Elliot is dabbing her bleeding lip with a wet cloth. She's slumped so far into the sofa she's bound to disappear into the cushions at some point.

"Stop laughing," Ethan snaps. "That shit ain't funny, Cade."

"What," I shrug, "you all look like you went to war or something." I drop my backpack on the floor and sit on the coffee table to face all of them. "So, I guess there's no need to ask how your day was."

"Fuck off," Elliot growls back at me. "Your new recruit did this. Did you know?"

My heart skips a beat just thinking of Billie. No one's even said her fucking name, and my chest is buzzing with excitement.

"Billie did that, huh?" I ask, incapable of stopping the corner of my lips from tipping up. I run my hand against my mouth to try and hide it.

Jade shifts to try and sit up and winces as she does so, bringing a hand to her ribs. She pushes Elliot's hand away and shoots daggers at me. "You better do something, Cade. She's not getting away with this."

"Now, why would I do that? When Billie does something wrong, she gets punished." And they all witnessed that last Friday when I was drunk off my face. Not exactly my proudest moment. "But as far as I'm aware, she did nothing wrong today."

"She did nothing wrong?" Elliot retorts. "Charlotte is at the hospital because Billie's dog feasted on her leg. Man, she *punched* the lights out of Reilly. Reilly!"

I nod, pride warming up my stomach. I knew Billie had a reputation. People tend not to want to piss her off. She's a fighter, after all. But Reilly is a huge girl. Fuck, even I wouldn't want a punch from Reilly. And she dabbles in amateur MMA, too. Obviously, that didn't stop Billie.

"My car is riddled with bullets. Two of our guys got shot when Xi and his men showed up."

I roll my eyes. "That's not Billie's fault."

"Stop defending her," Ethan jumps in. "Fuck, can't you see the state she put Jade in? We're your friends, Cade. Your family. She's just some girl you want to fuck."

"I'm not defending her," I snort. My eyes go to Jade, and she must see my deadly thoughts because she shrinks back into the sofa. "Tell me, Jade. What happened, exactly?"

She gulps and her eyes dart to the side. "I was with Reilly, Lea, and Charlotte. We were walking back from a race, and we saw Billie. I didn't know what she was doing on our turf, but we thought she was up to no good. When we walked past her, she jumped us."

I smile, and she squirms some more in her seat. "Oh, really?"

"Yeah," she sticks with her lie. "She punched Reilly, and when I tried to get in the way, she beat me up. She set her dog on Charlotte and—"

"Do you know what sounds a little strange?"

Her jaw tightens as she shakes her head.

"That Billie, a girl who is dying to move into professional MMA, would start a fight with not one, but *four* girls. That's a big risk to take from someone who shouldn't even be fighting outside the ring."

What I don't tell Jade, is that I had about a million missed calls when I left Stoneview today. Everyone wanted to make me aware of what had happened and ask where I was. I talked to Reilly and Lea, and both admitted the truth. They looked for trouble, and they found it. Of course, they want me to get back at Billie, but at least they're not lying.

"I don't know why she did what she did. The girl is fucking unhinged," Jade insists.

"Okay, I heard your story. Now here's what I think happened." I tilt my head to the side before saying, "I think Billie was on our streets, for what reason I don't fucking care, and you girls bumped into her. I think you picked on her because you're being a jealous bitch who can't accept that you're not getting my attention and that a girl from NSC is. And I think you started a fight, except it turned against you because she's much stronger than the four of you combined. Now you're scared to get in trouble with me, so you're lying to my face hoping I'll take it out on Billie. How does that sound for the truth?"

Her eyes narrow at me before she snaps. "She left me a fucking pathway of tears!" she yells. "If you don't take my side here, you're a fucking traitor, Caden!"

"She left you with what you deserved. You made your bed; now you fucking lay in it." I raise my voice only in the slightest, but she shrinks from it.

There's a long silence before Elliot says, "Is it true? You started all this?"

She looks away, tears shining in her eyes, and crosses her arms.

"Why did you lie to us, Jade?" Ethan asks softly.

When she turns back to us, she's fuming. "I'm telling Kay and Sawyer that you're defending some NSC girl, Caden. I'm going to say how she can get away with everything because you're letting her get under your skin."

I stand up so quickly she lets out a whimper of fear. Leaning over, I bring my face close to hers. "And I'm gonna have to tell them I've got four cunts on my payroll who can't even fight against one tiny fucking girl."

"Fuck you," she rages. "We all heard you call her pretty when you were supposedly teaching her a lesson on Friday. You were drunk and couldn't help wanting to see her on all fours, so you could imagine what it'll be like when you fuck her."

Her pointing out something very fucking true pisses me off even more. I press her temple, where the bandage is, and smile sadistically as she lets out a pained hiss. "Go home before I change my mind about not hurting you. And feel free to ask yourself if it was all worth it."

I straighten back up and move to the side to let her get up and leave. She does so in a storm of rage and slams the front door.

Elliot rakes his hands through his hair and shakes his head. "Jealousy doesn't suit her."

I roll my eyes. "What the fuck can she possibly be jealous of?"

I sit down on the armchair as Elliot and Ethan get their controllers and turn on their PS4. Grabbing my phone from my pocket, I google something before pulling up my conversation with Billie. It's not much. She only ever replies with a thumbs-up when I tell her something. Or an insult. Smiling to myself, I type,

> Caden: The Young and The Hopeless. Track 9, 0:18.

13

BILLIE

PLEASE - Omido, Ex Habit

Lying on my bed with my headphones in my ears, Good Charlotte sings: *"My girl's a hot girl who needs an attitude adjustment."*

My mouth falls open. Caden King is an asshole.

But I'm tired, and I want to give in to the distraction.

> Billie: You listen to Good Charlotte now?

His reply comes straight away.

> Caden: 0:28 to 0:43

The song's been going on, so I rewind to twenty-eight seconds in.

"My girl's a hot girl. A riot girl and she's angry at the world."

I bite my lower lip and keep listening until it stops at *"She wants a riot, she wants a riot."* It's hard to keep a smile off my face when I type back.

> Billie: I'm guessing you heard about Jade and her girls.

The fact that I see the three dots right away and know he's on his phone right now, thinking of me, makes my stomach tighten. What the fuck am I doing?

I'm furious at him. He humiliated me in front of his family and closest friends. I fucking *crawled* for him.

And yet what I remember the most is the way my heart jumped when he leaned in, smelling of alcohol and cigarettes, and his soft lips kissed my forehead.

I've seen some serious toxic shit on the North Shore...but never have I seen a girl falling for a guy who degraded her the way Caden has done to me.

So why, God, explain to me why, when his text appears on my screen, I lay on my front as my feet bounce on the bed, resting on my elbows and staring at my screen.

> Caden: I heard someone fucked a few of my girls up.

> Billie: What? Some hot girl?

I bite my thumb as the dots appear and disappear.

> Caden: I didn't send it for that part of the sentence. Rather the other half of it.

Going to my music app, I return to that moment in the song and my thighs tighten.

> Caden: Did you find it?

I gulp and text back.

Billie: Yes.

Caden: Tell me. What is it?

I don't know why I type it. Probably because I can feel my thighs trembling and my panties getting wet. So I keep chasing the feeling.

Or probably because I'm a masochistic idiot.

Billie: She needs an attitude adjustment.

Caden: Tell me, Billie. How am I going to adjust that attitude of yours?

Billie: I don't know...

Caden: Should I come around? Should I fuck you so hard your tight pussy will remember me for days?

My hands are shaking when I answer.

Billie: Everyone is home. You can't show up.

Caden: No?

Caden: Okay.

Caden: Touch your pussy, then.

My eyes widen, and I drop the phone on the mattress. He can't be serious?

When I don't reply for two whole minutes, he texts me again.

Caden: Put two fingers against your little clit. Right now.

Brain frozen, heart exploding, and stomach tightening, I twist and roll onto my back. I pull up my oversized t-shirt to my hips and slide my hand into my panties. I press two fingers against my clit and grab my phone again. There's another text.

Caden: Start touching yourself. Go slow until I tell you otherwise.

Slowly, I draw a long circle, pressing my fingers to my clit. I keep going until I moan softly and my chest rises and falls quicker.

Caden: Make yourself feel good. Imagine it's my fingers on you. Imagine I'm kissing your neck and sucking your pretty pink nipples. Feel the way they'd become so hard in my mouth as my teeth graze against them.

My nipples are so hard they could fucking break glass.

Caden: Pinch your left nipple.

I drop my phone on my stomach and drag my hand under my top. I pinch my nipple as he would. Hard and mercilessly. I cry out in the best way, and my lower belly tenses as my legs open wider and my thighs start to shake.

My head comes up so I can look down at my stomach to see his next text.

Caden: Go quicker, Billie. I know you want to.

My fingers accelerate, losing the circles I was making and rubbing with more intensity in multiple directions. As long as it feels good, I follow what my body wants. I'm getting closer and closer to exploding.

My phone repeatedly vibrates on my stomach and I almost have a heart attack when I see Caden's name appear on my screen.

I pick up, only to realize too late that it's a video call. I gasp at seeing his face pop up on my screen and, in a small square, my own flushed face against my pillow.

"*Don't you fucking dare hang up right now,*" he growls.

He's outside somewhere. A backyard I recognize but can't necessarily place. He's not speaking loudly, and I can tell he's alone.

"*Show me your whole body,*" he orders low.

Without stopping, I extend my arm and put my phone high above me. I pull up my top, completely exposing myself before he even asks.

"*Lose the virginal panties. I don't think they suit a little slut like you.*"

I moan at his words before lowering my panties just below my knees and spreading my legs. I go back to my clit and rub myself again.

"*That's a good girl,*" he smiles. "*Keep going. Faster.*"

I quicken to the point that my arm hurts. My hips are bucking against my own hand, and I'm ready to explode. When my moans turn into whimpered pants, and my voice gets higher, he says, "*Stop.*"

"What?" I groan, shocked.

"*I said stop. Right now. I swear, Billie, if you make yourself orgasm, I will come over and choke you with my cock.*"

I stop and pull my hand away, panting and frustrated. "What is wrong with you?" I practically yell at him as I bring the phone to my face. My cheeks are red, and my hair is a mess. My eyes are shining but my stare is deadly.

He smiles at me through the phone and runs a hand

through his hair. "*You're so hot like this. I want to fuck you right now*."

"Then fucking do it," I snap before I can control it.

There's a silence, his smile lost and his eyes widening slightly. There's a glimmer of hope on his face.

"I—"

"*Did you mean that?*"

"I mean..." I take a deep breath, the fog from my pleasure finally dissipating. "No. No, of course not. You left me hanging on the brink of..." I cut myself off, not because I don't want to say what happened but because of the look of disappointment on his face.

"Just don't come here," I confirm. "If you think I want you anywhere near me after what you did last Friday, you're sorely mistaken. Don't come here, Caden. I *mean it*."

"*Too late,*" he grins.

The knock on my window startles me. I hurry to open it, scared he will bring everyone's attention to this room. I can't have anyone seeing a King at my window. He climbs in right away, pushing me out of the way when I try to stop him. I only understand now that the backyard I recognized earlier was my neighbor's.

"You just can't take no for an answer, can you?" I hiss.

"Chill, I was already here. I'm not going to touch you."

A certain disappointment washes over me. One that I try to not think about too much.

His eyes narrow as if trying to see me better. We're in the dark and are only illuminated by the lamp post outside.

"Is your face okay?" The worry in his voice is evident, but the obsession is prominent.

I put my finger to my cheek and then my lips. Of course, his bitches did manage to hit me earlier. "It's fine. It doesn't really hurt. I'm more worried about my finger."

I don't know why I'm saying that. The truth, I mean. Caden is Kings crew. He's a bully, and he harasses me. Yet, tonight, I want to open up and tell him what the consequences of today truly were for me.

Maybe because we're in the dark. In the softness of the night, reality doesn't exist. When the moon shines and the monsters come out, I'm allowed to give in to them.

"What's wrong with it?" He grabs both my hands then drops the left one. He looks closer at the index finger on my right hand. It's still swollen.

"I don't know." My voice is barely above a whisper. "Probably strained it or something. It's not broken, at least. But I couldn't train tonight, and my coach was furious about what I did. He's...he's really helping me out, and I disappointed him."

I swallow the pain at the back of my throat from the anxiety of what Dickie told me earlier. Caden is looking closely at my finger, and it's easier to talk when the intensity of his gaze isn't on me. "If I can't win my next match, then I won't move on to the fight against Killer Clover, and...it's the end for me."

"It's not the end. I know you want to go pro, but there will be other fights," he says reassuringly.

He doesn't look up as I pause, taking his words in. "How do you know I want to go pro?"

"We live on the North Shore, little Scott," he smiles as he keeps observing my finger, "everyone knows everything about everyone else. It honestly isn't the end of the world if you don't fight Clover."

"Yeah, but my new agent will drop me, and I'll...I'll never get out of here."

His eyes flick up as he straightens. "Get out of here?" he sniggers. "To go where?"

I don't like the way I feel like he's mocking me.

"Anywhere," I retort. "Just not here. I want to be...*there*."

"There?" His lips curl into a smile, and I get frustrated.

"Just drop it, okay? Maybe you love the North Shore because your crew has authority over everything. Because you're a King. Because you can fuck around and not care about anything or anyone. But I hate it here. I've hated it my entire life and I want to leave."

I let myself fall back onto my bed, sitting in front of Caden. Why am I telling him this? I'm making myself vulnerable, allowing him to get to me and ruin me further than he already has.

At the same time, I keep wanting him to know. There's a part of my mind that keeps thinking if he sees how vulnerable I really am, he'll be nicer. What a joke.

He crouches between my legs and grabs my hand again.

"Someone's set on leaving," he says. "Here. Have a magic kiss. You'll be all healed for your fight and your plan to escape the North Shore won't go to waste." He drops a kiss on my swollen finger and I giggle like a fourteen-year-old.

I bite my lower lip as we both look at each other with wide eyes.

Then he throws his head back and laughs. I'd never heard such a genuine laugh from him. His Adam's apple is bobbing up and down and I want to bite his neck.

"Oh, I want to hear that again," he says as he brings his head back. He kisses my finger again, and I do my best not to react. To ignore the butterflies flaring up in my stomach and creating a tornado of feelings in my chest.

He pushes me backward, and I fall onto my bed, my legs bent at the knees and my feet still touching the floor. His mouth kisses my palm then my forearm. He makes his way up, his body moving until he's above me. It's slow and delicious.

Kissing my shoulder and then my neck...my jaw...the corner of my lips.

"I want to leave this hellhole, too," he murmurs against my lips. "I would give anything to have been born somewhere else. I don't care where. *There*."

There's a brief pause, my mouth agape at the revelation. His gaze goes from my eyes to my lips and he captures my mouth with his.

I practically gasp from the pleasure and perfect release I feel. He licks my lips and I open my mouth for him. His tongue comes to stroke mine and my heart explodes in my chest.

What am I doing?

What is wrong with me?

Everything.

And nothing.

The simple truth he just admitted is making me feel closer to him than I ever could have otherwise.

Ignoring the alarm bells ringing in my head, I let my heart take over and wrap my arms around Caden's neck. I bring him closer, and he holds himself with a hand on the mattress right next to my head so he doesn't crush me under his weight. His other hand goes under my top and grabs my hip tightly. The mere sensation of his skin against mine makes me tremble.

I'm not sure how long we've been kissing for, but I feel lightheaded from it. He pulls away and wraps a hand around my throat as his other one goes to my bare pussy. He strokes my clit slowly and reignites the fire he started earlier. It only takes him his thumb and brief focus to make me come under his touch yet again. I'm panting when he releases my throat to undo his belt.

"Wait," I whisper. "I..."

His confused stare makes me uncomfortable. There's a

certain impatience in it, and I'm terrified he'll use this moment of weakness to do things that'll make me hate him.

You're already meant to hate him.

"I don't...I mean, I'm not...ready." A beat. "To have sex again."

"Again?" The surprise in his tone makes me retreat. "When did you stop having s—" The evident truth in my eyes cuts him off. "Fuck," he releases on a breath as he jumps off me and stands up. He rakes two hands through his hair as he turns away from me and pulls at its roots. I sit up and cover myself with the blanket.

I don't say anything, because it's not my duty to make him feel comfortable in a situation that has always been entirely his fault.

He turns back to me, and his true self is more apparent than ever when he says, "You won't get a sorry from me, Billie."

"Sorry wouldn't fix anything. It can't." My voice has no anger, but the truth isn't easy to say or hear.

The truth never means anything. It's just there, existing to remind us that we're so terribly human and flawed.

"I really fucking broke you that night, didn't I?" For once, he doesn't say it offensively. He doesn't say it to taunt me and torture me. He's just realizing the extent of his actions.

Yes, he did break me. But I decide to lie. To not give him the satisfaction of knowing I'm a weirder, more fucked up version of myself since he assaulted me and made me come against my will. Since he made me realize that being forced could bring me pleasure.

"I'm not broken," I whisper. "You're not important enough for that. You're just a smudge on the canvas of my life."

"Good," he murmurs as he takes a step closer. "Because it

doesn't change anything. You'll be mine, Billie. If not now, then. If not here, in this shitty town that broke us...then *there*."

That fictional, magical place that we both long to go to.

I'm speechless that he dares tell me it doesn't change anything. I try to push a thought past my mouth, but nothing comes out for a few seconds.

"I don't understand you," I finally say.

"I'm obsessed with a girl I barely know and should hate. I killed three guys because they touched her. I'm turning against my own crew for her and don't even know her fucking middle name. Trust me when I say I don't understand myself."

There's a beat while I take in information that sounds so real and emotionally genuine.

"I mean, there are some people I know really well, and I don't know their middle names. I don't think it's a reference..." I pinch my lips, realizing it's not the time to get into this. "Three guys, huh?"

He shrugs.

"From that fight night?"

He ignores my question, but I know it's them because the Kings have been putting the blame on NSC. Turns out it was Caden.

"Get some rest," he finally says. "You need to get better for that fight."

He walks to my window, and just as he's about to climb off, I say, "Caroline. That's my middle name."

He laughs softly and leaves into the dark of the night.

If I thought hating Caden was bad, starting to like him is absolutely worse.

14

BILLIE

The Wall - PatricReza

"*Be careful,*" Caden says low on the other end of the line. "*As much as I like your smart mouth, I would hate for it to get you in trouble.*"

I roll my eyes but can't stop my thighs from tightening and the smile that tips at the corner of my mouth. "I don't have a smart mouth. I'm just telling you I don't need you to protect me."

"*I'm worried for you.*"

If he's so worried for me, maybe he shouldn't have started this whole thing. Maybe he shouldn't have humiliated me at his house, and I might have had a little respect from his crew instead of being called their pet.

"Please," I scoff. "You're worried Jade is going to kill me before you get to fuck me. If there's a risk of Kings girls jumping me when I come to drop off your cash, just do the jobs yourself instead of warning me."

"*So we agree that I will fuck you.*"

Yes, please! a voice screams in my head.

171

"There are more chances of me running away with the Wolves when they come drop your merchandise than my allowing you to have sex with me."

"*I don't really need you to allow me. You know that, right?*"

Lead drops in my stomach. Does he always have to go from easygoing to absolute asshole?

"Anything else you want from me? If not, I have to get your shit."

"*Don't hang up on me, Billie.*" The warning in his voice is sharp, but I don't care.

So I hang up.

I start my car, and it rumbles into the night before the engine finally decides to come to life. It always sounds like it's going to explode when I try to drive during cold nights.

I did four drop-offs for Caden in the last week and a half, and every time instead of just grabbing the bag of cash, he settled into my passenger seat, and we talked for hours. The first time, I was shocked. I was terrified of parking in front of his house and him asking me inside like the last time.

Instead, he came to my car. He opened the door and just sat there for ages in silence. I didn't know what to do. For long minutes he was talking to himself. Then, weirdly enough, everything flowed effortlessly, talking about anything and everything except our gangs.

Something must have shifted when he admitted he wanted to leave this town too. Because the moment he mentioned it again, I felt safe next to him. Like I finally had someone who understood me.

Rather than talking about our rivalries, I learned that he has two one-and-a-half-year-old twin nieces who live with him and his family and who he spoils to death. I learned that his favorite meal of the day is breakfast and that he'll sometimes have two, just for the sake of it. I told him about how Dickie got me off the streets and that I now have an agent, that MMA means the world to me. More than staying here with my family. I told him that my favorite thing to watch is animes, and we bonded over *Fullmetal Alchemists*.

The worst thing of all...we laughed. He made me laugh until I felt like I was choking, and tears were running down my face. He did, too, until his voice was raw and his eyes shone with happiness.

How can I do this to myself? Talk and laugh with someone who I know without a doubt is a merciless man? Who is still blackmailing me into doing a job for him that could send me to prison for the rest of my life. And who, when he loses patience with me, might make me do things I'm not ready to do.

The pickup is the same as usual. I put the bag on my head, wait until they're gone, and then bring my car to the other meeting point. I leave with the bag of cash, drive to Caden's house and let him know I'm parked on the street. Instead of coming to the car like usual, he texts me asking me to come to the door.

My heart drops, and my breathing halts.

No.

Everything was going fine. He didn't bother me for two weeks, didn't hurt me, didn't humiliate me.

Fear gripping my chest, I text back.

Billie: Are you drunk?

I take a deep breath when I see him type.

Caden: I know what you're thinking. I'm not drunk or planning on doing anything to you (if you behave, of course). There's no one at my house. I'm tired, just bring the bag.

Fuck this shit. Another deep breath and I open my door. If I die tonight, it'll be because of my poor decision-making and nothing else.

I drag the heavy bag of cash with me and knock on his front door. My jaw almost drops open when he answers. He was clearly sleeping and I woke him up when I texted him. His dark hair is messier than usual, and his green eyes are heavy and slightly swollen from sleep. He's wearing a *The Offspring* black hoodie and gray sweats that leave absolutely nothing to the imagination.

The outline of his dick sends a shiver through my spine. Is that thing asleep right now? Caden's tall but not bulky, and his dick doesn't seem to fit the rest of his appearance. My stomach tightens and I kind of want to push him to the floor and mount him.

"H-hey," I manage to say before swallowing thickly.

"Is that how you girls feel every time we look at your boobs instead of your eyes when we talk to you?"

My eyes snap up to his, and I have to scratch my throat before I can talk. "Sorry. Here's your cash." I drop it at his feet.

"Please," he smiles, "don't be sorry. I love when you look at my dick."

"I wasn't—" I stop myself before I get further into my lie. "Anyway, you've got your cash. Have a good evening."

"Hey, hey. Wait." He grabs my arm just as I turn and brings me toward him across the threshold of the house. "No one's staying here tonight. Kay is on a trip, and my dad is sleeping at his girlfriend's house. Wanna come in?"

My eyes dart to where I am now, which is inside the house. "A bit late to ask. As usual."

He chuckles yet doesn't lose his focus. "I mean, wanna hang out here? Better than your car, don't you think?"

"Not as safe, though," I say instinctively. The last time I was here didn't exactly feel like a fun place to hang out.

"More comfortable."

I bite my inner cheek because I don't want to smile at him. It's a dangerous thing to smile at Caden King. He might take it as a green light to do whatever the hell he wants.

"I'm meeting Xi for game night. I had to cancel the last two Thursdays because of you, and I told him we could move it to Sunday. Told him I'd be there tonight no matter what."

He raises an eyebrow and loses some of the sweetness that was present only because I'm here.

"You spend every Thursday night at Xi's?"

I shrug. "Yeah, we play PS4 and have some dinner."

"Do you sleep over?"

"Sometimes. If I'm too tired to go home."

His grip intensifies slowly but firmly. "That stops now. From tonight on, you're not spending time alone with him."

"What?" I scoff. "Have you lost your mind?" I shake my head, realizing what I just said. "No. Don't answer that question. I fucking *know* you have," I say more seriously.

He releases me and smiles. I can see he's trying to make it sickly sweet, but the fury is apparent. "I don't want to hurt him, Billie. I think it'd be better if you just do as I say."

"I think it'd be better if you lose the obsession over me. Or whatever it is you've got going on. I'm not the kind of person who waits around for a man to come and tell them how to act. I've got my own shit going on, and you can shove your order up your a—"

My rant is cut short when his lips slam against mine, and his hand comes to the back of my neck to press me closer. I'm pretty sure I order my hands to shove at his chest. Not for my arms to wrap around his neck and for my toes to push me up so I am closer to him. Not for my lips to part so I can deepen the violent kiss.

We carry on kissing as he drags me further inside the house and slams the door behind us. He keeps walking back, leading me with him until he falls back and sits on the sofa. He grabs my legs and straddles me on his lap. My hips roll against him and my head is above his now, so I grasp the sides of his face and tilt his head up so we can keep kissing.

He only pulls away to chase a greater high. His lips kiss my jaw before they follow the line of my throat and down to my collarbone. He bites my skin and sucks, putting new bruises where the old ones had faded from when he had come to my house.

I grunt in pain when he bites so hard I feel my skin tear.

"Caden," I cry out in a half moan.

He lifts his hips, pushing his hard-on into my core and making me groan in pleasure. But as he lowers his sweatpants and boxers, I freeze.

"No." It comes out in a panicked whisper. I push myself off him by putting my hands on his shoulders, but he grabs my hips tightly, raising my heartbeat in alarm.

"I won't fuck you," he says softly before kissing my jaw. "Just touch me." He grabs my hand off his shoulder and lowers it to his dick. It's so hard it could break me.

My fingers wrap around his girth as he keeps his hand on mine before we both start moving. He lets out a heavy breath and keeps up the movement until my fear dissipates, and we move in tandem, our breaths becoming one. Lust is running heavily through my body, causing my stomach to twist as I feel myself clench inside.

He lets go of my hand, bringing his thumb to my lips and pulling at the bottom one.

"Take me in your mouth," he whispers.

I go to talk, but my words don't come out. Instead, I struggle to take a breath as my chest freezes. My lungs are full of cement, and I have to push myself off him again. This time I throw my leg off and sit next to him. My back against the armrest, I bring my knees to my chest, my heart beating quickly and my body wrapped with terror.

"I can't," I heave. "Don't...don't make me."

From the corner of my eyes, I see his jaw clenching. Is that guilt? Or is it frustration for not being able to fuck me yet again? I'm about to put my feet on the floor so I can leave. I need to be away from him. Every time we get close to doing anything, that night comes back to the forefront of my mind. I hear his callous orders, his mocking voice. I see the flash of his phone in front of my eyes. How my knees hurt and how tight my jaw was. I remember the fear of dying and knowing that despite leaving without being physically hurt, a part of me stayed with Caden that night.

His hand locks around my ankle before I can move my legs properly, almost like he felt I was about to flee.

"Please, don't go," he says quietly.

I take a deep breath, doing my best to keep the tears at bay. "I can't do this, Caden." My voice is wobbly, but I do my best to make it clear. He's looking ahead of him, at his TV displaying a black screen.

"I know. I understand. Just...forget about what I just asked." He finally turns to me, and his hand slides up to my knee. "Let me make you feel good. You don't have to touch me."

I shake my head, hesitant. "I-I don't know if this is a good idea."

His hand slides higher, to my inner thigh. "I'll stop if you ask me to." He licks his lips, nearly uncertain. His green eyes come to mine as he adds, "Trust me."

I want to burst into laughter. How could I possibly trust a King? And not any. *Caden.*

Never.

But I don't need to trust him to spread my legs slowly. To let him unbutton my jeans and get rid of them along with my panties. To lay back as he settles between my legs and kisses his way up my inner thigh.

"Do you want this, Billie?" he asks low, his warm breath caressing my pussy.

"Yes," I breathe out.

When his lips meet my pussy, and he pushes his tongue inside me, I moan so loudly I'm afraid the neighbors will hear.

His hands slide under me, and he grabs my ass, tugging me closer to his face.

"Holy shit," I gasp as he eats me out like a starved man. This is nothing like two years ago. *Nothing.*

He had been violent, intent on humiliating me and doing it with sadistic, selfish pleasure. Tonight is all about me. About making me enjoy the ride for as long as possible.

My hands pull at his hair as I throw my head back, crying out from the pleasure. His tongue plays with my clit and my eyes roll to the back of my head. I gasp, having just realized I've not been breathing.

His tongue is merciless as he keeps going. One of his hands glides to my pussy and he pushes two thick fingers in, forcing me to realize how wet I am.

"Fuck," I pant. "I'm gonna come..." A shocking current travels through my entire body, the voltage too high to survive as I explode on his tongue and fingers. He tries to pull away, but my grip on his hair tightens as I buck my hips and ride the wave until I've got nothing left.

I fall back on the sofa, letting him go as my whole body relaxes. I barely have time to breathe when suddenly his lips are on mine. I gasp with shock when I taste myself on his tongue. He tears another moan out of me before pulling away.

"Was that alright?" he smirks.

I burst into a relaxing laugh that eases up the tension in the air around us. "Did you not just hear me come? Cause I'm pretty sure your neighbors did."

He chuckles then says, "I meant, are you okay? That I did that?"

Understanding he's checking if he didn't overstep my boundaries, I bite my lip and nod, unable to stop the smile that forces its way on my face. "I'm good."

He drops a kiss on my forehead and lets himself relax on top of me. Still between my legs, His head rests on my chest and I wonder if he hears my heart skipping a beat.

"Let's watch something," he says.

"Really?" I ask, surprised. "Don't you...want me to give something back? That boner looks painful." I don't know if I truly want to.

I feel him shrug against me. "Nah. It'll go away." He presses his hand on top of it before grabbing a pillow and covering his crotch. Then he grabs the remote and turns on the TV. "How about some *Fullmetal Alchemist*?"

"Oh, now you're just trying to turn me on all over again."

He laughs as he goes through the animes on Netflix. "Which of the brothers gets you all wet?"

"Edward. Of course."

"You sure?" he teases. "Cause Alphonse looks like your style."

I slap his chest as I giggle. "No, stop!"

He takes a deep, serious breath and peers up at me from where he's resting. "That giggle...It does something to me, woman."

"Are you making fun of me?" I snort.

"I wish I was."

Time stops, and I run a hand through his hair. "Stop it," I let out in a whisper. "You're going to hope for things that are impossible."

"Impossible doesn't exist in my world. I get anything I want. And believe me, I want you."

Now that he's made me speechless, he puts our anime on to fill the silence. We watch quietly, my hand caressing his hair all along. His head on my chest and his arm wrapped around my leg.

After three or four episodes, he stops it and looks up at me. "Do you wanna eat?"

I can see that he's scared I will say no and leave. Only the simple truth is...I don't want to. He would never admit it, but I think Caden was lonely tonight. I'm enjoying his company, and who knows when I'll ever be able to be this way again with him. So I smile and nod.

"I would like a burger."

He sits up and raises an eyebrow at me. "Oh, she wants a burger, does she? And who made you queen of our food?"

"Me," I say proudly, poking his chest playfully.

"Alright, then, if you want a burger. A burger you're getting. Do you have a favorite place?" He gets his phone out and my eyes widen.

"Delivery services don't come to the North Shore," I say as if he hasn't lived here his entire life.

"Thanks," he laughs without looking up from his phone. "I know. I'll just ask one of my guys to pick something up for us and bring it here."

My mouth falls open. Because I stay silent, he looks back at me.

"What?" he asks, confused.

"How important are you in the Kings' hierarchy?" His

name means a lot, of course. But Caden is not his dad, Sawyer, or even Kay. At the end of the day, no one has any obligation to listen to his orders. I guess everyone just does because they're terrified of him.

"No talks of that, Billie," he says sternly as his eyes darken. "I'm making it a rule from now on."

I swallow the ball of stress that has started forming in my mouth. "Okay," I nod. Not because I like when he tells me what to do, but because I wholeheartedly agree.

Less than an hour later, we're eating burgers on the sofa. We're facing each other, cross-legged, and sharing a massive bag of fries in the middle.

"No!" I shriek with a mouth full. "'On't mish!"

"What?" he cackles. "Try again with an empty mouth."

I gulp my bite. "Don't mix! The ketchup and mayo."

"Oh my god." He stops with the bottle of ketchup half tilted and only a drop mixed with the mayo. "How...*how* can you not like mayo and ketchup mix?"

"Ketchup is too sweet," I say with iron conviction. "Mayo tastes good enough on its own."

He shakes his head at me, mouth agape. "I don't think I like you anymore."

"Good," I smile. "I'll finish my burger and leave."

"You'll finish your burger first, huh?"

"Can't leave here on an empty stomach. I had an exhausting orgasm, Caden," I say as seriously as I can muster.

The corner of his mouth tips before he says, "You're not leaving."

"No?" I ask.

"Nah. Not until I give you an orgasm so exhausting, you'll fall asleep on me."

"But once I'm asleep on you, I can't leave."

"Maybe that's the whole point."

"What is? Sequestering me?"

He throws a couple of fries at me. "Stop fighting this. Right now."

"Why?" I grin. "It's fun."

"Because I'm doing my best to be nice and not just take what I want. And if you start fighting me on everything, I will lose it and just do it."

My heart accelerates. I'm not sure anymore if I want him to respect my wishes or just take without asking. Maybe I need that push. I could just give him control and enjoy the ride. Perhaps that's what I need to get over the fear.

The tightness in my stomach and the way my pussy sends a zap of electricity up to my heart tells me this might just be it.

I put my burger down and put my hands on my knees. "What would it be like? You just taking what you want."

There's a way his piercing eyes darken when his thoughts turn dangerous. A way his smirk becomes like one of a creature from the deepest depths of hell.

"You really wanna know?"

I nod sternly.

He shrugs. "Remember you asked." He wipes his mouth before talking again. "First, I'd make sure to get you alone and in a position where you're relaxed and let your guard down."

Time stops as I realize this is the exact situation he's put me in tonight. My heart is beginning to quicken, my hands clenching on my knees.

"Then I'd kiss you gently, run my hands from your hips all the way to your hair. Did you know I love your hair, Billie? It's so thick, so easy to grab." He leans toward me, above our food, as if he really is going to kiss me. I do the same, and we stop only a couple of inches from each other.

His voice is a low rasp now. "And when you're soft and pliable, I'd push you to the floor, flat on your stomach. I'd put a hand on your back to keep you there as I spread your legs with my knees. I'd ripped your jeans and underwear off and then slap your ass before spreading it. The thing is, you think you'd hate it, except I understand how your body works now. I've played with you enough to know. And when I push my hard cock against your entrance, you'd be so wet I'd slap your ass again for being such a dirty slut. Unfortunately for you, I'm big, and you're not wet enough for that. And since you're fighting me, it's even more painful when I shove myself into you. But don't worry. Your tears turn me on, and really, who cares if you're enjoying yourself, right? And as I thrust into you harder and harder, you will feel the pleasure spreading into your entire body. And, my god, will you hate yourself for loving what I'm doing to you. And when you come all over my dick, and I come too, when I pull out and you're nothing but a trembling mess on the floor, I'll make it worse for you and ask, '*Are you mine now?*'. You won't be able to answer through the tears and the pain in your body, but I don't need you to. I know the truth. That you are. Because trust me, Billie, after that outrageously good fuck, no one, and I mean *no one,* will ever compare. You'll just be mine and mine alone. Good thing since I'll do it again, and again, as many times as I fucking want to until you know that there's no point fighting me anymore. Until you understand that what I want, I get. Always."

Our faces are so close, I'm sure he's going to grab me, kiss me, and throw me to the floor. He's going to do every single thing he just said. And I want him to so badly. Fuck, I don't know why I'm so broken, but I want him to fuck me and make it hurt. To make me cry from pleasure and pain. To make it so that I can never move on from him. To make me his.

I shift. I'm wearing my panties and his hoodie now, but I'm

scared my wetness is showing. His eyes go down as I move away slightly.

There's no doubt anymore when he smiles widely and says, "You've got a spot there." He presses three fingers against my crotch, and I let out a strangled moan.

Then he pulls away and shrugs. "But, like I said. I'm trying to be sweet so you can see I like you. I'm making a real effort here, so don't tempt me to throw it all away."

I'm practically panting when I'm forced to come back to reality. "O-okay," I say before grabbing my burger again and forcing food into my mouth just to have something to do.

He changes the topic, and his explanation of how he would force himself on me, of how I would love it, becomes a dense fog at the back of my mind.

"So," he says casually as he dips more fries in the sauces. I can't help but notice he dips in the ketchup after the mayo now that he knows I don't like the former. Like he wants to make sure it doesn't mix. "How long until you leave the North Shore, you think?"

"Hopefully by the end of the year. If I win against Killer Clover, I'm off to fight small promotions on the East Coast." A thrill runs through my stomach as I explain this.

"Wow, that's soon."

I nod, my mouth now too full to add anything.

"I'm kinda jealous," he snorts. "I want to leave next year."

I swallow. "Do it," I say excitedly.

"I can't." He runs a hand through his hair. "Everyone knows I want to leave, but I just don't have the money yet. I need something to sustain me. I don't want to fail and have to return here."

I crumble my wrapper as I swallow the last bite of my burger. "I understand." I grab the cup of Coke Zero on the table and take a sip.

"Maybe when you're a rich UFC fighter, you can send me money to get me out of here?"

I chuckle as I put the cup back. He relaxes into the arm of the sofa behind him and crosses his arms. "What's so funny?"

"I might become a UFC fighter, but I'll still be a woman. I'm pretty sure the current highest-paid female fighter earns five-hundred grand per fight."

"Sounds like enough to get me outta here."

"I won't make that kind of money. Not until a very long time. I have dreams, but I also need to be realistic. My living conditions will be shit until I can make a name for myself. That's okay with me. I can live in a shed in someone's yard as long as I'm far from here. If you want a nice life, yeah, you're gonna have to wait longer."

He gathers everything on the sofa and throws it all in the trash before returning. "Come to my room."

"Now?"

"Yeah, now," he says. "I had a super long day of work and I want to rest with you."

"Okay," I nod.

I follow him to his room. His house looks the same as mine and most houses around him. Only one level, magnolia walls and rundown carpet. One bathroom, three bedrooms. All in the same hallway.

He opens his door and I'm surprised to find a double bed. It's dumb. Most people have double beds, even though I still have my old childhood twin bed.

I walk in first as I look around, but there's not much to see. The walls are the same as the rest of the house, with minimal furniture. There's a *The Offspring* poster on a wall and I smile.

"Weren't you the guy who made fun of me for listening to Good Charlotte? You weren't even born when these guys," I point at his poster, "dropped their first album." I look down at his hoodie I'm wearing. It's also *The Offspring*. "You get obsessed easily, don't you?"

Leaning against the doorframe, arms and ankles crossed, his lips are tipped. "You have no idea."

There's a desk with math textbooks and homework. "Is that what you study? Math?"

"Uh-uh," he yawns. I keep looking around, tracing my finger on the furniture.

"I see you sometimes at college. You don't really talk to anyone, do you?" I ask. "Always absorbed in your work."

"Yeah, I actually like college." His head comes to rest against the door frame, and I notice the eyebags. What does he even do all day to be so tired?

"What do you want to do when you leave?" I ask as I lean against his desk.

When you leave. We keep asking each other that, as if our lives are on pause right now and that nothing here counts.

He gives up on standing and goes to lie on his bed.

"I wanna be a math teacher. But it pays shit. Hence why I need as much money as I can get now."

I almost choke on a snort. "A teacher? You? I really can't see it."

"Hey. I tutor in Stoneview multiple times a week. They fucking love me."

"No way," I gasp. "Do you like it?" I come over to his bed and straddle him. "Do you see many of their mansions?"

He shifts, slightly uncomfortable. "Yeah, they're all unnecessarily big. Have you ever been?"

"A guy I dated super briefly two years ago lived in Stoneview. He was a foster kid who luckily ended up there. Man, his mansion. Could have fit my house about five times in there."

He laughs softly and runs his hands against my hips and to

my waist, holding me tightly. His gaze goes to my chest, covered by his hoodie, and then to my eyes. "Was that the last guy you had sex with?"

It's my turn to feel uncomfortable. "Yeah," I say. "Erm, so does tutoring make good money?" I change the topic as quickly as possible. I've been feeling safe with him tonight, and I don't want to bring up something that will change that.

His gaze goes to a spot behind me, avoiding my eyes now. "Yeah." I feel him shift uncomfortably again.

Why does he feel so awkward about Stoneview? Probably the reason we all do. Most families there have more money than all of us here combined. The unfairness makes us jealous and vindictive.

"It pays well, though I would never want to have their kind of money. Never want to live there. They're fucked up." His eyes come back to mine, haunted. "Truly fucked up. We might not have a dime to our names, but at least we have our souls."

I titter at the statement. "Sounds a bit dramatic."

"Shh," he smiles. "You know nothing, you're just a little baby." He pulls me down with his hands still on my hips until I'm lying on top of him, my head against his beating heart. The rhythm is uneven, and I can't help wondering if that's the effect I have on him. He's topless, his chest hard and his body warm. My stomach flutters before I can speak again.

"I could kick your ass," I mutter against him. "I'm no fucking baby."

"When you talk to me, it's like a little bee trying to shout at a giant. All I hear is *bzz bzz*."

I burst into a laugh, and he's close behind. "I hate you," I grin in the dark.

"I hate you too, little bee." His hand comes to the back of my head, and he undoes my ponytail.

"So soft," he comments absently as his fingers untangle my

hair gently, one strand at a time. "What will your new life be like?" he asks quietly. "*There.*"

"Simple," I say, listening to his heartbeat. "No drama. No crime. I might even garden or something. I'm gonna have the white picket fence kind of shit. A nice husband, even."

"Kids?" The interest in his tone is intense.

I have to think of that answer for a moment. We're in the dark again. Like every time we start sharing stuff about each other.

"I'm not sure. I only want kids if I know I'll be a great mom. It's complicated. Generational trauma and all. Who knows what kind of shit I can pass on to them. That'd be selfish."

He runs a hand along my back languidly and lovingly. "Is that how you feel about your mom?"

I shrug. "My mom could have been the best mom. It's not her fault that she isn't."

"What's wrong with her, then?"

Fuck, he's really going for my feelings tonight. How am I meant to resist him if he keeps asking questions like he truly cares?

"She's...ill." He stays silent, and I don't wait for him to ask the question I know he's thinking. "She has severe depression. She's on meds but always stops them, making her worse. Every time I see her, it's a gamble. Is she going to be herself today? Will she be so depressed she doesn't want to see her own kid? Emma doesn't even bother. She says it hurts her too much. I just...I can't leave her alone, you know? What if something happens one day, and no one has been to see her? What if I go just to find her...I don't know. Dead. What she really needs is to be in a psychiatric hospital so they can help her. But we can't afford that shit."

He wordlessly takes it all in, his hand on my back becoming more and more reassuring.

"What does it feel like? To have a mom with depression?"

Tears build at the back of my eyes. I can feel them trying to force their way through. I scratch my throat, swallow them, and admit the truth no one ever bothered asking for.

"It feels like I'm deeply hurt, and yet, no one hurt me. Like there's no one to blame for your trauma, and you just keep going around in circles wondering how to heal yourself. I know my mom did her best. I know it's a sickness. A black poison that infected her mind. Sometimes I want to hate her. Sometimes I wonder if I love her out of guilt for wanting to hate her."

After a beat, he drops a kiss to my hairline. "That's very sad, Billie."

"We live on the North Shore. We all have sad stories."

"I guess, yeah," he confirms.

"What about you? Where's your mom? I've never seen or heard of her." I remember clearly what he said to his dad when he was drunk. That he abuses his women because that's what his dad did.

He shrugs as if he's about to say something he doesn't care about. "My mom escaped my dad as soon as she could. He was an abusive fuck, so good for her that she left."

I raise my head, trying to gaze into his eyes despite the darkness around us. "Do you ever hear from her?"

He shakes his head, his stare on mine. "She left in the middle of the night so he wouldn't catch her."

My heart breaks, my brain trying to understand how she could leave them behind, knowing his dad was dangerous. "But...didn't she want to take you and Kay with her?"

He looks away and presses the back of my head so I lay

down on him again. It's like he can't even say it to my face. "She didn't want kids."

"A lot of women end up with kids accidentally. It doesn't mean she didn't love you."

"That's not what I meant. She didn't want the process of having kids. My dad just forced her."

"You mean, he..." Realizing what he's saying chills me to the bone. He doesn't stutter, either. Doesn't hesitate. It's just a fact to him.

"I'm not sure about Kay. Maybe my mom hadn't realized he was abusive back then. I don't know. But I do know she was deep into the abuse when he wanted another kid. I know he raped her to have me."

His entire body has stilled. I wrap my arms around him, my forearms crushed between him and the mattress. This doesn't excuse or explain anything he has done to me.

So why do I suddenly feel like it explains everything about him?

What must it be like to grow up knowing your existence happened only because your mother was raped?

"I'm sorry, Caden," I murmur against his chest.

"There's nothing to be sorry about," he says with a chilling voice. "I feel fine."

Of course he does. Because he has been made utterly emotionless about sexual assault. When he thinks about it, there is nothing but a cold, calm feeling.

We stay silent for a while. I don't even know how long passes, but I feel his breathing becoming even.

At some point, he startles, as if waking up from a dream.

"Are you scared of me?" he asks with a groggy voice. I can feel his heart kicking against his chest.

"Yes."

I don't need to hide the truth. I know how I feel about him.

"Don't be scared, okay? You won't end up like my mom. You'll fall in love with me, and you'll want everything I have to give you."

And isn't that the most terrifying thing I've ever heard?

I thought he'd fall back asleep, but he grabs my hips and flips us around so I'm crushed under him. "I promise it'll be nothing like that."

"You can't say that when you've already forced me in the past," I whisper against my own will. I shouldn't provoke him. I shouldn't even be here in the first place. So close to the man who fears nothing and no one.

He shakes his head before burying it in my neck, inhaling my scent. He then talks in my ear. "I make you feel good, Billie. You know I do."

One of his hands keeps a tight hold on my hip, but the other one slides under his hoodie and pushes my panties to the side.

"Caden," I hesitate. "You—"

"I promised you another orgasm so you could fall asleep."

"It's weird," I squeak as his thumb comes to brush my clit, sending a jolt of electricity through my body. "You just talked about...about..."

"Rape?"

"Stop saying that." I shift uncomfortably and try to pull away. But he comes up, his hard eyes on me. "Why do you insist on me hurting you?"

I just wish I could hear even the slightest bit of emotion in his tone. There's nothing.

"You're so wet," he notices while rubbing his index and middle fingers against my clit. I shiver under him, choking back my pleasure. "Why don't you just enjoy yourself?"

"Because everything you do is wrong." I try not to accuse him or push him further into his anger, though it's hard not to when he has no morals. My heart is beating fast, and my brain is confusing the rhythm of fear with the melody of arousal. Something is wrong with my reactions.

"Who says it's wrong?" His lips break into a smirk before his head falls to my neck. He kisses me, featherlight touches bringing goosebumps to my skin. He makes his way to my jaw and then the corner of my mouth.

"Me," I moan as his thumb keeps playing with my clit. "*I* say it's wrong."

He smiles against my cheek before biting it. "I disagree."

"Y-you can't di...aah..." My complaint turns into a moan as he pushes inside me with one thick finger.

"Do me a favor, Billie," he murmurs against my ear. "Shut the fuck up and enjoy how I put you to sleep."

He puts a hand over my mouth and, without warning, pushes another finger inside me as he keeps stroking my clit. He thrusts into me slowly with a patience I could never have. I push against his hand as my eyes flutter close.

"Open."

He stops and only starts again when my eyes open wide, silently begging him to accelerate.

"Look at me, baby," he taunts with a chilling smile. "I want to see what no other man will ever see again; that glint in your eyes when you come apart."

He still takes his time, slowly coaxing me into a soul-shattering orgasm. The whole time, he keeps his eyes on me, drinking my entire being and forcing me to accept the truth: Caden King does whatever he wants to my body, and I don't have a say in the pleasure he forces on me.

He lies back next to me and wraps his arms around my body, bringing me close. Silence stretches as I try to catch my breath again. I'm not even sure he's awake when I ask,

"Why me?"

He shifts, tightening his hold on me.

"Billie." He says in my ear with a serious voice that sends a chill down my spine. "I just want to make sure you understand something. I don't *need* a reason. Everything will be easier for you once you accept that I want you, and I will do absolutely anything I have to do to keep you. I can give you a reason if you wish, but reason or not, you're mine, and that's a fact."

"I just want to understand..." I whisper back.

"I've been thinking about it. I always think about you, so of course I've been thinking of *why*. And one of the conclusions I've come up with is... everyone says I'm certified crazy, and they don't understand why. They don't know how to control me."

He pauses, and I wonder if he expects me to say anything. I'm this close to agreeing that he *is*, in fact, completely insane, but then he keeps going.

"Maybe I am. And when I'm with you? I feel like I have a reason to be. It's you. You make me feel crazy in the best way. You've already seen the worst in me. You've seen the length I'm capable of going to to get what I want. There's nothing to hide now. Isn't that amazing? Isn't that so...*simple*?"

I can't find anything to say. My heart is pounding, and I wonder if he can feel it. I don't know if I want him to. Nothing about this is *simple*.

I shouldn't want to be the reason someone feels crazy. I shouldn't want to enjoy the fact that he is giving himself excuses so he can act any way he wants toward me.

But there's a certain power in that, isn't there? To know that I make Caden King lose his mind.

I startle as the sound of my phone ringing feels like a fire alarm in my head. "Holy fuck," I gasp. That scared the shit out of me.

I go to grab it before reality comes crashing into me. I'm not in my room. I'm in Caden's bed and can't move because his arms are securely wrapped against me. We were chatting and just fell asleep. We must have shifted during the night because he's now spooning me and holding me so snugly I feel like I'm a kid's blankie and he'll die if he drops me.

"Turn that shit off," he growls in my ear.

Someone doesn't like being woken up.

I reach for my phone. *Xi* is written on the screen.

Fuck!

I forgot to tell Xi I wouldn't go to his house yesterday. I pick up in a hurry.

"*Where the fuck are you?*" he barks into the phone.

"Oh my god, I'm so sorry. I—"

"*Do you have any idea how fucking worried I've been? You were meant to come at ten last night, and I called you about a hundred times, Bil's. What the hell happened to you?*"

"I'm okay. I'm sorry. I..." I'm out of lies. I have no idea what to tell him. "I was with..."

"*Where are you? Right now, where are you?*"

"On my way home," I lie, and I can clearly hear the panic in my voice. I'll be surprised if he believes me, so I add, "I slept at a friend's house."

"*Who? A guy friend?*" The jealousy in his voice is so apparent I recoil slightly.

"It doesn't matter if it was a guy or not. Look, I'm going home now. I'm sorry about worrying you and missing our game night. I'll see you at my dad's tonight, okay?"

I hang up before he can say anything and turn to Caden. His arms are still wrapped around me, although he's now wide awake.

"He wants to fuck you," he says, hushed. I can see so in his eyes that he's not happy about it. Caden wants me, and he's not the kind of guy who deals well with competition.

"Stop it. He's my stepbrother."

Another lie. Xi is my stepbrother, but we've always had an ambiguous relationship. Xi protects people. That's his thing. With me, he's always been a little too protective, and I've grown to enjoy it. His hands have lingered in inappropriate places in the last year, and I've let him.

And this summer, we crossed the line.

We didn't have sex because I wasn't ready, but we kissed during one of our famous game nights. It was ravenous and lustful. It was so perfect we couldn't stop there. I let him make me feel good with his fingers, and he asked for nothing in return except that we never mention it to anyone.

I've come to like his overprotective behavior and the way he's constantly checking up on me. The fact that it's annoying me right now just because I'm with Caden means something I wasn't ready to admit to myself.

I don't want Xi anymore.

Because I desperately want Caden. My ultimate rival.

I escape Caden's hold and gather my clothes. "I have to leave." I put my jeans on and zip them up.

"Billie, I'm serious when I say I don't want you to spend time alone with him any—"

He's up just as I take his hoodie off, revealing my bare breasts. He tilts his head to the side and cocks an eyebrow. "Are you trying to distract me?"

I check the time on my phone. "Fuck! It's almost eight. I have training in half an hour."

"Okay, I'll drop you off," he says as he grabs some clothes.

"Absolutely fucking not. I have my car anyway."

He spins around and marches back to me, grabbing me by the waist and lifting me so he can sit me on his desk. His stern face makes me want to retreat, but he grips me tightly. "I'm hearing a lot of *no's*. I think it's about time you change your tune, huh? I want more 'Yes, Caden. Anything you say, Caden.'"

He spreads my legs to settle between them and grabs one of my nipples between his thumb and forefinger. He starts rolling it, and I throw my head back in pleasure.

His other hand pops my jeans open, and he slides it beneath my panties to come and caress my clit.

"I can't hear you, little bee," he murmurs against my ear. I'm getting wetter by the second as he rubs his thumb against my clit. He lowers his hand and enters me mercilessly with one finger.

"Yes, Caden," I moan loudly.

He thrusts another finger into me and curls them, rubbing against my magic spot. "What else do I want to hear?" he growls low.

"Any..." I pant. "Anything you say, Caden—aah." I cry out as he relentlessly moves faster.

"I don't want you to see Xi alone anymore," he repeats with unwavering violence in his tone. I shake my head, but another moan pours out of me.

"Say it." I can sense him losing his patience just as much as I feel myself getting close to the edge.

"Yes...," I moan. "Yes...Yes, Caden!" I explode. My arms wrap around his neck to keep him close to me.

When we separate, and I come down to earth, he's donning his wicked grin. "Good girl," he says before dropping a kiss at the corner of my mouth.

"Ugh, get away from me." I try to sound mad, like I *truly* need space. But I don't.

I don't really want him to step away because it means going back to real life, and who needs that right now?

He grabs a t-shirt and throws the hoodie I wore all night on his bed.

"I'm gonna sleep with my nose buried in this," he tells me without an ounce of shame. "I like your smell."

"My smell? I don't have a smell. I don't wear perfume."

"'Course you do," he says as if I'm the crazy one. "You smell of raspberries and mint."

My mouth opens and closes a few times as I slowly slide off the desk. "That's just my shampoo," I ultimately say, confused that anyone could enjoy the simple smell of supermarket-brand shampoo. *Summer Cocktail.* That's what it's called. It's meant to be strawberries, raspberries, lemon, and mint. It just smells of chemical raspberries and mint. Exactly like Caden described.

I put on my bra and top and look at my phone again. "I'm going to be late for training. I didn't even run this morning."

"Don't worry. You got your dose of fitness."

I hurry to his front door, gathering the rest of my stuff and grabbing my car keys.

I'm about to leave when he grabs my arm and pulls me back toward him. "Not even gonna kiss me goodbye?"

"Stop," I whisper, eyeing the street. "Anyone could see us. Neither of us needs the Kings to know what happened last night."

Not caring about anything I just said, he grabs the back of my head and smashes his lips against mine. "If anyone has anything to say. They can come to me. I will gladly settle it with them."

I roll my eyes at him and hurry down the street. As I'm walking to my car, I cross paths with Sawyer. He narrows his eyes at me but manages to maintain a cold front.

"Been busy last night, little Scott?"

I ignore him, opening my car and trying to get in, but he

catches my elbow before I get to. "Not so fast," he hisses low. "What are you doing around here at this time?"

"Nothing," I say as I try to snatch my arm back.

Sawyer is probably in his early thirties, at the prime of his strength, and much bigger than me. But I'll be damned if I let him make me feel scared like he did in that kitchen the first time I met him.

"If we keep finding you on Kings' grounds, we might have to start punishing you for it."

"What? Like Jade and her girls did?" I snort. "Do you want your own trip to the hospital with my name on it?"

He releases his grip on my arm, but before I understand what he's doing, he grabs me by the hair above my ear and crushes the side of my face against my window.

"Don't play smart with me, little bitch. I didn't want this deal between you and Caden in the first place, and I'll kill you myself if you start bringing us more trouble than you're worth. This is my crew, and I take care of it. So let me not catch you causing us problems anymore. Or Caden's little protection on you won't matter. I will fucking kick your ass and send you back to your crew broken beyond repair."

He releases me before I can answer, and I flip around to face him. "Fucking asshole," I rage before grabbing the handle again and slipping into my car.

There's nothing more to say. He's made his point, and I have nothing to fight back with. Better for me to get out of his way.

After all, it was probably a needed reminder. Caden and I are not a thing. We will never be a thing. We're rivals. If we forget about it, our gangs will gladly remind us.

15

BILLIE

All In - Chri$tian Gate$

By the evening, I officially hate myself for staying over at Caden's last night. The short moments of bliss didn't outweigh the burden of reality.

Training was the worst it's ever been. Now that my finger and face are better, I was unfit from the lack of sleep, the fact that I didn't run before exercising, and the greasy food from the night before. My heart was beating fast from the memories of what I did with Caden and my stomach fluttered at the idea of seeing him again.

I didn't have the right clothes, no sports bra, and everything was a struggle. Dickie picked up on it, obviously, and made me work twice as hard for it. By the end, we had a talk about starting to take this seriously, or he would pull me out of the amateur tournament. The fear was enough to promise myself to stay away from Caden.

I wish my heart would just listen. I keep trying to rationalize this. Caden and I have never been close, we barely know each other, and yet he's the person I've opened up the most to in my life. I feel like he told me things he doesn't express to others too. I have seen a tamed side of him and know he's putting in an effort for me.

I keep having to remind myself that he is not a good person. That he's the same man who broke me two years ago, although my mind seems set on separating the two. How am I meant to hate him if I don't see him as the person who did me wrong anymore?

I'm coming out of the shower when I smell Aisha's Maghrebi food. At least one good thing tonight is that it's our family dinner. This week she felt extra motherly and wanted to do it on Monday and Friday. I guess it's a nice start to the week. We're all going to get to enjoy my stepmom's food and have a little chill time.

I change into jeans and a hoodie and walk into the living room.

"Ah, she's alive," Emma says as soon as she sees me. She and Dad are watching the football game as I walk over to where they're sitting. I squeeze myself between her and the armrest.

"Where were you yesterday?" she whispers in my ear so Dad can't hear.

"I see Xi snitched like a little bitch," I say.

Her pale eyes cross my brown ones, and I can see the annoyance in them.

"I'm joking," I ultimately add.

Her jaw tightens, and she looks at the TV again, not looking at me when she finally says, "I don't like how you've been behaving recently. And I told Dad about it."

"What?" I choke.

Someone knocks on the door, and a minute later, our

conversation is put to rest by Lik and his boyfriend walking in. Aisha is over the moon and I force a smile on my face. Lik hugs all of us, being his natural social self, while his giant of a boyfriend settles on the armchair and nods at all of us.

He's not exactly a talker. Sam is a big guy with dark eyes and dark hair, full of tattoos, and always silent. Not exactly the fun type. Lik and he balance each other perfectly since my stepbrother can hold a conversation with himself for hours on end.

Aisha asks where Xi is, and that's when I realize he's not here yet. My chest tightens and my heart accelerates. I hope he's not in trouble. I hate myself a little more for yesterday because that's probably how he felt all night waiting for my call.

Fuck, Emma's right. I've been a shit person lately.

We're already eating when Xi shows up.

"Ziad!" Aisha snaps his full name when she sees him. "Is this a decent time to show up? And covered in blood?"

My heart drops as I turn around and see he's got a bleeding nose. My eyes automatically go to his bloody knuckles.

He's talking to his mom and not looking at me, so he can't see my worried look and inquiring gaze.

He goes to the kitchen sink and washes his hands before taking his seat next to mine. He crosses his gaze with Sam, and the latter nods to him. A thankful nod. Maybe he was moving a body for him.

Sam is a hitman, after all. He used to be the enforcer of the Bianco family, but then the Bianco empire fell apart. Sam had already started seeing Lik by then. So he stayed around because they fell in love, and he became a hitman so he could work for himself rather than join another criminal family.

When Sam has a body to hide, he calls Xi for it. He pays him a hefty amount, and my stepbrother loves money.

"Are you okay?" I ask Xi. Instead of answering, he takes a violent bite of his food. Though under the table, he puts his hand on my thigh. I'm pretty sure I never minded him doing that before. I used to really like it, actually. When we overstepped what was appropriate for stepsiblings in public, it started naturally, and I thought it was fun. I never took it too seriously.

Now I feel strange about it as I shift in my seat. He realizes this right away and gives me a look. Under the table, I grab his hand and move it off me.

He practically chokes on his food and everyone turns to him.

"Sorry," he mumbles.

The conversation flows as we all eat together, and it's only after dinner that Xi corners me in the hallway as I exit the bathroom.

"What is wrong with you?" he asks me low.

"Are you okay? What happened to you?"

"I did a job for Sam," he says as if it was that simple.

"Yeah?" I reply as I cross my arms. "And did the body come back to life and punch you in the face?"

"It's worrying when you don't know what someone you care about has been up to, huh?" he snarls.

"You're a dick," I huff. I take a step to go past him, but he pushes me back and pins me against the wall with a hand just above my chest. His other one goes above my head and against the wall.

"Don't do this to me, Bil's. You've been in trouble and don't want us to know about it. Just admit it."

I shake my head. "That's not—"

"Caden King cornered me and started a fight out of nowhere. I was on NSC grounds. I was no threat, and he had no reason to do this."

"What?" I choke. "Are you for real? Are you okay?"

"Do I look okay? I'm fucking pissed," he seethes. The anger in his voice makes me tremble.

"Y-yeah, but did he hurt you?"

"No, of course not. He might be good, but I don't go down easy. Plus, I don't think he wanted to hurt me. No, he wanted to *warn* me."

"Warn you?"

"Yeah, to stay away from you. So, wanna explain?"

I am going to kill Caden King with my bare hands.

"I-I don't know!" Lies on lies on lies. That's all I'm capable of lately. "The guy is unhinged, what do you want me to say?"

"You've been disappearing a lot lately. Everyone notices that you look skittish and out of your depth. Your dad got you a fucking guard dog, for fuck's sake. You're in trouble, Billie. We can see it. Just admit it's him, and we can deal with it."

"There's nothing to admit."

"You're scared of him," he finally says. "You can tell me that."

"I'm not scared of anything," my pride snaps back.

"Okay," he nods. "Fine."

We look at each other for long seconds, and I feel him softening. "I'm just worried for you. You know I care about you." I nod, and he adds, "A lot."

"I know. I care about you too."

His head drops into my neck, and I barely restrain a gasp. "What are you doing?" I whisper in panic.

I go to push him away, but he keeps me flat against the wall. He kisses me from my shoulder all the way to my earlobe and whispers in my ear, "I care beyond friendship, Billie. You know that. How long do you intend on making me wait before you reciprocate those feelings?"

I gulp and push at his chest. "I can't give you a timeline on feelings," I say softly. "I love you deeply. And I know we've been walking a fine line between friendship and more. But I don't think it will ever go beyond that."

He takes a step back, clearly dejected. "You've not been yourself lately."

"Or maybe it's the opposite."

"Right," he snorts. "You keep lying to yourself."

He finally leaves me alone, walking back into the living room, and I follow.

We're mid-Monopoly, everyone shouting at each other, when I notice my dad slipping away discreetly to the back porch. I know Sam is out there smoking, and I doubt he's going there to have a friendly conversation with him.

"Is it true, Rose White is back?" Xi asks his brother out of the blue as the arguing dies down.

Lik plays with his nose ring before nodding. "Yeah. Sam's been going a bit insane from it." He turns to me next. "Happy your bestie is back in town?"

"Fuck off," I grunt low.

She doesn't belong to any crew; she's just a pathetic foster kid who ended up in Stoneview and yet somehow always found her way to North Shore parties. We had a huge argument at a party one day and then again at a lacrosse tournament. Neither of us seems to get over it, so we simply keep hating each other. I heard she was getting mixed up with Lik and his boyfriend, and if she ends up in my business because of that, I will probably lose my shit. I don't need any more drama in my life right now.

My eyes dart to the door my dad just walked through.

Lik notices because he attempts to bring me back into the game by pointing out I was cheating. I struggle to stay still, knowing he's up to something.

I get up, except he's quicker than me. He walks to the back door, and a few seconds later, he and Sam are walking back in. Sam's eyes dart to me, and he quickly says goodbye to Aisha before heading out. Lik hugs us all goodbye, and I don't even get to ask anything.

I walk to the back porch to talk to my dad. He's facing away from me but raises a hand before I can open my mouth. "Not now, Billie," he says sternly.

I let out a loud huff and hurry to the front door. I'm fucking fuming. I know they've all been talking about me. Sam and Lik's car is just leaving when I slam my hand against the window. My eyes widen when Sam takes his gun out, not even looking at who it is. Lik is the one grabbing his wrist and pointing at me.

As soon as he lowers the window, I talk. "What did he say?" He doesn't reply because he doesn't like talking and even less about stupid shit like this. "Sam. What did my dad ask you to do?" Ignoring me completely, Sam looks at Lik, expecting him to sort this out.

"Lik, what did my dad tell you? I'm fine," I insist, having a feeling I know what they're doing. They think they can protect me and go against the Kings, especially against Caden.

They can't. Our crew doesn't have that kind of power anymore, and if they try to threaten Caden King, it will start a war.

I will not be the reason people start dying on the North

Shore. We have it hard enough without needing a motherfucking gang war on our hands.

"Bil's—" He tries to sound reassuring, but I don't let him.

"I'm fine!" I nearly shout, sounding way too defensive to be genuine. My trembling hands come to rest on the windowsill.

"We're just trying to help," Lik responds.

"I don't need anyone's help," I snap violently.

"What's wrong with you girls and being too proud to get the help you need?" Sam finally joins in.

I rear back my head in surprise, not only because he's talking, but he's also angry. Someone is having a negative effect on him, putting him on edge, and I know precisely which bitch has that power.

"Damn, Sam," I jeer. "Rose White has been back for how long? And look at you, losing your patience and all." I let him swallow my words before I add. "Speaking of her, I want the bitch out of my town. There's something you can help with." Maybe if he keeps busy with her, they'll both leave me the fuck alone.

"Stay away from Rose," he orders calmly. "Let me handle her."

I shake my head. He's in love with the girl. He's always been, and she will cause absolute chaos in his settled relationship. But the true reason I know they're heading for failure? Her brother is Sam's best friend and he would never allow this. Lucky for Sam, the fucker is currently serving time for shooting someone. We all know Kayla King is the one who put him there, and she will suffer when he comes out. In the meantime, Sam is free to do whatever with Rose White. So I taunt him some more.

"Does he know she's back?" Meaning her brother, of course. If he wants to get in my business, I can get into his too.

Instead of falling for it, he rolls up his window.

"Hey!" I shout. "Stay the fuck out of my shit!" He probably can't hear me since he's already driving away.

I walk back inside, only to catch my dad, Xi, and Emma talking to each other in the living room. Hushed words and scheming whispers.

"Are you all for real?" I rage. "What the fuck is wrong with this family!" I stride to them, but they don't even look sorry. "I didn't do anything wrong. I don't deserve all of you going behind my back like this."

"You're in trouble," Emma says firmly. "We know it's Caden we—"

"Oh my fucking god, just stop talking about him," I practically shriek. "He doesn't. Scare. Me. Nothing is going on!"

"Look at the way you're reacting," Xi jumps in, shaking his head. "If the Kings want to threaten our family thinking they can come out on top, I can tell you right now that they're fucking wrong. We can stoop to their level. We can play with their families too."

"Lowering to their level is not the way to go," I fight back.

"So you do admit something has been going on," my dad says softly.

Fuck.

"No-I...No!"

The silence that follows makes me uncomfortable.

I shift awkwardly.

I feel uneasy in my own home, and I hate it.

"Go to your room," my dad finally says. "You're just a kid who's out of their depth. Let us handle it."

"I'm almost twenty," I snort. "Emma was involved up to her neck at my age." The quietness of the room is only broken by the sound of Aisha washing dishes in the kitchen.

"Dad—"

"Go to your room, Billie."

"Un-fucking-believable," I mumble as I head to my room.

I hear one last thing my dad says to the rest of them, and my heart drops. "We should deal with it tonight."

I grab my phone to see a message from Caden. He sent me a picture of his lower lip. It's split and there's dry blood on it.

Caden: I need a magic kiss.

So he really had a fight with Xi. Threatened him to stay away from me. My stomach flutters at the idea, but my heart tightens. This is wrong; he can't just threaten my family. I put my phone back on my desk and grab the split ends of my hair, pulling and breaking them. Anxiety has had such a strong hold on me lately that I forget what I feel like when it's not here.

I'm cuddling Murder in bed when someone knocks on my door.

"Come in," I mumble.

"Hey, Pumpkin."

I stare daggers at my dad, not over our discussion from earlier.

"I know you're mad at me, but I'm only doing this to protect you," he explains like I'm a five-year-old.

"I don't need to be protected, Dad," I huff desperately. "Please, you have to believe me."

He scratches his beard for long seconds before his apologetic eyes meet mine. "I want you to go sleep at your mom's tonight."

I sit up so quickly, Murder jumps off the bed. "Why?"

"Because I'm asking you to."

"What are you guys doing? What's your plan?"

"That's not for you to worry about."

"Are you seriously sending Sam after Caden?" Panic grips my chest, its claws ripping my lungs. "You...you're sending a professional hitman after him because you *think* he did me wrong? He didn't!"

"We're sending them a message. No one is getting killed. As much as I love you, this goes beyond you. The Kings have been walking all over us for two years. It's time to fight back."

"But—"

"I've called your mom. She's expecting you."

He grabs my gym bag from the floor and passes it to me. "Pack for a couple of nights. I don't want you here should things go south. She's in pretty neutral territory. No one ever goes and causes trouble in the trailer park."

I gulp as I stand up and grab my bag from him. "Please, don't do anything stupid."

"Emma has made a decision as the head of our gang. I think she should stick to it now."

"Then, at least let me be here. I'm part of this! You can't just keep me out. I've always had your back."

"You said it yourself, you want to become a professional fighter and can't be involved in this anymore. I agree."

I walk past him, "I need to speak to Emma."

"She's gone, Pumpkin. Now please pack your bag and go to your mom's."

I swallow the dread that keeps making its way up my throat and look at my dad, dejected. I don't say anything as I pack my bag. I'm too disappointed in all of them.

Just as I finish packing, he says, "Bil's."

I peer up at him, ready to hear he's changed his mind about this whole thing.

"Leave Murder with us, will you? We could do with the extra help."

I hate this. NSC is not strong enough to take on the Kings, and involving Sam is a stupid idea.

As soon as I walk into my mom's house, I know it's not a good day for her.

"I'm on a new medication," she slurs as soon as she opens the door. "It makes me sleepy."

She hugs me as I walk in, practically falling asleep on my shoulder. I love my dad for paying for treatment for her, but the truth is, doctors put her on meds and never look further than that.

"Aw, Mom," I say as I help her to the couch. I drop my bag next to it as she lies down.

"I left you the room," she yawns.

"You didn't have to. I can take the couch."

She waves a hand dismissively. "How's your dad?"

"I don't want to talk about Dad tonight." I grab the bottle of pills from the small coffee table in front of her and read the label. "Are you sure you didn't take too many of these?"

"Just one as indicated," she tells me as her eyelids start to drop.

"'Okay," I nod. "Get some rest." I draw the covers over her frail body and caress her hair until she's fully asleep. I turn the TV off and tidy the living room.

There are dirty dishes everywhere and piles of clothes on the floor next to the sofa. I wash them up, and that doesn't wake her up. These meds are strong. It upsets me that instead of giving her proper help, she's just given something that will make her sleepy and forget how she feels when awake.

I make sure I've cleared the floor around the sofa so she doesn't trip if she wants to use the bathroom during the night.

I fill a glass of water and leave it on the coffee table before heading to her room.

It's not really her room. She says she only sleeps on the sofa when I'm here, but the space is pristine. It's exactly how I left it last week and the week before. There's no bed, only a mattress on the floor. The sheets are clean, the shelves empty, and the closet only has two dresses she never wears. Everything else is piled up in the living room. All her stuff is close to her on that sofa so she doesn't have to move to grab anything.

I turn on the small lamp on the floor by the mattress and throw on a hoodie and clean panties before getting into bed. It's only a thin sheet since my mom uses the thicker cover. I regret not having grabbed proper pajamas.

I look at my phone and realize I never answered Caden's text earlier. I was too mad at him for attacking Xi. Now I don't know how I'm feeling anymore. Should I warn him that danger is coming? But then that would be betraying my family, my crew.

I find his contact in my phone and my thumb hovers over his name.

A small voice at the back of my head tells me he would do something if the roles were reversed.

No.

I can't do this. Not for him.

I go to Instagram and click on his account. The telltale colored circle around his profile picture tells me he's posted a story recently and I'm dying to know what he's up to. Just to make sure he's safe.

I click, not giving a fuck that he'll see I spied on him. He's at an illegal car race in Silver Falls. He's filming Jade in a tuned-up car. She's doing some sort of hand signs I don't get and then points her tongue at the camera. In the next story, her car is speeding down a long road, followed by another. It was posted ten minutes ago.

He's fine. There's no need to worry because he's not even on the North Shore right now.

I sigh in relief and put my phone beside the lamp before turning it off. It's late, and I just want today to be over. I close my eyes but can't find sleep for a while. Eventually, my body gives up on worrying about Caden, my family, and the feud that will forever separate the Kings from NSC.

16

BILLIE

Crazy - Jake Daniels

The sound of the mobile home's window being opened is what wakes me. It's not glass, and the plexiglass is old, so it always makes a loud squeaky sound when it slides open.

I sit up in bed as my heart drops, but I recognize all too well the man who's now slipping through.

Once he's fully inside, Caden faces me. The light of the moon is behind him and I can't make out his features.

"What the hell are you doing?" I say quietly. "My mom is sleeping. How did you even know where I was?"

He takes a step forward in complete silence and doesn't reply. I don't need him to, though. Fury and violence emanate from him, and my heart accelerates as I plaster myself against the wall behind me. The sheet drops to my waist, and I think I notice his eyes taking me in. I'm not sure, since it's too dark.

"Oh, little bee," he says in fake disappointment. "We were having such a good time."

I feel my eyes widen as he approaches. I need to run, move

out of the way, fucking do something. I'm not facing the Caden I've been getting to know over the last few weeks.

This is the wicked man who holds no pity for his enemies.

Maybe it's naivety that keeps me from moving. The fact that I think I can still bring him to his senses.

Or maybe it's fear that freezes me into place.

Either way, in two long steps, he's by the side of the mattress, staring down at me.

And it's too late for me to go anywhere.

"Caden," I try. "Talk to me."

His lips start spreading into a smile. Charming enough to lure his prey closer. So close that it's too late when they understand it was a lethal smile all along.

He crouches next to me and brings a hand to my cheek, caressing it softly with his thumb. He smells different than usual, but I can't quite place it.

"Did you know?"

"Know what?" My voice is wobbly, and fear so evident in it makes him smile wider.

"What they were gonna do?"

I shake my head. "I-I don't know what you're talking about." I knew they were going to do something, just not what exactly.

I still don't know what they did.

He chuckles softly to himself, shaking his head. Honesty rings in his words when he says, "I was so patient with you. Ready to minimize who I was, just so I could fit into that tiny box of things you can handle without breaking apart."

My gulp is loud in the room, and he brings his hand to my throat, grazing it with the tips of his fingers. "Now, I'm going to hurt you."

"No," I whimper. "Tell me what happened. Please, I want to understand."

The soft grazing turns into a handful. I gasp when he squeezes hard for a few seconds then releases, still keeping his hand around my throat. A rush of dizziness overcomes me before I can see straight again.

I put a hand on his forearm, about to speak.

"Tsk, tsk," he tuts me. "The time for talking is over. It's time to cry now."

He drags me along the mattress and flips me on my front violently. I gasp loudly as he forces me out of my hoodie. Just as I'm about to cry out for help, I'm the one who stops myself.

For what?

So my mom can wake up and see me in this position?

By the time she hears me, she'll be too late.

If—and that's a big if—she hears me through her meds' sleep, all she'll be able to do is watch as Caden King breaks me yet again.

All it'll do is make her worse. Push her deeper underwater.

And what if he hurts her? He's never had any problem hurting me, and he likes me. I know he does.

He doesn't like my mom. He doesn't care. He'll harm her, maybe kill her.

There is no limit for Caden. Nothing can stop him from hurting people but himself. There are no rules and no laws for him. No sense of decency or respect.

Caden breaks and destroys.

And tonight, I'm his victim yet again.

My time thinking put me in an even weaker position. He's holding my wrists against my lower back now. His other hand spreads my legs as he settles between them.

"Caden," I cry out. "Please..."

He leans over me, and his calm whisper contrasts drastically with his violent movements. "Do you remember how I told you I'd do it, little bee?"

I fight against his hold despite knowing there's nothing to do. He'd planned this all along, and I was the girl stupid enough to listen to him tell me how he would assault me and think I was safe from it since he cared about me.

He bites my shoulder and I whine loudly.

"Shh, your mom's gonna hear you."

"Please. Caden, this doesn't have to happen like this. I know you care..."

And that's when he flips. His anger takes over as he cups my pussy roughly from behind.

"I care?" he seethes. He leans back and presses the tip of his fingers inside me. Even from above my panties, I can feel the rough invasion. "Maybe that's what got us here. Because I. *Fucking. Cared.*"

He presses against my lower back with the hand holding my wrists. I wriggle against his hold to no avail.

"There were kids in that house. Do you understand that?" he hisses with fury.

"I-I don't know what you're talking about." My guilt doubles at the mention of children.

"I'm talking about the fire your crew started at my house, you little bitch." He presses harder against my core, and I want to die of embarrassment. He's going to feel how wet I am. How the panic of being at his mercy doesn't mean the same thing as it did two years ago.

"I'm talking about how my nieces could have died tonight if I hadn't come home just in time to run inside the house." That's when I understand the smell on him is of ash and smoke.

My heart drops so low in my stomach I feel sick.

Is that what Sam did? What Emma decided? To set fire to the Kings' house?

"I didn't know," I choke out through guilt and fear. His

216

nieces are just kids. Children who could have died in a war they don't even understand.

"My dad's dead," he drops just before ripping my panties off my body.

He grabs my ass cheeks one after the other before slapping them harshly. I hiss from the pain while doing my best to stay as quiet as possible.

"I didn't even like my dad," he says casually. "I just hate the fact that he got killed by insignificant NSC people. It's fucking annoying."

I hear the telltale of his belt unbuckling.

"Wait," I whisper in a panic. "I can't do this. I c-can't. Not after what happened tonight. Please…"

I feel the leather of his belt wrapping around my wrists and dread truly grips my stomach.

"What are you doing? What are…"

"Stay quiet now."

I shake my head harshly but don't dare make another sound.

He fastens the fake leather around my wrists and lets go of me. I try my hardest to untangle myself from this mess, but with the way he tightened his belt, it won't budge.

He grips my hips and tugs until I'm on my knees, my ass in the air and my cheek resting against the mattress. I feel humiliatingly exposed.

He runs his fingers against my entrance and mocks me. "This is going to be so hard for you. The fact that you will enjoy what I'm about to put you through."

"You don't have to—" His hand against the side of my face cuts me off as he pushes my head harder against the mattress.

"I told you to shut the fuck up." He searches for something on the mattress. The next second, he's shoving my ripped panties in my mouth. "I don't want you to wake up your mom when you come on my dick."

He spreads my ass cheeks, exposing me to the cold air. I feel it against my wet, burning core.

"I tried to be patient with you, baby. I tried to take my time and do good by you." I feel tears spring to my eyes as he tells me what could have been. "And you just went behind my back and betrayed me."

I didn't... I try to say. I can't even defend myself anymore now that he's gagged me.

Gone is the man who took his time turning me on. I'm already turned on by his forceful ways anyway.

Gone is the man who made me orgasm before trying anything else. No, tonight he holds my thighs widely apart, then grabs a handful of my ass cheek with one hand and my hip with the other before he forces himself inside me in one violent thrust.

And gone is the woman who hated him so much she couldn't find any of this erotic. She's been replaced by the woman who moans loudly against her own underwear as he starts moving inside her.

It hurts; there's no denying it. Despite being wet, I feel like he's ripping me open. I'm so full of him my tummy contracts and aches. And somehow, through the pain, I find a perfect rhythm as he violently abuses my body.

My moans are essentially shrieks when he pushes deep inside me. I hear him grunt at his own violent movements, and my arm muscles tighten from pulling at the binds.

"Why did you have to ruin everything?" he rasps, yanking at my unkempt hair. He presses the small of my back with his other hand, and I arch backward, my chin practically lifting off the mattress. He's relentless as tears fall down my cheeks. The tension in my body is ready to snap.

One hand leaves my hair, pulls out my panties, and instead, he shoves three fingers inside my mouth. I cry out against him, forced to swallow back my moans as he rubs aggressively inside me with his cock and somehow makes it feel sensual.

"Fuck..." he pants. His movements are cruel, but I feel the way his hand rubs my lower back in a reassuring gesture, helping me to take him. "You feel too fucking good. Look at you taking me in so well." He chuckles, mocking the way my body bends to his will. "What a dirty little whore."

I explode around his dick, feeling my lower belly fluttering and my body tightening around him.

I don't have time to take a breath as he pulls out and flips me around. He holds his dick firmly and thrusts into his fist before exploding all over my chest and stomach, his head thrown back. When he's finished, he grabs me by the jaw, pushing my head to the side and keeping me in place as he leans over me.

"Are you mine now?"

I squeeze my eyes shut, feeling more tears fall down my cheeks. I can't look at him, but he knows the truth.

"Do you hate yourself? For loving it so much." I feel his sneer against my ear.

His grip tightens as I nod, unable to keep the truth from him. He bites the skin just below my ear and sucks on it, making me gasp.

"What are you doing?" I panic.

With my hands still tied behind my back, there's nothing I can do as he bruises his way from my ear, all along my jaw, to my chin.

"Don't..." I whimper. He violently fucked me without asking for my opinion tonight, yet it's as he leaves his mark on me that I genuinely voice out my refusal. "Please, Caden... everyone will see."

I have no choice except to stay still, watching the opposite wall through tears as he takes his time fucking up my life.

He finally pulls away and smiles down at me. "Isn't that the whole fucking point, little bee? For your entire crew to see that you were in the arms of the enemy, being fucked senseless and coming hard on my dick while they were trying to take us down?"

I cry out as he releases me and stands up again. He flips me around, undoes the belt, and then uses it to whip my ass harshly. I have to bite my tongue to stop myself from screaming from the pain.

"Just thought I'd leave another mark," he says simply.

I turn over as he approaches the window. "So, is this it?" I rasp in a broken voice. "Is that all you wanted out of us? To hurt me?"

He turns around, and his white teeth almost appear sharp in the dead of night. "Oh, no. Don't worry, baby. I'm far from being done with you. Now that I've had a taste of the best pussy in the world, how am I supposed to leave you alone?"

I sit up, wrapping the sheet around me. "Do you even care a little about what I want out of this?"

"No," he says simply. "You had your chance to go out with the nice version of me, and you fucking blew it. So don't go crying to your daddy anymore because if something happens to my family again...what I did to you tonight will feel like the sweetest sex you've ever had in your life."

"Caden, I promise you I didn't know what they were going to do," I choke on a sob.

"But you knew they were going to do something," he says. He sounds so disappointed in me, so betrayed. "And you chose not to tell me. See, after Jade jumped you, I told everyone they'd have to deal with me if they touched you. You? You just let them come at me without as much as a warning. That's the difference between you and me."

"Please," I shake my head, refusing to accept that our good times are over. Tears stream down my face, and I do my best to wipe them as they come. "Don't leave me like this. Just stay. Stay, and we can talk through it. We can make this right. If you leave now, it really...it truly feels like..."

His smirk sends a chill down my spine. "Like you were my victim?"

I nod at the same time as I sniffle. I run my forearm under my nose and push some strands of untamed hair away from my face. I feel dirty, soiled by it all. His cum is still sticky on my breasts, and my whole body is aching. "Please..."

"You look beautiful when you're broken," he says softly. He turns to the window again and, like a nightmare disappears when you open your eyes, he escapes into the night.

Right where he belongs.

17

BILLIE

Follow You - Bring Me The Horizon

"And please go to bed early tonight," Dickie insists before sliding into his car.

This has been the most awkward conversation of my life. He's been eyeing my bruises all week without saying anything, too focused on training me. Tonight, he finally asked. And I had to explain that, no, I haven't been attacked. Rather a boy I had sex with left hickeys on me.

I'm not even sure if it was a lie or not. I've had rough sex before, even though that was more than that. That was Caden not holding himself back. It hurt, it was violent, and I enjoyed it much more than I should have. But at the end of the day, I still can't process whether I was attacked. I don't feel like it, and a part of me is ashamed of that. A part of me wants to say I was and that the fact that I didn't have a choice means it was wrong. It didn't *feel* wrong, though. It felt fucking fantastic. The only thing that felt wrong was the guilt because I didn't warn him NSC was planning something. Now his dad is dead, and his nieces were put in danger.

"Hey," Dickie says before closing his door. "You're going to be amazing. Get some rest, I'll see you tomorrow, Billie Unbeatable Scott."

I smile at him, but my stomach twists. It's always like that the night before a fight. I feel sick and useless, praying for the best. I will only feel my confidence returning once I'm in the cage.

Tomorrow is my last fight before Killer Clover. I'm fighting some girl from the south bank. It's going to be in the nice gym and it's probably going to be packed. The further I get to the finals, the busier the fights get. It's still a small amateur gym, although the feeling differs from the North Shore. It's more official.

I'm scared since I know I haven't trained to the best of my abilities recently. But Dickie has faith in me, and Taylor will be watching, so I'm going to give it all I have.

I just wish my mind wasn't always so distracted by Caden. The last time I saw him was Monday night when he sneaked into my mom's trailer. It's Friday, and I haven't heard from him since then, but I know the Kings have been busy sorting out the funerals.

His father died because of my family. Murders between the Kings and NSC happen. They're not exactly common, but when one crew tries to take over the other, it's bound to lead to serious shit. I wish it hadn't been Caden's dad. Even though he hated him, a cold-blooded man like him must feel emotions from time to time. Caden's not a psychopath. He is a man made of an intricate tapestry of feelings. He simply taps on the damaging ones more often than the sympathetic ones. And by more often, I mean most of the time. Always, actually. Regardless, I know there's more to him.

I get in my car and grab my phone before leaving just to look at our conversation. I've sent a few texts since Monday, but he's not responded to any of them. I wanted to check on him, to see if there was anything I could do for support. I know I shouldn't expect a reply; we're enemies, after all. Despite that, I'm dying to share something special with him. Something more than him just fucking me and throwing me away. Something that would mean he's forgiven me for not warning him NSC was coming after his family.

I hit my head against my headrest. Every time I think this way, I want to slap myself. Caden never apologized for the wrong he did to me, and yet here I am, feeling like shit for something I didn't even do.

I start my car and head home to my dad's. I need a hot tea and a calm night.

"Fuck my life," I mumble as I push my front door open. There's a raging party going on in my house. It's the first time I'm back home this week and I fully intended to run to my room and avoid everyone.

I've been sleeping at my mom's house and ignoring my sister's and Xi's incessant calls. Spending more time with Mom than usual has been nice, and her meds have been doing her some good now that she's getting used to them. She's been lovely to hang out with, and we enjoyed some much-needed mother-daughter time together.

"Whoa." Some guy's eyes widen as he sees me. His name is Logan, and one of Xi's dealers. "Did you get beaten up or something, Billie?"

Another small dealer is with him, Nolan. He looks at my bruises, and a smile consumes his face. "Damn, is that from boxing?"

My grimace is from confusion until I remember I'm still sporting Caden's hickeys. No one except my mom and Dickie has seen me this week. Since I can't see the bruises, I tend to forget about them.

I slap my hand against my jaw and shoulder him out of the way, hurrying to my room without stopping for anyone. The music is loud as fuck, and I find Murder on my bed, her head buried under my pillow.

"Hey, girl," I say as I close my door. The bass makes the window tremble, and she barks out a whimper. "Aw, no. It's nothing. It's just music, baby." I put a knee on the bed as I rub her back and she finally pops her head out. "Hey!" I smile at her. She is so happy to see me, her tail wagging as she jumps on me. "Oh yes, that's a big girl. I missed you too!" I laugh.

I jump when my door bursts open and Xi strides in. He grabs me by the upper arm before I can react and slams me against the wall by my bed, my head hitting the window behind me.

"What the fuck is wrong with you!" I rage.

"Let me see," he growls low. He grips my jaw brutally and turns my head to the side. Xi is so much taller than me, and he doesn't even realize I'm balancing on my toes as he pulls me up to see the bruises up close. "Was it Caden? Did he hurt you?"

"Xi, *you're* hurting me," I try to say past the pout he's forcing my mouth into.

"Answer me, Billie. Or I swear his house on fire will be the least of his worries."

"It wasn't him," I lie. "I…"

"You're so full of shit," he hisses. "You were protecting him so he wouldn't hurt you, and look where that got you."

"I'm not scared of him," I tell him again. They're all so sure he's been threatening me and I'm too scared to tell. Yes, of course, he has. But I'm not afraid anymore. I'm protecting him for other reasons now.

It hits me just now that I'm protecting him because I want him out of here. Because we share that need to leave this godforsaken town, and we understand each other. Which isn't something I have with Xi.

I've only ever shared sexual tension with my stepbrother, and now that I have found something deeper with Caden, I don't want Xi to touch me. Not even out of protection.

"Let go," I grunt as his grip squeezes. "Xi...It wasn't him." I keep lying.

He yanks my head again so I can look him in the eyes. "Who, then?"

I try to shake my head and that pisses him off even more.

"Fine. Don't tell me. Maybe you'll tell your sister."

He lets go of me only to grab my wrist in a deadly grip and drag me through the hallway and the living room. Nolan catches us again and waves at me. "In trouble, little Scott?"

"Bitch-ass snitch," I spit back. I can't stay long enough to say anything else because Xi hauls me to the kitchen, where Emma is making out with some random girl.

He pulls at the girl's shoulder and points at the kitchen door. "Leave and close the door."

She turns to Emma, and my sister nods her encouragement.

Fucking great.

"What the fuck happened to you?" Emma gasps as they crowd me.

"Stop it!" I snatch my wrist from Xi's grasp and shove past them before resting myself against the counter. "I need you two to let me fucking breathe for a second."

They don't. They corner me where I am, firing a hundred questions at me.

"She says it's not Caden, but I know it's someone from their crew."

"When did that happen?" My sister asks.

"Was it after the fire?"

"Talk, Billie," my sister orders seriously.

I look them in the eyes. One after the other, and keep my jaw shut.

Emma is six years older than me, and Xi never went to high school, meaning none of them ever saw the girls walking around our hallways with Caden's mark on them, showing everyone he had fucked them.

I'm sure they've seen some around the North Shore, but it would have been rare since we don't usually cross paths with the Kings. Even if they did, they wouldn't know what it means anyway.

"Call Lik," Emma finally says. "You're gonna talk, Billie."

Xi turns around and grabs his phone. It won't take long for Lik to show up and he'll know what this is. I'm fucked. I'm so fucked I'm starting to go back to hating Caden. He did this on purpose so that I would end up in this exact situation.

Emma keeps asking questions, shouting at me, unable to control her anger. I know it comes from a caring feeling. I know she's trying to protect me. I've made up my mind, though. With my arms crossed and my chin up, I stay quiet, my jaw aching from the way I firmly hold it shut.

But when Lik enters the kitchen with a girl I know too well, and he asks what's going, I lose my patience. She's tall, pretty much Lik's height, and he's just below six-foot. My eyes narrow on the girl the entire fucking planet falls in love with every time she crosses their path. Rose White disappeared for almost two years, but she hasn't lost that beauty everyone falls at her feet for. And she hasn't lost the danger in her eyes that tells everyone to not fuck with her.

But I don't give a shit. I don't like her, and she is definitely not welcome in this house.

"What the fuck..." I start.

"....is that?!" Lik cuts me off.

"Fuck's sake," I whisper to myself when I understand I'm not getting out of this mess anytime soon.

"Are you fucking kidding me, Billie!" Lik shouts at me. He's clearly also had a long night, and I can understand why if he spent it with the stubborn girl he brought here.

"Do you know who did this?" Emma asks him. I can hear how worried she is, and it distorts my mind with guilt. She's so focused on my problem, she's not even registering the fact that the girl she once fucked walked into the room.

"She won't talk," Xi tells his brother, making sure we don't lose the topic of the conversation.

"It's none of your fucking business!" I fight back.

For once, the attention is on someone other than Rose, and it makes me feel fucking uncomfortable. I need her to take it back.

I barge against Emma and walk toward Lik. "Bringing *her* here? Do you want me to commit a homicide tonight?" I ground out. I need everyone to focus on this problem. Not mine. It's embarrassing to be scolded like a five-year-old in front of her.

"Yeah. I know." Lik can see right through my attempt to change the topic, and doesn't bite.

"We know it's a guy from the Kings crew, Bil's," Emma says gently. She's attempting a new approach. "Just tell us which one. He'll be dead before you know it."

Lik is on me the next second, grabbing me the same way Xi did earlier. He pulls me up and looks at the horror on my face closely.

"Are you for real?" he whispers. I'm not sure if the others can hear or not, but the pleading in my eyes is loud enough for him to understand.

Don't do this. Don't tell them what it truly is.

My gaze darts to the side when his hardens, and I can feel my cheeks warming from the embarrassment. This is all Caden's fault. *Again.*

"Your guilty King is Caden," Lik says loudly enough for everyone in the room to hear. "And he didn't hit her. These are love bites. He leaves them on every girl he fucks."

Fucking traitor.

He finally lets me go, and I cringe at the silence from my sister and Xi trying to swallow the news. I just want the ground to open up and swallow me. Spending eternity in hell would feel less awkward than this situation. But then again, Caden would probably show up at some point, and I want nothing but to see him again.

The only thing that breaks the long silence is Rose's mocking laugh. It shatters the tension into pieces as everyone turns to her.

"This shit is just too funny," she mocks. "Who knew you could fall any lower, Billie."

"Bitch, shut the fuck up!" I shout back. I try to push past Lik. I need an outlet for my fury and I have decided it will be her.

Lik grabs me by the arms and stops me, a stern look on his face. "Worry about yourself."

"Billie!" Emma barks with a ferocity I'm not used to hearing from her. "What..." She lets out a long huff. "What is wrong with you?"

"I thought Sam scared him?" Lik says, trying to turn this into a helpful conversation.

"Yeah, he tried," I retort. I'm about to add that this whole fucking plan was a shit idea and that I was right all along. Only Rose is quicker than me.

"And it looks like he was successful," Rose jumps in with

her unwanted sarcasm. Her gaze falls on me, and she smiles brightly. "She loves going for guys she can't have. It's a pattern," she taunts some more.

Of course, she was going to bring this up. I dated her twin, Jake, briefly when I was in junior year. The last guy I had sex with—the foster kid who ended up in Stoneview. What I always try to forget was that he was using me to get over his ex-girlfriend, and it was never going to last. They were meant to be, and he and I weren't. I hate to admit it, but the bitch is right. I always seem to go for the guys I can't have.

I'm about to retort something, but instead Lik cuts in. "We're leaving." He pushes Rose out of the kitchen at the same time as he says, "Shut your mouth," to her.

As soon as they're gone, Emma and Xi turn to me again.

My older sister walks to me, skimming the bruises along my jaw with her thumb. "Was it consensual?" she murmurs softly. Like she's afraid to break me.

It's not until now that I have to downright force myself to think about that. I pinch my lips together, digging deep into my heart and soul. I coax my mind to face what happened on Monday night and tell the truth to the people who love me enough to compel it out of me.

I grab my sister's hand by my face and hold it tightly when I answer in an even quieter voice. "Yes."

The hand I'm holding turns into a fist, and she snatches it back. She does her best to control her anger, to not rage at the fact that I had consensual sex with our life-long enemy. Because any other answer would have been worse. Now she's frustrated at me, even if she doesn't want to be. I can see it.

"I'm glad," she says through gritted teeth. She spins around and walks out of the room, slamming the door shut behind her.

There is only Xi and me left. He's looking at me like I just killed a puppy in front of him. Slowly he approaches me and shakes his head, clearly not understanding my feelings. "I could have given you everything you wanted," he says low.

I peer up at him, a sob constricting my throat because we will never be the same way we once were. "But not everything I needed," I ultimately say. I realize that with unbreakable conviction. Only Caden can give me what I need, when what I need is him.

Him and the way he doesn't care when he forces me. Him and his dirty mouth and brutal tendencies. Him and his beautiful face and body. Him and the way he softens for me, turning away from the violence to open up to me.

My savage enemy.

My beautiful fiend.

Xi nods, noticeably dejected but not pushing it, and leaves the room too.

I let out a long sigh. Everything is fucked, yet somehow I feel lighter than ever now that they know I have been wanting Caden's attention.

I grab my phone from the pocket of my jeans, and my heart explodes when I see I have multiple messages from Caden, except my focus is locked on the last one.

> Caden: What are you doing tonight?

The message was sent fifteen minutes ago, and I quickly type out a response.

> Billie: I have a fight tomorrow, so I'm having an early night.

> Caden: An early night? With that house party going on? Come to mine you'll feel more rested.

I shake my head, smiling. He's turning into such a stalker.

> Billie: I can sleep through the noise. I'm used to it.

> Caden: My dad's funeral is over. I'm all alone and I could use the company.

I wonder where Kay has gone now and how livable his house is after the fire. Did it burn the whole house? Surely not if he's inviting me over.

Three dots appear again, and my heart squeezes from knowing he wants *my* company and no one else's.

> Caden: I think my cock down your throat could really help with the grief.

My lower stomach tightens with need, but I roll my eyes anyway, as if he could see me. I have to pretend his crude words didn't turn me on. Less than half an hour ago, I never wanted to see him again because of the situation I was in with my family.

Look at me now, virtually ready to give in to his request.

> Billie: I really can't. Fights are too important for me to jeopardize them.

Feeling like a dick because he did mention his dad, I add.

> Billie: I'm sorry.

He doesn't reply, and I feel worse, but I can't let anything hinder my success. Not even my need for Caden.

18

BILLIE

Pain - Jake Daniels

The party is at its peak when I walk back into my living room. I just said I could sleep through the noise, but this absolutely pushes it. Knowing there's no way to shut down a North Shore party before it ends, I grab a glass of water and sit on my sofa, watching everyone have fun while I long to see the only man who doesn't belong here.

Emma is nowhere to be found now, and Xi is talking to some girl I'm pretty sure came from Stoneview. Apart from me, he's always had a thing for the rich girls in short skirts who come to the wrong side of the tracks. That's fine with me. I don't get along with them, but I don't judge him for the fact that he does.

The sofa dips next to me, and I drag my gaze away from my stepbrother to Nolan.

"Hey," he smiles.

"Fuck off," I reply right away.

He laughs and wraps an arm around my shoulder. "I'm

sorry, okay? I didn't mean to snitch on you to Xi. I just wanted to make sure you're okay."

"I *was* great. Now, I'm not okay." I toss his arm off my shoulders, and he pouts.

"I'm sorry, Bil's. What can I do for you to forgive me?" He points at my now empty glass. "Should I get you another drink?"

"I don't drink," I huff. The guy calls me Bil's and doesn't know the first thing about me.

"Oh yeah," he chuckles. "You're a fighter."

"How long have you been working for Xi?" I ask.

"A few months," he shrugs. "Why?"

"'Cause his dealers usually know to leave his younger stepsister the fuck alone."

He bites his lower lip and smiles at me. "Maybe I know, and maybe I don't care." He brings his face closer to mine. "I like to live dangerously."

"You're not gonna live dangerously for long if you piss him off," I say casually. "And you're not gonna live at all if you piss *me* off."

"Rawr," he laughs. "You're feisty."

Someone kill me.

"Why don't you go grab me a Gatorade," I say to get him off my face.

"Sure thing."

He gets up, but I call for him again. "Hey, grab a new bottle from the fridge."

There's a rule everyone goes by at North Shore parties. You either open the bottle in front of someone or share it. No one truly trusts each other, and we prefer to always stay on the safe side.

Nolan returns a minute later holding a sealed bottle of

Gatorade in his hand. He opens it for me as he walks toward the sofa and smiles at me as he gives it to me.

"Here you go, unbeatable Billie." I take the bottle. "I heard what you did to those Kings girls," he adds as he sits next to me again.

I roll my eyes and down half the bottle so I don't have to talk to him.

"Look," he says more seriously. "I'm really sorry if I got you in any trouble."

I huff and put the cap back on. "Whatever, man. I put myself in trouble, don't worry."

The guy is annoying as fuck, but it would be very hypocritical of me to blame it all on him. I put myself in this situation in the first place. Well, Caden did. And when I played along, I knew I would get caught at some point.

"So, what is it?" he asks more calmly and with genuine interest. "Did you get in a fight or something?"

"It's nothing." I change the topic, knowing I'm heading to my room soon anyway. "So, what did you do before working with Xi?"

"I was doing drives for him, actually. But it's risky as fuck, and I wanted to do something more chill. So I asked if I could just sell and he was super understanding. He's a great guy."

"He is," I admit, my eyes darting to him now making out with the Stoneview girl. At least he's mending his broken heart rather quickly.

We talk for a little more before I feel my body giving up on this party. I can't control my yawns anymore, either. My eyes are practically closing on their own when I realize I haven't really been listening to anything Nolan has been saying anymore.

"I'm going to bed," I yawn. I want to also tell him to stay

out of my business from now on, but I'm so exhausted the words don't even come out of my mouth.

"Good night," he smiles at me. I get up and then fall back right away, my legs not carrying me.

"Whoa," he exclaims as he catches me before I fall. He's up now too, holding me against him. "You alright there?"

"I don't know what happ—" My vision narrows, and I can't finish my sentence.

What the hell is happening?

"Hey, Billie," Nolan says worriedly. "What's wrong?"

"Not...not feelin' well," I manage to slur.

"Let's get you some fresh air," he says quickly, wrapping an arm around my waist and helping me toward the door.

I try to look around for Xi. I would rather be with him right now than with Nolan. I need to be with someone I trust. Except I don't have the strength to call for him or look around. My head starts to fall against my chest and I can do nothing but allow Nolan to drag me out of the house.

The cold air doesn't help at all. I still feel entirely useless. My body is shaking from the freezing air and the fact that I'm wearing nothing but a tank top and jeans. The world turns blurry as I try to drag air into my lungs. The exhaustion turns to dizziness and I feel like I'm going to faint.

"What the hell?" Nolan panics. "Should I call an ambulance?"

"N-no," I force out of my cottonmouth. All I can see is the fuzzy ground going past me. Everything spins whenever I try to lift my head, and my neck immediately gives up. "Fight... tomorrow..." That's all my mind can focus on. I have a fight tomorrow, and I can't miss it.

Tripping over my feet again, I don't even think I'm walking anymore. It seems like Nolan is taking most of my weight and I'm hovering over the ground.

I'm not too sure what's going on. All I know is that I was outside, and now I'm sitting down in a moving car.

"What..."

"I'm taking you to the hospital," I hear next to me. "Did you eat anything today? Here, have more of this. At least it's sugar. Fuck, you're scaring the shit out of me."

With one hand on the wheel and one holding the Gatorade, he tips more into my mouth. Most of it spills on me, but I still manage to swallow some.

My eyes close for what feels like a second, but when I finally manage to open my eyelids again, Nolan is carrying me toward a building.

I'm still conscious enough to understand we're not heading to the hospital, but there is nothing I can do about it. Fear envelops me, yet I can't seem to consciously understand I'm scared.

"Where...we..." My voice comes out as a sob despite knowing I'm not crying. I can't control my emotions anymore. "Nol..."

"I'm just taking you somewhere safe," he says. Although, his voice is not panicked anymore, nor is it caring either. He didn't take me to the hospital.

He's not helping me.

"Wait..." My brain can only focus on one thing, and I can't stop running it over and over in my head. "Fight...my fight..."

He pushes a door open and we're in a small room. It's rundown and not well-maintained.

I'm on a bed, and his hands are on me.

His face is blurry now and tears are running down my cheeks, but I can't *feel* anything.

"My fight..." I repeat.

I'm not wearing my jeans and my top anymore. I can see them beside me on the bed as my head lolls to the side.

"Don't..." I choke. My thoughts blend, my words not coming out clearly. That's all I can repeat over and over again. "Don't..."

His hands are on my thighs, spreading them apart.

I try to lift my arm and push him away, but I can't even detect my own body, let alone his. And my arm feels like lead. My entire body does. I can't move any limbs whatsoever while he handles me like a ragdoll.

"Don't..." I repeat one last time before I give up altogether.

19

CADEN

Super Villain - Stileto, Silent Child, Kendyle Paige

When did I turn into a fucking stalker?

I used to barely remember a girl's name. I'd fuck her, mark her, and bump into her a couple of days later, only knowing I did so because she was baring my bruises on her jaw.

I wish I could forget about Billie Scott. I want to drill into my chest and rip out the bits of my heart that she's infected.

My dad's funeral was barely finished when my feet took me to my car. I drove fifteen minutes before I realized I was going to her house. I couldn't even control it.

I'm trying to feel sad for my dad, trying to think of all the things I will miss. But the truth is, we never shared anything, let alone love. Kay didn't cry, either. She was too busy sorting out what is going to happen moving forward with Sawyer, and who will take over. My dad would have wanted it to be Sawyer because my sister doesn't have a dick between her legs. But we're trying our best to avoid that.

There's no time to think of the bastard who slightly participated in giving me life when NSC started a war on us. I was more worried about my two nieces not being traumatized by the whole thing and making sure they get to a house where they'll be safe rather than grieving my father.

Now that burying him is out of the way and I had food with everyone who came to give me their condolences, I want to spend time with the woman who poisoned my mind with her doe-eyes and fucking tank tops.

So I'm standing right in front of her bedroom window, listening to the music shaking her house.

She just said she wouldn't see me tonight, and I'm not sure what to fucking do with myself. I don't want to go hang out with Ethan and Elliot. I just want to smell her raspberry and mint shampoo and bury my dick inside her again as I pull at her long ponytail.

Monday night was meant to be a punishment for her. I was raging and feeling betrayed, and I wanted to hurt her. Not only did she enjoy herself in the process, but I only plunged myself deeper into my infatuation with her.

Billie Scott gets wet from being tied up and assaulted.

Billie Scott fits perfectly with my violent tendencies, and now I'm fucked.

Because what's the point in looking for anything else in life when the woman of my dreams is at the tip of my fingers? I could hurt her, make her scream from pleasure all night long, and make her breakfast in the morning while we talk about what our lives could be far from the North Shore.

I could make her come over and over again before planning our future together. Her, me, and even that murderous dog of hers.

Fuck. I can really see us building something together away from here.

All that because I finally pushed her past the breaking

point. And instead of breaking, she flourished into precisely who I needed in my life.

I was angry at Billie that night, but how long can I hold a grudge against someone who didn't truly do me wrong? She was stuck between her crew and me. Who am I to be chosen over her family? I'm just the guy who ruined her life two years ago. Who changed the course of it and selfishly steered her back to me.

I was scared because my nieces could have died in that fire. But they're fine. The fear has passed, and Billie is still on my mind constantly.

I huff into the frigid night, condensation forming around me. I need to respect that she has a fight tomorrow and can't ruin her chances of getting out of here. Fuck, it's hard to be decent.

I don't know how long I wait in the cold outside her window for her to change her mind and send me a text.

It never happens.

I glance down at the box in my hand. The present I brought for her, a new pair of MMA gloves. Hers are old and falling apart. She'll need these for her fight tomorrow.

Eventually, I make my way back to my car. Just as I do, another car drives past. I would recognize her small form anywhere. Billie is passed out in the passenger seat with a guy I've never seen. My gaze crosses with his, and his predatory smile tells me he's up to no good.

Even if he wasn't. Even if he was prince fucking charming. There is absolutely no way in hell I'm letting another fucker near my girl in this lifetime.

I'm in my car in a split second, speeding after him.

I almost lose him, but eventually, I follow where I'm sure his car has turned and recognize it in the parking lot. It's a small motel in Silver Falls. They're not in the car anymore, and I bet my life he's dragged her into one of these rooms.

Except which one?

I jump out of the car and run to the motel.

It's late at night, and all the curtains are drawn. There's no way for me to see where he's taken her. I will kick down every single door until I find my girl and make sure she's safe in my arms. I don't give a shit.

I sprint up the stairs, walking along the balcony that leads to all the doors. There are only a few windows that have light seeping through the curtains.

I knock on the first one without hesitation. "Open the fucking door," I shout. The door is shaking under the strength of my fist.

It opens to show a middle-aged man. He's naked from the waist up, his fly down, and his belt hanging. It's not him, though I notice a hooker bent over the bed.

I leave his room and look at the name of the place. *Silver Moon Motel.*

It's that filthy Silver Fall motel all the cheap hookers from around here bring their jobs to.

Fucking. Great.

I always feel sick being around those girls. Not because I judge them but because I do the exact same thing. Sex for money. I'm a fucking boy toy, but I do it with wealthier people than they do.

My stomach churns, making it hard to focus. Billie is in here somewhere with some fucker who thinks he can hurt her and not pay the price.

Karma is about to knock on his door and show him how deeply wrong he is.

I slam my palm on the next door that still has a light on and, before they can even answer, I knock on the third one. In the second one, a woman opens, wearing underwear only. Not Billie.

I knock on the third one again and am still waiting for someone to answer. I bang against it, hitting it with my shoulder.

Still, he doesn't open and I just know it's him.

Taking a step back, I kick the door just under the handle. I repeat the process again and again, feeling a beast awakening in me.

On the fourth kick, the door budges. I barge into it with my shoulder a few more times and finally stumble through.

That sleazy guy from earlier has stepped away from the bed, halfway through putting his jeans back on.

"What the fuck?" he screams at me. He buttons his jeans and rolls his shoulders back now that he's half-dressed. "You knocked on the wrong door, fucker."

From the corner of my eyes, I can see Billie lying unconscious and naked on the bed. My heart is telling me to go to her right now. But the bastard in front of me is clearly some NSC cunt who thought he could touch what's mine. The second my focus goes to her, he's going to attack me.

The beast in me is begging me to tear him to pieces, which is what I must do before taking care of my girl. Can't save her if he kills me before I'm able to get to her.

"Right, let's get this done," I smile. "You die, then I need to get her to safety."

"You're Caden King," he says, trying to mask the fear in his voice.

"Ding, ding! Ten points for the dead man walking."

His shoulders relax, and he huffs out a relieved breath. "Has Sawyer not told you? I'm joining your side. I've been wanting to go after Billie for months, but Xi never allowed me.

I don't have to do anything he says now. I'll just have some fun before joining the Kings."

Seeing that his words aren't helping his case, he carries on, "Bro, do you understand what I'm saying? Fuck NSC. I'm with *you* now."

"No, you're not. What did you give her?"

He shrugs. "Bro, don't worry about her. She won't remember a thing."

I run my tongue against my teeth, trying my best not to turn this into the biggest blood bath in history.

"*Bro*," I repeat. "What did you give her?"

"Just a bit of Rohypnol. Not like she's gonna die or anything."

"You gave my girl date rape drugs? And admitting it?" I let out a bitter laugh. "She's not gonna die. But you sure as fuck are."

I stride toward him, grabbing the side of his head and dragging him, until I can slam him into the mirror on the other side of the room.

Dizzy, he stumbles back and falls onto the dirty carpet. "That's twenty years of bad luck for you," I say calmly as I grab a chunk of the broken mirror so massive I have to hold it with two hands. "And it starts now."

I slam the entire block on him. It's big enough that it smashes on his stomach and chest, cutting his naked torso in multiple places.

He screams in agony, and I shake my head. "Tsk, tsk. You're gonna wake up the neighbors."

I put a foot on his chest, feeling broken pieces and shards piercing into his skin, and then crouch down onto him before ripping a portion of the sheet on the bed next to us. I stuff it into his mouth and push it far in.

"This is going all the way down your throat unless you answer my next question."

I take a deep breath, my stomach coiling. "Did you rape her?"

He shakes his head wildly, attempting to talk.

"Tell me the truth, motherfucker, because I'll know as soon as I go over to the bed. So think real hard about your answer."

He shouts something behind the sheet, and I take it out.

"I didn't...I didn't have t—" A cough escapes him as I press harder on his chest with my foot. "You arrived before I could do any-anything. Please, I'm sorry, I'm so sorry." Big fat tears fall from his eyes, and I laugh.

"Why is everyone always sorry once they face me? Couldn't you be sorry enough to not drug a girl and get her naked in a motel room? What the fuck is wrong with you?"

He shakes his head, sobbing so hard my shoe bounces on his chest. He tries to raise a hand to my leg and shove me off, but I grab a mirror shard and stab him in the arm without hesitation. I put the cloth back into his mouth, forcing it further down his throat. The fear in his eyes gives me life.

"You say sorry to me," I hiss. "But are you even sorry to her?"

His choking and mumblings are unclear, but I don't care anymore. I keep pushing until the piece of sheet is so far down his throat that he can't breathe anymore. He panics, his arms flailing everywhere.

"Do you want to breathe?"

He nods, terror seeping from every single pore on his body.

"Wait," I hold a finger up. "There's something stuck in your throat, I think you need a tracheotomy or something. Just another little hole to help you breathe."

I stab him brutally in the hollow of his throat with the bit of mirror I'm holding. Blood spurts out, covering me in it. He can't make any noise anymore, but his eyes widen in horror when he realizes he will die for what he did.

He's choking on his blood, the sheet dying a deadly red.

"Everyone. Who. Touches. Her. *Dies*," I seethe. There's still some life left in him, so I stab the piece of glass further into his throat. "Now fucking die."

Not wasting another second. I jump on the bed where Billie is. Her soft brown eyes open and close, but she can't focus on anything. I must be a bloody, blurry monster to her right now.

"Little bee," I whisper softly. "Wake up, baby." I know she can't, that she's drugged, and it's impossible for her to fight it. But I need to know she's at least somewhat okay. I grab her jaw and force her lolling head to face me. "Come on, give me something."

She opens her mouth, yet only a pained whimper comes out. "Where are you hurting?" I ask. Dread is wrapping around me. My entire being was calm while murdering a man, but I now feel my heart kicking against my chest.

I look down at her naked breasts and notice the redness around her nipples. I put a hand on her right one, caressing it. "Motherfucker," I growl. A frustration comes over me, knowing that there's nothing more I can do to him. I can still hear his gurgling noises, and at least it brings me joy that he's still suffering.

She tries to bring her hand to mine, but her arm falls back against the bed. She mumbles something, but I no longer try to listen to her.

The problem is, Billie wasn't saved by a hero tonight. She was saved by me—the possessive devil who can't stand someone other than me touching or hurting her.

And I don't do gentle. I don't do hero-saves-the-girl caring and hugging.

No, I want to know if he lied, if he violated her. So, I sit back between her naked legs and spread her thighs apart.

She moans a protest but can hardly move me or even her own body. She's limp and defenseless as I stare at her beautiful pussy in front of me. I bring my thumbs to her nether lips and spread them apart. There's nothing. No blood or unusual redness. Nothing that indicates he touched her there. I press my index finger against her entrance, feeling the tightness and the way her body attempts to block me.

It doesn't feel like anybody has been able to push through, or surely within the short time, there would at least be a stretch for my finger. But everyone is different, and Billie's body will only let *her* know.

It feels like a knife is piercing my abdomen. I will never know the truth. Since she might never remember, or if she does, she could lie to me and never tell me. She could lie to herself. Her mind could protect her along with her body.

We're both just as helpless. But to keep going and not kill myself with that same broken mirror shard I used on the guy, I need to tell myself that I arrived in time to stop him.

Pulling away from Billie, I search for her clothes to find them discarded on the bed and floor. I put her in her jeans and top, not caring about underwear right now. I simply put those in my back pocket so they're not found at the scene of the crime.

I pick her up with one arm under her knees and one at her back, her head nestled against my chest. In the cold night, she's shivering against me and I tighten my hold. She keeps trying to say something but only mumbled words come out.

Once in the car, I blast the heat and turn it all toward her. Her ponytail is a mess, falling to the side of her head. Her eyes keep opening and closing slowly, still conscious. I can see the frustration on her features, the helplessness from being unable to control anything around her, not even her own body or mind.

I drive her to my house. No one's here anyway. Kay took the girls away from the North Shore now that NSC is after us.

I bring her to my room. There's still a nasty smell of fire in the entire house. Kay and the girls' bedroom is where they started it. The fire was contained in that room and my dad's room, so the rest of the house is still livable even though we got told we shouldn't reside here. That the foundations could be affected. Where the fuck else would we live?

I undress Billie, undo her hair, and put her in a pair of my boxers and a hoodie. She's so out of it she has no choice but to let me handle her body completely. I get her into my bed and hold her tightly.

"M....ight," she mumbles in such a weak voice I have to bring my ear to her lips.

"Say that again, baby," I tell her.

"My...fight," she finally manages to say.

Her fight. She's been drugged and assaulted, but that's the only thing she thinks about? Her fucking fight?

"Tomorrow's another day," I say softly. "Sleep for now."

Of course, she doesn't. Because that's not what usually happens when you're drugged, and she's clearly been given a hefty dose. First, her body fights her. She's sick a few times. Thankfully I succeed in getting her to the bathroom every time. I hold her hair and give her as much water as she can take. I rub her tummy when we get to bed again. And when she starts hallucinating that she can hear someone's steps in the house, I reassure her that it's just our boiler making weird noises like it always has.

When she finally falls asleep, it's six a.m. Her head is on

my chest, and one of her legs is around mine. Her arms are wrapped so tightly around my stomach I can barely breathe. I'm still covered in the fucker's blood, but I don't move because I can finally hear her breathing settle, and the cutest snore I've ever heard in my life is coming out of her mouth. I do something I realize I've come to love. I slip a hand in her hair and close my own eyes. Caressing the soft strands over and over again soothes me slightly.

I can't sleep, though. All I can think about are his hands on her body and that I want to bring him back to life again just to kill him a second time. And that I can't.

20

BILLIE

Freakout - Gianni Canetti

Nolan giving me a bottle of Gatorade and an Angel of Death covered in blood.

That is all I remember from last night.

I wake up with a sticky sickness seizing my body from the inside out. I feel like I'm on a boat, and the nausea only worsens when I try to move and can't.

Arms are wrapped around my body. A soft voice comes to my ears and makes my pounding headache heighten.

I groan, trying to escape the hold the arms have on me, and a panic overcomes me.

Is it Nolan?

"Let me go," I pant with difficulty.

"Calm down, little bee. It's me."

The arms let go, and I sit up, so dizzy I feel like I'm falling backward despite my back being against the wall.

"Caden?" I rasp.

"How are you feeling?" he asks as he sits up. I can't answer because his state shocks me into silence.

"Your clothes," I say, pointing a trembling finger at his chest, covered with blood. I can't control it; my entire body is aching and shaking.

He looks down at himself and back up. "He won't touch you ever again."

My stomach rolls, and I put a hand in front of my mouth, feeling the sickness coming. He immediately gets the message and grabs my other hand before dragging me to the bathroom. The second we're in, I fall to my knees and throw up in the toilet.

Everything is spinning. Still, I quickly put two and two together. The Gatorade. The memory loss. Caden covered in blood.

How far did Nolan go?

As soon as I can, I lean back against the wall, and Caden gives me tissues. I'm suddenly hyper-aware of the way my body is feeling. My breasts are sore, and my lower stomach is tight. The tightness is probably from fear and sickness. I don't hurt down there. Not at all. I could barely walk after Caden paid me a visit and I was fully into it. Whereas right now, it feels...*normal*.

I'm not entirely reassured. He obviously touched me without my consent in other places, and who knows if I can trust my own body right now. I can't even trust my mind and memories.

I look up at Caden. His apologetic eyes bring dread to my chest.

"Am I okay?" I whisper in a complete panic.

He squats in front of me and puts strands of my messy hair behind my ears. He wipes my sweaty forehead with his hand and kisses it. "You will be," he answers with his lips against my skin.

It shouldn't help, except it does. My heartbeat slows and the trembling calms. Then reality hits me all at once.

"My fight!" I gasp. I push Caden away and stand up. I have to put a hand on the wall to not fall back down. The room is still spinning, and my stomach threatens to puke up again.

"Billie, you can't fight," Caden says calmly, following me into a standing position.

"What time is it? I just need to shower, and I'll feel better." My heart is kicking against my chest. I cannot miss that fight. It's my only chance. It's everything. I turn on the shower, but he grabs my arm and turns it off.

"I didn't shower you last night because it's not advised when someone is assaulted. You need to go to the hospital and get checked." There is no hesitation in his sharp tone. He doesn't shy away from what happens. All he cares about is my safety.

I bark a sarcastic laugh and pull at my arm. "We live on the North Shore. Have you forgotten what it means? Even if I go to the hospital and bring them hard proof. Even if Nolan goes to them and admits he did me wrong in front of their faces, they'll put it on the gang-on-gang crime and push it to the side."

He lets go of my arm and bites his fist, clearly trying to keep calm under the circumstances. He brings his hand down by his side when he looks like he won't explode anymore.

"That's not why I want you to go to the hospital. Nolan already received justice." My eyes dart down to his bloody clothes as he says the words. "I want them to check that you're okay and if he dared violate you."

I rip the t-shirt off me. "He *did*, Caden." My sore nipples are proof of that, and as I look down, I feel like I'm going to throw up again. There are bite marks around them.

I swallow the sickness and shake my head, trying not to let

any tears fall. "He did," I rasp again. "It doesn't matter in what way." I turn the shower on again and take off the boxers.

A small whimper escapes me this time. The higher half of my inner thighs are riddled with hickeys and bite marks.

Get a hold of yourself, I order.

My fight. It's the most important thing right now. It's the only thing that can get me out of this town and away from this nightmare. I need to win.

I take a deep breath to ground myself and get into the bathtub, letting the jet fall onto my cold skin.

"I have to get to my fight."

"Fuck," Caden whispers to himself.

He gets rid of his clothes and gets in the tub with me.

"What are you doing?" I shriek.

He doesn't say anything. With gentle movements, he grabs a bottle of shampoo and pours some into his hand. I notice the cuts on his palms. They're crusted with blood.

"What happened to your hands?"

"I used Nolan's head to break a mirror then grabbed the pieces to stab him," he says with a steady voice, as if describing his morning routine. "Turn around," he adds softly.

I do, and he lathers my scalp with shampoo. His fingers are light, relaxing me instantly. He spends a long time running his hands through my hair, ensuring it's clean. I think this is to calm himself too. I noticed his slight obsession with my hair though I never mentioned it.

I feel the reluctance when he rinses it and grabs the shower gel. His scent invades the bathroom as he massages my entire body in that marine smell. I can't help but bring my back closer to him. I feel the hard-on against my skin, but he doesn't say anything, so I don't either.

I want to bathe in his scent and warmth forever. I want to clean myself of Nolan and wrap myself in Caden.

"Harder," I say as he washes around my breasts. I grab his hands and place them both on my tits.

He stalls to only slowly move in circular motions. "Harder, Caden. Wash him off me," I force through gritted teeth.

He rubs harder, but not nearly as much as I need him to. "Just fucking wash him off!" I shout at him.

And he does. He grabs a clean cloth and scrubs my entire body with it. My skin is red all over and stings, but I feel less and less like I want to rip it off my own body.

I grab his hand and bring his fingers to my pussy. "Does it feel different to you?" I ask tightly as I rub one of his fingers against my entrance.

He grunts behind me before rigidly saying, "It doesn't."

"It doesn't feel different to me either," I finally say. A wave of pleasure fills me as I bring his finger to my clit.

"Little bee..." His tone is a warning.

A warning that Caden isn't a good man and won't hold himself back for my sake.

Which is precisely what I need right now.

"Just let me do what I need to," I tell him. Using his fingers, I rub myself slowly for a minute before accelerating and bucking my hips against his hand.

It takes time to come, my mind protesting and my body clearly in pain. Caden doesn't move, doesn't fight me. Eventually, I let the orgasm supersede any other emotion I feel and the entire reality I want to avoid for less than a minute at least. I scream loudly, forcing feelings I don't want out of my throat before falling back against Caden's naked body.

I turn around, and in a moment of utter weakness, I wrap my arms around his neck and bury my head against his chest.

"Tell me he suffered," I say against him.

"He suffered," he replies firmly as his arms encircle my waist.

"How?"

"I pushed a sheet down his throat. Then, I stabbed his throat with a piece of broken mirror, and he choked on his own blood. He wasn't fully dead when we left because I didn't stab him in an artery. He must have suffered for a long hour or so before dying." He is utterly void of emotion when discussing murdering a man for me. There isn't an ounce of regret in his voice. Not even pride. He did what he did, and that's it. I can take it or leave it.

Taking it all in brings me whatever satisfaction I can take from it. That is to say, not much, though still enough to keep me going.

I look up at him and push on my toes to leave a light kiss on his lips. "Thank you," I say.

He stays longer in the shower after I get out, so he can get rid of all the blood. Finding a new toothbrush below the sink, I brush my teeth hard enough my gums hurt.

I'm in his bedroom, dressed in a pair of his gym shorts and a t-shirt, when he joins me. He's dressed and holding a bottle of water.

"I need you to—"

"Sit down," he cuts me off.

"Let me talk," I fight back with a stern voice. I need to get to my fight.

"Sit down, Billie."

His muscular body is blocking his bedroom door, and I already know I'm not getting out until he decides. I sit down and look up at him.

"Don't you know North Shore rules about sharing drinks?" he asks so calmly I know he's fuming.

"Of course I do," I seethe, hating the way he makes me feel like a scolded child. "I saw him open the bottle in front of me."

"Did you?" He turns to his desk, grabs a packet of sugar he

had there, and empties it into the bottle before screwing the cap back on.

He wraps his hand around the bottle he's holding, hiding the cap with his palm, and extends his arms toward me as he opens it in front of my eyes.

This is the exact same way Nolan did it. He walked back into the room, already hiding the cap within his hold, and like a rookie... I thought he was opening a new bottle in front of me.

How could I be so naïve?

"That was a sealed bottle. Drink."

"I get the message. I'm a fucking idiot, and you're a hero. Can I leave now?" I stand up from his bed and shoulder past him.

He grabs my arm and tugs me back, dropping the bottle and wrapping a mighty hand around my jaw. "I'm no fucking hero, Billie," he grits out with fury. "Don't you know that yet? I'm your worst nightmare. I'm the villain who will save you only to use and abuse you for his own pleasure."

I try to shake my head away to no avail.

"How do you know I didn't take my turn after I rescued you from Nolan, huh? You know I'm no good, little bee. How do you know none of these marks are from me? Stop being such a naïve little girl, and remember you live on the North Shore. No one saves you. You can only save yourself."

My heart sinks with disappointment and tears spring to my eyes.

"Did you?" I force past my pouted lips. "Did you assault me last night?"

He chuckles and shakes his head, his smile freezing every single atom around us. "Of course not, baby. I plan on doing much worse to you. And when I do, I want to feel you fight and hear you scream."

He releases me and I take multiple steps back. My head is still spinning from the drugs, and I'm sweating despite not feeling warm.

How could I think for one millisecond that Caden was the good guy? What went through my gullible mind to believe that?

Doing my best to feel even slightly alright, I take a deep breath. Rolling my shoulders back and crossing my arms in my own way to strengthen myself, I jut my chin.

"I'll save myself, don't worry. I always have. And I have my ticket out of this hell hole."

"Good. I like seeing you toughen up." He stretches his arms above his head before leaning back against his desk. "What's your plan now?"

"I need you to drive me to my house so I can pick up my gym bag and then to Silver Falls. I...I still feel too dizzy to drive."

He shakes his head. "When I said save yourself, I didn't mean by being outright stupid. If you can't drive, you shouldn't be fighting."

"I'm fighting. Period."

He licks his lips and tilts his head to the side. "Look, I've never seen any of your fights and don't know the exact level you're on, but if you get hurt—"

"I won't," I say firmly. "They don't call me unbeatable for no reason."

"A lot happened to you, little bee. It's okay to forfeit."

I almost choke on my own breath. "Forfeit? Do you know what I'd be forfeiting? My agent. My chance to leave the North Shore. My dreams. No. I am fighting with your help or not. So make up your mind. Want me to toughen up, or want me to be rescued? I've already missed pre-fight training, so I need you now or never."

He presses his lips together, clearly unhappy I'm using his own logic against him. His jaw tightens and the disagreement is apparent on his face, but then he finally nods. "Alright, get in the car."

I push the doors to the Silver Falls gym without much strength. I was sick again during the drive, right after I forced myself to eat a banana for energy.

I can hear the crowd in the main area and run through the hallways to make it to the locker room. Caden is right behind me. I turn to him just before going into the changing room.

"Don't come in." I shake my head. "Dickie doesn't want anyone in there."

"Little bee," he huffs. "I think you're making a big mistake."

"I don't care what you think right now." I take a bite of an energy bar and force myself to swallow it before hydrating some more.

"Okay." He nods, taking a second to calm himself. "Here, I got you these."

My eyes widen as he gives me a wrapped box. "It's a present for your fight."

Holding on to the energy bar with my teeth, time stops as I unwrap the box. My mouth falls open, shock turning my muscles weak. The bar falls to the floor in front of me.

"Caden," I whisper in disbelief. "These gloves are almost a hundred dollars. That's too much. I can't accept them."

He smiles softly. "Don't make me force you to accept a present."

"But...how?"

He shrugs and runs a hand through his hair. "I have a bit of money saved. I wanted to do something nice for you."

I gulp. "Thank you. I...wow. Thank you."

"I'll be in the crowd," he says.

I grab his arm before he can leave and go on my toes to give him a peck on the lips. "Come see me after the fight."

I hurry into the locker room.

"Billie!" Dickie rages as soon as he sees me. Taylor is with him. "I've been calling you all morning."

"I don't have my phone."

Taylor walks to me slowly, his hand in his suit pockets. His brows furrow as he observes the state I'm in. I feel sick and icky, sweat coating my entire body. Probably from the drugs that are still in my system.

"Are you hungover?" Taylor asks.

"No. I'm not. How late am I?"

"Too late for any warm-up," Dickie tells me sternly. "Get your hands wrapped right this second."

I sit on the bench and let him wrap my hands. My heart is beating crazily in my chest, and I keep getting moments of dizziness. Thank god I'm already dressed because all I can do right now is go into that cage and beat the shit out of that girl. I hope adrenaline will carry me through this fight.

"What's wrong?" Dickie asks worriedly. "Where were you?"

"No time for chit-chat. Just get me in that cage," I say as I stand up. I see black for a second and throw a hand out to catch myself.

"Whoa," Taylor catches me instead. "Are you sure you're fit to fight?"

"Will you represent me if I forfeit?" I ask seriously, feeling my strength is quasi-zero.

His eyes dart to Dickie and back to me. "I can't. The contract states—"

"I know what the contract states," I snap. "I'm not forfeiting."

Dickie puts the gloves on my hands and I'm in the cage

before I can even blink. This fight won't wait for me, and I know what I'm capable of. I'm Billie Unbeatable Scott. And this bitch doesn't stand a chance.

The crowd is bigger than I anticipated. Dickie is in my corner and gives me a pep talk just before the ref calls for us.

He offers us to tap gloves, but I don't, ignoring the girl's gloves in front of me. I never do. I am not a kind woman in the ring. I am here for one thing and one thing only: the win.

The girl doesn't even appear like the sort of bitch I normally fight. She's even smiling at me. She looks humble, kind, yet still a fighter. She's bare of any tattoos or any other gang-affiliated marks. Her shorts and bra look expensive, and I understand she's not from the same place I am.

She's fighting as a hobby. I'm fighting for my life.

The bell rings, and her smile drops to make space for focus. A chill crosses my entire body as dizziness engulfs me before I make a move. I swallow thickly and force myself to jump on my feet as she comes for me.

I manage to avoid her first hits out of pure luck. Despite feeling unwell, I'm quick on my feet and it's not uncommon in our low-weight class to move rapidly. But fuck, I can't find the strength to throw anything.

I hear Dickie shouting at me to wake the fuck up, but my muscles refuse to obey me. I can barely keep my guard up, let alone hit her. Sweat is dripping down my forehead despite putting the minimum effort into this fight.

I make it through the first round only taking a few hits and punching her once or twice. As soon as I'm in my corner, Dickie gives me water and a towel before putting gel on my eyebrow to stop the bleeding.

"Billie," he says desperately. "What is wrong? If you can't fight, I can't put you at risk by leaving you in this cage."

"I'm fine," I mumble as I pull the bottle away from my lips.

But I'm not finished with my sentence that I'm hunching over to the side and vomiting. It's off the ring, and the ref is too busy with something else to notice, but Dickie is on me right away.

"What's going on?" he insists. "You need to talk to me."

Everything is happening too fast, and there's only one thing on my mind.

"Is Taylor watching?" Panic takes hold of me as I force more water down my throat. My body is exhausted, and any strength I have is leaving me quicker than I anticipated.

"Y-yeah, of course," Dickie hesitates. "Billie, kiddo, I know you want to win, but you're extremely unwell right now. I'm calling it—"

"No!" I shout before I can stop myself. "You are *not* doing this to me, Dickie."

The bell rings to get back in the middle of the cage and I force myself to straighten up. It feels like I sat down for ten seconds.

I manage a couple of punches, but the other girl stops them easily. There's no strength behind my hits and she doesn't need to put much effort into fighting back.

I see black again. For a few seconds, the world disappears, and I feel myself lose my footing.

It's a real shock when her punch gets me right in the nose. I grunt as I stumble backward, and my vision finally returns. My arms are down, and I realize I'm not guarding myself anymore. I'm too slow to put my fists back up.

Her next punch gets me in the temple. I try to open my eyes and move, but I get a high kick in the head and fall back to the floor.

I don't feel physical pain as she rains punches on me. No, only the horror of my dreams shattering into pieces.

Only the understanding that I will never leave this shit

town. That everything I held onto, my reason to live and keep going, is burning to ashes.

My one and only dream is slowly disappearing and instead leaving space for the true nightmare that is my life.

Blood tastes like copper in my mouth.

And defeat tastes bitter.

The ref calls the end of the fight before I pass out, and I hear it all. The cheers for that other girl. Her crystal-clear shriek of happiness. The way she asks me if I'm okay, because she's a nice girl like that. I roll onto my side, curling into a ball as I put my gloves over my ears.

I can't fucking listen to this; the sound of her victory. The concerned tone in Dickie's voice.

My coach helps me up, grabbing me by the waist and keeping me standing up while they announce that the other girl is the winner by TKO and will go on to fight Killer Clover next month.

Really, all I hear is that Billie Scott wasn't so unbeatable, after all.

21

BILLIE

Ghost town - JVKE

My sobs are unstoppable in the locker room. Dickie is by my side when Taylor explains that he won't be able to take me on. Our contract was only viable if I went on to fight Clover and won that fight. My forearms are on my thighs, my wrists hanging between my legs, and my head down. I'm not looking at him, but I hear every word.

His voice is business-like, even when he announces that he's sorry. He does put a hand on my shoulder, though, telling me that professional fighting is not for everyone.

My eyes have been focused on the floor for so long, I can't lift my head anymore. Dickie insists that he wants to look at my face. Drops of blood are falling in front of me from my nose and eyebrow. I watch the blood landing on the floor, but I can't be bothered to take care of myself at this moment.

"Billie, come on. This isn't the end of the world."

No, it's the end of *my* world. Everything I worked so hard for. All the early morning runs, the hours at the gym, the dieting, the no alcohol and drugs rule. My whole life was built around professional MMA. And just like that, it's gone.

So what do I live for now?

Where's my ticket out of the North Shore?

"I need to look at your cuts," Dickie insists.

"Please, leave me alone," I say weakly as I inhale some much-needed oxygen into my lungs. Another sob wracks me, and it feels like I didn't even try to breathe, to begin with.

"I'll leave you alone as soon as I've fixed you up, kiddo."

"I got this," a deep voice says. "I'll make sure she's taken care of before she goes home."

Caden.

When did he come in? I don't want him to see me like this. I don't want anyone to see me ever again. The embarrassment of losing a fight is too much to take.

I sense Dickie's hesitation. Maybe because he notices Caden's crown tattoo on his neck. His allegiance to his gang. Maybe because he's never seen him before and doesn't want to leave me at the hands of a stranger.

I'm not sure what Caden says, I'm not listening, but Dickie leaves eventually.

I feel Caden crouch in front of me, and the next second he puts two fingers under my chin, forcing my head up. His piercing green eyes send my entire body into overdrive.

It was humiliating enough to lose. It's utterly destructive that it happened in front of Caden.

Without saying anything, he helps me up and gets me in the shower for the second time today. This time he's even the one who brushes my teeth. Afterward, he dries me and helps me into my clean clothes before sitting me on the bench again and taking care of my broken face.

The tears haven't stopped running, but the sobs are not

shaking my body anymore. I'm just silently letting the pain fall down my cheeks.

I wince when Caden pushes a little too hard on my eyebrow cut as he disinfects it.

"Needed to check you were still alive," he says casually.

"I'm not."

The thing with Caden is that he has his own manner of caring for someone and taking care of them. He is not the kind of prince charming that comes with sweet words and gestures when his princess is in distress.

I don't want him to take pity on me, even though I also don't have the strength to pretend I'm tough right now. I want to fall into a dark abyss and never come back out. I want to sleep forever so I can keep dreaming of leaving the North Shore and everything in it that has broken me.

And Caden is one of them.

He's the man who took a piece of my soul and crushed it under his stupid boot. The man who took a chunk of me for himself and never intends on giving it back. And when I tried my best to protect myself from him, he shattered my safe space and forced himself into my life. The worst part is that I've been stupid enough to enjoy it.

I stopped focusing on training. I betrayed my family. I thought myself invincible because Caden King had chosen to give me more than momentary attention, and he never does that. No, he fucks girls and throws them away. He tortures his enemies, kills them mercilessly. Only he didn't do that with *me*.

I thought I was special.

And tonight was a massively humbling experience for me.

I am not special. I'm just another girl from the North Shore who was born here and will ultimately die here.

"Do you need a magic kiss?" Caden asks me in that mocking tone he uses. Like my entire life falling apart is a little funny thing.

I don't reply. I stand up and walk over to my bag. I need out of his vicinity.

"Don't ignore me, Billie." His voice is turning that shade of dark that always makes me writhe with pleasure when it should remind me of the true monster he is.

I pack up my stuff and grab my gloves but stop myself. They won't be of any use to me anymore. Ever.

I hook my bag up my shoulder and turn around. Startled, I realize Caden is right there. His tall body is towering over me, a harsh frown hardening his features.

"Have you eaten anything today, little bee? Apart from that banana you threw up and the half-eaten energy bar."

"Get out of my way," is my only response as I try to walk around him. He steps to the side, and I try again and again, until he's got me cornered between two walls.

"Get out of my way, Caden," I repeat to his chest, not having the mental strength to stare into his soul-sucking eyes.

"Are you sure you want to push me away when I'm trying to help? Because there's no option in your life where I'm not part of it. Accept that I'm trying to care for you or be forced into accepting it. No promises that I'll be gentle for the second option."

"What a surprise," I say bitterly. "Caden King can't promise he'll be gentle. Tell me something I don't know, yeah?"

"Tsk, tsk," he tuts me mockingly. "Sarcasm surely doesn't suit my girl."

"I'm not your fucking girl."

I try to push past him again, but he grabs my ponytail this time, forcing me to look up before he talks again. "Look me in the eyes when you talk to me, Billie. I need to see the lies in them when you say you don't want me."

"Take your hands off me," I growl low, trying not to wince at how harshly he's holding me.

"You're upset, and I understand. But you can't push me away. This isn't my fault, and it isn't yours either."

"It's not your fault," I spit. "How dare you say this to my face?"

I put my hand on his that's wrapped in my hair, trying to loosen his hold.

"You fucking ruined my entire life, Caden." I twist, but he doesn't let up. "The illegal shit when I should be focusing on my career. The bullying like we're in fucking high school. Demanding every single one of my waking minutes. Demanding my mind and my body. You play me like a game, use me like a toy, and now look at me. I've got nothing."

The tears start falling again, waterfalls of pain draining my energy as I slowly give up on making him let go of my hair. "I've got nothing," I repeat. "Isn't that what you wanted, after all? For your lifelong enemy to lose everything."

"I'm not the reason you lost your fight. You were drugged and assaulted. I had nothing to do with it. I helped you today."

"Wow," I drawl with all the bitterness in my being. "My *hero*."

"Stop it," he growls. "You're pissing me off, and you know I'm not a nice person when I'm angry."

"I didn't need you yesterday," I rage. "No one was there when *you* assaulted me. *I* picked up the pieces and put them back together. Just me. I can do it all over again. But you're the one who made me weak. You're the one I missed training for. You're the one I slacked on the hard work for. I regret everything. You were the biggest fucking mistake I ever made."

His jaw works from side to side, and I see a glimpse of the monster before he flips me around and pushes my face against the wall, my bag falling off my shoulder in the process.

"Ah, you did it, little bee. You pissed me off." Why is it that he's a loud motherfucker when he's in a good mood, but as soon as he loses it, indifference creeps from his words.

"Let go!" I wriggle against his hold, but he doesn't relent. My cut eyebrow is pressing against the tiled wall and there's nothing I can do to move off it.

He nudges my feet apart with his boot and his free hand comes to unbutton and unzip my jeans.

"I'm a mistake, huh?"

"Don't you fucking dare," I hiss against the wall.

"Unless it's to scream my name, keep your fucking mouth shut."

I attempt to push off against the wall, but the hand against my hair slides to the nape of my neck and, with his better grip, presses me harder against the wall.

He yanks my jeans and underwear down to my knees and cups my pussy from behind. "Is you being wet a big mistake as well? Wanna have a discussion with your body before I keep going?"

He slips his fingers between my lower lips, parting me and stroking my clit over and over again until I'm writhing against him.

"Cad…" I struggle to take a breath, but his fingers don't stop caressing me, rubbing me in the best way, and my words keep getting cut short by moans trying to escape my lungs. "S-stop."

"Are you sure, baby? You seem to be enjoying yourself."

I open my mouth to say something, but he pushes two fingers inside me, and I gasp in shock and pleasure. He moves his hand from the back of my neck to the front of it and pulls me until my back is against his chest. I feel him caressing the edge of my face, exactly where his hickeys are still bruising me.

"Let's make a deal," he says into my ear. "If I can't make you come, I'll leave you alone. But if you come undone for me, little bee, I will take it as an invitation to never, *ever*, let you go. Sounds fair?"

"No," I moan. My body knows no shame.

"I'm giving you a choice." I hear the smirk in his tone. "Just control your body."

He keeps fucking me with two fingers, taking me to the edge of an orgasm before he pulls out, moves me around, and bends me over the bench. He pulls my hips up as my head and chest flatten against the wood. He lowers my jeans some more, and before I can think straight, he makes sure to turn me into putty again. I didn't even notice him undoing his jeans, but I know he did when I feel his dick pushing inside me. He takes his time, only giving me small thrusts and forcing me to move my ass back against him so I can take more of him.

I let out a mix of moans and whimpers when he starts increasing his pace. He shifts slightly and I scream when he hits my G-spot repeatedly.

"Scream my name when you come, baby. I can't have you forgetting who owns you."

"Fuck...fuck you!" I scream in a loud groan. As he keeps hitting the right spot, harder and harder, my anger disappears into dust, and I scream his name loudly enough to make us both come apart at the same time.

He grunts as his grip tightens on my hips just before releasing me, pulling out, and coming all over my back. I feel the warmth of his cum in the small of my back and dragging down my ass cheeks.

"You're not on any contraception, are you?" he asks, out of breath.

I shake my head as my whole body slumps against the bench.

"We need to change that. Because this wasn't the last time I fuck this beautiful pussy, was it?"

Stuck in my post-orgasm bliss, I simply nod, not too sure what I'm even agreeing with.

Using the towel he dried me with after my shower, he wipes his cum off me and pulls my jeans back up before helping me into a standing position. I can barely stand on my own two legs. The drugs from yesterday, the fight, the fuck. It's all taken a toll on my body.

Caden holds me by the waist as he drops kisses on my eyebrow, my cheek that is starting to swell, and finally my cut lip.

"Magic kisses," he finally says softly.

And that's my complete undoing. I've grown accustomed to Caden's roughness, to his brutality and the sickness in him...but fuck, the soft side of him is addictive, and it's easy to fall for it and forget everything else. It could so simply become someone's obsession.

Caden makes sure I'm fed by the time he drops me home. He doesn't walk me in, of course. Hell will freeze before a King walks through the front door of the NSC leader's house. It's late in the afternoon, meaning everyone is home, but I ignore them as I walk to my room.

They don't try anything. They know not to.

Murder is on my bed, curled into a ball like she's waiting to comfort me. I drop my bag to the floor, remove my clothes, and put my Good Charlotte hoodie on. I grab my headphones and find my charging phone on my desk. I'd put it there when we stopped by this morning. I place my headphones in, music on loud, and get under the covers with Murder.

Let the world forget about me and the darkness swallow me.

22

CADEN

Dangerous State of Mind - Chri$tian Gate$

My phone rings as I put a ready meal in the microwave, and I run to the table. A wave of disappointment washes over me when I see my sister's name on the screen. I was hoping it would be Billie. It's been two weeks since she lost her fight, and she won't talk to me.

I called and texted her countless times. I showed up at her bedroom window at her dad's and her mom's, but she didn't let me in or respond to my messages. She always makes sure they're locked now. If she continues, I'm going to have to break in. It's not decency that's been stopping me till now. Just the fact that I've been too fucking busy with everything happening between the Kings and NSC.

I want to give her time to recover from her loss, but my two weeks have been more than enough. I just need to find a way to make her mine without breaking her beyond repair. I had a delivery from the Wolves last night, and I didn't even send her. I went myself because I didn't want her to feel like I was using her again. I still need to talk to Sawyer about that. We need to find someone else to do the drives. I don't want Billie to do them anymore.

"Hello," I pick up.

"*Uncle Caden! Uncle Caden!*" The crystal voice on the other side of the line pierces my eardrum from her excitement.

"Huh...who's this?" I pretend not to recognize my niece.

"*Is Lia!*"

"I don't know any Lia," I keep faking ignorance.

I hear her little feet tap against the floor as she runs around. "*Mama...*" The rest of her words are unclear. She's only two and can almost have entire conversations, but she doesn't need to speak for her mom to understand her.

"*Okay, two minutes, and then you give it back to me,*" I hear my sister say.

A request for a video call comes on my screen, and I accept. Lia's little face comes on and I smile at her.

"Hi, beauty," I tell her.

"*Uncle Caden. Is Lia!*" She smiles at me and starts babbling incomprehensible words.

"Where's your sister?" I ask. "Where's Livie?"

She keeps going on and on because she loves talking, even with the little vocabulary she has. I think she's telling me about her dress.

"*Is pink, Uncle. Pink!*" She puts the phone down on the floor, and I can't see her any longer. When I hear her feet tap against the floor again, I assume she's doing a twirl. Then she grabs it back. "*See?*"

"Wow," I pretend I saw her dress. "So pretty." She scurries around the house, making the camera shake and sits down next to her sister before pulling it back up in front of her. "*Livie!*" Lia screams with excitement.

Livie looks at the phone and then at me, though she says

278

nothing. Her face twists, and she rubs her hands on her eyes before shaking her head.

Unlike her twin sister, Livie doesn't talk. Not a word. Not at all. While Lia is unstoppable and has taken the role of everyone's sunshine, spurting a thousand words a minute despite her young age, Livie looks at the world like she is already sick of it and can't be bothered to even speak to anyone. None of us seem to deserve her effort. My sister is scared she'll never talk, but I keep telling her that not talking at two years old is not a big deal. She's just worried because it's a huge difference between the sisters.

"*Nana here, Uncle Caden,*" Lia says to the camera. "*You Nana tak.*"

"Talk," I correct her. "No, I don't talk to Nana. Give Mommy the phone, now."

Kay finally takes the phone and looks at me. "Hey," she says. She looks exhausted, but at least I know she's safe. "Girls, Nana is gonna keep an eye on you while Mommy talks to Uncle Caden, alright?"

She doesn't really wait for an answer. She opens a door and closes it behind her before leaning on it.

"How's mom?" I ask. It feels strange to even say those words.

"She's not talking to me, but at least she's taking care of the girls."

"Not talking at all?"

"Bare minimum. She hates me. What can I do." She pinches the bridge of her nose as her annoyed voice continues, "At least she still loves her grandkids enough to welcome them here."

My mother never wanted kids. She was with my dad, who was an abusive dick. He got her pregnant twice before she managed to escape his clutches. She's never wanted to see us, and my dad never wanted to give us any information about her. I know her a little bit and remember her from when I was a kid. I mainly remember my dad humiliating her with his words and beating the shit out of her. Kayla spent more years with her, except they never formed a bond.

When Dad died, we found her number in his phone and contacted her from Kay's number. She seemed a little nicer to us since we called her to inform her that her old abuser was dead. And she agreed to help us. We need the twins away from the North Shore, but we have nowhere to go. She's our last hope.

"How long can you stay there for?" I ask.

My sister shakes her head. "I don't know." She takes a deep breath, and her voice wobbles. "But she said she'll take the girls."

"In that case, you can stay too."

"She lives in a one-bedroom apartment in a really shit building, Cade. She's got no room for me. She barely has any room for them."

"So what? You three come back here? All that for nothing?"

She shakes her head and tears spring to her eyes. "She said she'll take care of them for me for a little while."

I run a hand through my hair and run my tongue piercing against the back of my teeth before telling her what she needs to hear. "They'll be safe there, Kay. Safer than here."

The fear I went through the night of the fire must have been nothing compared to what Kay felt. She almost lost her two precious girls, and now she can't bring them back here.

"NSC wants a war," I insist. "It's getting violent here. Plus, they can't stay under our roof when we're not even sure it'll hold till tomorrow."

"I don't know her," she says quietly. "They're my babies, Cade. I can't leave my babies with a stranger."

I hesitate, working my jaw from side to side. There's another issue. "How long can you stay? The longer we delay appointing a new leader, the more likely Sawyer will take Dad's place."

She nods, and her mouth twists. "I'm staying as long as I can. As long as Mom lets me. I'm sorry, but I need to make sure my girls are in good hands when I do leave."

"I understand," I nod. "Give Livie and Lia a kiss from me."

We hang up, and I barely have time to put my phone down and check if Billie texted me before someone is knocking on my front door.

I open to Ethan and Elliot, then smile when I see Jade behind them. "Well, look who's talking to me again."

They all come in, and Jade puts a pack of beers on the coffee table in my living room.

"They made me buy this to make it up to you."

"Me? I'm not mad at you. You're the one who shouted at me."

"Okay, well, it's a sorry present."

"A sorry present," I snort. "I'm not the one you should say sorry to." I head to the kitchen and turn the microwave on since I left my meal in there.

"Are you saying I should say sorry to little Scott?" Jade snarls as I walk back into the living room. "NSC is starting a war on us, Cade. Maybe when you're done burying your face in her pussy you could look into that."

"I have a feeling this is not how your apology should have gone."

"Cade's kind of right," Elliot chuckles.

Ethan puts a calming hand on Jade's shoulder and leads her to the sofa. "Bad apology, indeed. But we still need to think about what's happening with NSC. While you fuck Billie, her sister is fucking us too."

"Real fucking deep," Elliot nods.

"She kidnapped a guy we'd stolen from them. I can't even imagine the sort of info they got out of him. We don't even know if he's alive," Ethan carries on. "Not to mention, Xi and his guys raided one of our dealer's houses."

"It was a fucking massacre," Elliot jumps back in. "Two of our guys died. They took all our supplies and that cop they bribed came right after them and arrested four Kings."

"But you're too busy sleeping with the enemy to know how bad it's getting," Jade concludes. She just had to add her grain of salt yet again.

The microwave beeps in the kitchen and I grab my meal before returning to the living room. I sit down and look at all of them before smiling.

"Thanks for the reports, the three musketeers. Rest assured, I'm not sleeping with the enemy anymore. Not that it would change anything anyway. I already knew all of that. The only reason we're not retaliating is because we don't have a leader at the moment. In case you haven't noticed, Sawyer is breaking my balls since he thinks he should lead after my father, and my sister isn't here to shut him up or take her rightful place."

"What about you?" Ethan suggests low. "Why don't you take his place?"

"Because this is not my life," I say to him. "I was born into it, but I'm not staying. I don't want any of this to be my fucking problem. All of this is temporary to me."

"You wish it was," Ethan retorts. "You're here, Cade. You're a King. You're not in some nice town, in a nice high school, being a nice math teacher, and going home to your nice wife in your white picket fence property. You're on the North Shore, and you're part of a gang that has your name on it. Fucking act like it."

Elliot opens a beer and falls back on the sofa. "How long until we can do something and actually fight back against motherfucking NSC?"

"I don't know. I'm waiting for Kay to come back."

"Well, maybe if Kay doesn't want to be here, and you don't want to be here, then Sawyer isn't such a bad choice after all," Jade suggests.

"Sawyer is a dumbass who doesn't know shit about business. He cares about instilling terror, not making money." The edge in my voice is hard to fight when I talk about the fucker. I don't like him. Never have. He's an opportunist, and he will step on anyone to get to his personal fame. "The Kings crew won't last three months with him as a leader."

I take a bite of my food and tilt my head to the side. "Don't worry. I'll talk to him, and we'll think of something to start keeping NSC in place. I'm not worried about them. If they come for us, we will crush them."

"They *are* coming for us," Jade snaps. "Open your fucking eyes."

"Fine." I stare at her and smile. The smile I know she hates, because she always says it gives her the creeps. "Then let's crush them."

We're driving Jade's car since mine is garbage, and Ethan's is at the garage after being shot up by NSC. Crossing over into their territory, we go straight to the liquor store we know some of them hang by. Unsurprisingly, the two guys we're looking for are in the parking lot, their backs against their car. One has his hands in his pockets, chilling without a care in the world, while the other is discreetly finishing a deal with a man, shaking hands as I'm assuming he's passing the drugs over. The man leaves, and we approach with our car.

"What're their names again?" I ask as Jade slows down just in front of them.

"Logan and Racer."

"Racer?" I ask surprisingly.

She shrugs. "He races a lot."

"The originality," I deadpan. "Come on," I tell Ethan and Elliot in the back.

We get out of the car and as soon as they see us, Logan goes for the back of his jeans. He doesn't have time to pull out his gun since I've already punched him in the face with my knuckle duster. The rush of pleasure coursing through my veins is better than any fucking drugs they deal.

Violence is the ultimate pleasure. Controlling it makes me a god.

Ethan and Elliot are on Racer. One grabs his arms, tying his hands behind his back with zip ties, while the other puts a bag over his head. Logan is on the floor, curled into himself with his hands on his face. I grab him by the back of his shirt and drag him back up before punching again. He passes out in my arms, and we hurry to put them both in the trunk of the car. Elliot grabs Logan's phone and passes it to me.

As soon as we're on the road again, I find Xi's number and text him.

> Logan: Where are you? I need you.

The response comes a minute later.

> Xi: What's wrong? I'm on my way to pick up Billie from work.

My blood freezes, and my limbs tighten. The fucker never

took my threats seriously, did he? What's the point in punching him and telling him to stay away from her if he doesn't listen? Do I have to kill him too? I didn't even know Billie had a job.

Completely forgetting about our plan, I send another text.

> Logan: What are you doing after?

> Xi: We're chilling at mine, so if something's wrong tell me now because I don't want to change my evening plans.

The world around me disappears as I taste acid at the back of my mouth. Is she fucking him? Is that why she ignores me?

> Logan: Where does she work now?

> Xi: Man, worry about yourself instead of getting in my stepsister's business.

My jaw tightens, and I call Xi as my blood starts boiling. The sound of Racer kicking at the trunk and screaming is really not helping calm my rage.

"*Logan, what the fuck is wrong with you?*" Xi's annoyed voice comes through the phone.

"Why don't you stay away from my girl like I fucking warned you, and I'll tell you what's wrong with your dealer?" I seethe.

There's a beat before Xi huffs. "*Caden.*"

"It's King to you, preferably down on your knees when you say it."

"*What the fuck do you want?*"

"There's quite a list. Why don't you meet me at tree number thirteen, and I'll give it to you. What I'll do is I'll get your boys to start digging their own graves. If you're there before they finish, I'll give them back to you. If not, I guess you can bury their dead bodies as soon as you arrive. Come alone."

I hang up on him and throw the phone on the dashboard.

"Fucking cunt," I mumble to myself.

"Your girl?" Jade asks. "So much for not fucking the enemy anymore," she tells me, annoyed. She rolls her eyes even though she's still looking at the road.

"What?" I say to her. "I'm not fucking her."

"Clearly not if Xi is," Elliot snorts from the back.

"Shut the fuck up," I say coolly. "He won't be able to fuck her once I cut his dick off."

The two men have been digging for fifteen minutes, with Ethan's gun pointed at them. I see a car coming our way. Tree thirteen is the tree that marks the area where we start burying dead bodies. The number came just because of its ominous meaning; it has nothing to do with the number of trees. It's deep into the forest and a place the cops never venture to. The ones who have ended up underground with all our victims. Law enforcement can't always deal with our violence, and they're better if they ignore it.

Xi comes out of his car, slamming the door violently, and walks toward us.

"Keep digging," I tell the two, who stopped when they saw their boss.

Elliot checks Xi for weapons and beams at us. "Such a good boy. Coming unarmed and all."

He ignores my friend's remark and talks to me instead. "I'm here," he shrugs. "What do you want?"

"We'll start with the fucking money we lost from you raiding one of our main dealers' house. Then with the fact that you think you can get near Billie without me ending you."

Xi laughs in my face, throwing his head back with a casual behavior that doesn't fit a situation he has no control of.

"You're so fucking pathetic, Caden. We're opposite gangs. I burn your house, and I kill your dealers." So it was him who set fire to my house. I should have known that was his idea. The guy is known for being a fucking arsonist. "That's how it works. I'm not stopping until you guys understand there's only space for one crew on the North Shore."

He steps toward me, ensuring I can see him clearly despite the night surrounding us. "And if I want to fuck Billie, then fuck Billie. That's how it's always been between her and me. All's fair in love and war. I thought you knew that." His satisfied smile wakes up the monster in me.

Calmness wraps around me, and my entire body relaxes as I grab the weapon at the back of my jeans. Xi has no time to react before I pounce on him. I grab the back of his neck and keep him close against me as I stab him in the stomach with my switchblade.

"That's for putting two defenseless little girls in danger," I say with unmatchable peace in my voice.

He grunts painfully when I pull out the blade. Then I stab him again.

"That's for stealing from us," I keep going.

I pull out again as he wheezes for air. His hands come to grab my shoulders to help himself stay up.

I stab him a third time. It's deep and violent.

"And that's for putting your hands on my girl."

I retrieve my blade for the last time and let go of him. He falls to the floor, grunting in pain as he tries to take a breath. His hands come to cover his wounds and I smile down at him.

"I doubt that'll help."

I turn to Racer and Logan. They're watching their boss die helplessly since Ethan is still pointing a gun at them.

"You guys should take care of him. I think he's feeling unwell. And next time you come for the Kings, remember we rule this fucking town and everyone in it. Including your pathetic crew."

We get back into Jade's car and drive away.

I keep running my hand through my hair, messing it up, and trying to put it back together again. The strands fall in my eyes, pissing me off and making me pull at my roots.

I can't get Billie and Xi out of my head. I can't stop imagining his hands on hers. Caressing her porcelain skin. Her big doe-eyes peering up at him from her small height as he grabs her waist. I keep thinking of his dick ramming inside her while she gives him the moans that belong to me. She sounds so perfect when she comes, too perfect to share.

I run my hand over my eyes and finally say, "How do you win a girl back?" I ask everyone in the car.

There's a beat of silence before Ethan slowly says, "I guess I would start by not stabbing her stepbrother."

I hit my head on the headrest and huff. "He fucking had it coming."

"You made the right call," Jade confirms. "NSC needs to know they can't fuck with us. And Sawyer would approve. He'll be happy when we tell him."

"I'm glad we sorted that out for you, Jade," I say bitterly. "Back to my problem now."

"Just take her on a date or something," Elliot finally says.

I look back at him, raising an eyebrow. I'm surprised he's on my side.

"Brother," Elliot laughs low. "We just want you to stop talking about her. If helping you get her back will do that, I'll fucking help you."

I grin at him. "A date, huh?"

"You're asking Cade to spend his money on someone? Have you forgotten how cheap he is?" Jade chimes in.

My friends love to remind me that I don't spend any money. What they forget is that I have a reason for it. I'm saving to leave. I never spend money on things that don't help me toward that goal. But Billie is different. A queen deserves all the gold in the world.

"A date sounds good," I nod to myself. "I can take her to a nice restaurant in Silver Falls or something."

Jade gives me a look. "Wow, you're actually gonna spend money on her?"

Ignoring her remark, I tell Elliot, "She's never gonna say yes to a date, though."

"When has that ever been a problem for you?" Ethan says with that seriousness of his.

That's true.

I want Billie back. And what I want, I always get.

23

BILLIE

November - PatrickReza

I rub my hands together and blow on them while waiting for Xi's car to show up in the parking lot. I'm in front of the diner I now work at. I changed back into my jeans and a black hoodie, but I still smell of frying oil. It's okay, I usually take a shower at Xi's anyway.

I've not slept at my house much lately. Despite turning him down, Xi's been here as my friend and stepbrother. He has been my lifeline since my dream was crushed. He takes me to work every morning and back every night, so I don't have to spend any money on gas. He lets me stay at his place and keeps my mind busy. He never mentions the growing war between NSC and the Kings because he knows I don't want to hear about anything that will remind me of Caden. He's also been trying to get me back into the gym, but I'm not ready. He takes my phone when Dickie calls and updates my coach on my state of mind. Often, it's not a good state. But he's here to hug me and soothe the nightmare away.

Dad was fuming when I told him I was dropping out of

community college, but I couldn't do it anymore. My brain will never take me out of the North Shore, and I don't want to waste my time trying. The only thing that was going to help was MMA, and that's over now.

So, I took a job as a waitress in Silver Falls. It's at the diner just before the bridge that separates the south bank from the North Shore.

I grab my phone from the jacket I'm wearing on top of my hoodie and look for Xi's number with my fingers trembling from the cold. They feel numb and I can barely move them.

What the hell is he doing? His last text said he was on his way. I call, only he doesn't pick up.

I read his text again, and an ominous feeling wraps like a heavy cloak around me. My heart accelerates, and I text my sister, asking her if she knows where Xi is. She texts back quickly, telling me she hasn't seen him today.

Maybe Lik and Sam needed him and asked him to hide a body or something. I call my other stepbrother, who picks up on the first ring. He goes to talk about something, but I cut him off. Once Lik starts talking, he's unstoppable, and it's better to stop him from the beginning.

"Is Xi with you?" I ask.

"*Last time I spoke to him, he was leaving his house to come pick you up,*" he answers me casually.

"He never showed up," I say knowing for sure something is wrong.

"*Did you try calling him?*"

"Of course I did. I'm not an idiot," I snap.

"*Are you at the diner?*" His voice is more worried now, it's lost the casualness he always has.

"Yes." I lick my lips and let out a short breath that steams around me before adding, "What...what if something happened to him?"

"I'll come pick you up. Don't worry, he wouldn't let anyone hurt him. You know he's a tough little shit."

Except I hear the slight trembling in his usually honeyed voice.

He's here less than half an hour later. My body is numb from the freezing air, yet I'm not feeling the cold. I'm too worried about Xi to even notice I'm shaking.

"You should have waited inside," Lik says as I get in the car. He's taken Sam's. The white Range Rover everyone on the North Shore recognizes as his boyfriend's car.

The hot air blowing in the car doesn't relax me in the slightest. "Have you had any news from him?" I ask. The anxiety quietens my voice.

Lik shakes his head, and we look at each other for a beat before he drives us to my dad's house.

He's clearly already mentioned it to Emma, because she's on me as soon as we get inside the house.

"What's the exact last thing he texted you?" she asks as I take my coat off.

"He just said he was on his way to pick me up. That he'd be there in five."

"It's been more than an hour," Lik adds.

Emma rakes her pink pointy nails through bleached blonde hair, pulling slightly at the extensions that run all the way to the small of her back.

My dad walks in from the kitchen with Aisha behind him. She's been crying, and I glare at my dad.

"You told her?" I whisper angrily as he gets to me. We both look in her direction again. Lik is holding her tightly, saying it'll be okay.

"I didn't have to say anything," he says low. "A mother knows."

Lik and I help Aisha sit on the sofa, and I get her a tea, putting it in her trembling hand.

"Malik," she cries loudly, as she changes her mind and puts the tea on the table. "Take me to the room. I want to pray." Lik looks around the room and nods to his mom, helping her to her feet again and taking her to the bedroom she shares with my dad.

This woman has already lost a husband; she can't lose a son too.

I run my hands over my cheeks and feel my throat tightening. "I told you you were starting a war we couldn't fight," I say to Emma and my dad. "I fucking *warned you*."

"Shut up, Billie," my sister snaps in return. "You don't get to say anything. Not when you have been fooling around with Caden King for god knows how long. We didn't start anything. You did by choosing to betray us."

A knife to my chest would have been less painful.

"I didn't...I..." I'm not sure what hurts more, the fact that none of them ever noticed he had damaged me beyond sanity —that if I'm broken enough to want him now, it's because of the things he has done to me—or the fact that they are putting this on me when I have been trying to stop them from going against the Kings.

"Why don't you call your boyfriend now and ask him where the fuck our stepbrother is," she twists the knife.

"Dad," I gasp as I step away from her, seeking comfort by asking him to defend me. My sister and I have a strong bond, but she is a cruel gang leader and I tend to always forget about it.

"You think you're so much better than us because you're trying to leave."

I pull at my roots, going completely insane at her stupidity. "What is so wrong about wanting to leave this shithole? God, you got your head so far up your ass you don't see there's a life outside of being in a fucking gang!"

"That's right, Billie. Everywhere," she spreads her arms wide to accompany her sarcastic words, "is better than here. You're in a town that raised you, where you learned to defend yourself and be independent. We've protected you from everything like a fucking princess. But no, she wants to leave. The North Shore isn't good enough for little miss professional fighting. NSC isn't good enough anymore, so she fucks Kings men behind our backs—"

"Emma, enough," my dad jumps in.

"What?" she practically shouts. "She admitted it to us. We wanted to get back at them because we thought they hurt her. Turns out she wanted it all along."

"What the fuck do you know?" I scream back at her. I push her, and she stumbles back.

"Bitch, don't," my sister warns me.

"You don't know if they hurt me. You don't know shit. Take care of your useless crew and leave me the fuck alone."

She comes at me, chest to chest. She's a lot taller than me. She gets her eyes from our dad. The beautiful blue that shows their shared DNA. I get everything from Mom: the wide brown eyes, the brown hair, the petite body, and the small height.

"Don't push me, Billie," she seethes.

"Don't make me beat the shit out of you for being so blind to what happened to me."

Her eyes widen, staring down into mine and searching for the truth in them. I can see the exact moment she understands. The moment she flashes into the past and remembers that fateful night.

"You said…"

"I know what I said," I tell her sternly.

"But—"

A loud knock on our door cuts off our stare down. She hurries to the door and opens it quickly. Racer comes in first. He's one of Xi's dealers. My stomach tenses, and my dad and I remain completely silent while we wait for someone else to come in.

My sister's hard eyes cross with mine after she sees what's on the other side of the door. I can't decipher any emotion in them.

Logan follows and is holding Xi, a hand wrapped around his waist. There's blood. So much blood.

"Oh my god," I gasp as I hurry to them.

"Dad, go make sure Aisha stays in her room," Emma says in a commanding voice. She's the leader of her gang right now, and emotions have no place in her role.

I help Logan bring Xi in. His t-shirt is soaked in blood and his head hangs in front of him, chin to chest. I'm not even sure he's conscious. His feet are dragging, his legs not holding him as we bring him to the sofa. His face is the palest I've ever seen; the usual North-African olive skin has lost its complexion.

Emma leaves the room and comes back just as we lay him down. She's got a huge pouch in her hands and talks quickly to Logan.

"Where are the wounds?"

"Three stabs to the stomach," Logan replies quickly.

The words only make me stumble back into Racer's arms.

I put a hand on my mouth as a sob tries to escape. I must keep calm, or they'll kick me out of the living room. This is not the time to panic; it won't help Emma if I do.

My sister cuts Xi's t-shirt open with scissors, and there is so much blood that it permeates the air with a coppery scent. Emma never went to college, she has no degree in anything, but she is the epitome of street-smart. She has fixed enough broken bodies in her lifetime that she could probably work at the hospital.

My sister gets to work quickly, disinfecting the three wounds. She leads a whole operation independently as if she were the head surgeon.

When Xi groans, I exhale a breath. At least he's alive.

I go to the end of the sofa and kneel by his head, putting a hand on his sweaty forehead before dropping a kiss on it. "You're going to be okay," I whisper. "Just hold on, please." A sob tightens my throat, and I repeat, "Please, just hold on for me."

I keep my cheek against his forehead the whole time Emma works on him. Blood has dripped on the sofa, and Emma's hands are covered in it. Lik joins us and I hold his hand as he settles next to me, his head falling on my shoulder.

"Xi, *WAllah*, if you die, I'm coming to hell and bringing you right back just to kick your ass," he says through gritted teeth.

I let out a short chuckle and sniffle. That's when I realize I have been crying silently for who knows how long.

Xi's eyes have been opening and closing, pain twisting his features as Emma works on him. I've lost track of time, but I do notice the second they don't open back up.

"Emma," I panic, straightening up and forcing Lik off my shoulder.

Her eyes snap to Xi's face and her lips part in shock. "No, no," she murmurs. "Xi..."

My heart kicks at my chest and my stomach twists painfully.

"Xi," I repeat after her. The panic in my voice is palpable. His eyes remain closed and Emma puts bloody fingers to his neck, checking his pulse.

"Ziad," she snaps. "Don't fucking do this to me."

Lik falls back on his ass, his gaze lost. I can see him refusing to connect with reality.

"No, please." A wail explodes out of my chest. I crawl in front of the sofa and grab his head, shaking him. "Don't leave us. Xi, don't leave us." My cries bubble out of my mouth, and I can barely breathe.

His head feels completely loose, and his body pliable. I drop my lips to his cheek, crying against him. "Please…"

I pull back, my heart shattering into pieces and that's when I notice it, one corner of his mouth tipping up slightly. His eyes stay closed, but he lets out a ragged whisper. "Are you in love with me or something?"

"Fucking…*bastard*," I huff a relieved laugh. Tears are still streaming down my face as I drop another kiss to his cheek. His eyes open slowly and he's clearly in a bad state, but he's alive.

Emma and Lik crowd us, and my sister blows out a long breath. "You fucking scared us, asshole."

"I'm going to kick your fucking ass when you're better," Lik adds.

Xi smiles at all of us, but he looks at me when he talks. "I just wanted to check how much you guys love me."

A few hours later, Xi is sleeping in our parents' bedroom. Lik called Sam to help us move him. He also brought drips of antibiotics to keep him from developing an infection. None of us asked where he got those; he wouldn't answer anyway.

My dad and Aisha went to sleep at Xi's house so we wouldn't have to move him there in his current condition.

Sam spent a long hour convincing Lik to go back to their house. They live in a cabin in the woods that separate the North Shore from the next town over. Not too far, yet far enough for it not to belong to NSC nor the Kings. Lik promises us he'll be back in the morning.

It's two a.m., and I'm lying in bed beside Xi. I can't fall asleep, needing to keep hearing his now steady breathing.

Three stab wounds.

He could have died.

Logan and Racer told us it was Caden. That he and his friends kidnapped them then forced Xi to come unarmed.

I turn to my side and nestle against my stepbrother. I'm keeping my phone in my hand in case I have to call someone urgently. We never know what might happen during the night. Xi is asleep, but his arm unconsciously wraps around me, turning his bicep into my pillow. Just as I'm about to fall asleep, I feel my phone vibrating in my hand. I pull away from my stepbrother and look at it.

It's a call from Caden.

I decline it, pressing my phone softly. I never want to talk to him again. He's taken this a step too far. I'm not in love with Xi, and I don't want to be with him. But I almost lost someone I love tonight because of Caden. I can't forgive that.

My phone vibrates again. I decline it *again*.

> Caden: I wouldn't test my patience if I were you. Pick up.

I huff and type a quick response.

> Billie: I'm sleeping.

> Caden: When I said 'don't test my patience' I meant because I have none.

He tries calling me again, and I decline.

> Caden: Alright, you fall asleep, little bee.

I look at the text, surprised, but don't reply anything.

> Caden: I'll just be waking you up in the middle of the night with my dick in that tight pussy of yours.

My mouth drops open just as my lower stomach tightens to the point I let out a short breath.

He calls again and of course, this time, I pick up.

"What is wrong with you?" I whisper angrily. I get up from the bed and walk to my room so I don't wake Xi up.

"I don't think we want to start that list right now. But we can tomorrow on our date, if you want."

"Our date?"

"Yeah. I'm taking you out. I'll pick you up from work at eight p.m."

"No," I shake my head as if he can see me. "Stay away from me and my family, Caden. I mean it."

"Huh," he pauses. *"It's funny because you're answering as if I made a suggestion."*

The mix of humor and threat in his voice is what always keeps me on edge, and tonight is no different despite everything that's happened.

I wish I could control it. Wish I could just hang up and it would be over.

But it's not only the blackmailing and the threats that keep me close to Caden anymore. It's the fact that I desperately want him.

He tried to kill Xi.

"I'm being serious," I say weakly. God, this is hard, but I have to. "You can't kidnap me to go on a date with you. I don't want to take this any further. I'm asking you to respect that."

"You know, Billie." He must be smoking because there's a short pause and a loud exhale. *"I've come to understand there are*

a few things I'm willing to respect for you. Like not making you suck my cock since it reminds you of that night. Or the fact that I could have killed Xi tonight, yet I let him off with a warning because I know he's your family. But if there's one thing you won't get out of me, it's to leave you alone. So why don't you be a good girl for me and tell me if you prefer Italian or Japanese food?"

I shake my head. "Three stab wounds. Is that what you call a warning?" I hiss with fury. "He almost died."

"But he didn't. I can change that."

"Caden...please," I huff. "We need to stop this."

"Fine," he drawls, and I can almost hear his wicked smile through the phone. *"Play hard to get. I will get you anyway. Tomorrow, eight p.m., after you finish your shift. I'll choose the food. You choose if I drag you there or you come willingly."*

He hangs up on me, and my mouth falls open.

How can he be fine with forcing a girl on a date with him?

My phone pings and I glance down to find a text from him.

Caden: 1:06 to 1:26 My Bloody Valentine.

Rolling my eyes, I still can't help but check what he means. I open the Good Charlotte album and tap on the song with my thumb. My throat tightens, and I gulp painfully. It's not because the song is about a psycho who killed the girl's lover so he could be with her. No, it's because he chose the bits of the lyrics that clearly say *I love you*.

Surely he didn't mean it because Caden can't possibly love. Especially not me.

24

CADEN

Bodies - Bryce Fox

Billie is wearing a short black dress when she walks out of the diner she works at. I can't help but smile, knowing I got what I wanted.

It wasn't hard to figure out where she worked. I just had to force it out of Racer while he was digging his grave in the woods.

She's holding her gym bag, where I assume she's put her work uniform, and is wearing her usual sneakers, but I know she made an effort for me. She stops before she sees me, pulling at her dress before looking down at her boobs and rearranging the dress around them. She pushes them up, pulls the bodice of the dress down, and attempts to show more of them before her shoulders slump as she gives up. Her boobs aren't big, that's for sure, and looking at the way they pop out of her dress right now, I understand she's probably put on a push-up bra.

She didn't need to. She's perfect as she is. Could have worn her work outfit, and I still would have found her irresistible.

I'm not sure when or how it got this bad. She haunts my thoughts, her big doe eyes always at the forefront of my mind. Her raspberry and mint scent is a need I can't satiate.

I play with the piercing on my tongue, running it against the back of my teeth. I keep wondering if I'd change anything if I could go back.

Suppose I should have stopped before it went too far. The thing is, there's no 'too far' in my perspective. I do what I want, and I do whatever it takes. Everything around me is for me to take and for people to give. Whether I take it forcefully or not isn't really my problem.

But I do wish Billie wasn't so scared of me. She saw the ruthless side of me—the Kings' man who does what he must to impose respect and fear.

I don't think I would change anything, though. Billie has seen the worst side of me, and if she can take it, if she can move past it and understand there's more to me, then we're settled for life. Because once someone has seen the worst of you, they can love you for everything you are. That's the beauty of knowing someone inside out. You can't hide anything, not even your monsters.

Billie finally notices my car and walks over to me. She opens the door and gets in, rubbing her arms from the cold. "Will you drop me off here, after? My car is parked in the lot."

"Hello to you, too, gorgeous."

"Yeah, yeah. Hi. Can you answer my question?" she says, annoyed.

"Depends," I shrug.

"On what?" she snaps.

"On when I want to release you from your kidnapping."

She rolls her eyes. "You're unbearable." She tightens her ponytail, and my dick somehow awakens from that gesture alone.

"And isn't it so annoying that you're into me, despite that?"

I turn the car on so she can warm herself. She's just wearing that tight black dress, the fabric looks thin and with spaghetti straps. She must be freezing.

"Why aren't you wearing a jacket?" I scold her.

"I forgot to grab it when I left the house and only had my Good Charlotte hoodie with me. I know you love it, but I thought it might not fit wherever you're taking me."

Before putting the car into gear, I wrap a hand around her jaw and bring her toward me. I lean to the side and take her plump lips hostage with mine. She tries to pull away, making me tighten my grip and her wince. I slide my other hand into her ponytail and undo her thick, long light-brown hair before releasing her.

"Don't do that," she pants as she sits back against her seat.

"I prefer your hair down. Though only because I'm the only one who gets to see it that way."

"I meant kissing me," she accuses me.

I start the car and turn to her one last time. "I do whatever I fucking want to you. Get that in your head once and for all." Then I drive out of the parking lot.

"You're an asshole," she huffs as she looks out the window and crosses her arms.

I chose an Italian restaurant in the end. I hold the door for Billie as she walks in, and the waiter leads us to a table at the back, a little isolated from the rest of the restaurant.

It's a round table for two, and I sit down right next to her.

"Just go on the other side," she orders.

"I don't think so." I grab her thigh and she turns to me. "I really do like it when your hair is down. You're gorgeous."

"I'm only here because you threatened Xi. Don't get the wrong idea."

"How is he?" I ask genuinely. I don't care about him, but I do care about her being upset.

"Bed bound because someone stabbed him three times in the stomach."

"Bummer." I smile. "That's definitely not gonna help NSC."

She grabs my hand under the table and pushes it off her thigh. "I hate you, Caden."

"That'll change by the end of the night, believe me."

Her jaw tightens, and she runs her fingers along the silver chain around her neck. Another waiter arrives, and he smiles at both of us. "Good evening, I'm Leo, and I'll be your waiter tonight. Can I get you anything to drink?"

"Just water, please," Billie nods.

"I'll have a Peroni," I tell him.

Billie looks at the menu silently and I watch her take her phone out. She murmurs to herself as she adds up numbers on the calculator app. At first, I think she's adding the prices to check her total in true North Shore style. It's only after a long minute that I understand she's counting calories.

My brows tug together, but I let her do her thing.

We're not used to this kind of fancy restaurant, so we both end up having to Google most of the things on the menu. Billie's face twists when she sees the prices, and she turns to me, her wide doe-eyes confused.

"Seriously," she whispers. "You're wasting your money. I don't even want to be here."

I get up slowly and stand behind her chair. To the room, I pretend to lean down and whisper some nice words in her ear. What I really do as I bring my lips to her ear is slide a hand up her thigh, hidden under the pristine white tablecloth, and push her panties to the side. Without warning, I push a finger into her tight pussy, and I feel her straighten up from being startled.

"Caden," she lets out in a half-whispered moan. She might not have been ready a second ago, but I already feel her wetness coating my finger.

"Shh," I smile into her ear. "Here are the options I'm offering you. Option number one, be a good girl, pick your food, and give me a chance to be nice to you. Option number two, be a little brat, let the whole room watch you come on my fingers, and once you've orgasmed and you're more compliant, you'll pick your food and have a nice evening." I start moving my finger in and out of her, her wetness now practically dripping onto the chair.

"So what will it be, little bee? Good girl, or brat?"

She bites her bottom lip and I insert another finger inside her. "I can't hear you."

I feel her tightening around me and her breath hitching. I see her losing her resolve as she slumps against her seat.

"G-good girl."

"Mm, that's what I thought." Sticking to my word, I pull out of her. She closes her eyes in a mix of relief and disappointment. My dirty girl wants to come, just not in front of the entire restaurant.

I sit back down and stare deep into her eyes as I bring my fingers to my mouth and wrap my lips around them. Slowly, I pull them out before looking at my menu. "Fuck," I huff. "Nothing on this menu is going to compare to the taste of you."

Glancing back up, I relish in her pink cheeks and red ears.

"You're beautiful when you're embarrassed," I say softly. I grab her hand on the table, and she doesn't pull away.

Leo comes back to take our orders and she only asks for

one of the many items I saw her adding up on her phone when she counted calories. I order a carbonara and give her another chance to ask Leo something. Only she doesn't say anything, shyly shaking her head.

And I know what that shake means. She's scared we won't be able to afford it. Remembering exactly what she wanted to pick initially, I order them for her—a small plate of tomato pasta, two different salads, and a side of steamed vegetables.

"And add some grilled chicken," I finally say. "She needs the protein. No soda, no alcohol. Thanks."

Billie's wide, innocent-looking eyes are still on me long after Leo has left, and I've stopped talking. "Y-you didn't have to order all of that for me," she says quietly, shifting awkwardly on her chair.

"Little bee," I say, peering into her eyes. "When you're with me, you can have whatever you want. I will give you everything you wish for. Anytime. Alright?"

I watch her throat work before she nods weakly. Her cheeks are still tinted, and her brown eyes keep moving between mine. She is stunning tonight. It's not just the dress; it's the fact that I know it's for me. I notice she's put on some mascara and a light pink lipstick. It's so light, it doesn't hide the dark freckles on her cupid's brow that contrast with her pale skin.

My eyes drag along her lean throat to the curve leading to her shoulder and down. Her small boobs are pushed up, and I just want to put my dick between them and choke it until I'm coming all over her chest.

I grab a strand of hair that's falling onto her chest and move it behind her shoulder. Her long hair is enchanting when it's not in her usual ponytail. She'll scream tonight when I grab it and force her head into the mattress while she comes all over my dick.

"How was work today?" I ask, reluctantly letting go of her hair. I grab my beer to busy my hands. Otherwise, I'll grab her and it won't be gentle.

"Shit, like every day. It's a problem when you work in a diner that serves crappy food. People tend to blame the waitress rather than the cook."

"Why did you start working there?"

"Gotta earn money somehow," she shrugs before taking a sip of water.

"How does it even fit with your classes?"

Her eyes stay on her glass, and she starts playing with the rim. "I dropped out."

I let a beat pass so I don't fire my answer at her and make her retreat. "You shouldn't have. College will help you get a better job than your current one. Not that there's anything wrong with waitressing, but I know how badly you want to leave. College can help with that."

"Alright, *Dad*," she snorts sarcastically before turning to me again. "I'm never getting out of here, Caden. There's no point discussing this."

Her defeat against that Silver Fall girl was two weeks ago, and she is still completely dejected.

"How's training?"

"I don't train anymore." Her answer is clipped, and she looks relieved when Leo reappears with our food.

As soon as he leaves, she stuffs her mouth with the spaghetti on her plate, not wanting to talk to me.

"Little bee," I say calmly as I put a hand on the back of her neck. "Your MMA career isn't over."

As soon as she swallows her pasta, she pushes more vegetables than she should into her mouth. Her cheeks puff from her full mouth, and I shake my head laughing.

"At some point there will be no food left, and you'll have to talk to me." She coughs after swallowing and drinks some water.

"MMA isn't my favorite topic of conversation. Change it."

I look at her features for a beat, not liking the sadness I see in them.

"Stop looking at me like that." She shifts in her seat, uncomfortable.

"Like what?"

"Like you pity me."

"I just don't like seeing you upset," I admit, my hand caressing her neck.

She barks a sarcastic laugh. "Liar."

"I like seeing you at my mercy, but I don't like seeing you upset. There's a difference."

She squirms, trying to nudge my hand away by rolling her shoulders. When she fails, she shifts her chair a little further away from me. I let go of her only to move my chair too, following.

"God, Caden," she huffs. "Stop this whole trying to be nice and seducing me thing. We're enemies. I know '*us*' almost happened, but reality has caught up now. We're never going to leave this place and be happy somewhere else. Do us both a favor and accept it. I'm going to serve in that shitty diner for the rest of my life, living with my dad, and you'll rule your gang until it kills you. That's just how life is."

My voice is a few shades darker when I answer. "I will not be ruling any gang. I'm *not* staying here."

"Sure. That's what you say. But you just stabbed Xi because he raided your dealer's house. Sounds like someone who's into gang shit to me."

"I stabbed Xi because he didn't listen to my warning. I told him to stay away from you. I told him whoever touches what's mine, dies. He's fucking lucky he's still breathing," I hiss low.

Her lips flatten together, and she goes rigid without saying anything.

"You're giving up, Billie. That's not you. Keep training, keep fighting."

"I don't want to," she snaps back.

"You say that, yet you still run every morning." She goes to say something, but I cut her off. "Yes, I fucking watch you like a creep. Get over it. You still don't drink any alcohol," I point at the glass of water she's holding firmly. "You still count your calories to make sure you don't lose weight. A portion of carbs, steamed vegetables, and protein. Sounds like someone who still wants to go through rigorous training to me."

"It-it's just a habit," she babbles her lie.

"You lost a fight, little bee. Everyone needs a humbling session when they think they're invincible. You got yours. Now get back out there. Because let me tell you something, I will keep saving and studying to leave the North Shore, and you will keep fighting. Oh, and I will also keep making you mine while you secretly enjoy it. These are facts. Don't just get familiar with them. Accept them."

She doesn't say anything, simply looks right at me. It seems we can't stop returning to each other's eyes tonight. I don't know what she sees in mine, but I'm starting to see the fire of hope lighting in hers as a proud feeling envelops me. I did that. I gave my girl hope.

25

BILLIE

Body - Rosenfeld

Caden is holding my hand as we walk out of the restaurant. There's a tension in my lower stomach from the simple fact that his skin is touching mine. The words he said during dinner made me feel all sorts of things.

I hate him for what he did to Xi. Although I've always hated Caden; there's nothing new there.

I thought I would lose that weird feeling I've started to have for him after he hurt my family. I'm ashamed that I didn't.

His dirty words still make me feel hot and bothered. My chest still warms when he speaks softly to me. And tonight... he made me feel hopeful again.

I feel like all I've done in the last two weeks is lose myself and my convictions, my dreams, my hopes. Caden reignited them with the fire in his voice.

How does he do it? Always getting through to me like he knows me inside out. I want to bathe in the hope he made me feel. I want to hold his hand tightly, to let him hug me, and use my body.

He is absolutely irresistible tonight, and it's entirely unfair for my heart. I made an effort because I knew he was taking me to a nice place, and he did the same.

He's wearing black slacks that stretch around his perfect ass, a simple white button-down with the sleeves rolled up. Tattoos are peeking out on his forearms and his strong hands. The first two buttons are open. He had a suit jacket on but he's given it to me since I had nothing and I was freezing. Good, because I love watching the shirt wrapping snugly around his shoulders.

The man coerced me into going on a date with him, and I'm leaving the restaurant as if it had been my lifelong dream to go on said date.

"Billie!" a hoarse voice calls behind us. We both stop and turn around, unsure of who it could be. We don't really know anyone on this side of Silver Falls.

My eyes widen as I recognize the man walking the same way as us. Tall with broad shoulders and a confident demeanor. His pitch-black hair is similar to Caden's, except his is shorter and better kept. His midnight eyes take me and Caden in before he looks at our joined hands.

"Now, that's unexpected," he says as his poised smile settles over his lips.

I hadn't seen Jake White in over two years. He never contacted me again after the night we all thought he had died. Jamie had told me he was alive. She had messaged me to thank me for all the help that night despite our differences and that she wanted to bury the hatchet. After all, her boyfriend had broken up with her and used me to break her heart. We weren't exactly best friends. Still, I appreciated her message. I never replied because I was too taken by my own grief. I was burying the girl I once was, the girl who Caden had destroyed.

"Billie, how are you?" Jake takes another step toward me, opening his arms to take me into a hug. Automatically, Caden's hand drops mine to grab the back of my neck and haul me back. He's a little taller than Jake, while my Stoneview ex is much broader.

"Weren't you meant to be dead?" Caden asks as a hello. He holds me closer to him as he throws a death stare at Jake.

Jake takes a good look at us and lets out a small laugh. "No, I just napped for a little while." I notice the way his voice isn't as smooth as it was before that fight. His opponent in the Death Cage strangled him, which must have caused severe damage.

"So, you two are...together?"

"No," I assert at the same time Caden calmly says yes.

Jake throws his head back, a throaty laugh resonating around us. "I've been there, man," he tells Caden. "Good luck."

I feel Caden tense before his wicked smile appears. "What do you mean you've been there?"

Realizing the misunderstanding, I jump in before this encounter turns into a bloodbath. "He means with his girlfriend, Jamie. Not with me." I put a hand on Caden's chest. "You're still with Jamie, right Jake?"

I don't even care if he's still with her or not. He better say yes.

"Still with Jamie." He nods. "She's waiting at our friend's house for her takeaway." He shows us the plastic bags he's holding.

"Nice," I say awkwardly. "Do you guys still live in Stoneview?" The more I point to the fact that he and his girlfriend are serious, the better it is for everyone.

"No, we moved to Philadelphia for colle—"

"My patience for you addressing my girl has officially reached its limit." His tone is cool, but his words are knives. "You've escaped death once. You shouldn't tempt it a second time."

"Damn, Billie," Jake chuckles. "I knew you needed a firm hand. Didn't realize you actually wanted a complete psycho."

I bulge my eyes at Jake, silently asking why he has a death wish.

"The psycho has a switchblade. Remember that before you mention knowing anything about her."

Jake doesn't lose his confidence. He smiles brightly at Caden and replies, "Nice. Do you use it on her? I tried a gun on Jamie. Highly recommend it."

Because like recognizes like, I feel Caden's attitude changes drastically. "Oh," he simply says, a malicious bell ringing in his tone. "I think you would love that, little bee. Wouldn't you?"

His sinful eyes come to mine, the green sparkling with excitement. He must notice the terror on my face. "We'll start small, baby" He grins down at me. "Don't worry."

He starts guiding me away as he says, "We've got things to do now. Nice to meet you, Jake."

I don't even think Jake understands what it means to hear that from Caden. *Nice to meet you.*

He's essentially telling him they're best friends now. Only because he understood they have the same type of evil inside them.

We walk to the car with his hand still on my neck. I used to dread the possessive gesture, but tonight, the warmth is reassuring me and making me feel comfortable.

Caden opens the passenger side of the car and helps me in. He fastens the belt for me, making sure to hold my waist and lower his other hand down to my pussy when he's done.

Then, he slides both his hands under my dress, grabs the sides of my underwear, and drags it down my legs before putting it in his pocket.

"Caden," I let out a half-sighed protest.

"I've got something for you, little bee." He opens the glove compartment and grabs something I can't quite see before closing it again. "Lean forward for me."

"Why?" I say, narrowing my eyes.

"Because I want to do dirty things to you, and I want you to agree. Don't worry, it won't stop me if you don't want to."

I gulp, swallowing what he might think is fear, but what I also know is anticipation. My thighs tighten as I shift, feeling a need growing in my lower belly.

I give him an almost imperceptible nod, and he offers me his most wicked smile. The one that makes me wet.

"That's a good girl. Now lean forward."

I do so, my forehead resting on the dashboard. He brings my hands behind my back, and I hear the telltale sound of a zip-tie tightening. My wrists slam together, and it cuts into my skin.

He helps me back into a normal sitting position, my hands at the small of my back and crushed between me and the seat.

His hand disappears between my legs, and I feel something against my wet entrance, though I can't see what it is with my dress hiding my crotch.

"What is it," I panic, but I'm cut off by my own moan when he pushes the object inside me slowly. "Caden..."

"Yes, baby?"

"Wh-what is it?"

He moves the item in and out of me, forcing me to buck my hips and follow his movement in search of pleasure.

"It's a G-spot vibrator."

I try to move my arms, except I can't. Of course, I can't. I'm tied up with zip ties in my enemy's car. His hand moves again, and the next thing I know, the vibrator is pushing inside me. Right on my magic spot.

"Oh god," I shriek with pleasure. "Oh..." I pant. "Caden..."

"Mm, I love it so much when you call my name."

He leaves the toy as it is and steps away from me. Without the aimed pressure of his hand, it isn't as intense. He drops a small kiss on my lips and closes the door, leaving me for the driver's side.

As soon as he's sitting down, he starts the car.

"Let's go for a little drive," he tells me. And I already know it's not going to be a casual drive.

I take a deep breath, trying to calm my raging heart. We drive back to the North Shore, but instead of taking me to my house or his, he takes the road that crosses the woods. In less than fifteen minutes, we're surrounded by trees only. No light but the moon shining down on us, its ominous brightness turning the forest sinister.

Caden slows down and grabs something in his pocket. I see the small remote in his hand and am about to ask what it's for when the toy starts vibrating inside me.

I gasp a breath and cross my legs. The vibration isn't intense, yet I can feel it pressing against my G-spot a little more.

"How does that feel?" Caden asks, not taking his eyes off the road.

"G-good." My voice trembles as my body heats up.

"What about this?" The vibrations intensify, along with the pressure inside me.

"Oh god..."

"Answer me." His voice is tight, and I wonder if it's because he's trying to control his own need for pleasure.

"Good," I say in a hurry.

"Who's making you feel good, little bee?"

"Y-you...it's you, Caden."

He keeps driving but doesn't lower the vibrations and I feel my wetness dripping.

It's already hard to take a full breath. I'm writhing next to him, shifting in my seat while he drives calmly, not even looking at me. There's a smirk on his face, and I can't help but look at him and nothing else.

The vibrations intensify some more, and I scream as I feel my stomach tightening.

"Caden..." I panic.

"Again. Who's making you feel good?"

"You!" I scream. I pull at my arms, dreading the intense need building inside me.

"Say it," he growls as his hands firmly grip the steering wheel. "Who is making you pant like a little bitch in need?"

"Y-you, Caden. It's..." I gasp. "Caden...please."

"That's right, baby. Don't ever forget it." He settles down slightly and looks at me with his frightening smile. "You're going to come all over yourself for me." He accelerates the car and my heart beats wildly in alarm, eyes widening as I see the trees outside blur.

"Too...fast," I pant. I don't even know if I'm talking about the vibrations or the car.

My entire body tightens as the toy keeps pressing harshly against my G-spot. I squeeze my legs together just before I feel a harsh slap on my naked thigh. "Open your legs. Right fucking now."

I do so reluctantly, feeling exposed and like I can't control my body as well now.

"Please," I cry out, feeling myself losing control. "I...I can't hold it."

"I know," he glances at me again, his eyes shining with a

sadistic need to humiliate me for his own pleasure. "You're gonna come on yourself, little bee. You're gonna squirt all over my car seat, and I'm going to rub your face in it while I fuck you from behind."

"No," I shake my head. "Please..." I try to move my wrists, knowing perfectly well it won't change anything, but I have to try anyway.

There's no way I can control my body's need for this intense release. I want to orgasm so badly, but I don't want the embarrassment of losing control.

Tears spring to my eyes as I feel the unstoppable intensity building and building. "Caden..." My breathing stops and I choke on air for a few seconds, my body coiled tight. And then, I explode.

The scream that leaves my lungs resonates in the car. My knees come up and I fold onto myself, my head coming to the dashboard. I scream into it, biting into the plastic. The pleasure doesn't stop, and I feel the wetness squirting out of me. It's wholly unstoppable, and the humiliation is just as intense as the pleasure. I'm crying now, tears running down as my body spasms.

I don't know how long it lasts, but even when Caden turns off the toy, groans of pleasure spill out of my mouth as my pussy keeps pulsing around the toy.

I hear the car door, and only realize now that we've stopped. My side opens and Caden's hand is in my hair, dragging me out of the car. He flips me so I'm facing the car and bends me over, pushing my face onto the seat. It's drenched in my wetness.

He slaps my ass as I try to take a normal breath. "Dirty slut came all over herself. Look at what you did to my car." He slaps my inner thigh. One then the other. The wet sound brings me even more embarrassment. "Look at how much you've wet yourself."

I startle when I feel his tongue running on my inner thigh until it meets my pussy. "You're so fucking delicious." He pushes his tongue inside me and my knees buckle. His hands are the only things keeping me up.

He stands back up and takes the toy out before grabbing my hips tightly, and the next thing I know, he's entering me in one violent thrust.

I am so wet and swollen, my scream is pure pleasure only. He slaps my ass again, and I shriek from the intensity it brings.

"Whose body is this?"

"Yours," I cry out.

"Who fucking owns you?"

"You..."

"Let me hear it, baby. Give me what I need."

Need. He *needs* me.

His thrusts are merciless. I feel them so tightly inside me that another orgasm builds in my lower belly.

"You own me, Caden," I moan. "You. Just...aah...you."

"That's right." He increases the pace and my entire body electrifies. Harder thrusts, violent delights.

I moan loudly, and he pulls at my hair, forcing my head up from the wet seat. "Scream my fucking name when you come, little whore."

"Caden!" I explode. I scream loudly, the woods swallowing my sound.

He pulls out, flips me around, and comes all over my chest. Before letting me go, he bends over me and grabs my jaw tightly. He bites just below my ear, and when I understand what he's doing, I try to fight him.

"No," I writhe under him.

"Don't fight me," he growls. "I want everyone to know I'm still fucking you."

He leaves his mark from my ear, along my jaw, and all the way to my chin.

And I decide to let him.

We're just in the middle of nowhere, still panting from sex. There is no one to witness our madness, but *we* know.

We know this night is the night I truly give myself to him.

He was going to have me anyway. I'm all too happy to oblige.

26

CADEN

Baby - Elvist Drew, Avivian

"...and then that means we'll take over that store dealing spot, too."

I ignore Jade's voice, scrolling through Billie's messages on my phone. I smile, gazing at the selfie she just sent me of her and Murder. She's got an ice cream in her hand, even though it's cold enough outside to freeze her fingers, and Murder is trying to lick it.

I text back as people keep talking around me.

"We tried to take back the alleyway behind the cemetery. Xi killed two of the guys. Bare hands and all."

Sawyer's voice is merely background noise as I open the next picture from Billie. She's pushing her bottom lip out, pouting as she gives the cutest puppy eyes. Murder is licking the ice cream happily.

> Little bee: Noooo. She stole it!

A soft laugh escapes me and the room around me goes silent.

"Something funny, Cade?"

I peer up only to find four pairs of eyes staring right at me. Jade is sitting on the armrest of Sawyer's seat, and I cock an eyebrow.

"Are you two fucking now?"

"Caden," Ethan snaps next to me, not liking that I'm pointing out that his ex-girlfriend is obviously fucking his boss. "Can you focus on the task at hand?"

"We just told you Xi killed two of our dealers. Beat them to death." Jade pauses for effect but doesn't understand I don't care. "Lea was there, she saw everything. Said he only spared her so she could run back to us and let us know."

"That guy," I snort. "He just hates being alive."

"He's rubbing in our face that he doesn't give a shit about anything you said. And how did the fucker even survive three stab wounds?" Sawyer sneers.

I can't really hear him. My eyes are back on the picture of Billie.

> Caden: Baby, do I tell you enough that you're the most beautiful woman I've ever seen?

She replies right away.

> Little bee: What about all the ones you haven't seen yet? What if they're more beautiful than me?

I chuckle to myself, biting my lower lip as I reply.

> Caden: I don't want to see them. I've got everything I need.

> Caden: I want to bite that pouty lip and kiss it better.

> Little bee: I'm not working tonight. We should meet up. There are a lot of people at my house, though. We can't go there.

And there are people in my living room currently scheming against NSC. No way to meet here either.

"...den. *Caden!*" My eyes flick up, Jade's furious gaze on me. "What the fuck are you doing on your phone?"

I shrug. "Ignoring you." Returning to the question I last heard, I add, "He survived because I didn't want him to die. That's all."

"Yeah," Jade scoffs. "'Cause you didn't want to hurt Billie Scott's feelings." She puts on a fake pout and tilts her head. "You're so good to your girlfriend."

"Not my girlfriend," I lie a little too quickly.

She is. She's my girlfriend, my future wife, my everything. Not that any of them need to know. I don't want to put her in any more danger than she already is. What's pretending we're not together when we have the rest of our lives to make up for it?

Ethan tries to come in as the voice of reason, his calm demeanor helping to keep my own anger at bay. "You might think all these problems are beneath you because you're so desperate to get out of this town. But if NSC takes over, you'll be dead before you even finish college."

I huff, running a hand through my already messy hair as I lock eyes with Sawyer. "We were never able to take over the alley behind the cemetery. Xi holds on to it just as hard as he holds his dick when he jerks off over his stepsister. Why do you want it now?"

"To prove a point," Sawyer admonishes as he stands up. "This town belongs to us."

"Don't let NSC make you believe they can start a war on us, Sawyer. We already know they're useless fucks, but your pride is a very dangerous thing."

"My pride? What about your fear? You don't want to see what's happening right before you." He takes on a girly voice. "You're too scared it'll break you and your girlfriend up." Hardening his voice again, he adds, "What will happen when she chooses her crew over you, and you're too pussy-whipped to get over it?"

"Not my girlfriend," I rebuke a little harsher this time. I get up and slowly walk to him.

Chest to chest, he's glaring at me while I feel the glint of malice glowing in my eyes. "Let me make something clear. The only thing I've ever been scared of is myself. Because no one can stop me when I lose control. You know that, right, Sawyer?"

I feel the need he has to take a step back when his body tenses from alarm. "Don't push me," I say with a chilling tone. "Don't make me lose control." I notice goosebumps appearing on his neck as I observe him. Bringing my gaze back to his, I smile. "I don't give a shit what you do with NSC, but don't waste precious energy and resources on them. There's no point in our men dying. We already have the upper hand. Let them come to us if they want. They'll quickly realize it's a suicide mission."

Looking down at the phone in my hand, I notice another text from Billie. "I gotta go. Tutoring and all."

"I thought you stopped tutoring," Jade calls my way as I head to the front door.

"Mind your own business, Jade," I throw back as I start

typing back to Billie. "Who knows what I'll do to you once I'm truly sick of you."

I leave and keep typing as I walk to my car.

> Caden: Remember how I promised to do wicked things to you?

> Little bee: Yes…

> Caden: Meet me where the road turns into gravel in the woods. I have a game for us. Wear a skirt and no underwear. And I want your hair down too.

> Little bee: I'm gonna freeze to death in a skirt and nothing else.

> Caden: I'll warm you up, baby. Don't worry.

I go to my car and open the glove box. Rummaging through it, I find a piece of black cloth I keep there for when I've kidnapped NSC guys in the past. There's also a bottle of whiskey, a gun, and zip ties.

I won't use the gun because it reminds me too much of what her Stoneview ex did with his other girlfriend. I don't want Billie to think I had any inspiration from him. Although I think we could have been good friends if only he hadn't fucked my girl at one time. He's got that spot of darkness that dirties the blue of his eyes. There's something deeply wrong with him, just like me.

I drive to the meeting point I gave to Billie and recognize her car parked there. The road is the end of civilization when it comes to these woods. It turns into gravel and then slowly into nothing but forest ground. That's the beginning of the end. Where monsters hide and no one can hear you scream.

Night is falling, and it brings a peace over me. My favorite part of the day.

I belong to the night, and Billie knows that.

I open the bottle of whiskey and take a swig. Relishing in the sweet burn going down my throat, I take another one and smile. I am going to have fun with my little bee tonight.

Typing on my phone, I stay in my car as I send a new message to Billie.

> Caden: Get out of your car and wait, facing away from me.

> Little bee: What have you got in mind?

> Caden: Why don't you do what I tell you and find out?

I watch her exit the car and stand by it, facing the darkness of the forest. Following, I get out of mine. Keeping my steps light, I approach until I'm standing right behind her.

I know she senses me because her body relaxes slightly. "Okay, can I turn around now?" I can hear the smile in her voice.

"Not yet," I purr in her ear. I put the bottle of whiskey on the ground and grip the cloth in both hands. Without warning, I put it in front of her eyes.

"Caden," she panics, bringing her fingers to the cloth now covering her eyes.

Fisting both ends, I pull until she crashes against my chest. "Shh. Calm down," I whisper. "You're safe, okay?"

I can feel her heart beating through her back and against my chest. "You've been drinking." It's not a question, and I sense her tensing.

She's only seen me drunk once, and I'm not exactly proud of what I did to her that day. But we've been seeing each other for three weeks now and she's not scared of me anymore. Like a little lamb who falls in love with the wolf that could eat her, Billie has been lowering her defenses for me. This new version of our relationship makes my heart melt every single time I see her.

It's dangerously addictive to receive Billie Scott's love. She doesn't have much of it to give, and it's a privilege that she's chosen me to do so with.

It's also a precarious situation for her because while I was obsessed with her before for the simple fact that I wanted her, I am now consumed by love and euphoria at knowing I will never let her go. She agrees to that now, but if she changes her mind, it won't mean anything to me. She belongs to me forever, and there's absolutely nothing she can do about it.

I'm hyper-aware of every single one of Billie's trembling breaths as I tie the cloth at the back of her head. I make sure not to pull at her beautiful long hair.

"I'm going to do something with you I've never done before, little bee," I whisper in her ear.

Looking down, I can see her tapping her fingers against her thighs. A discreet dance of apprehension.

"I'm going to give you a way to stop what I'm about to do."

She freezes from the surprise. "W-what?"

"If it gets too much, I want you to tap out. The exact same way you would do in the cage."

"I never tap out in the cage." Her voice is strong, her pride unshakable.

I chuckle softly, before kissing her neck. "I know. But you know you can if you really need to. Okay?"

"Okay." She nods a few times before I wrap a hand around her throat from the back. "This will be valid for everything, forever. If I'm too much, tap out."

"You've never done this with me before," she points out as her body relaxes.

"I've never done this with anyone. I don't care if others can't take me, but I care about you. I would rather you tell me that I'm out of control rather than realizing too late that I've lost you."

My hand stays around her neck as I slowly run my other along her petite body. I palm her ass, the back of her thighs, and bend so I can grab the bottle of whiskey. Putting it in front of her, I bring it to her lips and make her drink.

"God," she chokes out, spluttering and spilling whiskey on herself. "That's whiskey!"

"Yeah. And you practically never drink, so you're a lightweight."

She clutches the hem of her skirt firmly. She's wearing a simple white skater skirt that makes her look angelic. I can't wait to soil it and her.

Keeping the bottle close to her lips, I bring the hand around her neck to her breasts.

"Billie," I growl low as I start to lose rationality. "You're not wearing a bra." I can feel it through the oversized sweater she's wearing. It's a simple beige sweater of mine that she stole from my closet. It's so large that one side is falling off her shoulder, and she had to tuck the bottom into the waist of her skirt.

I untuck my sweater and slide my hand under until I reach her perky nipples. I play with them, alternating and not stopping until she squirms under me. Her heavy breaths blow on the open bottle I'm holding in front of her, playing a beautiful melody that translates her need for more.

I tilt the bottle, making her drink again. She splutters again, and when she turns her head to the side, more spills over her. "T-too much."

She takes a deep breath, hissing through the burn.

"Here's what I want to do," I tell her low. "I'm going to turn you on slowly." I accompany my words by rolling her nipple between my thumb and forefinger. "Every time you want more, you ask for a sip. And when I deem you inebriated enough, I'll give you what you truly crave. How does that sound?"

She shakes her head, shuffling on her feet. She scratches her throat through the uncertainty before she talks. "I-I don't know."

I kiss just below her ear, following the trail of her neck until I gently bite her shoulder. She lets out a soft breath, and I ask. "Do you want to tap out?" I'm not playing fair, giving her a taste of the pleasure I'll bring her if she *doesn't* tap out. I don't really care. I also know how powerful 'tapping out' is in her mind. For a fighter, it's defeat. Admitting that you've been beaten.

Billie wants to be unbeatable.

"N-no," she huffs. "I'm not tapping out," she adds between clenched teeth.

"Then play by my rules."

I pinch her nipple and watch how she curves her back to press her chest to my hand. I play with her until she's writhing, and a breathless moan escapes her.

And then I pull my hand away.

She lets out a wordless complaint. "More?" I ask.

She nods, but I insist. "Say the words."

"I want a sip."

She can't see the wicked smile on my lips, but it's like she can sense it. I feel her shiver as I bring the bottle of whiskey to her lips. I force her to drink bigger gulps than she usually would, and she takes them.

When I'm satisfied, I pull the bottle away and slide my

hand between her legs. "Mm, no panties," I murmur in her ear. "You listen so well."

I run my fingers along the seam of her lower lips before breaching the barrier and grazing her clit. She pushes her hips forward, and I press my thumb against her clit. With balanced pressure, I start rubbing her slowly. She chases every one of my movements for a long minute. Her hand slams on mine when I pull away, but the pleasure weakens her muscles and she doesn't manage to stop me.

"Another sip," she whimpers.

"Anything for you, baby." Bringing the bottle to her lips, I force her to drink some more.

Now used to the burn, she drinks more greedily, surrendering completely.

I count three more times she begs me to continue and instead I make her drink some more. She starts shuffling on her feet and resting more on me, her body heavy from the alcohol.

"Caden," she slurs. "J-just fuck me."

"I have to tell you a secret, little bee." I take a swig of the whiskey, realizing there isn't much left in the bottle. It wasn't full, but there must have been just under half a bottle in there. She drank a lot.

"That time I found you drugged up and lifeless in that hotel room. Remember? Once I knew you weren't in danger anymore...I was so fucking turned on, Billie. I lied the next day when I told you I liked you fighting. I do, but that night, seeing you there, all lethargic and helpless...it made me hard for you. You're a strong woman, and having you in a state where you can't fight back makes me ecstatic."

She tries to pull away, but I hold her back. She can't do much, too drunk to defend herself now.

"I'm going to hunt you before enjoying you."

I look at the dark forest ahead of me and grind my hard cock against her ass.

"That's not funny. I..." She sways, and I catch her. "Caden, that's not okay."

"I know," I say as I breathe her scent. She smells of raspberries, mint, and whiskey. "I know it's not fucking *okay*, Billie. But I want to do it. It's not too late to tap out."

As I say that, I press a finger to her wet entrance.

"No," she pants. "I want you. I want you, and all the dark things you like to do to me."

I press a little harder against her pussy before retreating. "I'm going to fuck you. But first, I'm going to chase you."

I rip the blindfold off and let go of her. She shifts on her feet as she tries to catch her balance. She turns to me, her eyes glossy from how much she drank.

"Run."

27

BILLIE

DIE4u - Bring Me The Horizon

I trip on myself the moment I attempt to run. Managing to catch myself against a tree, I glance back at Caden. He's a being of the night, fitting in with the darkness like a demon fits in hell. His black hair is messy, thick strands falling in his moss-green eyes. The only light around us is the moon shining above us, but I know the moment I run deeper into the forest, that will disappear, too.

He flashes me his most wicked smile as he slowly walks toward me. The devil is silently telling me he is going to make me his.

Inhaling a sharp breath, I face forward again and start running. I was freezing cold when I arrived, but the whiskey and the fact that Caden has just spent nearly half an hour touching me and bringing me close to the breaking point have warmed me. I'm already out of breath despite having barely started. I'm drunk. MMA training keeps me away from drugs and liquor, but now that I have nothing to look forward to, I don't really care anymore.

Fuck, I had completely forgotten how lethargic my body can feel from drinking too much. My legs weigh a ton, and everything around me is fuzzy. I don't think I've run five minutes when I must stop. I brace a hand on the closest tree, bending over as the world tilts around me.

I didn't even know this was something Caden wanted to do. Having me completely helpless so he can use me? Of course, he would want that since he loves abusing me.

The fact that he gave me an out for the first time makes me feel safer with him. I glance around and see trees among trees, among more trees. That's all there is. The forest is alive, branches creaking, owls hooting. I laugh to myself. Safe? With Caden King? Who the fuck am I kidding?

Something snaps behind me, so I twist around. His shadow walks through the trees like a monster coming to get me. I'm little red riding hood, and Caden is the big bad wolf.

A giggle escapes me, excited by the chase. I start my race again. My belly is heavy from alcohol, my clit sensitive in the cold air, and my mind entirely free.

My foot catches around something, and I practically watch in slow motion as I fly forward and crash against the ground.

I grunt as my knees and hands are cut from landing in muddy soil. Going on all fours to catch a breath before getting back up, I look down at my pale hands against the dark ground. My hair is falling in front of my face, and I shake my head.

"What a stupid idea to wear a white skirt," I mumble to myself, my mouth feeling like cotton.

"I agree."

I shriek from fear. Turning around, I fall onto my ass in the mud. Caden is right behind me, a foot on the huge root that must be the reason I'm not standing anymore.

The fall reminds my brain how drunk I am and my ears

ring. I can barely discern Caden from the trees surrounding him. Everything is fuzzy, and I squeeze my eyes shut before opening them again.

"Your hair down gives you an even more innocent look," he tells me randomly. "It's beautiful."

Everyone knows I'm not innocent. But my eyes, my body shape, and my hair all make me look like I've never caused harm in my life.

Bringing the bottle of whiskey to his lips, he takes two large gulps. I watch as his Adam's apple bobs up and down before going to his eyes. They're staring right into mine. He runs his forearm against his mouth, wiping the liquid from his lips before lowering the bottle. His eyes go up and down my body. He walks toward me slowly, and I try to crawl backward, but my muscles feel useless.

"I'm drunk," I slur.

"You are." He smiles, and a chill runs down my spine.

"Don't hurt me," I say in a moment of weakness. I can feel the way I'm unable to defend myself.

Now right next to me, he squats and observes my entire body. He runs his knuckles against my jaw. "Now, that I can't promise."

Before I can take my next breath, he wraps his hand around my jaw and pushes me until I'm completely lying down on the forest ground. There is so much strength in his gesture that my head snaps to the side, my cheek pressed against the pine needles and mud. I can't do anything except lay there as he pins me down. My body is refusing to respond to the calls from my brain, and I look at Caden's blurry, strong form through the corner of my eyes.

There's a low growl in his chest before he lowers his mouth to my ear. "What happens when the hunter catches the prey, Billie?"

With his other hand, he presses the cold bottle of whiskey against my wet pussy. A sharp whimper escapes me. "I-I don't know..."

"It plays with her. Tortures her." He bites my neck sharply, making me cry in pain. I don't miss the fact that the prey is a *her*. "And then it kills her."

Fear grips my stomach, but I know I can tap out anytime. I will if I genuinely need to. I don't feel like it...yet.

He licks the exact spot where he just bit me and lets go of my face to lower himself between my legs. He lifts up my skirt and tilts the bottle just above my mound.

"Ca—shhhit! It's cold!" I try to push him away, but my muscles are not responding.

Pouring the liquid over my pussy, he buries himself against me. I feel his tongue lapping at the whiskey against my clit and let out a low moan.

His warm mouth soothes the cold of the liquid until it must run out because I hear him throw the bottle away. As he keeps licking my clit, I feel two of his fingers pushing into my pussy and grazing against my G-spot.

"Fuck!" I cry out, incapable of keeping quiet. My voice resonates in the forest around us, and I hear a flock of birds flying away.

His incessant tongue lapping at my clit brings me close to exploding. I feel my toes curling in my shoes and my hands grappling with the wet soil around me. Until he pulls away, extracting a scream of frustration out of me.

Grabbing my hips, he flips me around and crushes my face to the floor with a mighty hand at the back of my neck. Again, my cheek is against the cold ground.

I hear the buckle of his belt and the sound of his zipper. His hard cock presses against my entrance, and he pauses.

Time stops, the forest quietens, and the wind around us

halts.

Caden's whisper is as loud as a scream.

"I'm in love with you, Billie."

He pushes into me so violently my stomach lurches forward. I grip pine needles, attempting to crawl away.

Everything is blurry. Did he just say he's in love with me? I cry out as he thrusts into me harshly again. My body is on fire, my soul floating above us and looking down at the savages we've turned into.

The air wheezes out of my lungs, but Caden continues relentlessly. I feel my pussy tightening around him as my heart beats harshly, ringing in my ears. My stomach contracts, my chest desperate to drag in air.

I gasp as my entire world erupts into a million pieces.

I think I blackout for a moment, but it doesn't stop Caden from thrusting inside me like his life depends on it. He continues fucking my limp body as I crash back down from the most beautiful agony I've ever been through. He flips me around again, and I can see the glint of the hunter in his eyes. The monster grins at me, loving the fact that I'm just a lifeless doll for him to use.

He pushes my knees to my chest, getting deeper inside me, and slows down his movements as he starts rolling his hips. Against anything I thought possible, my body warms up again, my muscles tightening, and a band clenching my lower stomach.

I groan as I feel another orgasm building up. I think I tell him I can't do it, though I'm unsure if the words actually come out or just another moan.

Keeping his pace slow, Caden brings me to another climax. He falls onto me as whimpers push past my lips and he swallows them. His tongue caresses mine, and I feel him hiss into my mouth as he releases inside me.

I'm so dead after that; I don't even know how he brings me back to his car. Once inside, he turns it on and blasts the heat toward me.

"Little bee," he says softly, bringing messy, muddy strands of my hair behind my shoulders. "Say something."

I stay silent. My gaze is lost on the forest, the alcohol starting to wear off. Being drunk feels like nothing after the orgasms I just experienced.

I wrap my arms around my stomach, noticing that I'm wearing his leather jacket. When did he put it on? I feel dirty, cold, and sticky between my legs as his cum runs down my inner thighs.

And I know something must be truly fucking wrong with me because I turn to the man who broke me and put me back together, and I smile.

"I'm in love with you too," I murmur so low it's barely audible above the car heating.

I don't miss the way his shoulders relax or how he runs a hand through his messy hair. He grins at me with such genuine happiness that it brings tears to my eyes.

"No one knows me the way you do, Billie. From the worst to the best. You've seen it all, and I would never want anyone else to know."

I swallow, taking my time to digest his words.

"I love it all." I lean toward him and put a hand on his chest before giving him a chaste kiss.

He deepens it, sliding his hands into my hair and forcing his tongue inside my mouth until I'm breathless.

He lets go and frowns. "I want to spend the night with you. The *whole* night. Not bits of it until one of us has to escape because the other's crew is around."

I sigh, dejected. "Me too, but we can't go to my place."

"Not mine either. Sawyer has been busting my balls,

mentioning you too often for my liking."

We stay silent for a few minutes, until an idea comes to my foggy mind. "I know someone who could give us a place for the night."

He turns to me and cocks an eyebrow. "Who?"

"You're not gonna like it." My mouth twists, knowing what his reaction is going to be.

"Who?" he insists.

"Jake." He's about to say no. I see it from the way his lips press together before he talks, so I cut him off. "It's his old foster parents' house. He used to live in the pool house, completely separate from the mansion. He hasn't lived there since senior year. I'm sure he could give us the privacy we want."

"Ugh, Billie," he huffs, raking his fingers through his hair. His posture stiffens, and he shakes his head. "Why are you trying to turn me into a serial killer?"

"I'm not," I laugh, throwing my head back at how extreme he is. "We probably won't even see him."

He takes a deep breath, his nostrils flaring as his jaw tightens. "Fine," he snaps. "Call your fucking ex for a favor."

"Always with the big words," I snort. I grab my phone from the pocket in the sweater and look for Jake's number, hoping it's still the same one. I keep talking as I look through my contacts. "We just fucked a few times. I wouldn't call it a relationship. Ah, found it." My eyes snap up only to cross gazes with a furious Caden.

"Mention you guys fucking once more. Just *one more time,* and I will put a leash around your neck. Every time you say something I don't like, I'll pull hard enough for you to choke."

I gulp, the seriousness of his voice twisting my stomach. "Sorry," I mumble.

"You will be."

28

CADEN

Avril's Song - MOD SUN

"You said we wouldn't see him," I mumble, wrapping a hand at the back of Billie's neck.

In front of us, Jake White opens the front door to what I've been told is his old foster parents' mansion. His eyes grow twice their size when he sees the muddy state we're both in.

"Someone had a lot of fun." His cocky smile spreads across his lips, and he winks at me.

"Look, I don't want to have to kill you. I just want a calm night with my girlfriend. Thank you for giving us a place to stay, but let's walk in silence."

Jake chuckles to himself, and before we can go anywhere, someone calls out from behind him.

"Hi, Billie!"

A small woman about the same size as Billie rounds Jake to stand in front of him. She's Asian, with beautiful dark skin. Her green eyes glint with specks of gold, and she smiles brightly at the both of us. Her head reaches Jake's chest, and I can see the possessive look in his eyes the instant she stands in front of me.

"Jamie," Billie responds, a dash of awkwardness in her voice. "Erm...hi."

"Now, who do we have here," I purr, extending my hand. "Caden King." Jamie's almond-shaped eyes round, and she shifts uncomfortably.

"Oh, hi." She smiles politely and extends her hand, but Jake is quick. He wraps an arm around her from behind and brings her back against his chest.

"We're walking in silence. Remember?" he says low. He lets go of Jamie, puts a hand on the small of her back, and says softly, "Back inside."

"Bye, Jamie," I croon as she retreats inside.

Jake's death stare practically kills me. "Don't make me change my mind."

"About hosting us?" I smile.

"About murdering you."

I cackle a genuine laugh as Billie and I follow him to the backyard from the side of the house.

He leaves us in front of the door.

"She was scared. Why was she so scared of me?" I wonder out loud.

"Jamie?" Billie answers. "Do you not remember her?"

I cock an eyebrow and she continues. "You met her. You even offered to *ram your cock down her throat* if I remember correctly. The night..." She tilts her head to the side, clearly waiting for me to understand what she means.

She crosses her arms over the messy sweater, not impressed.

When it finally comes back to me, I shrug. "I guess I only had eyes for you that night."

"Sure," she snorts. She walks in and throws a *whatever* my

way. It's almost as if that night wasn't as difficult to think about as it used to.

As soon as we're inside, I grab my girl by the hips and lift her until she wraps her legs around my waist. We kiss passionately before I push her against the wall. "Let's shower," I say low before biting her lip.

She grinds her pussy against my belly and sighs. "Okay."

"I'm going to fuck you in there. Then on that kitchen counter behind me. And then in bed."

"Okay," she breathes.

"So agreeable." I smirk against her lips.

"The man I love wants to fuck me three times in a row. Who am I to say no?" She giggles against my mouth, and I want to die and come back to life.

"God, Billie. I love your giggles."

Since neither of us knows the place, I walk around with her petite body hanging onto me. It's not very hard. There's a living room, an open kitchen, and one hallway leading to two bedrooms and a bathroom. As simple as they come.

Just like I promised, I fuck Billie in the shower and on the kitchen counter.

In bed, I make love to her like I never had to anyone. Her gentle moans and whimpers when she comes all over my dick could be the end of me.

In fact, I have no doubt that Billie will be my demise. If we don't leave this town soon, we will both be each other's downfall.

I don't have to think about this tonight, though. For the first time, we can sleep next to each other without worrying about anything. We can just relax and pretend the North Shore doesn't exist.

"Where should we go on vacation?" We're both under the covers naked. She's resting her head on my chest and has a leg curled around my hips. Because I'm obsessed with it, I keep playing with her soft hair. Braiding it, untangling it, rolling and unrolling it around my pinkie.

"Vacation?" she snorts. "Did you win the lottery?"

I shrug. "I'm pretending we made it out."

"Caden," she sighs. "Please, you're hurting both of us when you do this. I'm not competing anymore. It was my only way out."

"I know," I answer tensely. I clench my jaw and release, trying not to snap at her. "But I also want to leave. I have my plan, too."

"Your plan is for one."

"Billie, *please*," I let out in a desperate tone. "Play along. We're in a Stoneview mansion. Just amuse me for *one* night."

She stiffens, staying silent until her shoulder relaxes. "New York City."

"Come on, at least leave the country. It's a big vacation. Unlimited money."

"Fine," she huffs. "Canada. Ontario. I want to see Niagara Falls."

I grin to myself. "Think bigger, baby."

"Caden," she snaps. "You fucking choose since you have big dreams."

I chuckle, and my hand leaves her hair to grab her jaw, pressing her cheeks tightly, a gentle warning to be good.

"Alright," I let my head fall back and close my eyes. "Japan."

"Japan?" she chokes. "That's so far."

"Yeah. First, because we would *have* to take a plane. How cool is that? First time on a plane, and we'll get our membership card to the Mile-High club."

She giggles and turns until she's lying perpendicular to me, the back of her head on my chest, gazing up at me.

"Intense for your first flight ever." I open my eyes and look down at her.

"Go big or go home, baby. Then we'll land in Tokyo and get to a super cool hotel. The kind where we can have a huge suite. I want a sofa in my hotel room."

"And a jacuzzi," she adds.

"Oh yeah. We'll try all their food. Imagine the sort of things they have over there that we never tried here."

"All the mangas we never heard of and won't even understand because we can't read Japanese," she says excitedly.

"We'll find lots of Full Metal Alchemist merch," I add. My stomach flutters with butterflies of hope. It warms my chest and pains my heart because a part of me knows it's just a dream.

But hope is gleaming in Billie's eyes right now, and I grin back at her.

"Oh, oh, I know!" she exclaims. "We can go on the bullet train! Oh my god, that would be crazy." Her delighted voice makes my entire body feel light. I love her, and I want nothing but the best for her.

"That would be so cool," I confirm. "What else?"

"Umm," she quietens while thinking. "I don't know. The night markets?"

"Fuck yeah."

Her voice is lower now. I suggest a few more things, and she nods. Her eyes get heavier and her breathing deeper.

"I wonder if they do an excursion to Mount Fuji," I add as I yawn.

"Uh-huh." She nods as her eyelids drop. Smiling, I run my hand through her hair.

"Do you like sushi?" I ask quietly.

"Don't know." Barely a murmur now.

"What about ramen?"

She's fighting sleep, but her eyes are closed and her voice quasi-inaudible. "Don't know."

I want to google all the Japanese food and keep asking her just to hear her softly spoken words as she tries to stay awake with me.

"We're going to do so many things together, little bee. I promise."

A small smile pulls at her lips, but her breathing is slow, and her head heavy on my chest.

"Goodnight, baby. I love you." She can't hear me, but I like knowing I said it again.

I want to repeat it until my voice is raw and she can't stand it anymore.

I love you.

I love you.

I love you.

29

CADEN

Problems - Jake Daniels

I park my car in front of the three-story house and look around me. They're not Stoneview rich around here, but they've got it good for sure.

The South bank of Silver Falls is mainly for middle-class families and the house I'm looking at screams upper-middle class. I leave my car and check the address I've been texted. Dylan, that kid who thinks of himself as a TV presenter and films all of Billie's fights to put them on his channel, *FollowTheFight*, has been helping me. When I told him what I was up to, he found all the info I needed. It seems he genuinely likes Billie—a little too much, in my opinion. But the kid is helping me, so I can't really kill him.

Now that I'm sure I'm at the right place, I walk to the gated property and ring their bell.

"*Yes?*" A sweet voice comes through the interphone.

"Hi, my name's Caden. I was told Carla Rupert lives here?"

"*What is it for?*"

"I'm coming on behalf of the Silver Falls MMA gym. It's regarding her next fight with Killer Clover."

"*Oh! Come on in, then!*" The voice says excitedly as the gates open for me.

I walk to the entrance and a middle-aged blonde woman greets me. "Hi, I'm Lana. I'm Carla's stepmother. Carla is in her gym training right now. I'll walk you to the back."

The girl has her own personal gym. While Billie must count her cents to put gas in her car and get to the shitty boxing gym Dickie owns, Carla Rupert has her *own gym*. Talk about unfairness.

I smile politely and let her walk me to the back of the house, into the backyard, and to their small guest house. The one they turned into a training gym.

Lana knocks on the door, but the loud music must mean Carla can't hear anything. She opens the door and waves me in. "Just go in. She is somewhere in there."

"Would you like to warn her I'm coming? I don't want her to think a stranger broke in."

Honestly, I don't give a shit, but I have to keep up appearances.

"Oh, I'm not allowed in there. I'm her stepmother...you know how kids are at that age."

What fucking age? I've got no idea how old she is.

"Ain't that right," I smile.

Turning my back to Lana, I walk into the gym and notice Carla hitting a bag at the back. Before going to her, I grab her phone connected to the speakers and turn off her music.

She looks away from the bag and at me.

"Who are you?" she gasps. Her eyes look me up and down, taking in the tattoos on my arms and scarred knuckles. She notices the letters I've got there. K.I.N.G.

She gulps, understanding who she's facing, whereas Lana had no clue.

"I'm Caden," I smile. "I want to talk about your next fight."

She puts two and two together quicker than I expect her to. "You're here because I beat up Billie. I won fair and square. You can't retaliate after a fight—"

"I'm not here to hurt you," I cut her off. "I'm here to ask for a favor."

"A favor?"

"I want you to pull out of the competition."

She chuckles and takes off her gloves slowly. "If I forfeit, Killer Clover will be the winner. Not Billie."

"Not forfeit. Pull out and put in a special request to give your win to Billie."

"It's just an amateur boxing competition," she mocks me.

"For you," I snap.

Narrowing her eyes at me, she takes her time to think. She drops her gloves to the floor and comes closer to me.

"What do I get in return?" she finally says, looking me up and down.

"That's a question only you can answer. What do you want?"

"Thirty thousand dollars." Her answer is so fast I almost lose my breath.

"*Thirty*—are you out of your fucking mind?"

"You clearly love the girl to come all the way here and ask this. I think thirty grand will be my cheapest offer."

"I could simply kill you next time you go a little too close to the North Shore. Problem solved. So how about you rethink that offer?"

She laughs and turns her back to me to grab a bottle of water and a towel. "Yeah, you could do that..." She dabs the towel on her forehead and leaves it around her neck. "But then again, our security cameras probably have you walking inside this house. My witch of a stepmother talked to you, and," she points at a camera in the corner of the room, "that one saw you, too. It'll be a bit weird if I suddenly disappear, won't it? Surely the cops' first instinct will be to look at the gangbanger who visited me in the days prior to my death."

I put my hands in my pockets and tilt my head to the side. "You're a little bitch, aren't you?" I observe casually.

"No, actually, I just know an opportunity when I see one." She cocks a hip and takes a sip of her water.

"What the fuck would you need thirty grand for? Doesn't your daddy buy you anything you wish for? Don't you have an unlimited bank account or something?"

"God," she snorts. "I know you guys on the North Shore probably have never heard of it, but see, there's this thing called a trust fund. We usually don't have access to them until a certain age. Mine is twenty-one, and I want to leave this shithole before then, so I need that kind of money now."

"Shithole?" I choke. "You live in a fucking mansion on the south bank."

"Gilded cages are still cages," she spits with venom.

"Please, what could you possibly need 30k for?"

She comes face-to-face with me, her cheeks red. "I'm being married off to the first Stoneview douchebag they found since my fucking evil stepmother wants to climb up the social ladder. Not that it's any of your business, but I'm using the money to join my girlfriend on the other side of the country, and I'm never coming back here."

I lick my lips and let a chilling smile spread on my lips. "Ever met that girlfriend?"

"We've been talking online for years."

"Your *girlfriend* could be a fifty-year-old pervert. Did your parents never teach you about online safety?"

Her eyes narrow at me, and she retreats back. "Guess I'm staying in that MMA tournament, then."

"Little bitch," I say calmly, the tone of my voice showing that I respect her for standing up to me. "I'll get you your fucking money. Just give me a week or two."

"Take all the time you need. I'll be here."

The moment I'm back in my car, my mask falls. My heart accelerates and my hands turn clammy. I don't have that kind of money, although I know exactly how to get my hands on it. I'd never done it before because I still had some self-respect left in me, but I don't fucking care about myself anymore. I just want Billie to reach her full potential. Nolan tried to take that away from her, and I can't accept it. Killing him wasn't enough. I also need to get her back on track to leave our hellhole.

In the three weeks following our date, Billie and I have become inseparable. So much that we both sneaked out of our respective parties to spend New Year's Eve together.

In the new year, I convinced her to get back to the boxing gym. I drive her every morning after her run. She didn't go back to college, but she did cut her waitressing job to part-time.

And me? I stopped 'tutoring'. Meaning I also stopped seeing the Stoneview moms who use my body for themselves. Over the last year, they've offered me to participate in the parties organized by one of the Stoneview couples. Rich people exchanging partners and wanting a young man desperate for money to participate...how bad can it get? The money is big—twenty-five grand. I can add five thousand of my own savings to that, and Carla will let Billie back into the competition.

Grabbing my phone, I call a couple I've never actually had sex with but that I know organizes those parties.

"*You've reached Gerald Baker,*" a man says as he picks up.

"My name's Caden King. I know Chantale Malone well. She told me about your parties."

The mic on the other side scratches before I hear a door, and then he talks again.

"*Who sent you?*"

"I told you, Chantale Malone. She said your parties pay well."

I can hear a smile in his voice when he finally understands I would be part of the entertainment, not of the participating audience. "*I see. How old are you?*"

"How old do you want me to be?" I try to say as calmly as possible. I fucking hate these people.

"*That's what I love to hear,*" he cackles loudly on the other side.

"How much?" I ask to double-check.

"Twenty-five thousand for the whole night. Eight p.m. to six a.m. You'll sign a non-disclosure agreement. You see nothing, hear nothing. You'll be there for our pleasures, and that only. No safe words, no backing out."

I run a hand through my hair, messing it up. My jaw clenches and unclenches, and I close my eyes. My car smells of Billie from when I dropped her off this morning. If I focus, I can almost hear that giggle of hers I love so much.

"Alright," I say through gritted teeth. "Just send me a date and an address. I'll be there."

"*Not so fast. Send me a picture of yourself.*"

"Are you for—" I cut myself off, not wanting to lose the job.

This is already fucking embarrassing, and it hasn't even started.

I open my camera and take a selfie, adding as much as possible of my torso before sending it to him. A few seconds later, he talks again.

"*Very good. You'll hear from me soon.*"

He hangs up, and I'm already left with an icky feeling.

30

CADEN

Night People - You Me At Six

She's so beautiful when she trains. Billie is the strongest woman I know, and I love that it doesn't show when you see her. Her big doe-eyes and her small size make her look bite-able. But in the ring? No one stands a chance against her. I'm not sure how long I stand at the back, biting my lip as my gaze travels up and down her body while she spars with Dickie. I am so fucking glad when he finally leaves. Especially since I'm rock-hard under the black ripped jeans I'm wearing. I barely don't even give her time to take her gloves off when I jump in the ring. She's focused on staring at the pictures on the wall, her back to me and her earphones in. I bet she's torturing herself thinking of the professional MMA fighters and knowing she's not one of them.

Yet.

"Hi, little bee," I whisper in her ear as I take out one of her earphones. She startles and turns around, a smile brightening her features when she sees me.

"Hi," she says, still panting. "When did you get here?"

My eyes go down to the hard-on in my jeans and hers follow. "Long enough." I smile wickedly before grabbing her leggings at the waist and dragging her to me.

"Caden," she giggles. Fuck, that's exactly what I needed to hear. She looks up at me with her big eyes and goes on her toes, so I bend down to catch her lips with mine.

"Who knew this ring would ever see you get fucked on it," I growl against her lips. She smiles and takes a step back.

"It's not going to see me get fucked. This is Dickie's gym, we're not having sex here." She tries to take another step back, but my other hand grabs her waist, pulling her to me. "Tsk, tsk. Where do you think you're going?"

She starts trying to remove her boxing gloves, but I stop her. "Keep them on."

"You want to have sex?" she says with a cheeky smile. "Fight me. If you win, I'll let you do whatever you want to me." She points to a box with two pairs of gloves in it. "Those are clean. Dickie literally bought them this morning. Completely unused."

I lick my lips and tilt my head to the side. "Anything I want?"

I watch her squirm on the spot as she nods. "Anything."

"Remember you asked for it," I chuckle.

"What? What's that for?" Her voice is stern, challenging me.

"Nothing." I shake my head as I separate from her and grab the gloves.

"You're either laughing because you think it'll be too easy for you or because you're scared to take me on."

"Billie." I smirk softly. "How could I be scared of a little thing like you?" I mock her.

She snorts at my words and nods like she hears this all the time.

"You're gonna get hurt," I reply while still putting the gloves on. "And you know how much I love hurting you."

We tap gloves, and a second later, we're dancing around each other. I can't be the first to attack since I have that alarm at the back of my head telling me that I should not be hitting a girl about half my size. I avoid her first punch and gently tap back on her ribs. She doesn't wince, barely even felt it.

"Come on, Cade. Fight me," she growls.

Billie isn't the kind of girl who likes it when people go easy on her. That much I've learned since meeting her. She grew up on the North Shore, after all. She understood from a young age that if she wasn't strong, she was dead. Or worse.

"Come on," she shouts as she punches my shoulder. "Hurt me!"

My cock stirs at her words. It enjoys hurting her way too fucking much. God forgive us, we are so fucked up. I pounce and hit her a little harder. We both delve into it, both getting a few punches. I feel fine, barely breaking a sweat until she gets me right in the cheekbone, making me stumble back.

Fuck, she's fast.

"What's wrong, baby?" she mocks me with a pout. "Scared someone my size is going to hurt you?"

She's on me again the next second, hitting me in the stomach and then the eyebrow.

"Shit," I hiss when I finally manage to counter her blows.

"I must admit," she says playfully, bouncing on her feet. "It gets me wet to punch you. I think you deserve it."

My mouth drops open and she uses that moment of shock to strike again. I get a punch to the jaw and have to take another step back. It wakes me up, and I get back at her. Straight. Straight. Hook. Uppercut. I only put half of my strength, even though Billie is now sweating and panting.

"It makes me hard when you pant, Billie." Her eyes widen

slightly, and I strike her stomach, struggling to hold back on that one. She hunches over with a pained grunt. She falls to the floor, into a ball, and rolls onto her side.

My heart drops from my chest as I run to her.

"Shit, you okay?" I kneel by her side and lean over. She sounds like she's struggling to breathe. I quickly take my gloves off and try to roll her onto her back so I can see her face. "Billie, say something."

"Boo!" she screams as she suddenly turns around, giggling. She wraps her gloved hands around my neck and pulls me down on top of her. "That hurt," she murmurs once our mouths are close, lips brushing.

Fuck, she nearly gave me a heart attack. I thought I'd broken her.

"I thought you liked it when I hurt you," I whisper back. Only now I'm a little lost in my own thoughts.

Since when did I start fearing for her safety so much? When did I start falling so badly I wanted to punch myself for hurting her?

Hell, I'm going to sell my body for her to get out of here.

It's bad how much I'm into her.

"I fucking love it," she grins. Her big brown eyes are hooded. They're so huge it's the only thing on her body that makes her look innocent. "Hurt me more."

"This fight is over."

"I wasn't talking about the fight." Her voice drips with sexual need and my cock hardens again.

"You want me to make you hurt, baby?" I rub her pussy roughly through her leggings, and she lets out a quiet moan.

"You want me to make you my little slut in this ring? Do whatever I want?"

She tries to answer, but instead, a louder moan comes out as I drop my head to her neck and start biting.

I lift her sports bra in a quick gesture. I only briefly stare at the NSC dagger tattoo between her breasts before dropping my teeth to her nipple. I bite hard enough to make her gasp. She pulls at my hair, but I don't let go. She can't do much with her hands still in her gloves anyway.

"Don't beg for things you can't handle," I say when I finally release her. I lick the reddened bud that's got the mark of my teeth and she shivers under me.

"I can handle it," she whispers. "There's nothing I can't handle."

And isn't that what makes her perfect for me?

Gripping her leggings, I pull them down before ripping off her panties.

"Why do you always wear those little cotton panties like some sort of innocent girl?" I lean down and bite her other breast. "You know you're a little slut for me, Billie."

I kiss my way down her body until my head is between her legs and I take her clit into my mouth. I suck, nip, and bite until she's writhing under me, her hips bucking against my mouth. Her wetness coats my lips and I lick it off with my tongue. There's more though, she's dripping onto my face and I delight in the fact that I'm the man who makes her so wet.

Pulling away, I undo my jeans and stroke my cock, watching as her eyes stay fixed on it.

"Something you want, maybe?" I say as I watch her stomach trembling from uneven breaths.

She bites her lip and nods. "Yeah," she finally puffs. "You."

I'm not in the mood to make her beg when I can barely hold myself back from destroying her. I enter her in one sharp thrust and sigh in pleasure when she gasps. She feels so tight, accommodating to me like she was made to have me inside her.

I move in and out of her in a hurried rhythm, not hiding

how much I need her and the effect she has on me. I lust after this girl, I just want to bury myself inside her forever, and physical touch is the only way I know how to show her for now.

The moment I feel her breathing shorten and the way her body spasms around me, I allow myself to explode inside her. I wrap her arms around my back, forcing her to hold me tightly as I thrust one last time and pull out before falling on top of her.

I'm dressed and ready to go while Billie is still blow-drying her hair, when I receive a text. It's from Gerald Baker. I had to wait less than twenty-four hours before he contacted me. I only called him yesterday. My muscles tense as I read.

> Baker: This week, Friday.

Checking that Billie can't see anything, I text back.

> Caden: I want half the cash now. Rest after the night.

> Baker: Come pick it up at my house like a good boy.

I'm gonna fucking throw up. Do I get to kill the fucker at the end of the night?

He sends me his address in the next text, and I use the occasion to be on my phone to message Carla. I ask her to start talking to the organizers of the tournament if I give her half the money before Friday. Her 'okay' comes instantly, and I feel a wave of relief wrapping around me.

"Caden?"

I pocket my phone as Billie comes to me. "Yes, little bee?"

She grabs my hand and peers up at me with puppy eyes.

"Can we get milkshakes on the way back?"

This. This is why I'm doing it—the simplicity of her happiness.

It'll all be worth it when she leaves this shit town and blossoms into the woman I know she can become.

"What about your fighter's diet and all that?" I say as I grab her duffel bag.

She shrugs. "It's calories. I'm not too worried, anyway. I won't be fighting anytime soon. It doesn't really matter which weight category I'm in."

I nod, not mentioning that it will matter very soon. One milkshake won't change anything.

"The only problem with your milkshake is that you get strawberry, and that's disgusting," I laugh.

"*You're* disgusting," she fights back, pretending to be hurt.

"Are you trying to get yourself in trouble with me?" I bend down, putting my shoulder against her stomach and grabbing her as I stand back up with her over my shoulder.

"Caden!" she shrieks.

"Alright, I think I've got all my stuff," I say calmly.

"Put me down. I hate being carried."

"Little bee, I'm just grabbing all my possessions and going to my car. What are you talking about?"

"I'm not your possession, Caden. Put me down," she growls.

"I'm loving the damsel-in-distress look on you," I laugh as I walk out of the gym, not putting her down until I sit her in my car.

She goes to punch me in the stomach, but I grab her wrist and kiss the inside of it. "You taste delicious," I say, before inhaling her scent. "I want to eat you right now."

"Can it wait until after my milkshake?"

I chuckle against her skin and nod. "Whatever you want, baby."

I walk to my side and we're off for milkshakes. I have to drive all the way to the south bank, so we don't go anywhere that's either her crew's territory or mine. I don't care, it's worth it, and it's more time with her.

She slides into a booth while I order our milkshakes and return to the table with her strawberry and my chocolate.

"Are you fighting at the warehouse?" she asks, her brows furrowed and her eyes still on her phone.

"Oh, yeah. Tomorrow night. It's not the Death Cage or anything. It's just easy money against some loser from NS—" I cut myself off, pinching my lips when I realize what I'm saying.

I'm sitting next to her rather than on the other side of the booth, and I can practically feel her anger simmering beneath her skin. Her jaw works from side to side as she looks up at me with a deadly stare. "And who's the loser from NSC?" she says spitefully.

"I don't know," I shrug. "Look, I'm not doing this because it's NSC. I'm doing it because it's money, and I'm guaranteed the win."

"That sounds pretty cocky, don't you think?"

"You're not the only unbeatable fighter out there, little Scott. I've never lost a fight, and I'm not about to start tomorrow. I'm sorry, but your NSC boys can't do shit against me in the ring."

"You're fighting Xi!" she rages. "Emma just told me."

I can't help the smile from spreading on my face. "Am I?"

"Caden," she says sternly. "He's barely recovered from the stab wounds. The ones *you* inflicted on him."

"Then I guess he shouldn't be fighting," I say calmly before drinking from my milkshake.

"Don't be a dick," she continues. "Just don't do the fight."

"Tell your stepbrother not to fight me. Who knows if I'll feel as generous as the last time I saw him."

She nods, not saying anything further. We finish our milkshakes in silence and I know I haven't heard the end of this, but I don't add anything.

We're in front of the diner when I can't take the silent treatment anymore. "Nothing else to add about that fight, then?" I ask while closing the door behind me.

"Nope."

"Come on, little bee. Let it all out."

"I have nothing to say," she smiles innocently. "You go ahead and fight Xi. And when he gets hurt, I'll go home with him to help heal his wounds. He can stay with me in my room while he gets better."

I stop in my tracks, and a step later she stops too, turning back to me. "What?" she asks, pretending she didn't say all this to piss me off.

"Oh, little bee," I smile. It's when she sees that smile that she retreats, unsure she's safe with me anymore. "Who else but you would be silly enough to try and make me jealous?"

I wrap an arm around her shoulders and calmly walk her to the car. As soon as we're inside and I lock the doors, she gives me a frightened stare. Her expression is like a deer caught in headlights.

Pretty sure Bambi never looked as scared as she does now.

I put the car in drive and get on the road again.

"Are you taking me home?" she asks quietly after a few minutes of driving. She knows I'm not. We're not going her way at all.

"I think you know the answer to that question."

"Where, then?"

Choosing to let her simmer in her fear for a little longer, I don't answer.

"Caden, I've got a morning shift tomorrow. I can't stay out forever."

"Not forever," I taunt. "Just enough for me to teach you a lesson."

She shifts in her seat, and I glance at her, watching the way her thighs tighten.

"Do you get turned on knowing you're about to be punished?"

"No," she huffs out. "You're crazy."

"I am so fucking crazy when it comes to you, baby," I mutter. "Obsessive jealousy, keep-you-to-myself-forever crazy. You've seen nothing till now. But you just wait."

Ten minutes later, we're parked in front of the place I've been dying to take her to for weeks. I'd managed to keep hold of myself until tonight. I guess no more.

I walk to her side and grab her upper arm tightly, forcing her out of the car. "What are you doing," she hisses.

"Making sure you don't run away."

As I expected, her eyes widen when she sees the tattoo parlor. She tries to stop, but I keep walking, and she's forced to follow.

"What the fuck!" Her attempts to get away from my hold are getting my dick hard.

I push the door open, and I'm greeted by Nick, the man who has done every one of my tattoos.

"Caden," he cheers. "I wasn't expecting you, man."

"Cancel the rest of your night."

He looks at Billie then back at me. "You or her?"

"Her."

"Absolutely fucking not," Billie resists some more. She glares at Nick. "Touch me, and I'm punching your lights out."

There's a slight pause while I smile to myself. "She's capable," I tell Nick. "But she won't because I'll be holding her down."

"Caden," she snarls. "Get this idea out of your head. Right now."

I drag her to the tattoo chair at the back of the shop, and her fighting gets more resilient. "Stop...I'm serious, *stop*."

It's so easy to force her small form onto the chair that I almost feel bad. I watch Nick lock the shop and draw the blinds before coming to the back.

"Stop fighting me, little bee," I threaten low.

"You're about to mark me permanently," she fumes back. "I'll fight all I fucking want."

"But it's so useless," I say deadpan. "I'm just dying to see what will happen when you try to make me jealous after tonight."

"I wasn't trying to make you jealous," she grits.

"That's a lie, and we both know it."

Her eyes go to my belt as I slowly unbuckle it.

"W-what are you doing?" She tries to get off the chair just as I place myself by her head and grab her hair. I tug her back down so quickly she shrieks from the surprise.

"Caden," she huffs. The panic is starting to settle now that she realizes this is going to happen and there's nothing she can do about it. "I was...I was just annoyed. You know I would never let Xi stay in my room. I just wanted to convince you not to do the fight." She winces when I yank harder, forcing her to stay lying down.

Letting go of her hair for a split second, I slip my belt out of the loops and bring it around her throat before pulling at both ends.

"Now, if you don't want to choke, you'll have to lay down and let Nick tattoo you. Can you be a good girl for me?"

"I don't want a tattoo," she coughs. She brings her hands to the belt, trying to ease it off her neck, but I don't relent. "Please, I got the message."

"No, you didn't," I say low. My voice is hoarse from the need to teach her how badly she belongs to me.

Nick settles next to her and glances up at me. "Alright, what do we want?"

"Nothing!" Billie shouts back.

"Don't make me gag you," I growl then look at Nick again. "She's got an NSC tattoo between her tits. I want you to add a crown to it."

"No!" She twists. "Caden, don't fucking do this."

"Go on," I tell Nick. "Cut her top open."

As soon as Nick gets close to her with scissors, she grabs his wrist. "Do this, and you're dead."

I grab both ends of the belt in one hand and grasp her jaw with the other. I tighten my grip on the belt until she's peering up at me, choking.

And I smile down at her.

"Do you want to die, Billie?"

Her cheeks are getting red as she unsuccessfully tries to breathe. She shakes her head and lets go of Nick before tapping aimlessly at her neck.

"No?"

"C—" she tries to cough my name.

"Fucking sit still before I choke the life out of you."

Squeezing her eyes, she nods desperately, and I loosen my hold slightly. She takes in a ragged breath, tears lighting up her pretty eyes. "Please," she whispers.

Ignoring her plea, I nod at Nick, and he starts cutting her top open.

She's not wearing a bra, and I can't stand my tattoo artist seeing her that way. "Hide my tits, Billie. Cover them with your hands."

This time, instead of fighting me, she's more than happy to listen as she cups her small breasts with her hands.

I hate that tattoo of a dagger that marks her as NSC, but I can't do anything about it. It's the gang she was born into. I can add my mark to it, though. And it's not the only ink she's getting tonight.

"Caden," she tries one last time as Nick dips the needle in the ink. "Please, I'm sorry..."

"Here she is," I sigh softly, caressing her hairline. "I love to hear you apologize for being a bad girl." I smile down at her before turning to Nick and nodding.

"No," she cries out as the buzzing resonates around us.

It takes him about twenty minutes to add a crown around the handle of her NSC dagger.

Billie cries silently the whole time, and I know deep down I should feel bad. Except all it does is get me rock-hard.

He puts a sticky protective film on top of it and then looks at me for the rest. "I texted you what I want on her ribs."

A minute later, Nick is back at work. Billie keeps avoiding my gaze. She's looking at an imaginary point in the shop, wincing when Nick starts tattooing her rib just below her left tit.

When he's done, he puts a film on that area too, and I take a picture of it. My hands are practically shaking from the high of knowing she's now marked as mine forever, and there's nothing she can do about it. I show the picture to Billie and smile at her.

"So? Do you like your new tattoo?"

Her eyes grow so wide I'm worried they might pop out of her head. She whispers as she reads, "Owned by Caden

King..." All the hope leaves her body as her head hits the chair and she closes her eyes tightly. "Why?" she rasps.

"Keep-you-to-myself-forever kind of crazy, little bee," I murmur before dropping a kiss on her forehead.

"I hate you."

"Hate me all you want. You're still mine." I buckle the belt around the head of the seat rather than letting it go.

"What are you doing?" she panics.

I ignore her. "Give me some tape, Nick." He rolls his chair to the side and throws me some duct tape.

I bind each of her wrists to the arms of the tattoo chair and she starts fighting me with all she has. "Caden!" she screams with fury. She twists, only there's nowhere to go with her arms and neck fastened to the chair.

"Is it uncomfortable?" I say, pointing at the tattoo on her ribs. "Did it hurt?" Nick had to press his fingertips to her stomach to do his job since she was trying to move. He had to press hard to make sure she wouldn't mess up the art, and now there are little red dots where he touched her. I don't like that.

I don't like that another man touched her skin.

Fuck. I'm deep into this shit.

"It's a fucking tattoo. Do you honestly think it was comfortable?" she seethes.

"Do you need a magic kiss, little bee?"

"Fuck you and your magic kisses!"

I lick my lips, not able to contain my hunger for her. "Why do I love it so much when you're mad at me and can't do shit about it?"

"Because you're *fucked in the head*!" she shrieks.

I nod. "I agree. I was a little crazy before I fell for you. Now I'm completely deranged. I'm a maniac for you, Billie."

"This isn't falling for me," she pants, still fighting her bonds. "This...is...it's..."

"Crazy? Obsessive? Wild? I fucking feel it all, trust me."

She screeches in frustration when I lower her jeans. "Don't you fucking dare."

"I think we both know that you not wanting something never stopped me." Going on my knees in front of the chair, I rid her of her jeans and panties before spreading her legs.

"I'm going to kill you," she snarls. Her eyes go to Nick, but mine don't leave her beautiful pussy when I say. "Go write up my bill, Nick."

He leaves the room in a split second. He's barely gone when I dip my tongue in Billie's pussy.

"Fuck," she groans, trying to fight the pleasure.

"What made you wet, little bee?" I could drown in her all day. I want to spend the rest of my life on my knees in front of her, making her crazy from orgasms and forcing her to love me despite everything working against us.

I push my tongue in and out of her before pulling away slightly. "Is it because I've made you mine completely? Because you know I've ruined you for anyone else?"

I lick her clit slowly, making her squirm with need. "Is it because you really, truly love it when I force you to do things out of my infatuation for you?"

She doesn't answer. She can't because my tongue unleashes on her clit before alternating between dipping inside her and flicking her bundle of nerves like a starved man.

She moans loudly under me when I finally take it between my lips and start sucking, applying slight pressure with my teeth. She screams my name, coming undone on my tongue as her hips push into my face.

I can barely stop when she begs me to, shouting that it's too much. I just want to stay here forever. I just want her to understand how much she means to me. That if I force my love on her, it's only because that's all I have in me. Love for her. Passion for her body. Fascination for her mind. Lust for her soul.

When I pull away and gaze up at her, she's a mess on the chair. Her pussy is so wet it must be uncomfortable. She fought the tape and the belt, and her skin is now reddened on her wrists and neck. Her cheeks are flushed, her ponytail a mess falling to the side of her head, and her chest is heaving. But her eyes? They're bright from the orgasm. Vivid from new feelings flooding her body and her brain. Feelings I'm sure, just like me, she can't control.

"Fuck, that was hot," I hear behind me. Billie freezes at Nick's voice. Her legs cross, and she fights the tape around her wrists again.

"Oh my god," she panics.

My eyes narrow into slits as I slowly stand up and grab my switchblade. I cut off Billie's binds and undo the belt.

"Cover yourself," I say calmly. "I thought I told you to leave," I add, turning to Nick.

"Man," he chuckles. "You're eating out an NSC girl on my tattoo chair. Right after having me tattoo between her tits. I think I deserved a tip."

"You think?" I ask slowly. "I guess we have different opinions, then."

"I guess," he shrugs. His eyes go to Billie behind me. "Into sharing?"

Nick is a big guy. Tattooed from head to toe, obviously. He killed a few men for us in the past. We bring them here, and he takes care of them in the back.

"No." My voice has dropped so much I could swallow darkness and spit it back in his face. "Not into sharing."

"Eh," he slaps his hands to the side of his thighs. "Next

time, maybe. I got your bill ready at the front, man. Feel free to...finish whatever you started."

"Yeah, I was planning to," I grunt. "I was going to fuck my girl while I had her tied to your tattoo chair, but you kind of got in the way."

Nick lets out a throaty laugh, missing the fact that I don't find any of this funny.

"Now," I add. "You've touched my girl. Seen her tits and watched her orgasm. And the funny thing is," I laugh to myself. "You think you're gonna live after that."

"Caden," Billie tries to intervene as I sense her standing up.

I point a finger at her, not even bothering to look at her. "Sit back down."

I hear her slump back into the chair and point my opened switchblade at Nick. "I don't even know how some of the Kings still haven't heard our new rules."

I take three steps toward him, grab the back of his neck and stab him in the stomach. "No touching her." I pull the knife out and stab him in his ribs. "No watching her." The next stab is right in his heart. "No disrespecting her."

Just for the sake of it, I slash his throat. His blood splashes onto me, and I'm forced to take a step back and let him fall.

I turn to Billie. She's sitting on the stool next to the chair and staring at me with wild eyes and her mouth agape. She's holding her ripped top to her chest and has buttoned up her jeans.

"You—"

"Take your clothes off," I cut her off.

"You can't just kill people for—"

"Did you not hear what I just said?"

I point the knife at her, and she shoots up. Putting one hand in front of herself. "You're insane. You've completely lost it, Caden. You *asked* him to tattoo me. *Asked* him to cut my top. Of course, he was going to see me topless!"

"No one listens when I tell them not to fucking get close to you. What else do you expect me to do? They should have spread the word by now."

"No one can spread the word because you're always killing them. Dead men can't talk and warn others that Caden King has lost all sanity. You make no fucking sense!"

The fear in her beautiful brown eyes feeds the monster in me. It feeds the wicked, possessive being I can't control around her.

"No, baby. I make no sense anymore," I growl low. "It's you. Don't you get that? It's you messing with my brain, messing with my sanity. I had so little of it and look at me now." I smile widely, and I can't even imagine what I look like to her. "Utterly in love."

31

BILLIE

SWEAT - PatrickReza

His smile is demonic. He looks like the devil, covered in blood and proud of it.

Caden feeds from people's fears and mistakes. He waits for anyone to provoke him in any way and pounces to nourish the monster in him. And the way he's looking at me right now? I'm his next prey and am not getting out of this tattoo parlor before he gets his way with me.

If Caden is the devil ready to destroy me, and I'm dying for him to devastate me, what does that mean? If he's crazy, what am I? Like him?

Worse?

"Your clothes, little bee," he says impatiently. "I want them off, and I want you on all fours. I'm going to fuck you covered in his blood." He grabs his dick through his jeans and his crazy eyes meet mine.

I drop my top to the floor and undo my jeans.

What am I doing?

Constantly jumping to action when Caden orders

something. Getting wet from him forcing me to do things I don't want to do.

He tattooed me.

Marked me as nothing but his. I'm not a person, not a human being with feelings and needs and wants. In his mind, I'm just his property, and he marked me as such.

Owned by Caden King. That tattoo on my ribs and the crown added to my NSC dagger make me want to cry...and yet I've let him fuck me and make me feel all sorts of ways.

And I want more.

So much more.

Finally naked, I lower to my knees in front of him. When he gets close to me, I put my hands on the button of his jeans.

"Would you look at that," he says as his hand grabs my ponytail. "I've finally made a good, obedient girl out of you."

I pull his throbbing dick out of his boxers, and my heart speeds up. How can I have gone from being scared of it to salivating in front of it? What has this man done to me?

"Open, baby," he rasps.

I brush my lips against it and slowly open my mouth. Hesitantly, I wrap my tongue against his tip, then move to the underside before looking up. His eyes are bright from lust and impatience, though he doesn't move and doesn't push me. He knows this is a big step for me. This is how it all started. And he's not forcing me anymore.

No matter how fucked it is, I'm doing it out of my own need, and I don't even want to think about what that makes me.

I wrap my lips around him and take him into my mouth, running my tongue under his dick as I feel his hand tighten in my hair and the hiss from his mouth warming the top of my head. I look up to watch him looking down at me, so much love in his gaze I feel it all the way to my toes.

There is a dead man behind him. A man he killed for me. Out of his own irrationality, but for me nonetheless. And it warms my stomach all the way down to between my legs.

I feel my pussy tightening as I take it further into my mouth and down my throat.

"Fuck," he rasps.

Keeping my lips firm around him, I pull forward and back, bobbing my head up and down as I do so and making sure to keep my tongue running along his shaft.

"Shit," he grunts after a minute. "You're gonna make me come." He pulls away from me in a sudden movement. Completely out of reality, I follow and end up falling on all fours.

"Don't you move," he says in a rush. He walks behind and lowers himself to his knees.

"Oh my god, Billie. You are so fucking wet. You're dripping down your thighs."

"I know," I moan as he runs his fingers against my clit. "I need you."

"Need me to what," he says low as he inserts a finger inside me. He's so slow, torturing me with a promise of pleasure.

"To...to..." I pant.

"Say it."

"I need you to fuck me, Caden. Please just...just fuck me the way I love."

"How is that, baby?" he says, now a finger deep inside me. He inserts another one and my elbows buckle below my weight.

"Hard," I moan slowly. "Please..."

He removes his fingers and I feel the tip of his hard dick against my entrance.

"Oh god," I breathe out. "Yes." I try to push against him, but his hands come to my hips.

"Tsk, tsk. You've not been good enough yet."

"Caden," I huff with frustration.

"Mm, my name on your lips when you're desperate, is priceless."

"Caden," I groan as he shifts and his dick slides between my pussy lips. The tip hits my clit and I see stars.

"Who does this pussy belong to, Billie?"

"You, Caden." He thrusts inside me slowly, and I want to die from need alone.

"Who does this body belong to?"

"You, Caden," I groan as he pushes some more. "Oh my god..." I can hardly breathe from the pleasure overwhelming me.

"Who do you belong to, Billie? Who fucking owns you? Who's got their name tattooed on you? Their mark on your *fucking* heart?" His growl is animalistic as he moves deeper inside me.

"You!" I scream from pleasure. "You, Caden," I pant as he starts moving inside me.

He slams in and out of me, using so much strength I almost fall right on my face. My muscles are turning into jelly from the pleasure, and when he curves his hips and hits my G-spot, my arms give up as I moan loudly.

He catches me at the waist and wraps a hand around my throat, bringing me up so my back is to his chest. He continues fucking me relentlessly. I can feel sweat coating my back as I get closer to coming. It's when he drops a featherlight kiss in the crook of my neck that I explode.

We got tested and I got the shot, so it's without any guilt that I come undone as he comes inside me. He groans and stills just before we both fall to the floor, and he flips me over.

He doesn't give me any respite. Climbing on top of my naked body, he grabs my wrists in both his hands and places them on the floor on either side of my head before unleashing his mouth on my breasts. He bites and sucks, covering me in hickeys. He's a starving beast as he makes his way up my neck and redecorates my jaw with the necklace he always leaves. It was starting to fade; better ensure people can still see it.

"Enough," I grunt, bucking my hips. "Caden, that's enough marking me."

"Never," he rumbles in my ear like a madman.

"If we're going to give this a real shot, I can't always be walking around town with hickeys on my jaw."

He pauses and straightens up, peering down at me with a confused face.

"Say that again."

I frown as I repeat, "I can't always be walking—"

"The other bit."

A smile tugs at my lips as I repeat myself. "If we're gonna give this a real shot."

"Yes," he smiles wickedly. "I want to hear that again."

I giggle, and his eyes soften. The gentle, human version of him is coming back to reality. He lays down on me, nuzzling against my neck. He releases one of my wrists and undoes my ponytail, bringing my thick hair to his face before he inhales deeply. He keeps a hold of it and looks at me.

"Say it again."

"We're gonna give this a shot, Cade. *Us.*"

The things this man gets me to say when I've just had an orgasm...it's almost like I meant them all along. Almost like I can only be myself in his arms after he's pushed me to see the truth.

"Mm, my girl." His hand tightens around the ends of my hair, and he breathes me in again. "Mine."

We hug for long minutes until I start shivering from being naked on a cold floor. Caden helps me up and back into my panties and jeans. I have no top anymore, so he takes off his t-shirt. My eyes stay stuck on his abs for a few seconds before something else catches my eyes.

"What is that?" I ask, my eyes stuck on the bee tattooed on his chest, right where his heart is. He must have had it done recently because he didn't have it the last time we had sex completely naked.

He looks down at it then back up at me. He slides his t-shirt over my head, and I inhale deeply, relishing in his fresh scent.

"Caden," I insist. This time I touch the tattoo. "What is this? When did you get it done?"

He takes my fingers in his hand and brings the tips to his lips, kissing them one by one. "You said it earlier, baby. I'm fucking crazy. A maniac. Unhinged. I found what I need. And what I need is you, little bee."

"You...got tattooed...for me?"

"So did you," he smirks. "Aren't we the cutest couple?"

Letting go of my fingers, he grabs my head and kisses me deeply. When he takes a step back, he says. "I'll cancel the fight, baby. Don't worry about it."

This man...he will be the end of me.

32

CADEN

Only - NF, Sasha Alez Sloan

Sawyer opens his front door, and his puzzled gaze makes him look dumb. I hate every time I have to come to his house, but I do enjoy the stupid look on his face.

"Unexpected," he says as he steps aside to let me in.

"I'll be quick. I got somewhere to be tonight."

We walk to his living room, where he sits on the sofa. I stay standing, looking down on him.

"Arms dealing is going on hiatus until further notice," I say. "No more picking up from the Wolves."

He rests his ankle on his knee and spreads his arms on the back of his sofa, trying to act relaxed, but I can see how confused he is. "Why's that?"

"Because I said so."

"Because your dick is addicted to an NSC bitch you mean?"

I chuckle to myself, then tilt my head to observe him. He's the biggest coward I know, and yet he still gets to stay at the head of our crew until my sister comes back. Now I have to let him live after insulting Billie. Fucking ridiculous.

"Call my girl a bitch again, Sawyer. Just to see what happens."

He's not stupid enough to do it twice in front of me. Instead, he moves position again, showing he's anxious about the situation, and rests his elbows on his knees as he leans forward to talk.

"Look, I'll give it to you. I was dumb for not wanting to do get into arm's dealing before. You were right, it was a great idea. We're doubling our money, and we're all profiting from it. You know what that means. We can't stop now. Everything is working perfectly."

"If you want to keep doing it, find a new mule."

"Absolutely fucking not," he snorts. "You found the perfect one. Why would I change that? There is no one else from NSC who will ever do this for us."

"Billie won't be moving anything ever again. You heard me."

I don't need to convince him. She won't do it, period. I turn around, ready to leave, when he talks again.

"You're the one who put her in this situation, Cade. You're the one who assaulted her and filmed it. Who blackmailed her into working for us. Just because your dick convinced your dead heart that it cares, doesn't change anything for our crew. That's your problem, not the Kings'. You don't want her to do it? I don't give a shit. I can blackmail her. I can make the bitch do anything I fucking want."

Two steps, and I'm on him, smiling down as I punch him three times in the face. He grunts, falling back on the sofa, but I grab him by the t-shirt and hit him another two times. Just in case he didn't get the message. He's a big man, but I'm too fast for him to do anything.

"That's what happens when you call her a bitch twice. Wanna try again? See what I do next?"

As he gets his bearings again, I pull my phone out. The fucker just made me realize something.

"You're right, Sawyer. I blackmailed her."

I pull up the videos I have of her. I might have shown them to him in the past, but I'm the only one who has them saved. I wave my phone at him before deleting them.

"Gone. What are you gonna blackmail her with now, motherfucker?"

I hit him one last time before I leave. If I don't go now, I'm going to kill him, and it'll fall back on me. Plus, I need to be somewhere else.

I park my car next to the ones I would never be able to afford and look around. The Bakers' residence is not something I could even dream of. I didn't even know this kind of shit existed. I was here last week to pick up the first half of the cash, but I think this kind of mansion never ceases to impress. The grand, French-Chateau style would look tacky anywhere else, but in Stoneview it just makes them fit in even more. The larger the house, the bigger the privileges.

I slither my way between the parked cars and look inside. If I could steal even one of them, I would probably be set for a few years.

Ringing the doorbell, I tilt my head to the side as I observe the intricate carvings in the thick, double-wooden doors. Who the fuck puts dogs, hunting foxes and deer on their front door? It makes me cringe at how rich they are.

A butler opens the door, his nose up in the air and his eyes looking down at me.

"Welcome to Mister and Misses Gerald Baker's residence,"

he says haughtily enough, where you'd think he's the one who lives here and I'm the butler.

"I'm working the party," I tell him as if this whole situation didn't affect me.

"Right," he says with a pinched smile.

"I got it, Fred," a bright female voice calls behind me.

He steps to the side and bows his head at the young girl behind me. She can't be more than sixteen or seventeen. Are these guys hiring underaged girls? Fuck, that shit isn't gonna run with me, and I can't afford to leave this party with a murder charge rather than the money I came for.

"Miss Baker," Fred says as he disappears further into the hallway. That's when my eyes take in the huge family portrait behind them.

Gerald is in a suit, sitting down on a throne-like armchair. Behind him, his wife has a hand on his right shoulder, and a young teenage boy is on his left, his arms limp by his side. He has the same look as his dad; light blue eyes and blonde hair so light they could be white. The forced smile on his face makes me twist my mouth. Rich people are so unhappy. On the floor, her legs under her and her arm resting on her father's lap, is a little girl who looks exactly like the woman in front of me. She's older now, but she still has that look in her eyes—fear masked by fake sweetness.

"You're his family?" I can't help but choke out. Why would she be involved in this in any way, shape, or form?

She shakes her head and gives me a small smile. "I would suggest not talking to anyone if you want to have a half-decent night."

Her baby blue eyes darken slightly, pity clouding the color. She puts a strand of white-blonde hair behind her ear and jerks her head. "Come. I'll show you where they want you to get ready."

We start walking and she tries her best to make me feel comfortable despite it being completely impossible.

"What's your name?" she asks in a sweet voice.

"Caden. You?"

"Ella." She keeps walking ahead of me, knowing her way perfectly in the long hallways and complicated architecture. Gold, cream, and dark wood are the only three colors they use in this house, and everything looks like it belongs in an antique shop.

Apart from the painting in the entrance hall, this house has no personal belongings. It all looks expensive and portrays their wealth, but there is no fun, no life. It's all so bland, so sad. My house has colors on the walls from drawings Kay and I did as children. Markings that have witnessed our heights over the years. Even the holes in the walls and stains on the carpet remind us of the darkest moments that have shaped us. Moments when we felt alive. This place feels dead. Like the souls of the people who've been here are stuck in the walls and secret passages.

Ella stops by a door and turns back to me. I don't know the girl, and I don't care about her, but I need to know. "Are you even eighteen?" I ask with disgust.

She smiles, lips tight but making it as genuine as possible.

"This is your room," she ignores my question. "There are four other people in here. You don't have to talk to them or give them your identity, but it's not forbidden either. There's an outfit for you to wear. It'll have a sticker with your name on it. Just...wear it. There's no point in having any sort of rebellion. To be honest, that's what they want out of you. They'll love making your night worse than it is." Her shoulders hunch slightly, and a certain shyness comes over her despite the strong face she's been keeping until now.

"There is, um, lube. I would suggest using it now so you

can," her gaze is glued to the floor as she looks for her next word, "prepare yourself."

Knowing the rules and the game I agreed to play in there, none of this surprises me. No, I'm stuck on one thing I desperately want to know.

She opens the door, and I ask as casually as I can, "Do you go to Stoneview Prep?"

"Yea—" she stops herself, realizing she answered without thinking just to tell me the truth I already assumed.

Putting my hand on hers on the doorknob, I stop her from opening it any further. "What year?" I say low, closer to her ear. I'm behind her, my chest to her back, and I feel her shiver.

"Uh..." she hesitates.

With my other hand, I grab her arm softly. "Senior?"

She shakes her head slightly. "Junior?"

"I retook a year," she says in a trembling voice. "I should be in senior year."

"Fucking hell," I hiss as I let go of her and step back. "You need to get the fuck away from this place. Your dad's money isn't worth your sanity."

Ignoring me, she pushes the door fully open. She's lost her fake smile and her kindness. "Good luck tonight," she says tightly before walking away.

I step in, finding three women and one other man. I nod my head as I walk to the last outfit I see on a rack. My name is on it, and I take the sticker off before taking a good look at it. I run my free hand against the leather harness and leather pants. My heart skips a beat when I realize they're crotchless pants. The lube on the table next to me is sealed closed, and I grab it. Fucking. Great.

. . .

It's Billie's text I received before they took my phone that gave me courage. A simple *I miss you tonight.*

I told her I was spending the evening with Ethan and Elliot. As if I would purposely spend time without her. I'm so fucking addicted, my heart feels heavy every time I drop her off at her house. Every time she goes to work, or I go to college. I smell her on my sheets and hoodies, and I bathe in the raspberries and mint.

I run a hand through my hair as I enter the room where the main event unfolds. Naked women are walking around with platters, gags in their mouths as they offer champagne that must cost more than I'm making tonight. They're forced to hold their platters with two hands since their wrists are in cuffs linked with a chain.

As we have been ordered, the five of us walk to the back wall where five small stages are set, and we step up on them. For now, all we have to do is stay there, move around the stage and present the goods.

I do that for what feels like hours. While the billionaires eat and drink, while they talk business, and laugh loudly. I feel like I'm in The Purge. Except I won't be killed by the end of the night. It'll be much worse.

Gerald Baker comes to me personally, showing me to his friend. "Poor boys are always so cheap," he cackles loudly.

There are only about twenty of them in the room, but there are so few of us. I don't know how long I'll last before my teeth shatter from tightening my jaw or before my body jerks into action and I punch someone to death.

"How much did you pay for him?" his friend asks.

"Twenty-five," Gerald shrugs. They both laugh. At me. At the fact that I was ready to do whatever they wanted for that kind of money.

Gerald points at one of the girls who was in the room with

me. Her stage is right next to mine, and she's on her knees, wearing nothing but a collar and leather cuffs on her wrists and ankles. Gerald steps to the side so he's right in front of her. "Whereas I paid almost a hundred grand for a night with this beauty," he says as he rubs his thick thumb against her lips.

My heart stops for a few seconds. *A hundred. Fucking. Thousand. Dollars.*

I hate that he's right. That I was so cheap. It makes the humiliation that much worse.

"She goes to Silver Falls University," Gerald smiles. "She's a rich little bitch just looking for a thrill. Aren't you, pet?"

"Yes, sir," she murmurs.

"Is that so?" The friend smiles. "Open wide, whore. Show me how dirty you can get."

I tear my gaze away from them as soon as they both take their dicks out to fuck her mouth. My eyes stop on a woman who's staring at me. She smiles and comes to me with her husband.

Let the descent to hell begin.

"Hello, pretty boy," she smiles kindly as she approaches me. "My husband and I have been watching you since you arrived. You look absolutely delicious."

I don't say anything, not trusting what would come out of my mouth if I unclenched my jaw.

"Don't worry," she says as she runs her arm against my abs, to my pecs, and against my throat. "We just like making love as a three. Vincent and I are very gentle."

And they are.

Billie is on my mind the whole time Vincent and I double penetrate his wife. It's slow and so loving I want to puke pink and purple hearts on them.

The rest of the night is nothing like that. It changes as soon as another couple comes to me. Her gaze tells me that she wants her husband to hurt me. I can tell in his that he loves pleasing her.

She runs her hands through my messy hair before grabbing the harness and putting me on my knees. "On all fours," she smiles wickedly. Unlike some others, she doesn't introduce herself or him.

She grabs a gag from a platter a woman is holding for her and shoves the ball in my mouth. She pushes so far my gag reflex kicks in. "You're going to be such a good boy," she smirks. "I can already tell." She tightens the ball gag and turns to her husband before grabbing a tiny key in her purse. Undoing his pants, she pulls them down and makes him step out. I don't know what she does with them; I'm too focused on his cock and, more particularly, the fact that it's currently straining against a cock cage.

I want to look away, but the morbid curiosity at the back of my mind watches as she undoes the cage and rubs the fucking monster that is his dick, now allowed to grow thicker.

"You've been dying to come. Haven't you, baby?" she tells him sweetly.

"Yes, Mistress," he rasps.

"On your knees, boy," she says like she would a dog. "Bark for your Mistress."

He executes quickly, barking loudly, and I know what's coming next. I close my eyes, imagining Billie and me in our small house far from here. On the sofa together, watching TV and cuddling.

The woman snapping her fingers forces me to open my eyes again, but it was for her husband. "Go, boy. Go fuck the other puppy."

Panting like a fucking dog, her husband crawls to me on his hands and knees until he settles behind me and parts my legs.

Think of Billie. Think of being far away. Think of your perfect life.

I'm glad I followed Ella's advice and spread some lube on myself before coming in. Because with the way it fucking hurts as he roughly thrust inside me...I can't imagine doing this raw. Fuck, I already feel like I'm dying.

"Mount him, boy. Fuck him like the dogs you two are."

I close my eyes tightly, but I can't do anything about her words. They poison my ears, piercing my drums and making everything worse.

"That's right. Good puppy, good puppy. He's not hard, grab him. Grab his little cock and fuck him harder. *Harder*, I said. I want you to make the other puppy cry."

I signed something that said I couldn't contact the guests after the event. That I wasn't allowed to find them. But once Gerald's given me the money, what can he do about it?

I already know I'm gonna find this woman and her husband and kill them. I'll make sure it's painful too.

That's what helps me not break down completely as he keeps thrusting inside me.

33

BILLIE

Where Were You - girlfriends, Travis Barker

Lik releases a loud laugh as Xi's face falls. We all explode into giggles, following Lik.

"Do you want to fucking die?" Xi snaps as he gets up from his seat. We're having dinner all together, and Lik just ate the last Moroccan meatball on Xi's plate while he was in the bathroom. The one Xi said looked the best and that he was saving for the end.

"Ziad," their mom snaps. "Sit back down. Dinner isn't over."

"I'm not leaving the table, *Mama*. I'm killing your son."

Our laughs double as Xi tries to grab Lik, and he gets up to go hide behind Aisha.

"*Mama*, save me," Lik cries out.

Xi grabs him by the back of the neck and shoves him against the wall. Sam lifts an eyebrow silently, not enjoying his boyfriend being manhandled but unable to get in the middle of a sibling fight.

"You fucked up. Mom can't save you now."

"It wasn't me!" Lik screams. "*WAllah*, I don't know what happened. You left, and it just disappeared off your plate." Emma is crying from laughter as Lik blurts out his lie.

"Malik!" Aisha snaps loudly. "Don't lie swearing on Allah, *ya h'mar*," she calls him a donkey like always. She gets up, taking her time, and grabs both her sons by the ears, dragging them back to the table. One by one, she sits them back down. They don't do anything to defend themselves. They would never.

As soon as they're all at the table and settled back down, Xi can't do much more than stare daggers at his brother. I grab my plate and scoot my meatball onto his.

"Here, have mine. I'm not hungry anymore."

Stabbing into it with his knife and fork, he keeps staring. "Learn," he tells Lik. "That's what love looks like."

Because I'm sitting on his left, he easily leans over and drops a kiss to the side of my head. It's a friendly kiss, I know it. A normal peck step-siblings would have. Since I told Xi I didn't reciprocate his feelings for me, he's been respecting our platonic relationship—the one we should have had all along.

After dinner, I run to my room to grab my phone and send a quick message to Caden.

> Billie: I miss you tonight.

He's hanging out with his friends tonight, which I'm not used to. He always chooses me over anyone else. I'm trying to be okay with the fact that sometimes he'll be with his friends, and that said friends hate me because I'm NSC.

And because I gave Jade a pathway of tears. I guess that really didn't help.

He doesn't reply, and I'm about to put my phone to the side

when it rings. An unknown number appears on the screen, and my hand comes to my chain, playing with it as I pick up.

"Hello?"

"This is Sawyer."

I sit up in my bed and look around my room as if he's hiding somewhere in here. Whenever this man talks to me, I feel uneasy.

"What do you want?"

"We need you to do a move for us tonight."

My hand grabs my comforter, twisting it until it's cutting off the flow in my fingers. "I don't do moves for you anymore. Caden knows."

"Well, you're back at it, sweetheart. Caden's order."

"He didn't say anything to me."

"He's busy tonight. He can't always be on your case. He needs to do things he cares about sometimes. Or do people he cares about," he adds with a mocking snort.

Caden and I are the closest we've ever been. I always feel weird admitting it, even to myself, but he's my boyfriend. I know how we feel about each other. He told me he loved me in his fucked-up way. He wouldn't go behind my back and tell Sawyer to contact me.

"I want to talk to him," I say firmly. "He's the one who gives me the jobs. Not you."

"He's busy, and I'm telling you to pick our shit up from the Wolves in half an hour if you don't want me to leak your videos. You know Caden sent them to me, little Scott. I've seen you naked, on your knees, sucking his cock. Do you want everyone else to see that too? You're gonna look amazing on porn sites."

I struggle to swallow the anxiety that comes with his words. I'm so close to leaving this place. Having a fake sex tape of me everywhere would be the end of me.

"Whatever," I say to minimize the fear. "I'll be there."

I tell him that, but I don't really believe it. Caden wouldn't do that to me.

"*Atta girl*," he concludes before hanging up.

Instead of getting to my car, I try to call Caden. Three times he doesn't answer. So I send him a text asking if he's the one who wants me to go move merchandise for them.

No answer.

Fear grips my stomach. Did he really order this? Is he too busy with someone else to even tell me about it, so he sent Sawyer?

I don't have time to think about this. Sawyer has the videos, and I can't reach my boyfriend. The only person who could stop this and protect me isn't getting back to me.

Disappointment is such a small word for how I feel.

Not wanting to take the risk, I grab my car keys and leave the house without anyone noticing. Whatever, I can do a drop and talk to Caden about this tomorrow. I'm sure he's not with someone else. He's busy, and there must have been a misunderstanding. Either way, I have to keep Sawyer from sending the videos. I can talk to Caden about deleting them. I know he'll do it for me.

I speed all the way to the meeting spot, too scared I will be late and accidentally see one of the Wolves providing NSC with whatever they hide in my trunk.

I put the bag on my head, and with everything that's happened between Caden and myself, it feels like I haven't done this in years. I have to remind myself it's only been just over a month since the last time.

My heart starts beating faster. I'm now starting to feel like it's insane to think Caden could have fallen in love with me in such a short amount of time. But I did, and that's even more ridiculous.

Was this all a trick? Has he been playing me all this time? That's what he's always done with me.

Oh my god.

He has.

Two parts of me are fighting themselves, and the realistic one is starting to win.

How could I think Caden King could fall in love with me?

I shouldn't be surprised, but I am. I thought what we had was genuine. I don't know why. Maybe because of the obsession, the possession. He tattooed his name on me, for fuck's sake. It doesn't get more irrational than that.

The knock on my window comes quicker than I thought. I must have been profoundly lost in my thoughts to not even realize how long it'd been. I wait until I hear their car leaving and take the bag off. Everything seems foreign to me.

We were past this.

Why is he doing this to me? The threat of the videos had been completely forgotten, and now the wound has been reopened.

It fucking hurts.

I'm on the highway when my phone rings. I see Dickie's name on the screen. He never calls. Even less in the evening.

"Isn't it a bit late for a grandpa like you?"

"Here I was thinking you'd want to hear about a second chance in professional MMA. But I guess grandpa is gonna go to bed."

"What? Dickie, don't fuck with me."

"I would never, kiddo. I'm serious. Come to the gym now. We need to talk."

My eyes automatically go to my mirror even though I can't see the heavy bags in my trunk.

"I...I'm busy," I say in a huff. "Doing some work stuff."

"Billie. Did you hear me or what? This is your chance. Second chance. No one ever gets that lucky."

I take a deep breath. I can't let this slip through my fingers. I'm feeling alive for the first time in weeks. I need to hear what Dickie has to say. The Kings and their buyers can wait.

"I'm on my way."

I practically ran to the gym door. Pushing it open, I walk in and sprint to Dickie's office.

"Give it to me, old man," I say with a massive smile on my face.

"Carla Ruppert left the competition," he answers casually. Leaning back into his old chair.

My heart drops in my stomach, my shoulders deflating. That's why he made me come here?

"Yeah, but that just means Killer Clover wins by forfeit."

"That's the thing. She didn't forfeit. She gave you her spot."

"What?" I start pacing, still not convinced this is possible. "She can't do that."

"This isn't professional. We're talking about an amateur competition organized by a few gyms in a small city. It's big for you because you could get an agent, but other than that, it doesn't mean much. There are no solid rules."

I bite my thumb between my front teeth, pacing quickly and making myself dizzy. "Dickie, am I fighting Killer Clover?"

"In two months, kiddo. Taylor already knows, and he's coming to see you."

"Oh my god." My knees give up as tears of happiness fill up my eyes. I sit on a chair beside him and look up at him. "This is it. Dickie...*fuck*!" I shout from happiness. "I'm going to win this fight. I'm going professional. I can already see it."

He smiles at me wisely, knowingly. Then he confirms, "I can see it too, Billie. The universe is on your side, kid."

He grabs a beer and gives me a small bottle of orange

juice. "No alcohol for my best fighter," he happily teases before opening his beer.

We drink and talk some more about the intense training I'm going to be doing in the next two months. I'm glad Caden convinced me not to give up, or I wouldn't have trained since my last fight. I would be in deep shit right now.

It's bittersweet to think that he's one of the best and worst things that's ever happened to me.

I leave before Dickie does, and I'm alone in the parking lot when my jaw drops open.

"Fuck!" I hiss to myself as I run to my car. The back window is shattered, and unsurprisingly, the merchandise is gone. "No," I choke. "No, no, no."

How much shit does the old man up there still have in store for me? Because I'm not sure I can take it all.

I run my hands through my ponytail, pulling at it before rubbing my eyes. "Come on," I rage. "This isn't fucking fair!"

Bad news always follows whatever happiness I'm going through. I just can't catch a fucking break.

I settle in my car, hoping it still starts because they fucked it up real good. It does, and I notice one of my lights is broken again. The same one Caden had gotten repaired for me.

Back when I truly hated him. When I knew who he was. How could I forget?

Despite hating the guts out of him right now, I grab my phone and try calling him. If anyone can help me out of this situation, it's him.

"Please, pick up. Please, please..."

"*Caden*," his voicemail tells me.

"Caden," I say into the phone, hurry and panic clear in my tone. "Please call me back. I...I know you wanted me to do this move, but something happened. Please just pick up."

Tears fill my eyes when I hang up. I send a text.

> Billie: Where are you?

I try calling again.

"*Caden.*"

"Caden, you can't do this to me. I...he's gonna kill me. *Please*, pick up."

As soon as I hang up, I send another desperate text.

> Billie: Please...pick up. I'm begging you.

I bet he's looking at his phone next to whoever he's with right now, laughing his ass off at the stupid NSC girl who fell for him.

> Billie: It doesn't matter if you don't love me. It doesn't matter if this was all a joke. This is my fucking life. PICK UP.

I call again.

"*Caden.*"

"I hate you!" I shout into the phone. "You fucking bastard. I hope you're having the time of your life. I...how could I have been so stupid! How...I hate you, Caden. I hate you so much for sending me on this job tonight. You could have had the balls to at least ask me yourself, you coward. I hope Sawyer kills me because I can't stand a life knowing I fell for your stupid shit."

I hang up, fuming and heartbroken.

And I do the only thing I can.

I drive straight to Sawyer's. He needs to know. If I disappear, he'll come for me, or worse, my family.

I'm shaking when I knock on his door.

What am I going to say? What am I going to do?

He's going to kill me.

How ironic is that? Just when I learn that I have a second shot at leaving this shitty town.

It's not Sawyer who opens the door, but a man I don't know.

"Who are you?" he rumbles. I notice the gun in his right hand and regret not arming myself before coming here.

"Billie. I'm here to see Sawyer."

"Ah, you're that NSC bitch Cade's been fucking."

I grind my teeth, trying to keep myself under control.

"Is Sawyer here?" I insist.

"Yeah, yeah. Come in."

He steps away from the doorway, but I don't move. "I'd rather talk to him out here."

"Nah, I don't think so."

It's like he knows I've got news that'll give them a chance to hurt me. He wants me inside with them. I glance out at the street before walking in. No one is going to save me in Kings' territory.

What choice do I have?

I follow that guy into the living room. Sawyer is lounging on his sofa in sweatpants and nothing else, a beer in his hand and a couple of empty ones on the table in front of him. His abs tense when he laughs at something on the TV. He'd be so hot if he wasn't a fucking asshole. Elliot and Ethan are next to him. Caden's best friends fucking hate me since I hurt Jade.

This is not looking good.

"Yo, Hook," Sawyer says without looking at us. He runs a hand through his blond hair, laughing again. "You need to watch this shit, man."

"Someone's here to see you," Hook says, settling behind me in a way I know means I'm not getting out of here until he lets me. He feels gigantic behind me, his head well above mine, and I feel myself shrinking when Sawyer's eyes fall on me.

"Little Scott," he smiles. "I was starting to get impatient. Was about to start watching your sex tape with everyone here."

I do my best not to cringe and run a hand behind my neck, massaging the stiff muscles before saying, "The stuff is gone."

"What stuff?" he asks without giving a shit.

"The," I hesitate. I was being vague on purpose. I can't fucking get myself to say it. "The stuff the Wolves put in my car for the move. I—My car got broken into. It's gone. All of it."

There's a tense silence as he puts his beer on the table and slowly gets up.

"Tell me you didn't lose my merchandise, Billie," he says quietly as he walks to me.

"It was stolen," I try to defend weakly. "Look, I'm here, coming to you and being honest. I could have run or killed you or something. I don't know. I'm here because I want to sort this out fairly. This wasn't my fault."

"You lost my shit, but it wasn't your fault, so you came here?" He fakes a pout before smiling. "Coming here doesn't make you innocent. It makes you fucking stupid. You should have run, little Scott. Should have given yourself a bit of a head start before I killed you."

"Sawyer." I take a step back, only to bump into Hook. "I can make this right." I look at Elliot and Ethan, talking to them now. They're still sitting on the sofa, watching the scene silently. "I...is Caden here? Can I talk to him?"

In front of me, Sawyer shakes his head like I'm stupid. Like I don't get it. "Caden doesn't give a shit about you. Why can't you get your head around it?"

He's so close to me now, I can barely take a breath without my boobs hitting his stomach.

Perfectly timed, a mocking laugh rises in the room. "Please, she's not actually asking for him, is she?" I don't have to look behind Sawyer because Jade comes right next to him, proudly showing the hickeys that go from her ear to her chin.

I shake my head, refusing to see what's right in front of me.

"No," I mumble, my voice choked down by a sob that's desperate to come out.

How could he do this to me?

"Come on," Jade snorts. "Tell me you didn't think he actually cared."

The tips of her fingers come across my jaw, where Caden left the same hickeys on me as he did her. "We match," she smiles wickedly. "Ain't that fun?"

"Where is he? I want to talk to him." My attempt at a stern voice doesn't alarm any of them.

"Cade isn't here," Sawyer jumps back in. "But even if he was, he wouldn't do shit. No one can lock that boy down, little Scott. Everyone knows that."

"You were the only one stupid enough to get played," Jade sneers.

"Now, back to my merchandise." Sawyer's voice isn't mocking anymore. It's deadly.

"I'll do other jobs," I whisper desperately, but I don't know if I care about them killing me anymore.

I fell for Caden when I should have known all along that his aim was to hurt me. My sweaty hands close into fists. My nails dig into my palms, leaving bloody crescents.

"She'll do other jobs." Sawyer lets out a loud laugh without an ounce of humor in it. "Oh, man. She's fucking hilarious."

His punch comes with no warning. I'm forced to the floor by the strength of it, dizzy and confused.

I inhale a deep breath as I roll onto my side.

"Little bitch thinks we're gonna go easy on her because Cade used her for a bit."

I spit blood on the floor, going on all fours to try and get back up, but he kicks me in the ribs, sending me back down again. I grunt, my body crashing down face first.

"Fuck," I choke as he puts his foot on my back. I can barely breathe.

"What are you gonna offer me now, huh?" He presses hard, crushing my lungs. "The same you did with Caden? A blowjob? Should I film it too?"

"Stop," I beg. I'm suffocating from the weight he's putting on my back. I have no strength in me. It's not the hits, it's the heartbreak.

I never truly had a will to live, but I had the strength to survive.

It's all gone now.

"Should we all take a turn on you? Fuck that pussy Cade kept going back to?"

I shake my head, tears welling up in my eyes. I will them not to come, but I feel like I'm dying. This is it. This is how I die.

"You'd need to be a whore for me for years before I get that money back. Put you on the street, in clubs. Sell you to high buyers in the Wolves' club. That what you want?"

"No," I cry out. "Please." I attempt a breath that gets stuck in my lungs. "It wasn—It wasn-t...wasn't my fault."

I vaguely hear Elliot's voice rising. "Sawyer, man. Let her go."

Instead, he presses harder, and I explode in a loud sob. I need to fucking breathe.

"What are you gonna do for me, little Scott?"

He lifts his foot and grabs me by the ponytail, pulling me back up as I choke on air, trying to regain full consciousness.

The house tilts, my eyes rolling to the back of my head as I try to stand up while he drags me across the room.

When he's got more space, he throws me to the floor again.

"What do you want, Hook? Ass, mouth, or pussy?"

"Pussy," he answers without hesitation.

Fear grips my entire body. Can't they just kill me?

I whimper, trying my best to crawl away. Sawyer grabs me by the ankle and drags me back before kicking me again.

"Hey, hey. Stay here. We'll just fuck the shit out of you, little Scott. Might beat you up a little more to make sure you don't run away while we take breaks between rounds."

"Sawyer." It's Elliot again. "What are you doing, man? Caden is going to k—"

"Sit your fucking ass down!" he barks at him. Back to me, he drawls, "We'll let you go in the morning, okay?" He grabs my ponytail again, pulling my head up. "Whatever's left of you, I guess."

"No one is fucking touching her," Jade intervenes. Hope rises to my chest even though Sawyer doesn't let go of me. "You dogs keep your dicks to yourselves. I have unfinished business with the bitch."

Sawyer releases me, my head falling to the floor, my muscles giving up on me. With a kick to the ribs, Jade rolls me around until I'm on my back.

"Remember when you left me a pathway for tears?"

My heart kicks so hard in my chest I feel like it's going to explode at any moment. People can die of fear. The Kings crew pride themselves in their violence. Some of their victims die before they're even done with them. Caden is the proudest member of what he calls 'the coward way to go'. A heart attack from fear or pain. When the mind can't keep up, the heart fails.

Is this my fate?

Jade kicks me in the face. My cheekbone feels like it's splitting into a million pieces. Blood spurts out of my nose, pouring onto the side of my face.

Then she does it again.

I feel it on my cheek, my lips, my temple. The side of my head.

I can't do anything while she beats the shit out of me to make sure I don't escape.

After what feels like ages of Jade beating me up—but must have been less than a minute—I can't move anymore. I'm stuck on my back, blood pouring down my throat from my nose and my bloody mouth. My face has fallen to the side, my cheek against the floor.

I'm not crying anymore. I have no choice but to accept my situation. I feel Jade straddle me, but I don't look. I already glanced at the cutter she was holding, and I don't want to see it again. At best, she will carve a Kings' crown on my neck. The other option is her cutting an artery.

"You're gonna love your new scar," she sneers above me. "You've been trying to get under our skin by fucking Caden. Now we're getting under yours."

If only she knew how much Caden is already under my skin. How he slithered his way through my veins and poisoned my heart.

I didn't ask for it, and yet I took it willingly. Every time he hurt me and scared me, I allowed him to steal a part of me and keep it to himself. Every time he stepped over a new line, I followed with excitement in my heart.

He lured me in, kept me to himself, and I begged him to never let me go.

Now I'm paying the price for my stupidity.

My eyes are practically swollen shut from the beating, and I can't do anything but look to the side where my head has fallen. I feel the cut into my neck. I feel Jade writhing from the pleasure of hurting me and my inability to do anything about it.

I know how it feels because I did it to her.

I can barely feel the pain; everything is mixed into one horrifying numbing feeling. Something catches my eye, though. On the floor, not far from me, are the bags that were in my car.

The exact bags the Wolves put in there and were stolen.

"It was you," I whisper past my swollen lips. "You set me up..."

They stole the bags, so I would have to come here. So they could attack me.

And I fell for it like the fucking idiot I am.

"Yeah, we did," she says so effortlessly. "Just to show you how much Cade doesn't give a shit about you. Where is he now that we got you all to ourselves, huh? He's not coming to save you. He's too busy fucking someone else right now."

I pass out before she's even finished carving my skin. Maybe I'm dying, I don't know.

I don't care anymore.

My shoulder shakes, and my entire body screams in pain.

"Little Scott. Come on."

This time someone grabs my jaw and turns my head left and right. "You're not dead, so fucking wake up."

Slowly, I attempt to open my eyes. They're swollen, sticky.

I can feel the side of my neck burning, and I bring my hand to it, hissing from the searing pain when I touch the crusted blood.

"Yeah, I wouldn't touch that if I were you."

Two hands help me sit up, and I try to open my eyes again.

My left one is swollen shut, but the right one seems fine. I look at the person helping me and almost fall back down from shock.

"Ethan?" I rasp.

"Don't get too excited. I'm just getting you out of here."

I realize I'm still on Sawyer's living room floor, but no one else is here anymore.

"They're sleeping," he explains as I keep looking around. "You need to leave. They aren't done with you, and you don't want to be here when they wake up."

I let him help me up into a standing position. At least they didn't break my legs.

Ethan takes me outside, and to my surprise, to his car.

"Come on, get in."

I look around, but I don't get in. The last time I saw his car, NSC was riddling it with bullets.

"I'm not going to hurt you, Billie," he finally says reassuringly. "I don't like you, but I also don't think you deserve this. What, because Cade loves you? That's none of our business."

He opens the door and invites me to go in with a jerk of his head.

"He doesn't love me," I mumble as I settle into the passenger seat.

Ethan is a quiet man, so he doesn't say anything else during the ride. It doesn't take too long to get back to my house. The Kings own most streets, and he doesn't have to take detours to cross the town.

He parks a little down the street, not going quite all the way to my house.

"Are you okay walking the rest?"

I nod, but just as I'm about to open the door, he gently touches my forearm.

"They lied." At my silence, he adds, "When they said he doesn't care about you."

I shake my head, tears burning my eyes and falling down my broken face.

"What they said doesn't matter. He didn't come when I called for help. He wasn't there. That means everything."

I have hope that he's going to say something. Defend his friend, tell me there indeed was a reason he wasn't there tonight.

He's got nothing else to say. Because I'm right.

"Thank you, Ethan. For getting me out of there. I owe you."

Owing someone in our world means everything, and when Ethan nods, I know it's because he will get his favor back one day.

For now, I exit the car and walk to my house.

The sun is attempting to rise behind dark clouds; it must be around six or seven. Rain starts to fall just as I get to my door. When I enter my house, my sister is coming out of the kitchen.

"Fuck, Bil's!" she gasps, running to me. "Dad!" she calls out.

I'm too exhausted to even explain what happened. For now, I just let my older sister take care of me.

I've got nothing but my family. My crew.

I'm back to where I started; broken by the North Shore Kings, only now with heartbreak weighing heavy on me. That hurts much more than any physical wound they could ever cause.

34

CADEN

Can You Hold Me - NF Britt Nicole

I don't turn my phone on until I get home. I'm fucking limping as I walk into my house, the pain tearing me apart.

The longest night of my life, and yet, I would do it all over again for Billie.

I throw my phone on my bed while it turns on and go to the bathroom. I scrub myself raw in the shower, making sure to get rid of their touches. My brain is burning up from all the thoughts going through my mind. From the flashes of their hands on me.

Nausea overtakes me and I have to swallow back bile. The only way I can get through this is by thinking of Billie. I imagine the warmth of her small body against mine, her Bambi eyes peering up at me, and her bright smile whenever she sees me.

I think of her tough voice when she's unhappy about something and the way in which she can fight anything. Her strength makes me stronger.

As soon as I walk back into my bedroom, I grab my phone,

wanting to call her. To hear her voice. A deathly grip takes hold of my stomach as soon as I open her texts.

> Billie: Is it really you who asked that I go on a job tonight?

> Billie: Where are you?

> Billie: Please…pick up. I'm begging you.

> Billie: It doesn't matter if you don't love me. It doesn't matter if this was all a joke. This is my fucking life. PICK UP.

I go to my voicemails, listening to her panicked voice when she talks about a job I supposedly wanted her to do. And when she mentions Sawyer, I see red.

The bastard sent her to the Wolves after I told him she would never do another job again.

I try calling Billie right away, but she doesn't pick up. Fuck.

Sawyer is fucking dead.

Before I can get to him though, I have to check if she's okay.

I must call her twenty times on my way to her house. I can't really feel the pain in my body anymore, too anxious to know what happened to the girl I love. It's pouring out, and I'm well over the speed limit in our town streets. It doesn't matter, though. All that matters is getting to her.

I turn the corner to her street with my tire screeching behind me before speeding down to her house. I leave my car in front of the house, barely parked, before running to her window. Inside, her blinds are down but enough slats are broken so I can see her sleeping on her bed. Her back is to me, and her long light-brown hair is the only thing showing as the comforter swallows her.

"Billie!" I scream as I hit her window. At least she's alive and home.

I try to open the window, but it's locked, so I knock again. She can't hear me. I'm soaked from the rain by the time I notice the wires of her earphones and realize she must have fallen asleep with her music on.

I run to the front door, not caring that her family hates me, then violently knock many times. It's her sister Emma who opens the door.

"You've got some fucking nerve, King," she hisses.

"I need to see her. Please." I push past, not caring that I might hurt Emma in the process. She grabs me by the arm, but I shrug her off easily.

Their front door opens into their living room, so I'm not far from the hallway that leads to Billie's bedroom. But once I'm past Emma, I come face to face with Xi.

"The fucker truly got a death wish," he snaps, advancing toward me. I put my hands in front of me, but he doesn't stop. His punch is swift and strong.

I stumble back, not defending myself.

"I'm not here to fight. I just want to see Billie."

"Fight?" Emma seethes. "You're lucky we haven't killed you yet. With the state she came back in—"

"What state?" I ask, but Xi is on me again.

"Get the fuck out of here." He pushes me. "If I see you near her again, I swear you're dead, King."

"Just let me see her!" I rage.

"You're never seeing her again," Emma tells me. "Was it revenge for the fire? Is that why you did that to her? She wasn't involved in any of this."

"Did what?" I choke. "What happened?" I try to shove past them, but Xi punches me again. My entire body is dead from the night I just had, and I can't find the strength to fight back.

Worse, my mind is crushed by what happened at the Bakers' house. I just need to see her. I just need to see the light of my life. She'll give me the strength I need to make it right.

Someone else comes in from the hallway, closing the door behind him. I recognize Lik, Xi's brother.

"Would you look at that? A dead man walking."

He and Xi are on me the next second. I take the hits because I somehow feel like I deserve them. I didn't hurt Billie last night, but I'm the one who put her in this situation, after all. All the bad things that happened to her happened because of me.

It's nothing to take a beating compared to everything she took for me.

As soon as they give me a break, I spit blood on their floor, doing my best to stand back up.

"Fight back, motherfucker," Xi pants. "Give me what I want, so I can rightly fuck you up."

"I just want to see her..." I repeat. "Just talk—"

"Get out."

Her broken voice makes me look past the two men. She's wrapped in a blanket, her tiny body trembling.

This time, I bulldoze past them. No one can fucking stop me when I want to get to my girl.

I freeze when I see her face up close. He broke her. I know it was Sawyer.

"Little bee," I push out in a trembling voice. "What happened?" I try to grab her, but she retreats back.

"Don't touch me," she says, her voice cracking. I move my hands away, fisting them as I force myself not to touch her.

"Billie, talk to me."

"Where were you?" she croaks. One of her eyes is swollen shut, but the other fills with tears she doesn't hold back.

I don't find the strength to answer. She couldn't take the

truth. She would never let me sacrifice myself for her. She couldn't live with it because she's good. She grew up just like me, and I turned into the biggest asshole while she became a good person.

When my silence stretches for too long, she gazes right into my eyes and kills me.

"Leave."

I don't know what it is exactly—the look in her eyes or her cold tone—but I fall to my knees in front of her. The toll of yesterday and seeing her like this is too much for me. I can already feel I'm losing myself without her.

"Little bee, I beg you don't do this to me. Don't give up. I'm going to fix this."

She shakes her head, determined.

"I love you," I say, staring up at her. "I know this has been hard. I know everything is against us, but I'm in love with you, Billie. You can't take this away from me. You can leave me, but you can't take away the love I have for you. That's never going to end."

"Caden, stop," she chokes as she moves backward. I grab her legs, wrapping my hands on the side of her thighs.

"Tell me you don't love me. Tell me this was nothing to you and you can live without me."

"You're embarrassing yourself, please." She doesn't say it in a mean way. More in that she feels bad for me.

"Breaking up with me won't change the fact that our love is forever. You can't end a love as strong as ours, Billie."

"Please...leave."

"She said leave." I feel Xi grabbing the back of my shirt and hauling me up. He shoves me away from her and toward the door.

"I'll wait," I tell her as I pierce my eyes into hers. "I'll wait until you're ready to love me again."

I let Xi kick me to the curb. There's no point fighting. Not here, not now.

But fuck that, if she thinks this is over.

It's never over.

I knock so hard on Ethan and Elliot's door it's impossible for them to ignore me. Elliot is the one who answers. He's in his boxers, his hair a mess, and I can only assume he was sleeping since it's barely eight.

I shoulder past him right away, storming into his house.

"What the fuck happened?"

Ethan comes out of the kitchen with a cup of coffee in his hands and is ready for the day.

"Man, where have you been?" Elliot asks, pinching the bridge of his nose. "Shit's been going down."

"And by that, do you mean Sawyer beat the shit out of Billie, and neither of you told me?"

"We tried calling you," he defends himself. Ethan stays silent, not feeling the need to justify anything.

"Why call me when you could fucking intervene? Did you see what he did to her?!" I bark. "What the fuck even happened? Was it just him?"

I'm barely sane on a good day, but their silence tips me over the edge. "Fucking answer me!" I rage as I flip their coffee table over.

"Take a seat," Ethan says calmly. "And stop breaking our house."

I'm panting, ready to punch him in the face, but I manage to hold myself back. I need them on my side. So I sit down with Elliot while Ethan settles on an opposite armchair.

"Sawyer fucked up," Ethan says.

There's a silence, the brothers exchanging a look before Elliot adds, "And so did Jade."

I run my hands against my face, trying to check if this is reality.

"What the fuck happened," I growl. I haven't slept in more than twenty-four hours, and nothing makes sense anymore. I'm running on adrenaline, not even feeling the bruises on my face from Lik and Xi. I want to fucking die and go to a different universe where none of this happened. Where Billie and I can simply be. Without anyone getting in the way.

"From what I understand," Elliot starts. "Sawyer told Billie you were sending her on a job last night. So she went. I'm not sure, I wasn't there for any of that. All I know is Sawyer called me and told us to come over. When we arrived, Jade and Hook were there too. They had bags of weapons in the living room, and I could tell by Jade being all excited that they were up to no good."

"Yeah. I believe they fucking were, Elliot," I snap. "Why would Billie go on the job? She knows I don't want her to do them anymore."

"I don't know. All I know is that Billie showed up at Sawyer's saying her car had been broken into and the merchandise was gone. She didn't know it was Sawyer who stole it. He clearly had planned it all."

"Him and Jade," Ethan adds. He's calm. Deadly calm. I can tell he is fuming at his ex-girlfriend.

"Yeah," Elliot huffs, running a hand through his bed hair. "Him and Jade," he confirms. "They made Billie believe it was her fault and..."

Since Elliot doesn't have the courage to keep going, Ethan takes over. "Sawyer beat her and wanted to rape her. He was making a point to show her you weren't there when she needed you the most. They told her you were with someone else. Jade even had the necklace of hickeys to prove it. Obviously, Sawyer must have been the one to give it to her. Jade stopped Sawyer from raping her. She wanted her own revenge. Beat her up instead. Carved the Kings' crown into her neck because Billie had given her a pathway for tears."

I'm yanking at my hair now and need to get up. Anxious energy zaps through my body, forcing me to pace around the room.

"What...what the fuck?!" I rage. "What the fuck were you two doing? Watching the show and enjoying yourselves?"

"Man, I tried," Elliot fights back, getting up too. "Have you ever tried to get past Hook? He's a fucking mountain. He pushed me back once, twice. Threatened me. When Sawyer asks what crew you're defending, you shut the fuck up and sit down like everyone would have."

"No," I seethe as I grab him by the collar of his shirt. "You fucking do something about it when an innocent girl is being beaten up."

"Wake up, Caden!" he rages as he shoves me off him. "Billie is not *innocent*, she's fucking NSC. The only person who put her in danger is *you*. At least I calmed them down. As soon as she passed out, I convinced them to leave her alone, to wait until the morning to do anything else. I bought her time. We defended your girl."

Finding nothing to blame him with anymore, yet refusing to give up, I turn to Ethan. "Where the fuck were you, huh?"

"Where the fuck were *you*?" he says in a dangerously low voice. Ethan isn't the kind to get fired up like Elliot or me. He's the one who calms us down. He's the kind who kills people silently. "Cause I went off looking for you as soon as it started. You weren't answering your phone. You weren't at your house. I called your fucking sister, Cade. I even checked Billie's house and her gym. You were nowhere to be found. So, tell me.

Where were you while we were trying to save your girl from Sawyer?"

I can't reply, frozen by the reality of everything. I let men and women rape me last night to give Billie the chance to escape this hell hole.

And even that wasn't enough.

I gave the money to that bitch so she would give Billie her spot in the tournament. In the end, I wasn't there when it mattered the most. Who knows if she'll ever be able to fight again after what happened. Who knows if she still wants to live?

I don't know.

I might not ever know if she doesn't speak to me again. She doesn't want me anymore. She doesn't want anything to do with me.

I understand the reason.

But I can't accept it.

"Brother," Elliot says softly as he puts a hand on my shoulder. "Where were you?"

How long was I out? Lost in my thoughts? Pressure is building behind my eyes and a headache strengthening in my skull. I'm exhausted, everything is too heavy. My throat is tight, and I'm choking on my own thoughts.

My legs give out on me, and I fall back. Thankfully I had paced until the sofa was behind me again, so it ends up catching me.

"Cade," Ethan says as he slides nearer to me. "You can tell us anything. We've got your back."

My head falls back, and I look at the ceiling. I failed Billie. My entire world is falling apart. Now is the time to open up to my best friends, my brothers. Now is the time to tell them the truth about what I've been doing in Stoneview for the last few months.

So I do.

It's the most liberating thing I've ever done. To tell them what the tutoring indeed was. To tell them how I got Billie back into the boxing competition. That I would do anything for her, including losing control over my body for one night.

A silence overcomes us all when I'm done.

"That's where I was," I conclude. Tears are shining in Elliot's eyes even though he's not crying. Ethan wrapped an arm around my shoulders at some point, and I let him hold me close.

"Fuck," Elliot whispers.

"Desperate times call for desperate measures," Ethan says steadily, keeping strong for all of us. "You did the right thing."

I look at him. "How? I fucked it all up. It was all for nothing."

"Don't blame yourself for the greed of others. Whether it be the Stoneview billionaires or Sawyer. This was out of your control, and we will fix it, Cade. All together. I promise you."

I nod, wiping my sweaty forehead. "Sawyer is going to die. Slowly and painfully. *Today*." I get up and sway slightly.

"Sawyer is gonna die slowly and painfully," Elliot confirms. "After you've rested. What you did last night...it's heavy, Cade. Billie's stuff has taken a toll on you too. You might be strong, but you need rest. Put all the chances on your side."

I turn to Ethan, and he nods. "Have one of our rooms. Sawyer isn't going anywhere, and we'll be here when you wake up."

35

BILLIE

The Raging Sea - Broadside

"The strongest fucking girl!" Xi shouts as I hit the bag again. "Come on, Bil's!"

Even though Dickie hates having him at the gym, his words give me strength, and I accelerate my punches as the ten seconds bell rings out.

"Come on, come on! Quicker, kiddo!" Dickie shouts over Xi.

The bell rings at the end of the five minutes, and I step away from the bag, panting. I wipe my forehead with my forearm before letting my gloved hands hang by my sides.

"Fuck, I'm exhausted," I huff as Xi comes over with water.

"No water!" Dickie barks as he slaps the bottle away. He doesn't allow water between rounds during training. That way, it'll feel like a real help during the competitive fight when I do get water. "How long will you keep coming to my gym?"

"Until she feels safe going out on her own," Xi snaps back.

"I can pick her up from your house and drive her back after training."

My stepbrother crosses his arms and juts his chin at Dickie. "The fight is in two days. You lasted almost two months, you can last another forty-eight hours."

"Please, can we focus," I intervene, putting myself between the two.

They silently stare at each other before Dickie finally turns to me. "Alright, get in the ring. Let's spar."

I remove the boxing gloves and put my MMA mittens on, but Xi's words stick in my exhausted mind.

It's already been two months since I broke up with Caden. Two months of ignoring his constant calls and messages. Of sending Xi or Dad to the door every time he comes to the house.

Everyone has grown so protective around me I don't do anything on my own anymore. And Xi has become my personal bodyguard. The worst thing is, I'm so grateful for it I don't know how to thank him.

After what happened with the Kings, I'm terrified for them to come back for me. They were going to end me, I know it. Jade and Sawyer's hatred for me knows no boundaries. I was ashamed to admit it to Xi. When I finally opened up to him about my fear of being alone on the streets, he swore he'd be glued to me until I was ready to be on my own again.

Nothing, and I mean *nothing*, stops me from thinking of Caden. Not when I'm with my loving family. Not when I'm fighting. Not even when I'm asleep.

My dreams are too often his body against mine, his wicked smile, his magic kisses. I've woken up too often from touching myself while moaning his name. He's cursed me to love him forever, to a broken heart and an aching need to be near him. He's put his mark on me, more than literally.

No one has seen the tattoo saying he owns me under my right breast. Practically everyone has seen the crown that's been added to my NSC dagger because it's glaringly visible when I wear my tank tops or sports bra. While most people stayed silent, Xi lost his shit. I couldn't tell him I didn't even want it on top of everything. I just stayed quiet and took his wrath about how I was the worst decision-maker, that I couldn't have gone for a worse boyfriend, a worse person to fall in love with.

Thankfully, he didn't add that he would have been a much better choice. He knows where we stand on that, but he only stopped scolding me when I exploded into sobs.

He apologized many times for going too hard on me, saying that he was just furious on my behalf and couldn't stand to see me heartbroken. I let him spoil me with food for upsetting me. Even though it had to fit within my diet.

When my round of sparring is over, I'm bent in half, wheezing, while Dickie talks harshly to me. "Two days, and you're dead after a few rounds? I hope for your sake you're planning on knocking out Killer Clover in two."

After the Kings beat me up, it took me three weeks to get back in the ring. And even then, I couldn't spar and risk being hit in the face. I fully healed two weeks ago since nothing was broken. I'm fucking tough; that was my only luck. That and Ethan getting me out before they could do more damage.

I've only had two weeks of actual training. Dickie doesn't say it, but I can see he thinks it's not enough. He thinks I'm going to get crushed in that cage.

What he doesn't understand is I need this more than I've ever needed anything in my life. This is not about escaping the North Shore anymore. It's about leaving Caden behind. If I ever want a normal life again, I have to.

We train for another two hours. Until I'm so exhausted my legs are shaking. After a shower, Xi drives me home.

We settle for dinner in the living room together because

421

Dad and Aisha are out, and Emma is dealing with whatever shit she needs to deal with for NSC. She no longer shares anything with me, keeping me away from any news on the Kings.

We're eating some leftovers and watching TV, but I can feel the way his eyes keep coming to my neck, so I finally turn to him.

"Will you fucking stop?" I snap. "I know it's there. I don't need your eyes on it all the time. Fuck, I can feel you seething silently, and it's a constant reminder."

The Kings' crown that Jade left on me doesn't hurt anymore unless I'm showering with hot water, or if I scratch it by accident. The scars are still an ugly red. They'll turn white with time, leaving me with their mark forever. As if the tattoos Caden had given me weren't enough.

"You know I tried to find Sawyer," he says low. "The motherfucker has been hiding, knowing we'll end him as soon as we find him. Fucking coward."

"Jade did this. Not Sawyer."

"Jade is untouchable."

"Why?" I snap. A certain rage engulfs me. "Why can't she fucking be killed?" My arms swipe the entire coffee table, sending the plates and glasses flying before I stand up, pacing the room. "The bitch has had it out for me for months. She attacked me with her friends. She tried to fucking *end me*. You keep talking about Caden and Sawyer, but it's *her* fault."

I don't know why I put so much of the blame on her. Growing up as a girl, we socialize in a society that blames everything on women. We learn to condemn each other for the mistakes of men. For the times they purposely hurt us.

On the North Shore, the violence between women is like nothing I've ever heard of anywhere else. It's more than cattiness and gossip. We go for each other's throats. We go for the kill. I was hurt when I was just a teen because my sister and Kay were arguing over a man. Sawyer beat me up and threatened to rape me, but it was Jade who carved my skin. And I am raging at her. Because—no matter how much it shouldn't be this way—that's my first instinct.

It's not right, but she's the one I can afford to blame. She's the one I could kill with my bare hands. She's an easy target for me and anyone else around me. It's so wrong for me to think this way. I am aware of it, but at the end of the day, I'm not trying to be the bigger person. I'm trying to survive in a patriarchal, broken town.

"Billie," he scolds me. "Keep your energy for your fight."

"Fuck!" I scream, throwing whatever was left on the table against the wall. "Why?"

"Because," Xi says calmly as he gets up too. "No matter how mad they are at her, the brothers love the fuck out of her." And by the brothers, he means the stepbrothers, Ethan and Elliot. "And they're not letting anyone near her. I'm pretty sure they're planning their own type of punishment for her."

He approaches me carefully and wraps his arms around me. "We'll avenge you, Bil's. I promise," he whispers as I let myself fall into his embrace. My head lands against his chest, and I feel the tears returning.

I can't fucking stop crying. That's all I've been doing for two months. People are walking on eggshells around me, avoiding the topic, but I'm the one who always ends up bringing it up. I'm the one who ends up in tears.

Because that night was fucking traumatic.

Because I want revenge.

Because I miss Caden.

Every time he sends me song names and a time, I go to check it. I'm weak, and I check exactly what the lyrics say despite ignoring him and never answering. I know how sorry he is and how much he misses me. That's what makes it the hardest. We could have had it all. And he fucking ruined it.

"Let me kill Caden," Xi whispers against the top of my head. "Just give me the go-ahead, Bil's."

I give him the same answer I've given all of them a hundred times.

"No," I rasp. "Leave him alone."

And he will, like every other time. Because he doesn't want to break me further than I already am.

When I go to my room, I open my conversation with Caden. It's just texts from him. He sends me something almost every night at the same time, and I watch as, without fault, the three bubbles pop up at the bottom of my screen.

Caden: 1:15 to 1:33. Say Anything.

I know the song he's talking about. Like the heartbroken girl I am, I go to my music app and put the Good Charlotte song on.

I listen to the lyrics he mentioned and don't even stop the tears when they spring to my eyes. I click the repeat button on the song and lie down in my bed.

Fuck you, Caden King. For making me love you so much that I suffer every day.

"Oh my god," Emma says, bouncing on her toes and shaking every single one of her limbs. "Bil's, I'm so stressed right now. I can't take this."

I roll my eyes at her, shaking my head despite a small smile spreading on my lips. "I'm the one going in the cage, not you."

"Yeah, I know." She stops jumping and starts biting one of

her acrylic nails instead. "But this is everything. Your whole life depends on this."

"Not helping," I mumble.

"I'm pretty sure they don't call her Killer Clover for no reason, you know?"

"Alright, that's enough," Dickie growls. "You're out."

"What?" Emma snaps. "Dickie, I'm her sister. She needs me right now."

"You're freaking her out. Plus, I need to wrap her hands." He steps to the side, and I say hi to the referee behind him. "Come on. Out of here," he insists.

"I think it's best if you go to the main room." I nod at Emma, agreeing with Dickie. "I need to get my focus on."

"Fine. I love you. Good luck. I'll be out there the whole time. Blink four times in a row if you need me to come help kick her ass."

"I love you," I laugh as she exits.

I show my hands to the ref, proving I'm not hiding any weapons and then Dickie starts wrapping me up. We're being watched the whole time. Taylor comes in at some point, wishing me good luck, and to say he'll be watching me. That he's excited to see me kick her ass and get the contract started. It warms my heart that he's got so much hope in me.

When we're done and the ref leaves, Xi comes in. Dickie glares at him. "You better not distract her before her big fight."

"Only here to wish her luck," he smiles. "Can I have her for a minute?"

Dickie turns to me. "I'm gonna settle in your corner, kiddo. You got this." He grabs my shoulders, leaning down and looking into my eyes. "Who's the best?"

"I'm the best," I smile.

"I said, *who's the best?*" he repeats.

"I'm the best!" I say a little louder.

"I can't hear you!" He starts shaking my shoulders from side to side, and I giggle.

"I'm the fucking best!" I shout.

"That's my girl. I'll see you out there with your guard up or your fist in her face."

He gives me a huge papa bear hug, and I feel the emotions ready to wreck me. "No matter what happens out there," he says, my head buried in his chest, "I want you to know I'm so proud of you. You're the daughter I wish I still had, Billie."

Tears prick my eyes, and I hug him tightly before pushing him away.

"Get outta here," I rasp before the tears come falling.

As soon as he's gone, Xi takes my wrapped hand. I can't move it properly with the MMA gloves now on, but I feel his warm skin against my fingers.

"You're gonna destroy her," he smiles. "I can't wait to celebrate."

"I'm fucking unbeatable," I chuckle. "Almost."

"Everyone falls down at some point. It's all about how you get back up."

I nod. "Yeah," I exhale loudly.

Feeling my uneasiness, he tightens his hold. "You've got nothing to be scared about."

My nodding increases as I let myself believe it, my head getting back into the game.

"I love you, Bil's. I know you know...but I fucking love you. Even if I never have a chance with you again, I'll always be there for you. No matter what."

"How could you fall in love with me?" I laugh as I shake my head. "I'm not right for you. You love the Stoneview girls. The preppy bitches who will wreck your back with their manicured nails."

"Mm," he nods as he bites his lower lip. "Those fucking Stoneview uniforms. They kill me, you know?"

"Aren't you too old to love girls in uniform?"

"Come on, I'm not a creep. Silver Falls Uni still has a uniform. And they're very legal girls."

"Okay, I'm done trying to save you. You're gonna end up with a real bitch who will hate all of us, and we're gonna have to tolerate her at family dinners. Fucking great."

He explodes in a laugh and hugs me.

"You didn't answer my question," I say softly against him. "How?"

"How could you fall in love with Caden?" he returns. "He's not right for you."

I stay silent. He really shut me up there.

As soon as he leaves, I go to look at myself in the mirror above the sink. My hands grab the edge of the sink, and I stare into my own eyes.

"You got this," I tell myself. "This is it."

"I really think you got it," a voice comes from behind me.

I gasp as I turn around. Ethan is standing right behind me. I attempt backing up further, but I'm already against the sink.

"Xi!" I call out, except Ethan is on me the next second, his hand slamming against my mouth. I grab his arm, yet I don't defend myself. I can't risk it, not minutes away from the fight of my life.

"I'm not here to hurt you. I swear. Just calm down and hear me out."

My heart is hammering against my chest, but I nod slightly.

"I'm going to take my hand off. Do *not* scream."

I nod again, and he lets me go.

"I'm sorry I scared you," he says calmly. "I had to talk to you."

"What do you want?"

He steps away, giving me space so I'm no longer stuck against the sink.

"I can't watch my best friend be so miserable another minute, Billie. He would kill me if he knew I'm telling you this, but—"

"Why are you defending him now?" I snort. "You hate me. You never wanted us to be together in the first place."

"He fucking loves you, that's why. Everyone has only ever met unhinged Caden when he had no reason to be. The scary guy who destroys everything in his way just because he feels like it. Suddenly he has a reason to live. And it's all because of you."

"He killed four people since he met me, Ethan. He hasn't changed."

"But now he's deranged because everything he does is for you. You've given reason to his insanity. Do you even understand what that means?"

"It doesn't mean shit," I whisper more to myself than him.

"It means you control him. It means you've got his heart in your clutches, and there isn't shit he can do about it."

"I'm done with this conversation. You can leave now."

"I know where he was."

An ice-cold grip gets hold of my heart, making it so heavy I can barely breathe.

"I don't need to hear any lies," I shake my head. "I don't need any of this right now. A few months ago, I was *kicked out* of this competition. Now I get to fight again. Fuck, do you even understand what kind of chance the universe has given me?"

"The universe," he snorts. "How naïve are you? It was all Caden. He'll deny it if you ask him, but I know the truth."

I still for a moment, not truly understanding. The interest

he's sparking in me is too intense to ignore. "Fine. Where?" I snap, pretending I don't care.

"Did you know about his tutoring jobs in Stoneview?"

"Fucking hell," I snort. "Yeah, I'm sure that's where he was. Teaching some kids math while your bitch was carving me." I push him away and go to my gym bag, pretending to look for something. "Thanks for helping him out. You can leave now."

"Rich Stoneview women paid him for sex. That started before he met you. He was so desperate to get out of here that he did it."

A sickness I can't control envelops me. My entire body freezes, and my movements of rummaging in my bag are cut short.

"That...that can't be true."

"But it is." He's right behind me now, and I force my frozen body to turn around. "You were losing yourself after your defeat. He wanted to get you back into the competition. He convinced the girl who beat you to give you her spot, but she asked for a lot of money. Much more than he could afford."

He takes a deep breath, and I shake my head. My brain refuses to see where he's going with this, opting for denial.

"No. That's not true. No."

"Fucked up people in Stoneview pay men and women to participate in their orgies. They offered him the money in exchange for a night. That's where he was. He always had the option to do this job but never took it for himself despite his need to leave the North Shore. He did it for you, though. Didn't hesitate one second."

I'm so cold. Why is it suddenly so cold? The shock of it all weakens my knees, and I fall onto the bench, my body trembling.

"He didn't want you to know because he knew you couldn't take the guilt. But fuck, I'm done seeing him hurt. I know you're hurting too. He came back from that night only to find the woman he had sacrificed everything for had been attacked by his own crew. Only for you to shatter his heart when he wanted to make it right. He's broken, Billie. He's crushed, and nothing matters to him anymore."

"That's not true," I burst out in tears. "Tell me that's not true?"

His mouth twists since he can't actually say that. "Do you know where Sawyer is?"

I shake my head, more tears running down my face.

"He's in my basement. That's where Caden's been keeping him for two months. He tortures him whenever he feels like it, just to avenge you."

"Fuck," I sob, my head falling into my hands. I struggle to take a breath before getting up. "I need to see him. Right now." I'm walking toward the door, my gloves still on, when Ethan grabs my upper arm.

"No. You're going to fight, and you're going to win. He lost everything for you. So don't you fucking give up now."

"I never wanted him to do this for me," I cry. "He...he's crazy. I would have never agreed."

"Of course, he's crazy. It's Caden we're talking about. He's fucking insane. So get out there, and show him you were worth it. Then you guys can make up."

"We can't make up," I sniffle. "I can't live every day by his side knowing I'm the reason he's broken. We're cursed, Ethan. Everyone wants us apart. No one ever approved of us."

"You owe me, Billie," he says calmly. "I'm using my favor, and I want you to go talk to Caden after the fight. I want you to give him another chance."

With nothing to add, he lets me go and leaves the room without looking back despite having just destroyed my entire world.

36

CADEN

Hurt Me - Suriel Hess

She's indestructible. Billie's been going at it for two rounds and the bell just rang, signaling the beginning of the third and final round. She was crying when she came out, and I wanted to get up there and take her in my arms. To tell her that everything is going to be okay as long as we're together. Only I couldn't, so I watched Dickie ask her a few questions and her shake her head before starting the fight of her life. She didn't touch the other girl's gloves. Billie isn't nice in the cage. She's a destroyer.

I've watched every single one of Billie's fights in the last two months. *Followthefight* has become my most-watched channel on YouTube. That guy has got it bad for Billie, too, since he's always at her fights and supporting her. He's here tonight as well. I can see him filming from just in front of the cage.

I'm further back because I don't want her to see my face and get distracted. This is everything to her, and I won't ruin it.

I know her fighting techniques now, and she usually bets everything on her small height and speed. She can punch someone's lights out in less time than it takes them to realize she started moving. And she's good at avoiding hits.

Fuck, Killer Clover doesn't get her name out of nowhere. It's been hard for Billie to avoid her destroying kicks. My girl can't afford to kick her in the face since she's too short, but she's kneed her in the stomach enough times that Clover is forced to take a few steps back, hunched over. Billie doesn't give her time to breathe though, seizing the occasion to punch her right in the face. Her hook is deadly, with a precision like I've never seen. We're all used to underground fights on the North Shore. Nothing with rules or skills.

Billie is proof that it's nothing to be a tough girl when it comes to making a career out of her passion. It's all about practice and performance.

The crowd starts to cheer Billie's name as she hits Clover with punch after punch. The reigning champion of this small-town competition is getting a run for her money.

Clover falls to the floor, and everyone goes crazy. Although as soon as Billie tries to straddle her and put her in a weak position, she rolls away and kicks her in the face. Wincing, Billie falls to the floor as well, making the whole crowd gasp.

"Fuck." I can't help but get a bit closer. Billie's floor fighting isn't as good. I remember her telling me she didn't enjoy Brazilian Jiu-Jitsu training as much as Western Boxing. Mainly since she wasn't as good at it. She explained she was too light and easy to manhandle once she wasn't standing on her feet.

As soon as she hits the floor, Killer Clover gets her in a chokehold with her legs. Stuck between her thighs, Billie is in a compromising position. This could be the end. MMA fights have finished quickly that way, people tapping out to avoid losing consciousness.

But this means the world to her, and the fight isn't done. Billie hits Clover repeatedly in the ribs and wherever she can reach.

A raging war cry escapes her as Billie rains punches on her opponent, her need to keep on living taking over.

I scream at the top of my lungs when Clover can't take the punches anymore and is forced to let her go. "Yes! That's my fucking girl!" I don't even notice I'm telling lies as I roar into the crowd.

People are shouting; everyone is getting excited. I'm too focused on the fact that the two girls are now back to standing positions, catching their breaths, to notice I've made my way to the front. They exchange more punches, getting closer and closer to where I'm standing. People are screaming 'unbeatable Billie' so loudly. I wonder if she can hear them. She looks too focused to hear anything.

She's crying as she keeps hitting Clover, but I don't think she realizes. There's rage in her eyes, and it appears like she can't feel the pain despite her bleeding eyebrow and swollen cheek. Her face is the epitome of confidence, her body moving with accuracy. Her braided hair flies every time she moves too quickly for Clover to follow.

Billie takes a step back, avoiding a punch, her speed still incredible even though she must be exhausted. Killer Clover is getting slow and tired. Her hits are growing more sluggish.

Billie moves to the side, avoiding another punch, and hits Clover right in the nose. The latter falls against the grill of the cage right in front of me. I scream for her to keep going and her eyes flick to me, as if my voice was the only one she could hear amongst the countless others.

Her eyes widen, and I shake my head.

"Don't lose your focus!" I shout. "End her, little bee. Fucking. *End. Her.*"

A small smile pulls at her lips, her eyes not leaving mine as her arm pulls back. We lose eye contact as she looks at her target for a split second. Her punch is swift, confident, *unstoppable.*

She hits her right in the chin with her fist, followed straight away by a deadly hit with her elbow. A general hiss takes over the room as Killer Clover's jaw clicks to the side and she falls to the floor unconscious.

Billie takes a step back, jumping on her feet with her guard up. She doesn't see the way we all hold our breath. She doesn't realize or understand Clover is down, and doesn't sense the beat of silence. It hasn't hit her yet.

The ref is on Clover, and the next second he's standing up again, waving his arms to announce the end of the fight.

The crowd erupts into screams. Yelling for unbeatable Billie. Dickie is in the ring the next second.

Billie doesn't move, her mouth hanging low, her arms falling by her sides. She can't believe it, and I fucking love her for it.

They're so close to me that I hear everything when she stumbles back. "W-what?"

"You won, kiddo," Dickie yells at her. "You fucking did it!"

Her knees buckle, and her trainer catches her. Her gloved hands come to her face, hiding herself as she starts crying. She lowers them only for her gaze to return to mine, and I smile widely at her.

"You did it, little bee," I say just before beginning to move away from her. I know she doesn't want me here. She wants me to let her go.

I wanted to see if what I did was for something. If she would finally win the fight that would get her out of here. She did it, and the best thing I can do now is to let her live the life she's always deserved. Away from the North Shore.

So I let the crowd engulf me and disappear from her life forever.

I owe her at least that.

37

BILLIE

I miss you, I'm sorry - Gracie Abrams

"The winner by knockout...is Billie *unbeatable* Scott!"

My ears are ringing as my hand is lifted into the air. I can hear the screams, feel Dickie's happiness, and sense my whole body trembling.

All I can think about is Caden, and how I can see him making his way through the crowd. Unable to wait any longer, I snatch my hand back, get out of Dickie's hold around my waist, and climb the fence to jump out of the cage.

"Caden!" I scream into the crowd as I shove people out of the way.

Someone tries to grab and congratulate me, but I slither out of their hold.

"Caden!" I repeat, running through the crowd. "Wait!"

I run after him outside. It's pouring with rain, hitting against my hot, sweaty skin. He's just a tall, dark form barely visible through the curtain of water the sky is dropping on us. Just a shape walking out of my life.

"Caden!" I scream with despair. The heavy drops against

the asphalt of the parking lot make it sound like a low whisper. So I run. I sprint to him with the little energy I have left, and when I'm close enough behind him, I say, "I know everything."

He freezes on the spot. His car is nowhere close, so he can't escape the situation easily. He turns around, confusion twisting his features.

"What?"

"I know, Caden. Where you were that night."

He glances away, his jaw locking tightly. In the pouring rain, black hair sticks to his face, long enough to fall into his eyes. His dark green eyes would look black in the night if it weren't for the yellow lamp post flickering not far from us.

When he looks at me again, he takes me in, his gaze going up and down a few times.

"You should go in, Billie. It's freezing, and you're barely wearing anything."

I'm trembling from the cold, only wearing my gloves, MMA shorts, and sports bra. I'm soaked to the bone, yet I shake my head. "I'm fine."

He takes a step closer to me, like he can't stop himself, and I do the same because I *know* I can't stop myself.

Only a few inches away from me, he raises a hand to my chin, tilting my head up so he can look at me comfortably. Rain is falling in my eyes, making me blink up at him. With his other hand, he wipes some blood and water from the corner of my eye.

"Caden," I say softly. "Ethan told me everything."

A grin spreads on his lips. The kind that chills me down to my core. He's trying to detach himself from the situation, and I refuse to let him.

"Can't trust a friend nowadays," he says low.

"He did the right thing. I-I'm sorry. For what you've been through. What you did for me."

He ignores my words. Instead, he leans down, dropping a kiss to the skin just below my ear. "You were amazing tonight."

My lower stomach tightens, his warmth bringing back a need for him I can't control. When he pulls away and lets go of me, I shiver from his absence.

"I love you, Caden. I wish I'd been there for you like you were for me." My throat tightens. "I was so focused on myself." A sob explodes from my throat. "You sacrificed everything for me, and I was too *selfish* to see it. But the win, the career...none of it matters if you can't be by my side. I told Ethan the universe had given me a chance because I didn't know it was you. I wasn't wrong...you *are* my universe, Caden."

"I hurt you, Billie. If it helps you to say goodbye, if it helps to hate me so you can move on, then remember all the times I hurt you. The assault. The videos. When I made you crawl in front of my crew. Remember the times I forced you and made you cry. Remember that you had reasons to hate me."

"No," I shake my head, fat tears stinging the wounds on my face. "None of that matters if it brought us together. I don't...I don't care. I've forgiven you for that, and it's my choice to make, not yours."

"You know what I think about your choice," he sneers.

"You said you'd wait until I was ready to love you again. Except you hid all the reasons for which I could love you. You've always let everyone see you as a villain. You never let anyone see your sacrifices! I see them now. I see *you*."

"Heroes get the girl. Villains sacrifice themselves," he shrugs. "Go find your hero somewhere far away from here, little bee. You deserve it."

"No." My voice is so hard his eyebrows rise all the way to his hairline. "Be mine, Caden. Be *my* villain. Take my heart and keep it for yourself. Tell me you still love me, and we will fix this."

Coming close again, he kisses the corner of my lips.

"You want to know if I still love you?" He chuckles against my skin, like it is a ridiculous question.

I wrap my arms around his waist, making sure he can't go anywhere this time.

"Yes. I want to know if after everything we've been through...if you still love me," I whisper, my voice disappearing under the electricity he's sending through my body.

He pulls away from the corner of my lips and buries his face in my hair. Inhaling deeply, he exhales and says, "Tell me. On a rainy day, when the skies flood the world with despair... does the sun stop shining above the clouds?"

My heart explodes in my chest. Hope is a traitorous feeling. Your heart wants to believe the possibilities you're dying for, wants to read between the lines. But the brain needs cold hard proof before handing out your beating organ.

"Caden," I choke as I feel the tears coming back. "Just tell me you still fucking love me."

He pulls away but wraps his arms around my waist too.

"How could I stop loving you? My heart is yours, little bee. It only loves because you showed it how to." He wraps a hand around my jaw and brings our faces only an inch from each other, looking deeply into my soul when he adds, "And now that I've got yours too...you're mine forever. Understood?"

I nod, my lips parting slightly from the need to kiss him. "Yes."

"Good girl."

His lips crash against mine just before his tongue invades me. The world stops, and the pouring rain disappears. It's sensual, loving, and possessive—only the way Caden King knows how to kiss me.

He pulls away, and his eyes dart down. "Billie," he snarls, frustration coming out of him. Panic holds me again before he looks at me. "Did you run after me barefoot in the fucking rain?"

"Oh," I breathe out, reassured that it's nothing important. "I came straight out of the cage."

"You're gonna catch a deadly cold," he seethes.

"Worth it." I smile up at him and give him a peck on the lips.

He leans down, slides an arm under my legs and one under my shoulders, and lifts me off the ground. "Let's get you back inside." I sneeze from the cold as he starts walking, and then he adds, "I'm going to spank your ass so bad for damaging what's mine."

38

CADEN

Back in My Arms – Carlie Hanson

After grabbing her stuff in a hurry, trying to avoid anyone wanting to see her, Billie and I ran back to my car, holding each other's hand in the rain as we sped across the parking lot.

She asked me to drive her to her house so she could shower, and we could hide in her room before anyone came back.

She went through the front door and told me to go to the back because Aisha would be back from her evening walk.

"Sorry," Billie whispers as she opens her window. "Aisha hates violence so she never comes to my fights. She's in the kitchen right now."

I climb through her window and look around. "I am never going to reach your room through the front door, am I?"

"Not in this lifetime, no," she laughs. "I'm gonna have a shower. Stay here." A low growl grabs our attention, and I take a step back as Murder takes a dangerous one toward me.

"Did you not teach her yet that she must love me?"

"Murder!" Billie whistles and taps on the bed. "Come here, girl. You know Caden." She rubs her back and behind her ears, as the dog starts lying down. "He's very mean, but we like him anyway."

"Well, that's simply not helping," I deadpan as I cross my arms.

She goes to leave, but I stop her. "Wait."

She walks back to me. Probably because she hears the lack of confidence in my voice. "Are you okay?"

I nod. "Can I..." I grab one of her braids. "Can I undo your hair?"

She smiles softly at me and touches my cheek, caressing my face. "Yeah, of course." She grabs a chair where a lot of her clothes are piled up and sits down on it, her back to me.

I take the elastic off the first braid and take my time undoing it, relishing in the way her thick, light-brown hair untangles as I comb my fingers through it.

"I want to do them for your next match," I whisper before I can stop it. I undo the other one, and my fingertips tingle from the softness of her locks.

"You know how to do French braids?" she asks, surprised.

"Yeah. I do them on my nieces sometimes."

"That's so cute. Yeah, you can do mine next time."

Even when I'm done, I fist the strands gently without pulling just to feel them in the palm of my hand. I grab her brush on her bedside table and run it through her hair, making sure to start at the ends and find my way back all the way to her roots the more I untangle. It's so thick and strong.

"I love your hair," I breathe out.

"I know," she lets out on a soft breath. "I noticed. Why do you like it so much?" she questions softly.

I shrug. "It's so pretty and...I don't know." I'm surprised at the lightness in my chest when I approach a subject I usually wouldn't. "I just...when I was a kid and was too out of control, my mom would sit Kay on a chair and put a brush in my hand. 'Brush your sister's hair. If you don't calm down, you're going to hurt her. Is that what you want?'" I stop brushing, looking at the simple object in my hand. "I was already so violent as a child, but everything would disappear when she put me behind my sister and told me to brush." My thumb comes to play with the soft spikes of Billie's hairbrush. "And I'd feel in control of my own emotions because I knew I didn't want to hurt Kay."

I put the brush to the side and roll my head to ease the tension in my shoulders. "It's so dumb." I smile sadly. "It's just the only memory I have with my mom where she doesn't hate us or is being beaten up."

Billie stands up and rounds the chair. She wraps her arms around my waist and cranes her neck to look into my eyes, but my gaze darts to the side focusing on the window behind her. "That's not dumb at all, Caden. I think it's beautiful."

She puts two flat hands on my cheeks and draws me back to her, pulling down so I'm locking my gaze with her. "Hey," she smiles. "It's okay to talk about her. Even if it's the bad memories. Whatever you need to get off your chest, I'll always listen."

I nod and feel my lips break into a grin. The happy kind that softens my features and that no one ever sees except Billie. "I'm gonna wash your hair." I nod to myself, glad to have come up with an amazing idea.

"If we get caught on our way to the bathroom, it's your problem."

"I take full responsibility," I titter as I grab her hand and nudge her to lead the way.

I'm good in the shower and stick to washing her hair and body without turning her on. As soon as we're back to the bedroom and she closes her door, I grab her hips and drag her to the bed with me. I fall on my back, and she straddles me.

She throws her towel to the floor and unwraps the one around my waist. She's about to press her pussy to the tip of my hard cock, but I stop her.

"Sit on my face."

"What?" she chokes out, retreating slightly. "No."

I grab her waist tightly and start moving her toward my head. "Don't be shy. I've eaten your pussy before."

"Yeah, but not like that. That's...what if you can't breathe?"

"Then I'll die a happy man." I grin as I drag her closer again.

"Caden, that's not funny. I'm not sitting on your face. I'll suffocate you."

"Baby, that's the whole fucking point. Now stop fighting me, or we'll go back to me forcing you to do things. I'm happy either way."

Not even listening to her next answer, I shift her until her pussy is right above my face. "Let go," I growl, feeling tightness in her thighs so she can hover just above my mouth. "Fucking *sit*."

I pull harshly until she falls on my face and straighten my tongue to push into her tight hole. She breathes out sharply, her hands going to the wall by my head. I bring her tighter against my mouth and lick at her until her muscles turn into jelly, and she can't hold herself anymore. She's forced to let go completely, and her full weight presses on top of me.

I devour her, and she screams like never before. She rides my face without a care in the world, and I give her everything she needs.

When she explodes on me and I taste her climax on my

tongue, I moan against her. I feel her as she shivers above me. Grabbing her hips, I move her down to my dick and impale her in one move.

"Fuck!" she pants. "Be c-careful...you're big."

Instead of letting her ride me, I hold her in place and thrust up violently. Her mouth slackens, and her head falls back.

I play with her tits as I ease my movements and she curves her back, pushing her chest into my hands. She starts moving herself the moment I'm too slow to her liking. Riding me like a goddess, I watch her taut stomach and abs, then go lower to where her pussy meets my dick.

"Fucking hell," I groan. "You're so beautiful, baby. You take me so fucking well."

I sit up, bringing her closer to me and wrap her long hair around my fist. It's still dripping from the shower. I pull until she cranes her neck to look up at me. "I love you, little bee," I murmur as our rhythm gradually fades. Instead of thrusting in and out, I'm deep inside her while she rolls her hips.

"I love you too," she pants, her eyes fluttering open.

"You're getting out of here, baby." I smile softly. "The world is ours."

"The world is ours," she repeats. Her cheeks are flushed, her eyes shining. I can feel her pussy so tight around my cock, her small breasts against my hard chest.

I press my lips to hers, and her mouth opens as she comes from riding me. My hips thrust up, elongating her orgasm as I find my own release.

We pull away from each other, her body rolling off as I grab the towel she discarded and put it between her legs.

"Thanks," she breathes out. She rolls onto her side, watching me intently.

"Our future starts now," she smiles.

Butterflies explode in my stomach, flying to my chest and lifting my soul.

I have never felt so free.

39

BILLIE

Somewhere Only We Know - Keane

Caden goes through the window, and I lock it before leaving my room. Aisha is in the living room, reading a book in Arabic on the sofa.

"Hey. I'm going out. Where is everyone?"

She looks up and smiles at me. "They went for dinner. I thought you were with them."

I shake my head. "I was tired after my fight. Why aren't you going?"

"Eh, you know I prefer home-cooked." Her features twist as she looks away. "Ah, your face, Billie. I don't like seeing you like this."

I graze the bruise I feel on my cheek with the tips of my fingers. "I won. Did Dad tell you?"

"*Mashallah.*" Her bright smile brings me pride. "Well done. No more fighting now."

"Sure," I chuckle. "In your dreams, maybe."

"How is Caden?" she asks, the shadow of a smile tipping her lips. "It's nice that he can fit through the window."

"Oh…" My face is still warm from the incredible fuck we just had. I feel my cheeks heating so much we could probably cook an egg on my face. She must have heard *everything*. "I—"

"Isn't love so beautiful?" she hums calmly as her eyes go back to her book. "The way it can defy everything. Have fun wherever you're going."

I smile to myself. "Thank you."

Caden knocks on the stepbrothers' front door, and I hold his hand tighter.

"It's fine, little bee. It's only Ethan and Elliot in there."

I nod, but it feels strange to go willingly into a house that belongs to the Kings crew. I'm not here because I'm being forced, stealing something from them, or for revenge. I was invited, and I accepted.

Before coming here, I had dinner with my family and brought Caden. Everyone was waiting for me in a restaurant in Silver Falls. Dickie and Taylor were there. So were my sister, Xi, Lik, and my dad. Aisha's words made me realize that we can genuinely defy anything. Even our crews' beliefs.

Xi almost said something, but Emma put a hand on his arm and he retreated. After that, no one said anything. Everyone pretended like our life-long enemy wasn't eating at the same table as us.

We popped a champagne bottle Taylor bought for us, and I signed my contract with him. He didn't waste one minute, saying he would contact me with the exact details for the first minor league professional championship but that we would be going to the state of New York for now.

I've only ever been to Los Angeles in my life, and that was because Bianco's mafia had sent me there for underground fights. Other than that, I've never seen anything outside of Silver Falls and Stoneview.

When we left, my dad did mention this wouldn't be happening regularly and that he never wanted Caden in the house.

I don't care. It's a step in the right direction.

I feel euphoric, everything surreal and the happiness overwhelming. Caden's hand in mine the whole night has been grounding me. His soft words and praises keep a constant smile on my face.

When Elliot opens the door, he smiles brightly at me. "Welcome to the enemy's house, little Scott. Please, come in."

I open my mouth to retort something but decide against it. Elliot has already disappeared into the kitchen anyway, and we make our way to the living room.

"Would you look at that," Ethan says from the sofa. "You did give him a second chance after all."

"Well," I shrug. "I owed you a favor, didn't I?"

"You know you're dead for snitching, right?" Caden jumps in. "She wasn't supposed to know anything."

"You can't kill me," Ethan smiles gradually. "I'm the one who got her out of Sawyer's house. If anything, you owe me your life," he adds dramatically.

"Not killing Jade is plenty enough," Caden mumbles low. "You guys are lucky I fucking love you like brothers, or your bitch would be six-feet under."

"I heard that," Elliot exclaims, coming back into the living room with a pack of beers. "Jade's punishment is for us to worry about."

"She better fucking suffer, Elliot," Caden rumbles, getting heated.

"I've been wanting to make her pay since she went from

me to Elliot," Ethan admits. "This is just another thing to add to the list. Trust me when I tell you Jade will pay."

"And I'll get proof?" my boyfriend insists.

"Caden," I jump in. "I'm over her. Okay? I know what Jade did, but if anything, it stopped me from being raped by Sawyer." I shake my head. "We're moving on to greater things. Just leave her behind."

Elliot gives Caden a knowing look before he turns to me, pointing the beers in my direction. "So, I hear you're a professional MMA fighter. Let's celebrate."

We all pop open a beer, even me. I get to let go tonight.

I feel Caden hesitate a few more seconds before he nods to himself.

"To Billie," he says as we all join our beers up in the air. "Billie Unbeatable Scott. My fucking girl."

"To seeing Billie in UFC!" Elliot adds before we all drink a sip.

By the end of our beer, Caden is getting restless, and I put a hand on his knee as it vibrates up and down while we sit on the sofa.

"What's wrong?"

"I'm excited, that's it."

"Excited?"

"Yeah, I want to show you your celebratory gift. Come."

It's only when he opens the door to a basement that I remember Ethan's words about Sawyer.

He's in my basement. Because that's where Caden's been keeping him for two months. He tortures him whenever he feels like it, just to avenge you.

I'm shaking as we walk down the stairs.

"Oh my god," I gag as the smell of piss and sweat hits me. Then Sawyer comes into view. He's only skin and bones.

"Caden," Sawyer rasps. His ankle is shackled, and the chain is nailed to the floor. "Please."

"I brought you a little present," Caden smiles wickedly.

When Sawyer sees me, he retreats into a corner and starts to cry. "No, please, please..."

"Get up," Caden snaps.

"Please..." he sobs.

"Get the fuck up before I cut off another one of your fingers."

Sluggishly, he gets up, helping himself by leaning against the wall.

"I brought Billie so you could apologize to her."

"Caden," I grab his arm as I feel my face twisting. "This is... too much."

"Help me, Billie." Sawyer falls forward, not able to stand on his own two feet, and wraps his arms around my legs. "Please, help me."

Caden is on him the next second, grabbing him by the back of the neck and pulling him away before throwing him against the wall.

"Don't fucking touch her," he seethes. "You will never touch her again, you hear me? I said I brought her so you could apologize. Now get on your knees and *apologize*."

I've never seen such fury on his features. Even when he hated *me,* he never had that kind of rage toward me.

"I'm sorry," Sawyer cries. "I'm sorry, Billie. I'm sorry for what I did to you. I never had the videos in the first place. Caden had deleted them...I lied. I'm bad, *bad*!" He hits his palm against his head and then slams his head against the floor. "Bad! Bad! I'll never hurt you again. Never, Billie. Never."

I struggle to swallow. "Caden...what have you done to him?"

He appears so relaxed now that he gets to talk about what

he did. A playful grin tips the corner of his lips. "Ah, well, see. I've been a little on edge these last two months. Sawyer here might have been a way for me to simmer my anger."

Sawyer is naked and so thin I've been avoiding looking at him, but when my eyes go to him again, I notice the cuts and bruises.

"You tortured him."

"Little bee," he sighs. He lets his head fall forward and brings it back up. "When will you fucking understand that no one touches you without paying the consequences? He did more than hurt you, he took you away from me. For Two. Whole. Fucking. Months."

He grips the back of my head, his fist closing on my hair, forcing me to look up.

"I'm glad he finally apologized and told the truth. Sawyer never had the videos. Okay? I deleted them that same day I told him you'd never go on a job again. I want you to know that."

"Okay," I rasp, the position uncomfortable and cutting my voice. "Okay, I trust you. If you say you don't have them anymore, then you don't."

"Good. Now what happens to anyone who touches you?"

My eyes widen slightly. "Don't you think he's been through enough?"

"Little bee." He shakes his head, that unhinged smile scaring me to my bones. "Just answer the question."

After a few seconds of silence, I give him what he wants. "They die."

"That's right. Sawyer trapped you. He beat you up, threatened to rape you. Or have you forgotten?"

"I haven't forgotten," I hiss, rage for Sawyer burning up in my body.

"Then kill him."

He lets me go softly and moves back so he can look down at me. "I can do it if you wish. I'd kill anyone for you, but I want you to have the chance to get your own revenge."

My hands start to shake, and it takes me a minute to realize it's not fear.

It's excitement.

"Do it, Billie. Get it out of you."

Caden is the devil on my shoulder. The one who worships me. Who wants every piece of me, especially my soul. I'm more than happy to give it all to him.

"No one can ever know," I whisper. "My career would be over before it even started."

"This is between you and me. The boys upstairs don't have to know you did it. I'll tell them it was me."

Leisurely, I approach Sawyer who's still on the floor. "No," he shakes his head. "Please...I'm sorry. I'm sorry..."

I don't hear him anymore. I jump on him, falling onto his body as my hands wrap around his neck.

I'm completely silent as I end his life slowly. He chokes and tries to fight me, except he's too weak from two months of torture.

"Maybe Caden will let you go in the morning," I sneer as his eyes start rolling to the back of his head, repeating the exact words he said to me. "Whatever's left of you," I growl before putting more pressure on his neck.

He turns all shades of blue and purple before he's motionless, and his heartbeat stops beating frantically against my palms.

With sudden realization, I jump away from him, but Caden is ready to catch me.

"Shit," I panic. "Shit, shit, shit...he's dead."

"He is," Caden says softly as he hugs me against him. His

hand caresses my hair softly, and I feel him lower his head to breathe me in.

"I'm scared," I admit in a trembling voice. "I'm scared someone will know."

"Don't be," he whispers in my ear. "Nothing will ever happen to my queen again."

"Let's get out of here."

Only once we're upstairs do I allow myself to take another breath.

"Done?" Ethan asks.

"Done," Caden confirms.

The two brothers look at me, small smiles on their faces.

"I'm sure Kay will be happy to know she can take her rightful place as the head of the Kings," Elliot says.

"You two need to get rid of the body," Ethan adds more seriously. "I'm not keeping a dead man in the basement of a house the cops love to raid."

Caden nods and turns to me. "Ever been to tree thirteen?"

"No," I shake my head. I've heard of it, of course. It's where we bury the North Shore bodies. Xi spends a lot of his time there.

"First time for everything." Caden wiggles his eyebrows at me from the excitement.

It takes us almost two hours to get the body in my car. Caden and I are taking it to tree thirteen while Elliot and Ethan clean their basement.

"I like when you drive me. Who fixed your car?" Caden asks as we drive alongside the forest.

"One of Xi's guys changed the windows for free, but he didn't have the bulb for my light. I need to get that fixed at some point."

"I'll take you to Ashley again. She'll fix it in no time."

"Last time we went there, I hated you."

"What about now?" he asks with a smug voice.

"I guess you're okay."

"Okay? How about I ask your little pussy what she thinks, huh?"

He wraps a hand behind my neck, and I glance at him before looking at the road again. We're in the exact same position we were in only a few months ago. I was terrified of him then. Terrified of the things he had done and what I knew he was capable of.

Five months later, I've seen the worst Caden King has to offer...and I love him for it. The bastard ultimately made his way under my skin, slithered all the way to my heart, and made a home there.

"She can't be trusted. Leave her alone," I laugh.

"Sure thing. Count on it," he says deadpan, knowing perfectly he will never.

A cop car drives past us, and I tense, my hands tightening around the steering wheel.

"Don't worry," Caden says softly. "They have no reason to stop us."

But in the mirror, I see them stopping to turn around and putting their lights on.

"Caden," I panic.

"Shit," he hisses as they turn the siren on. "Your light."

"What?" I sit upright, my knuckles white from clenching the steering wheel.

"It's your fucking light. Motherfucker! Even in death, he is going to come at me."

"Now is not the time to hate Sawyer for breaking my car." I try not to hyperventilate while waiting for him to say something else. He hesitates for a second, and I read the danger on his face.

"Caden..."

"Floor it."

"I-We can't..."

"Floor it, Billie. *Now!*"

I don't even think about it, my body just follows his voice, and I press the gas pedal so hard we're crushed against our seats.

"This is stupid," I shout at him.

We never get into car chases on the North Shore. The town is too small, it's too risky. By foot, yes, because we know the secret places we can hide. But in a vehicle, you easily end up blocked between two cop cars and at the mercy of their easy triggers. We're never in these situations because we're too smart to get chased in the first place.

This is not good.

He grabs his phone and starts sending texts, although I'm too focused on the road and the police car accelerating behind us.

"Turn right," he says calmly. So calmly I barely heard him. "Don't slow down."

He pulls the handbrake just as I turn right, and we skid across the road before he undoes it and I accelerate again.

"Holy shit!" I scream. I'm losing all sense of direction as a feeling of dread takes hold of me.

"Stay focused, little bee," he says calmly.

The cops are still behind us. Softly, with no fear whatsoever, Caden guides me across the North Shore. He knows the town like the back of his hand, barely keeping his eyes on the road while he texts and indicates where to go.

"I think we lost them," I breathe out since I can't see them behind me anymore. I barely believe it myself. I have never heard of one single car chase that ended well in our town.

"Don't slow down. You're going to take the next left."

Nodding, I press the pedal until I turn into a rundown road. There's only space for one car here, and we're at the back of buildings. It's not even a road; it's an alley surrounded by brick walls only.

"Caden," I snap as I reach the alley's end. "This is a dead end."

We're facing two garage doors I recognize. That's where Xi locks stolen goods to resell them. We have no way to go forward or even turn around. How could he fuck up like this?

"I know."

"What?"

"Get out of the car."

I look around, utterly confused. "What are you doing?"

"The cops are going to find us either way, Billie. Right now, they're filtering every street to find us. You think we know the North Shore? They spend their lives chasing after us. They're not far. Now get out of the car and leave."

"Okay, you too. Come," I say as I undo my seatbelt in a hurry.

"I'm not coming. These guys have been looking for Sawyer. I'm going to give him to them."

I blink at him, trying to understand what the hell is happening.

"No." I shake my head so harshly I see spots at the edge of my vision. "What the fuck are you talking about? I'm not leaving you here."

"We've got a body in the car. They're going to want someone to take the fall."

"Fine. Let it be me, then!" I say, throwing my hands up. "I killed him, so I'll take the fall."

In a split second, he's out of the car and opening my door.

"Get out," he hisses.

"I'm not letting you sacrifice yourself for me again!" I fight back as he grabs my arm and drags me out of the car. "Stop! I killed him. I should be the one—"

He tugs my hair harshly, bringing my back to his front and slamming his other hand against my mouth.

"Shut the fuck up," he barks. "You did not kill him. I did. Got it?"

I shake my head, tears welling up in my eyes. I try to fight him, but I know there's no point. I've never been able to make him see reason. Why would it start now?

"I was jealous and furious that he had attacked you. So I kidnapped him, held him hostage for months, and tonight, I strangled him to death. Do you understand?"

"Please..." I yell out, my sounds muffled by his hand.

"I killed him." He lets go of my mouth and wraps his hand around my throat. "Say it."

"Caden, please," I whimper. "They'll put you away for life. I can't...I can't live without you. I can't live knowing you took the blame for me."

"I *said*," his grip around me tightens, "I killed him. Now, say it."

"Don't..." The moment a sob comes out, numerous others follow. I'm shaking so violently, his hard chest hurts against my neck.

I choke when his hand grips harder on my throat. "Say it, Billie."

The edge of my vision narrows, and I shake my head again.

A siren is heard down the street, and I feel his head snapping to the side, probably looking at the other end of the alley.

"Say it!" he rages, crushing my windpipes.

"Y-you..." I cry, "k-killed...Caden, I love you, please."

"Finish that sentence," he says, death controlling his voice.

"You killed him," I blurt out. If this is our last moment together, no matter what happens next, I want to be able to look into his eyes.

"Good girl," he exhales, anxiety seeping out of him. He lets me go, grabs my shoulders, and turns me around. "Good girl," he repeats with a broad smile on his face. "You're so strong, Billie. Fucking unbeatable."

"Stop," I shake my head.

"Billie," someone calls out as they run down the alley. My face snaps to Xi running to us.

"No..." I sob. "Don't. Caden, *don't*." He must have been texting Xi in the car. He knew what he was doing all along.

"I love you so fucking much, you know that?" he rasps.

"No!" I shout, anger coursing through my body. I hate him for sacrificing himself again. Behind us, Xi uses his keys to unlock one of the garage doors.

"There." I point at the garage hopelessly. I already know he's going to refuse. "We can all hide in there."

"Billie," Caden shakes his head. "If they don't find someone to blame, they will keep searching. I can't risk your career, your chance to get away, your *freedom*. The world is yours, baby."

"I don't care about any of that!. You can't do this. You said the world was *ours,* you...fucking liar!"

Smiling softly at me, he squats and brings his palm to the ground, tapping twice.

Our gesture to stop it all. Our version of a safe word.

"No," I force between clenched teeth. "You don't get to tap out."

Instead of defending himself, he wraps an arm around my

waist and cups the back of my head with his other hand. He slams his lips against mine and kisses me like there is no tomorrow.

Like it's the last time.

"Remember, baby. The sun never stops shining above the clouds," he whispers against my lips as we separate. "No matter what comes our way, I'll never stop loving you."

Xi grabs my upper arm and drags me away. "Come on, they're going to be here any second. Let's go."

"No, no, no," I explode into tears again. "Caden!"

"We're going to meet again, little bee. I promise you," he smiles. "Somewhere far from this shitty town. *There*." True hope shines in his eyes. The misleading kind. The betraying hope that makes people do crazy, unfixable things.

I fight Xi, but he doesn't even give me a chance. He grabs me by the waist from the back in a bear-like hug and lifts me off the ground, carrying me with him. He holds me tightly as he pulls the garage door down.

Caden is smiling as he disappears, and I take him in one last time. His beautiful, messy hair, and those piercing green eyes. I don't think he realizes that he's rubbing his hand just below his heart, exactly where his tattoo of a bee is.

Just as the door shuts, as if they had all conspired against me, the siren gets louder, and I see blue and red lights from under the door.

All I can do now is listen.

Screeching tires.

Doors slamming.

"Hands behind your head!" someone shouts. "Turn around and get on your knees!"

A whimper escapes me, forcing Xi to slam a hand against my mouth. He's holding me so tightly I feel his heartbeat raging against my back.

"Gentlemen," Caden's calm, mocking voice rises.

"Fuck!" one of the cops shouts. His radio crackles. "419. Calling for backup. I repeat 419. We've got a dead body in Greenfield Alley. A known gang member is present at the scene."

My eyes squeeze shut, tears falling onto Xi's hand.

My heart shatters into a million pieces knowing this is it. This was the last time I ever felt Caden against me. The last time his lips touched mine. The last time I heard those three magic words from him.

We fought all we could against our tragic fates.

And yet, it wasn't enough.

EPILOGUE
BILLIE

Two Punks In Love - büllow

A year and a half later...

The pre-fight anxiety never gets easier, and the hits in the ring never get less painful.

Every new win is a step closer to making everyone around me proud, to earning more money, and to helping the ones I love.

Fame, or whatever people like to call it, doesn't really make me feel anything. People recognize me when I go to a gym or if they're fans of MMA and bump into me on the streets.

Interviewers are not from the same place as me anymore, and they often want to know about my past. What it was like where I grew up. They want to know what the scar of a crown on the side of my neck means and if I was ever affiliated with a gang.

I ignore them. People don't care about us when we're in our shitty town. Why would they care now, apart from gossip?

I also often get some screen time when I go watch a fight. The camera pans to me in the crowd to put me on the big screen. But at the end of the day, I'm not really recognizable yet to the average Joe.

It might all change after tonight.

After over twelve months of fighting my way from more minor to bigger leagues, Taylor finally got me a fight for the Contender Series. I just need to win by TKO, KO, or submission, and I'm in. One win, and I will get a UFC contract.

I'm so fucking close as I punch my opponent in the head, and she falls to the floor.

I'm on her instantly, but so is the ref. He forces me to back off when her arms don't come to defend herself, and waves his hands in the air, announcing the TKO.

Cheers explode around me.

The lights are much brighter in UFC venues. The crowd is much louder, and my name is so distinct from their mouths. Despite everything, I always look for his face in the crowd. Sometimes I even imagine it. Tonight again, I was sure I saw him just before I knocked out my opponent. Just like I did that night on the North Shore.

But I can't see him now. He's not really there, and I know it.

No, Caden King is serving a life-long sentence in prison for first-degree. Nowhere near Las Vegas, where I am fighting tonight, and nowhere near my apartment in New York City.

He won't be here tonight like he wasn't in the many other fights I've won.

Dickie is still there, in my corner, holding my waist when they pull my hand up. The feeling never gets old, even though everything feels a little duller since Caden was put away.

I never got a chance to see him again. He refused to see me when he was being tried, and Xi had promised him he'd keep me away. He never put me on the visitor's list and won't take my calls when I phone the prison.

Talks of contracts, champagne, and random people partying are what I find in my changing room as I come out.

Taylor and Dickie stay true to themselves, congratulating me while keeping me humble. I don't really need it. Nothing can truly make me happy anymore. Not when I had the ultimate joy at the tip of my fingers. Love in my clutches, and it all went away because the man I love sacrificed himself for me.

Everything around me, I owe it all to him.

UFC flies us back to New York City in a private jet, and I'm moody the whole way.

"Come on, Bil's," Taylor laughs softly. "Just enjoy it. You don't ever have to take it again."

"This is rich people shit," I mumble. "No one needs a fucking private jet. Think of the environment."

"I'm pretty sure you're part of the rich people now," Dickie cackles.

I rarely touch my money. There's too much for one person, so I send a lot of it to my mom. I got her out of the trailer park as soon as I could and checked her into a psychiatric hospital. She spent six months there. After that, I got her a cottage in the middle of nowhere, since that's what she wanted.

My dad and sister refuse to take any of the money I offer. I think it's because that would mean leaving the North Shore Crew behind, and their gang is their reason to live. They don't want to let it go.

Which is fine. I bought myself a nice apartment. I spoiled myself on some nice vacations with Emma and Xi. Mainly, I put it all into a savings account for Caden. What if he gets out one day? I don't want him to have nothing left to his name.

Not after what he did for me.

Five months ago, I sent some money to his sister and asked her to get him a new attorney. I never heard anything else from her except when she gave me her bank details.

We land in New York City around four a.m., and I get in a taxi to my apartment in Brooklyn. I don't live anywhere fancy. I would have felt weird to suddenly buy a penthouse. My place is nice, in a decent neighborhood, but I don't need anything gigantic.

I walk into my two-bedroom apartment and lock the door behind me. Letting out a long huff, I make my way through the dark hallway and enter my living room, dropping my bag before I even turn the light on.

When I flick the switch, my heart completely stops, and I fall a few steps back from the shock.

"You think they'd give such a famous fighter a little more protection," he smiles.

It's not the wicked one. It's the same smile he showed me when I gave him a chance. The smile he reserves for truly happy moments.

"Caden," I gasp.

His hair is the same black mess on top of his head. His eyes are eating me alive like they always used to, calling my soul and demanding I respond to him.

"Hey, little bee," he says, standing up from my sofa.

"Oh my god!" I cry out as I run to him. I fall into his arms, tripping on my own feet, and he catches me.

He holds me so tightly against him, I can't breathe. I do the same, my arms wrapping around him, my heart beating in unison with his.

"I don't understand," I cry on repeat. "I don't understand..."

He pulls away in the slightest, only enough to slam his

mouth against mine. We devour each other, but he's the one who steps away and looks around.

"What are you doing?" A small laugh escapes me as I watch him look for something in the living room.

"Looking for your boyfriend's belongings. Although there better be no other fucker in your life." Of course, that's his number one priority. "'Cause I'm back, and I'm not scared to go back to prison if anyone else touched you while I was away."

I shake my head. "No one." I grin, still not believing what's right in front of my eyes.

"Ever?"

"Ever," I confirm.

"Mm..." He bites down on his lower lip. "This pussy must have been missing me so much, baby."

He takes a dangerous step toward me, as I take one back. "Wait. You...how?"

"Explanations later," he says faintly. "Right now, I want my girl."

"But how did you get out?" I take another step back as he keeps advancing toward me.

"Billie, baby," he says in his mocking voice. "I know I've been gone for a long time, but did you forget who calls the shots?"

I pinch my lips, tilting my head to the side and putting my hands on my hips. "Excuse me. I've been very independent without you. You can't just come back and order me around."

"That's very funny," he chuckles, that sinful smile back on his lips.

"It's not a joke," I defend as I take yet another step backwards, only to hit the wall behind me. He brings his arms on either side of me and looks down at me.

"Do you know what I was secretly hoping for? For you to have moved on."

"Moved on?" I choke.

"Yeah. Just so I could convince you all over again. Just so I could assault your tight little body and remind it who it belongs to. Oh, little bee, I'm going to spend hours teaching you how to take me again. I will use and abuse you until you're nothing but my little slut. All. Over. Again."

I gulp, my heart kicking at my ribcage. My entire body is on fire from his words alone. A year and a half is a long time. A very long time. My lower belly is twisted, and my legs are practically shaking as I feel the wetness invading me.

"Maybe I don't want you anymore," I lie, in a whisper. "Maybe...maybe I don't want you to touch me."

Caden loves the chase. He likes forcing his way. Isn't it just so convenient that I love when he forces me?

"Oh yeah?" he growls low. "You don't want me to touch you?"

I shake my head, trembling when one of his hands caresses my inner thigh. Despite wearing jeans, I feel his touch all the way to my core.

"Officially a UFC fighter, and you still wear your simple jeans and tank tops, huh? How humble. And that fucking ponytail." He lowers his head, burying his nose in my tied-up hair. "Mm," he delights. "The same shampoo. You know that's my favorite smell."

"I'm still the same person," I squeak past the need building inside me.

"Me too," he says wickedly. "And do you know what that means?" His hand between my thighs gradually trails higher.

I shake my head.

"It means I still don't give a shit what you want. You're mine, little bee, and you'll take everything I fucking give you."

He harshly cups my pussy, and I cry out in pleasure.

"Exactly what I wanted to hear." His voice is barely above a growl now. He undoes my jeans at the speed of light, and I do the same with his. Our tops are next, and before I can do anything else, he grabs the back of my legs, lifting me up and settling between my thighs, crushing me against the wall as I wrap my legs around his waist.

The tip of his hard dick touches my wetness, and we both release a satisfied moan.

"Fuck," he hisses. "You're not ready. I've waited so long for this."

"Me too," I whimper as I start rubbing myself against him.

"Let's do a quiz. I want to hear my name on your lips when you answer."

I nod, dropping kisses everywhere I can reach.

"You couldn't get with anyone else while I was gone. Could you?"

"No, Caden," I shake my head.

"Because you belong to me."

"Yes, Caden," I nod, desperately moving against his dick. "Please..."

I'm not done begging as he slams into me. I scream in both pleasure and pain. I feel so tight. It's been too long.

"Who do you belong to, Billie?" he says as he stays buried deep inside me.

"You..."

He starts moving, grabbing my ponytail, and pulling my head back.

"What's my fucking name?" he snaps, thrusting harshly.

"Caden!"

"So, who do you fucking belong to?"

He slams harder, his movements accelerating and becoming harsher by the second.

"You, Caden!" I cry out. "You...fuck...fuck...it's you!"

He keeps fucking me against the wall, grabbing my legs around his waist and moving them until they're by his shoulders. I'm folded in half between him and the wall. He's so deep inside me that I can barely breathe.

"I have a secret for you," he rasps against my ear. I'm panting, stuck in ecstasy, barely able to hear him.

"W-what..." I moan as he thrusts at an angle that perfectly hits my G-spot.

"I belong to you too. You've been on my mind every single day I was in that hell hole, Billie. You're the one who kept me alive. You're the reason I didn't lose whatever little sanity I have. It was all for you. 'Cause I fucking. Belong. To. You, Billie Scott." He punctuates his words with harsh thrusts.

"I love you," I scream as I explode around his dick, feeling my entire body float into nirvana.

"I love you too," he grunts, coming inside me.

He pauses after, his forehead falling on mine. One of his hands comes to caress the scar on the side of my neck; the Kings' crown that Jade marked me with. There's a moment of silence as we both seem to be remembering that night.

What strikes me, though, is how far we've come. "It's all behind us," I whisper reassuringly. "It's just you and me now."

Caden inhales deeply, taking in the truth.

"You're my everything," he murmurs.

I've never believed him more than I do now.

We settle on my balcony afterward. It's a warm evening, the end of August, and I'm only wearing his t-shirt with nothing else. I just went to get him a bottle of water and observe him as I walk back. His gaze is lost on the view, watching the city from the fifteenth floor.

It's only now that I realize, even though he hasn't truly changed, he looks more tired. Older. Like he's got more experience and isn't just the unhinged boy who ruled the North Shore. He's a little bulkier too, and has more tattoos.

I can't wait to discover him all over again. To spend every waking minute loving him like he deserves to be loved.

He turns around, probably sensing my presence, and smiles at me. "How long have you been standing there?"

"Enough to remind myself yet again how much I love you."

He lets out a small laugh and grabs the bottle from me. He's topless, wearing only his jeans, and I relish in observing his prominent abs.

"Caden," I say as I sit down next to him on the small sofa I keep on the balcony. His eyes are back on the city now. "How did you get out?"

"The city is so bright and loud," he simply replies. "So many people here."

Realizing he's ignoring my question, I rub my hands against my face. "Caden, please tell me you didn't break out of prison," I exhale.

"Of course not," he snorts. "It was all thanks to you."

"To me?" I say, rearing my head back.

"My sister got me a new attorney with the money you sent. Just like you said."

"She did? She never said anything."

"I told her not to. I didn't want to give you false hope. Our new attorney asked to reopen the case based on the fact that they hadn't looked at all the evidence. She got the judge to open the investigation again, and they found that the marks around Sawyer's neck didn't match my hands. Not only that, but it was most likely women's hands. My attorney appealed my sentence, and a month later, here I am. Free. All charges dropped. All thanks to you, little bee."

I gulp, swallowing anxiety and sadness. "It should have been me in there in the first place. Even if you had been freed and decided not to come back to me, it was the least I could do."

"You're the first person I came back to. I got out yesterday afternoon."

"You got out yesterday?" I choke.

"Yeah." He nods, finally turning his head to me. "I called Xi for your address. Took Kay's car, and I drove here."

My mouth falls open. "You're crazy."

"For you? Always."

My cheeks burn as I understand my heart never got over Caden King.

"So what now?" I ask, a shyness coming over me as I look down at my hands, picking my nails.

"Now I try to start all over again. I will probably have to get a job or something. Save some money so I can finish college."

"I meant...us."

"Us?" he chuckles. "There is no thinking needed when it comes to us. I am never letting you go. Ever. Again." His eyes are hard when he grabs my hands and stops me from avoiding his gaze. "You're mine. How could you ever think I'd choose any path in life other than the one that leads right to you?"

Happy tears spring to my eyes. I suddenly feel silly for thinking otherwise. "You need to move here," I say. "I'm away often, and the little time I have, I spend it in this apartment. I want you here with me."

"If that's what you want, then I'll be here. I'll be the best stay-at-home boyfriend the universe has ever had. Anything else?"

"I want you to finish college and become a math teacher like you always dreamed."

"Done. What else?"

"Marry me one day. When you're ready."

His brows shoot up. "Marry you?"

I nod, biting my lower lip. "You know I want that stupid, typical dream of a husband, a nice house, and kids. You're mine. I want you to myself, forever."

He licks his lips, a smug smile spreading on his face. Grabbing the water bottle again, he gets down on one knee in front of me.

"I don't have anything to my name right now, but I promise I will get you the beautiful ring when I'm back on my feet. Fuck, I'll get you the entire world." He undoes the cap and removes the sealing ring attached to the plastic bottle. "Billie Scott, will you marry me and become Billie King?"

"Caden," I burst into a blissful laugh as he presents the small plastic ring to me. It's way too big for my finger, of course, but I don't care. "Yes...give me the fucking world already."

He puts the oversized plastic piece over my ring finger, and we kiss passionately before exploding into laughter again.

We talk all night. About everything like we used to. His time in prison, where he said he's feeling lucky to have come out without being sexually assaulted. My time as a fighter. He says he followed all my fights one way or another. Either smuggling phones in or anything else he needed in there to know what I was up to.

We talk about our future. It takes me hours to convince him to accept the money I put aside for him. I ended up having to tell him I'd give it to Xi if he wasn't going to take it for him to finally say yes.

We're cuddled together, watching the sun rise on the city, when he whispers to me, "The sun is shining again."

I smile at him knowing exactly what he means. I take in his gorgeous face. It's always been too beautiful for such a wicked man. He's *my* wicked man, though. And I'm starting to realize we're truly reunited. For good.

I play with the big plastic ring around my finger, knowing I won't be able to keep it there but loving that I know I will be the wife of the man I love.

"The sun is shining again," I confirm in a murmur. "Despite everything."

The end.

ALSO BY LOLA KING

STONVEVIEW STORIES

Stoneview Trilogy (MF Bully):

Giving In

Giving Away

Giving Up

One Last Kiss (Novella - includes spoilers from Rose's Duet)

Rose's Duet (FFMM why-choose):

Queen Of Broken Hearts (Prequel novella)

King of My Heart

Ace of All Hearts

NORTH SHORE STORIES (interconnected standalones)

Beautiful Fiend (enemies to lovers)

Heartless Beloved - (good girl/bad boy) coming August 2023

ACKNOWLEDGMENTS

Thank you to my readers for sticking with me through thick and thin.

Thank you to everyone who made this book possible. Every books is life-changing, but this one hits different.

Thank you to my partner Jay for being always my number one supporter and picking me up when I'm down. Nothing would be the same without you. I love you.

Thank you to the amazing team behind me for everything you do so I can write and not worry about anything else. My assisstant, Nikki. Lauren, who always has the heart of the book in mind. Kat for the beta reading. And all the girls at Valentine PR for your amazing work.

Thank you to my pretty girl, Jess, for the sprints, the time together talking about books, and for being there through all the ups and down of publishing. Love you.

Printed in the USA
CPSIA information can be obtained
at www.ICGtesting.com
LVHW091432290524
781286LV00001B/21